DEATH THROES

DEATH THROES

Clive Egleton

St. Martin's Press
New York

Library of Congress Cataloging-in-Publication Data

Egleton, Clive.
Death throes / Clive Egleton.
    p.   cm.
ISBN 0-312-11774-4
    I. Title.
PR6055.G55D4   1995
823'.914—dc20   94-45771
        CIP

First published in Great Britain by Hodder and Stoughton Ltd.

First U.S. Edition: April 1995
10 9 8 7 6 5 4 3 2 1

This book is for our very good friends,
Stuart and Audrey Marsee
of Redondo Beach, California

Chapter 1

The man Ashton had been told to meet lived in the old quarter of Sofia near the fruit and vegetable market on Georgi Kirkov Street. Like the two neighbouring houses which had been built around one of the small courtyards off the cobbled alleyway, number 23 Car Simeon was in a poor state of repair. Subsidence had opened fissures in the outside wall, there were signs of rising damp, the wooden shutters and windowframes hadn't even received a lick of paint to help preserve them, and several dislodged roof tiles had come to rest in the sagging gutter. Number 23 wasn't unique; the whole backstreet neighbourhood was a far cry from the new housing estates in the outer suburbs and was likely to be demolished in the not-too-distant future.

Ashton tried the rust-pitted doorknocker, found it wouldn't budge and rattled the letterbox instead. Getting no reaction, he used a clenched fist to hammer on the door and was mildly surprised when it swung back on its hinges to reveal a gloomy hallway. It was only then that he noticed the claw marks on the jamb and realised the lock had been sprung with a jemmy. He stepped inside, closed the door behind him, then called out in a voice loud enough to carry upstairs. But there was still no response.

The kitchen was at the back of the house; to his left, a narrow staircase led to the upper floor, while on the right, a door opened into a living room that looked as if a tornado had swept through it. The contents of the writing bureau had been tipped out onto the floor, burying the Turkish carpet under a pile of bills, old letters, photograph albums and back numbers of *Time* magazine. Both

1

armchairs in the room had been disembowelled with a knife, the horsehair stuffing protruding from the upholstery like the entrails of a dead animal whose belly had been ripped open. A large amateurish watercolour of some monastery up in the mountains had been removed from the frame and separated from the mount before being cast aside.

The kitchen had also been turned over but unlike the living room, there was no evidence to suggest the furniture had been deliberately vandalised. The intruder had however been into every cupboard and drawer and in addition had dumped all the pots, pans and cooking utensils into the sink after removing them from the shelf above the kitchen range. From the tacky mess on the stone floor, it was evident that the fire in the wood-burning stove had been doused with a bucket of water before the ashes had been raked out into the hearth.

Ashton opened the door to the store cupboard and found the housekeeper sitting on a sack of potatoes, her back resting against a marble shelf, her head drooping forward onto an ample bosom. She was wearing a soiled white apron over a shapeless black dress and thick woollen stockings which failed to conceal a network of bulging varicose veins. The cotton scarf which at one time had covered her hennaed hair had been used to secure both wrists behind her back. Then the intruder had executed her Spanish-style, tightening a thin piece of electrical cable around her throat with a wooden ladle in lieu of a garotte. The dead woman had worked for Henry de Vries; closing the pantry door on her, Ashton went in search of him.

In London, de Vries was known as the indestructible pensioner. He was seventy-six years old and had arrived in Sofia in the spring of '39. Of Dutch extraction, he had been born in Leeds, the only child of a watchmaker and a hospital cleaner. His mother had died of septicaemia shortly before his sixth birthday; two years later de Vries had ended up in a Dr Barnardo's Home after his father had gassed himself while he was in school. At fourteen he had started work as an office boy with the Municipal and General Insurance Company, then moved to a similar job with the local Co-operative Society before finding a niche at the *Yorkshire Post*, which had lasted until he had joined the merchant navy in 1934. He had signed on as a deckhand with the Royal Mail Line on the South

American run, the first of many sea-going appointments with various shipping companies in a career that had ended abruptly when he had been put ashore at Istanbul with a suspected duodenal ulcer.

Discharged from hospital seven weeks later, de Vries had become a courier for Thomas Cook, travelling all over the Middle East and the Balkans before settling down in Sofia where, with his gift for languages, he had eventually found employment as a translator. Somehow he had gone through World War Two without being interned, somehow he had managed to supply the Allies with valuable information throughout the conflict without arousing the suspicions of either the Bulgarian authorities or the Gestapo. But now his luck had finally run out.

According to Ashton's philosophy, the old had a God-given right to die in bed peacefully and quietly. Henry de Vries was old; death had come to him while he was lying on his bed upstairs and possibly he hadn't cried out even though his demise had been anything but peaceful. Before garotting him, the killer had whipped the soles of his bare feet with a bamboo cane until the skin had split open like an over-ripe peach.

Ashton walked over to the bedroom window and looked down into the small courtyard. The cobbled alley was only a dozen strides away; unfortunately, a woman from the neighbouring house on the right was on hands and knees busily scrubbing her front doorstep. He checked the back hoping to find an alternative exit but the passage behind the next cluster of buildings had been dug up and three workmen were endeavouring to repair a burst water main.

He returned to the front bedroom to keep watch on the woman, mentally urging her to finish what she was doing and go back inside. When finally she did get to her feet, a young mother leading a small boy by the hand emerged from the house to his left and passed the time of day with her. The exchange lasted no more than a couple of minutes but it seemed an age before they parted company to leave the way clear for him. Taking advantage of the opportunity, Ashton went downstairs, let himself out of the house and walked away.

Judging by appearances, he thought Henry de Vries and the woman had been dead for at least twenty-four hours, which meant they had probably been murdered long before he had boarded the

3

Balkan Airways flight from Heathrow yesterday afternoon. At least two men had broken into the house, most likely under cover of darkness. One of the intruders had dealt with the housekeeper while the other had taken de Vries upstairs and methodically tortured him. The way the kitchen and living room had been ransacked was indicative of a burglary that had gone terribly wrong when the thieves had found there was nothing worth stealing in the house. It was, Ashton believed, precisely what the intruders wanted the militia to think.

He walked on through the fruit and vegetable market, took a side street into the Boulevard Georgi Dimitrov and hopped a south-bound tram. Alighting one stop beyond St Nedelya Church, he retraced his steps to the Largo, the elongated plaza fronting the Sheraton Balkan Hotel which had been built on the ruins of central Sofia pounded by British and American bombers in the autumn of 1944. Although it was his first time in the city, Ashton knew his way around the centre; time devoted to preparation was rarely wasted and he had spent a couple of hours poring over a street map of the capital before venturing out of the hotel.

He crossed the plaza, went through the underpass below the Avenue Dondukov and entered the Central Department Store. The merchandise was displayed better than in Moscow's GUM on Red Square, but that wasn't saying a lot. There was still the same lack of choice, the same poorly finished products, and the same inattentive sales staff. He rode the escalator up to the top floor and came back down again to wander aimlessly from counter to counter on the ground floor. Finally satisfied that no one was following him, he then left the department store by the side entrance and hailed a taxi.

The British Embassy in Sofia was located on Marshal Tolbuhin Boulevard in a modest-looking town house down the avenue from the university and facing the monument to the Soviet Army near the Eagle Bridge. In keeping with its appearance, the embassy was also staffed on a very modest scale with just two First Secretaries, one Second and two Third Secretaries, one of whom looked after administration while the other was responsible for consular affairs. The armed services were represented by a lieutenant colonel in the Royal Engineers who held the combined appointment of Defence, Naval, Military and Air Attaché which effectively made him a jack of all trades. There was no officer from MI6 on the diplomatic staff; Intelligence matters were handled by Michael Pearman, the senior First Secretary and Head of Chancery.

Pearman was forty-two, eight years older than Ashton and at five feet eight, a good three inches shorter. A stranger meeting him outside the workplace would never suspect he was a diplomat; with his cheerful disposition and plump figure, he looked the part of the irrepressible salesman, the friendly proprietor of a small hotel or even a professional entertainer at a holiday camp. Ashton hadn't met him before but he had read the photocopy of his personal and security file belonging to the Foreign and Commonwealth Office. In it, Pearman was described as shrewd, intelligent, totally reliable, a family man whose only known vice was doing the football pools. He was also said to be unambitious and content with his lot, which was just as well since the promotion board had decided he had reached his ceiling.

'How did you find the indestructible pensioner?' he asked after they had shaken hands.

'Dead,' Ashton said bluntly. 'Along with his housekeeper. They had been strangled.'

'Jesus.' The smile vanished from Pearman's mouth. 'That's a bit of a shaker,' he said quietly.

'Did Henry de Vries have anything worth stealing?'

'I wouldn't have thought so. I mean he was hardly living in a palace. Of course, he might have had a few gold bars tucked away under the floorboards; my predecessor was certainly convinced that he was an out-and-out miser.' Pearman frowned. 'I assume the house looked as if it had been burgled?'

Ashton nodded. 'That's the impression they were trying to create.'

'So what happens now?'

'I don't see any point in my hanging around.'

Henry de Vries had been the go-between, the contact man who was going to put him in touch with the 'Insider' from Moscow. Only he knew where the Russian who had asked for a meeting was hiding himself.

'But there's a problem,' Ashton continued. 'London allowed three days for this job and changing my flight may not be easy.'

Pearman opened the top drawer of his desk, took out a copy of the British Airways worldwide timetable and opened it at the appropriate page for Sofia. 'All the direct flights are in the morning before midday,' he said presently. 'However, there is an Austrian Airlines to Vienna departing at 16.20 hours which connects with a BA flight to Heathrow. Usually, it's booked solid to Vienna, but you might be lucky.'

'It's worth a try.'

'Would you like my assistant to ring the airline now?'

Ashton shook his head. 'I think it would be more discreet if I did it from the hotel.'

'You're probably right. What exactly will you want from us?'

'A blow-by-blow account of the police investigation once the bodies are found. For all that he'd lived in Bulgaria for the last fifty-odd years, de Vries was still a British citizen at the time of his death, so I doubt the Bulgarian authorities will think it strange if the embassy enquires about the case from time to time.'

'I agree. Is there anything else you'd like me to do?'

'It might be an idea if you didn't classify any of the reports you send to London. I'm not saying the Bulgarian Intelligence Service will intercept any cables you dispatch but it's best not to take any chances. One other thing, don't address anything directly to me, route everything through the FCO. Okay?'

Pearman said he quite understood, wished him bon voyage and shook hands again before they parted company.

Out on the street, Ashton walked up the avenue as far as the university, then cut through the small park behind the National Assembly to the Alexander Nevski Cathedral honouring the two hundred thousand Russian casualties of the 1877–1878 War of Liberation. Crossing the open plaza to the taxi rank near the tomb of the unknown soldier, he took a cab back to the Sheraton.

He wasn't sure what story to give the hotel. Most guide books recommended that a tourist should spend up to a week taking in the sights of the city; if he left on the Austrian Airlines flight to Vienna, his stay in the capital was going to be one of the shortest on record. Yesterday, the Tu154 of Balkan Airways had left Heathrow three hours later than the scheduled departure time and midnight had only been half an hour away when he'd checked into the Sheraton;

DEATH THROES

now, as far as the staff were concerned, he was about to pack up and go almost before the ink was dry on the registration slip. In the event, no explanation was necessary. When he went to collect his room key from the desk clerk, he was informed that a young lady was waiting for him.

'A young lady?'

'From the tourist agency, sir.' The desk clerk pointed across the lobby. 'She's over there.'

Ashton turned about and received a tentative smile from the girl on the couch as she got to her feet. She was very young, no more than eighteen and modest with it. Not for her an abbreviated mini which barely covered her bottom; instead she chose to wear a calf-length floral silk dress with a black crocheted shawl around her shoulders. Long dark hair framed a heart-shaped face and she had the bluest eyes Ashton had ever seen. High heels made her appear taller than she actually was and emphasised her thin body. While not a candidate for famine relief, he doubted if she weighed more than eighty pounds.

'Mr Ashton?' She offered him a slender hand. 'I am Denista, your guide.'

'From which travel agency?'

'Interbalkan,' she told him with a puzzled frown.

'This may come as a surprise to you but I'm not planning on doing any excursions while I am in Sofia.'

'But I was asked to meet you . . .'

'Not by me.'

'I am sorry, my English is not good.'

'It's excellent,' Ashton assured her. 'Where did you learn the language – at the university?'

'High school. I am not speaking it well enough to go there yet.' The tentative smile made another brief appearance. 'That is why I got a job with the travel agency – to improve my English. Also to earn some money.'

'Well, I'm very sorry but I don't need a guide . . .'

'Mr de Vries said you would.'

The name brought Ashton up with a sharp jolt. 'Mr de Vries?' he repeated slowly.

'Yes – the Englishman.'

7

'How do you know him?'

'He lives in Car Simeon Street, near my grandmother. They are good friends.'

'I think you had better tell me all about it, Denista.' Ashton led her back to the couch and signalled a passing waiter. 'What would you like to drink?' he asked.

'May I have a Coke?'

The universal soft drink. At McDonald's in Pushkin Square, Ashton had seen Muscovites drink it by the bucketful in preference to anything else. Of course, sometimes they spiked the Coca Cola with vodka to give it a kick.

'And I'll have a lager,' he told the waiter. 'Heineken, if you've got it.'

The really skilful interrogator was friendly, understanding and sympathetic, like the priest in the confessional in whom it was natural to confide. Ashton had been trained by the best and was no slouch at the craft. Denista's parents, he learned, lived in the Ivan Vasov District of the city but she had always visited her grandmother three times a week after leaving school before catching a number 7 tram home. However, since graduating from high school and obtaining a job with Interbalkan, Denista had been living with her grandmother in order to be nearer the travel agency. As a result of this move, she had seen more of de Vries and had got to know him quite well.

'And he told you where to look for me in Sofia?' Ashton suggested.

'No, he had no idea where you were staying. I had to find that out for myself. Fortunately, that was not difficult; Westerners are not allowed to stay at the cheaper hotels.'

'And what interesting places are you going to show me?'

'Places?' Denista frowned. 'I am not understanding.'

'You're a tour guide, aren't you?'

'Yes . . . but . . . what . . .' The frown suddenly lifted and was replaced by a warm smile. 'Oh, now I see. Forgive me, I should explain. I am not taking you on an excursion; Mr de Vries said you wanted to meet his friend Valentin.'

Valentin was the name of the unknown Russian whom the Secret Intelligence Service referred to as the 'Insider'. Apart from certain desk officers at Century House, only Pearman and Henry de Vries had been privy to the information.

'And you know where he is?'

'Yes, I take you there like Mr de Vries said.'

'Why did he ask you to do that, Denista? Why didn't he come to the hotel himself?'

'He is an old man, sometimes he gets sick.'

'I had heard he was pretty frail,' Ashton said drily.

'Frail? What does that mean, please?'

'Delicate, in weak health. When did you last see Mr de Vries?'

'Yesterday morning; he was not feeling well.'

He was a damned sight worse now, Ashton thought grimly. 'And that's why you are here now, is it, Denista?' he asked.

'Yes, to take you to Mr Valentin whenever you are wanting to.'

'Where is he staying?'

'At a house in the Suhata Reka District.'

'I see. How long will it take us to get there?'

'Half an hour.' Denista shrugged her shoulders. 'Perhaps forty minutes if we have to wait for a tram.'

Ashton studied her thoughtfully. She was a very young eighteen and, as far as he could tell, completely without guile. He believed her story because she had given him no reason to suppose she was lying. 'All right,' he said, 'let's drink up and go.'

Denista nodded. 'As you wish,' she said gravely and downed the rest of the Coke.

They walked out of the hotel into the bright sunlit plaza, together yet apart. Wheeling left, Denista led him towards St Nedelya Church, which at one time had been the southern boundary of Lenin Square before Communism had become a dirty word throughout Eastern Europe. At 1.30 in the afternoon, the Largo was not exactly bustling with life.

'The tram stop is only a few minutes from here,' Denista informed him, an apologetic smile hovering on her lips.

'I dare say I'll survive.'

'Survive?'

'Never mind,' Ashton said hastily. 'It was an English-type joke.'

'Ah.' Denista cast around for some other topic of conversation, then said, 'This is your first visit to Sofia, yes?'

9

Ashton didn't get a chance to answer. Two militiamen and a muscular civilian who had been leaning against a dark blue Volkswagen mini van which was parked in the pedestrianised square by the church, suddenly straightened up and moved purposefully towards them. As they drew nearer, the tough-looking civilian pointed an accusing finger at him and started yelling at the top of his voice. Ashton couldn't understand more than one word in every three but it was evident that his excitement and undoubted hostility were rubbing off on the two militiamen who began to look equally intimidating.

'What's this all about?' he asked Denista.

'It is bad . . .' Denista stared at him, her face white as chalk. 'Mr de Vries is dead,' she continued with an effort, 'and this man is saying that you killed him.'

It was bad all right. The militiamen had grabbed his arms and were dragging him towards the Volkswagen and everybody in the immediate vicinity was looking anywhere but at him because they didn't want to know. Ashton fought them all the way, tugging, kicking out, doing everything he could to break free. As they shoved him into the back of the van, he called out to Denista, urging her to phone the British Embassy and tell them what had happened. Then suddenly he was lying face down on the floor of the Volkswagen, his arms pinioned behind him, and one of the militiamen was holding a sickly smelling pad over his nose and mouth. And, as he lost consciousness, he thought that this was how it must have been when the KGB had lifted Greville Wynne off the streets of Budapest back in the bad old days.

Chapter 2

A pneumatic drill was hammering away inside his head. He felt nauseated, which was hardly surprising because there was a revolting taste in his mouth and he could smell the vomit on his shirt front. Ashton had no idea how long he had been unconscious but he had been kidnapped in broad daylight and now it was pitch dark. Then he started thinking more clearly and it dawned on him that they had bandaged his eyes. The militiamen had also trussed him up like a chicken, roping his hands and elbows together and securing his ankles to the wrists until he was bent double.

He didn't know whether they had used chloroform or ether to put him out. As a layman who hadn't been exposed to either anaesthetic before, he couldn't distinguish between the properties of $CHCl_3$ and $C_2H_5OC_2H_5$, but he'd heard that it was not unusual for people to be sick when they came to. Since he was lying on his left side in the recovery position, it seemed this possibility had occurred to the militiamen. If nothing else, it showed they were concerned for his welfare, at least to the extent that they were anxious to ensure he didn't drown in his vomit.

There were no other comforting thoughts to be had. Pearman didn't know what had happened and would remain in ignorance because Denista wasn't going to phone the British Embassy. She might have looked frightened when the goons had pounced, but she was no innocent. Denista had set him up and that was the thing that really rankled. Ashton couldn't understand how he could have allowed himself to be so completely deceived by an eighteen-year-old nymph merely because she had looked vulnerable. It was an error of judgement that was best forgotten, especially as dwelling on it served no purpose.

He listened to the swish of their tyres on the asphalt surface and occasionally picked up the sound of another vehicle heading in the opposite direction. The road was obviously in a good state of repair and he calculated they were doing something in the region of seventy miles an hour. Their high speed, the absence of any sharp bends and the relatively smooth conditions suggested they were travelling on a motorway. The small number of vehicles they had encountered while he had been listening could mean that it was late at night. On the other hand, the Bulgarians simply didn't have a traffic problem. Ashton hoped the night had not yet drawn in; if it had, it meant they had been on the road for a minimum of five hours and Sofia was a long way behind them.

He had no idea in which direction they were heading and no way of telling. He just hoped they weren't going east towards one of the Black Sea resorts to keep a rendezvous with a Russian fishing boat. The noise from the engine underwent a subtle change as if the driver had had to put his foot down to maintain their present speed. Convinced he wasn't mistaken, Ashton started counting because it seemed important to keep account of the time from now on. It also gave him something to do and took his mind off the mounting pain in his swollen fingers.

The Volkswagen began to slow down gradually, dropping from seventy to sixty then fifty over something like a couple of miles. He listened even more intently, uncertain at first whether it was his imagination that made him think the engine was labouring, then the driver shifted down a gear and he knew for sure that they were climbing. Some fifteen minutes later by his reckoning, they made a left turn off the highway on to a much rougher surface.

A three-way conversation started up between the Bulgarians. He could only pick out a word here and there from what they were saying but it was possible to work out the location of each individual. One man up front, two behind sitting either side of him, one of whom was smoking a pungent cigarette which meant he frequently cleared his throat as a result of his addiction to tobacco. While his companion possessed a high-pitched voice, the driver had no recognisable characteristics. The 'Smoker', the 'Squeaker' and the 'Nonentity'; he thought it was as well to identify them by appropriate nicknames if they meant to keep him permanently blindfolded.

The driver was now alternating between third and second gear, confirmation if Ashton needed it that they were climbing up into the mountains. The deduction however didn't leave him any the wiser; Bulgaria was full of mountain ranges and he still had no idea where they were taking him. They weren't making for the Black Sea, but neither were they heading for the nearest police station, that was for sure.

Roughly half an hour after he had started counting off the minutes, the Volkswagen turned off the road, bumped along an even rougher track for a short distance, then stopped. The driver cut the engine and got out of the vehicle, slamming the door behind him before moving round to the back. The 'Smoker' dropped his cigarette onto the floor of the van and crushed it underfoot, then leaned over Ashton and gagged him with a piece of cloth. The same man subsequently cut the rope around his ankles before dragging him out of the van with the assistance of the 'Squeaker'. There was no feeling in his legs which threatened to buckle under him with every step he took so that, like a paralytic drunk, he staggered along between the two guards. The house was some twenty-eight paces from the Volkswagen, another nine put Ashton at the top of a flight of steps leading down to a cellar. Neither Bulgarian bothered to help him on the way down. His wrists and elbows still tied behind his back, they sat him on a wooden stool, then removed the gag and blindfold.

Ashton found himself sitting between two long wine racks that contained very few bottles. Facing him at the far end of the cellar was a portable movie screen mounted on a tripod. The only source of light came from a naked forty-watt bulb suspended from a length of flex in the ceiling directly above his head. Somewhere in another part of the house he could hear the hum of a generator.

'Good evening, Mr Ashton.'

The newcomer spoke English with a mid-Atlantic accent and Ashton had a gut instinct that this man whom he couldn't see was a Russian.

'Please don't turn round. You will find the pictures on the screen much more interesting.'

'Yeah? What are you showing tonight – *The Battleship Potemkin*?'

'No, this is a different sort of feature film. If I were to give this movie a title, it would be *Goodbye, Mr Valentin*.'

'Who?'

'Valentin, the man you hoped to meet in Sofia.'

'I haven't the faintest idea what you are talking about.'

'Really? Next thing I know you will be telling me that your name is not Peter Ashton, that you were not a member of the Officers Training Corps when you were reading German and Russian at Nottingham University.'

'I must get you to write my CV sometime,' Ashton said.

'What else do you want me to say? That you left Nottingham with a good upper second and got a job with British Aerospace as a technical author and translator only to be sacked less than a year later? Should I disclose how you came to join the British Secret Intelligence Service and how in 1991 you blotted your copybook and were shunted off to a dead-end post at Benbow House?'

Although the Russian clearly knew a good deal about him, there were obvious gaps in his knowledge. Had he known the whole story, the Russian would surely have mentioned that he had also joined 23 Special Air Service Regiment in the Territorial Army when he had been taken on by British Aerospace. And no one had sacked him; bored stiff with his job, he had volunteered for a nine-month tour of active duty with the regular army's Special Patrol Unit in Northern Ireland. Nothing the Russian had told him had come as a surprise; he knew precisely when and how the information had been obtained.

'Nothing to say for yourself, Mr Ashton?'

'I thought you were doing all the talking.'

'Oh, I think I will let the movie do that.'

The light went out, plunging the cellar into darkness, then somewhere behind Ashton the projector started running, casting a blue-white square on the screen. Several frames later, the head and shoulders of a male Caucasian appeared five or six times larger than life-size. With his round face, small eyes, heavy jowls and short neck, he looked like a younger version of Khrushchev with a full head of hair. His name was Alexei Leven. Back in 1991 when

Ashton had met him, he had been a lieutenant colonel in the *Glavnoye Razvedyvatelnoye Upravleniye*, the Military Intelligence Directorate of the Soviet Armed Forces. In those days, he had been commanding the GRU cell at Potsdam who were supposed to liaise with the Arms Control Unit from the British Army of the Rhine.

'Your *bête noire*,' the Russian observed from the back of the cellar.

Ashton saw no point in denying it. He had got too close to Alexei Leven and had become contaminated in the process, at least in the eyes of the SIS. There had been no formal Board of Inquiry; instead, he had been quietly removed from the Russian Desk and transferred to the Administrative Wing at Benbow House. To ensure that he had no access to Top Secret material, they had put him in charge of the Security, Vetting and Technical Services Division.

'If it's any consolation, you didn't exactly enhance Alexei's career either, Mr Ashton.'

The camera moved in on a close-up. Leven had never been handsome or even personable but in the last two years his physical appearance had deteriorated significantly. He looked haggard and downcast; there were dark hollows under his eyes and the left corner of his mouth had developed a nervous twitch. The camera panned slowly downward to linger on the handcuffs manacling his wrists before focusing on the leg irons around his ankles.

'Now perhaps you are beginning to understand what this is all about, Mr Ashton.'

There was no voice-over commentary, no word of dialogue, only the noise of the film passing through the gate and the clatter of a spool. Then suddenly the sound track came alive with a familiar metallic shunk-shunk of an automatic being cocked that made Ashton's stomach drop because he knew what was about to happen. Leven was sitting in a wooden armchair looking straight at the camera when his forehead exploded spraying blood, pieces of bone and the grey ooze of brain matter into the lens. The crack of a pistol shot followed a split second later.

'The cameraman was protected by a sheet of bullet-proof glass,' the Russian informed him calmly. 'For the technically minded, Alexei Leven was executed with a 5.45mm PSM automatic using a special low-velocity round of six hundred feet per second.'

A second camera had captured the former GRU officer in profile with the executioner standing directly behind him, right arm extended like a nineteenth-century duellist to point the small-calibre pistol at the head of the condemned man. The replay of the execution in slow motion was the ultimate obscenity. To his horror and disgust, Ashton found he couldn't take his eyes off the screen. He saw the slight upward kick of the automatic when the trigger was squeezed and the wisp of smoke escaping from the muzzle at the moment of discharge, saw Leven slump in the chair and jerk his head involuntarily when the bullet impacted and witnessed the cloud of debris that accompanied its exit. Then mercifully it was over, the last of the film passed through the gate and the screen went blank. There was a moment of total darkness after the 16mm projector had been switched off before one of the Bulgarians thought to put the cellar light back on.

'Now maybe you can appreciate why *Goodbye, Mr Valentin* is such an appropriate title for the movie, Peter.'

Ashton didn't say anything. The sudden use of his first name was another ploy to throw him and it failed because the element of surprise had been missing. Although the Russian hadn't yet said what he wanted from him, it was obvious that the film had been part of the softening up process.

'The question is, what did Valentin give your superiors at Century House which proved to be so mouth-watering that they decided you should meet him?'

'Are you saying that Alexei Leven is Valentin?'

'I thought we had already established that.'

'Then you should have asked Alexei before you shot him,' Ashton said.

'We did, and he was extremely co-operative. What we want from you, Peter, is corroboration.'

They had tried to get the information they wanted from Henry de Vries before killing him and had come away empty-handed because the old man had no idea what the 'Insider' from Moscow had to offer. De Vries was simply the go-between Valentin had chosen, and all he had been able to tell them was the name of the man whom London was sending and where the meeting was to take place. If they hadn't already been aware of that, it could only mean Leven was not the 'Insider'. Although based on pure supposition, it was the only explanation Ashton could think of which made any kind of sense.

'I'm waiting, Peter.'

'For what?'

'To hear what you have to say.'

'You don't seriously believe that I know what information Valentin passed to the British Government as evidence of his good faith, do you? I mean, as you have already pointed out to me, I'm not exactly the flavour of the month with my superiors.'

'You are being difficult.'

'I have that reputation,' Ashton told him.

'And also obtuse.'

'Look, you want to know why London picked me for this job? Because I'm already compromised, because my face is known to you people. And for the last sixteen months, I have been denied access to sensitive material, which means I can't inflict any damage on The Firm under hostile interrogation.'

'That remains to be seen,' the Russian informed him, then issued a string of instructions to the militiamen.

Closely allied to Serbo-Croat and Russian, the Bulgarian language also contains local admixtures of modern Greek, Turkish and Albanian words. As before, Ashton understood very little of what was being said but he found out soon enough what they had in mind for him. The 'Smoker' and the 'Squeaker' grabbed hold of his legs and pulled him off the stool he'd been sitting on with such force that he was almost knocked unconscious when his head struck the floor. While he was still dazed, they raised both feet above the bottom shelf of the nearest wine rack and lashed his ankles to the wooden uprights. A towel was thrown over his face and the ends tied behind his head to ensure he couldn't shake it off. He knew what was coming before he heard someone take a bottle of wine from the rack and break the neck against the shelving.

'Bulgarian Cabernet Sauvignon and not a particularly good year,' the Russian said as he poured the contents of the bottle over the towel.

The red wine seeped through the material and went into his eyes, nose and mouth, making it impossible for him to breathe properly. He coughed, choked, spluttered and in mounting terror shook his head from side to side in a desperate effort to escape from the sodden towel that was slowly suffocating him. He heard another bottle shatter, and then he was drowning and there was a rushing noise in his ears as he went under for the last time and the darkness closed in.

Ashton had heard it said that a drowning man was supposed to see his whole life passing in front of him, but no last-minute images entered his mind. All he experienced was a searing pain in the abdomen and he came to with his head over to the left side, bile dribbling from his open mouth. The towel had been removed and he sucked in great gulps of air, filling his tortured lungs. He was still lying on his back, arms and elbows tied behind him, legs up in the air and lashed to the wine rack. He raised his head off the floor and discovered that after unzipping his pants, the 'Smoker' had burned his stomach with a cigarette.

'I imagine you are feeling some discomfort,' the Russian said casually. 'But we neglected to bring a bottle of smelling salts and we had to revive you somehow.'

'Why bother?'

'Well, the last thing we want to do is send you back to Harriet Egan in a seriously damaged condition.'

Ashton told himself it was just another ploy to make him think there was very little they didn't know about him, but it was still unnerving to hear her name from the lips of a stranger. Forthcoming Marriages: that was how the Russian knew about Harriet. Her mother had put a notice in the *Daily Telegraph* when they had got engaged way back last September. All the same, it was somewhat disconcerting to realise just how much time and energy the Russian Intelligence Service must have spent compiling a dossier on him.

'As I have said before, Peter, all we want from you is corroboration of Alexei Leven's statement.'

'We're comparing notes, are we?'

'Yes. So let's start at the beginning with the briefing you received from the Assistant Director in charge of the Eastern Bloc.'

'I think you should go first.'

'That isn't the way it works,' the Russian told him.

They put the towel over his face again and cracked another bottle of wine. The instructors who had trained Ashton when he had attended the Resistance to Interrogation course run by 22 SAS up at Hereford had told the student body that, ultimately, no matter how brave they might be, everybody had a breaking point. Ashton discovered the truth of this for himself after they had revived him for the fourth straight time when he then happily told the Russian everything he knew about the mission. When he finished, they put out the light and allowed him to sleep.

The intercept station on Mount Olympus in the Troödos mountains was manned by a mix of soldiers and civilian personnel drawn from 9 Signal Regiment based at Ayios Nikolaos in Cyprus. Before Gorbachev, the primary Intelligence-gathering activity of the regiment had been directed towards locating the tactical disposition, fitness for war and state of readiness of Soviet naval, military and air force units in the Black Sea Command, embracing the republics of the Ukraine, Georgia, Armenia, Azerbaijan and Moldavia. Post-Gorbachev and the disintegration of the Soviet Union they had only modified the primary task, not changed it. Nowadays, they were monitoring the communication networks of the independent republics with a view to ascertaining the military capabilities of individual nations in both the conventional and nuclear fields.

Far from shedding any commitments as a result of the break-up of the Warsaw Pact, the regiment had been obliged to take on additional tasks while simultaneously having its establishment reduced under the so-called peace dividend. With a three-way war raging in Bosnia Herzegovina between the Muslim, Croat and Serbian elements of the population, 9 Signal Regiment had been directed to monitor the command nets of the Yugoslav National Army to obtain early warning of troop movements should Belgrade be tempted to reinforce the local Serbian militia with units from the regular army stationed outside Bosnia. And because traditionally Russia had always supported Serbia, diplomatic wireless traffic originating from and addressed to the Russian embassies in Belgrade, Bucharest and Sofia were routinely intercepted. However, with only limited resources available, blanket cover of every target was impossible.

It was therefore something of a fluke when one of the special telegraphists with the Mount Olympus detachment picked up a signal from a previously unidentified station south-west of Sofia in the Rila Mountains. The operator appeared to be using the equivalent of the MANSAT portable satellite communications terminal developed by Ferranti, but was having problems establishing contact. When he did succeed in doing so, the receiving station only got part of the transmission, which meant that certain groups had to be repeated. The exchange continued long enough for the Royal Signals detachment to get a fix on the other station which proved to be in the Moscow area. For some reason, the originator of the message had used a low-grade cipher, and while it would be necessary to await confirmation from the code-breakers at Government Communications Headquarters in Cheltenham, the radio supervisor in charge of the detachment was fairly certain that the Russian operator had been asking Moscow for disposal instructions.

Chapter 3

Cramp overcame exhaustion and roused Ashton. He was still lying as they had left him, flat on his back, feet up in the air, ankles lashed to the wooden uprights of the wine rack. He could only guess how long he had been asleep but in such an uncomfortable position, he doubted if it could have been more than an hour. The nagging headache continued to plague him, kept alive by the bump on the back of his skull and the amount of corked red wine he had swallowed rather than the after effects of the anaesthetic.

Fully alert now, he listened intently while his eyes gradually became accustomed to the prevailing gloom. He could detect no sound which would indicate the presence of another person and it looked as if they had left him on his own in the cellar. But for how long? And what were they likely to do with him when they did return? Ashton doubted if they proposed to run him back to the Sheraton Hotel in Sofia; what had happened to him thus far was a throwback to the bad old days. He hadn't been around when Stalin was alive, hadn't even emerged from the womb until five years after the dictator had been buried in the Kremlin Wall, but he had read the dead files at Century House and had a vivid picture of the literally murderous atmosphere in the immediate postwar years. The only reason the Russian had left him in peace was to contact Moscow and ask for instructions for his disposal.

The thought acted like a stimulant on Ashton. Knowing that if he wanted to see Harriet Egan again, he would have to do something about it, he went to work on his wrists, twisting his hands this way and that in an effort to loosen the knots. When that failed to have

21

the desired effect, he tried rubbing the cords against the rough stone floor, only to end up skinning both palms. Frustrated at every turn, he summoned up the will to keep calm and think clearly.

The wine bottles. The Russian had smashed them against the rack and no one had bothered to sweep up the broken glass before they left the cellar. Maybe he would get lucky, maybe some of the shards had landed near him? There was only one way to find out. Somehow he would have to manoeuvre the upper half of his body in a clockwise direction because the Russian had been standing on his left side when he had poured the wine over his face. Using his arms for leverage, Ashton raised himself off the floor and immediately groaned in pain as the abdominal muscles stretched the cigarette burns on his stomach.

He tried again because the only alternative was to accept defeat and that was something he couldn't do; wriggling like a snake, he inched towards the wine rack. He found the nearest shard accidentally, though with his swollen and numbed hands it was some time before he associated the stickiness on both palms with blood flowing from a slit finger. When he did make the connection, he didn't bother looking for it. The tiny piece of glass which had inflicted the injury was of no use to him, his eyes were on the jagged neck of one of the bottles the Russian had smashed. He had nudged it aside with his foot and it had struck one of the wooden uprights and rolled back again, coming to rest about eight inches out from the bottom shelf. To reach it, Ashton had to turn over as far as possible on to his right hip, arch his body like a drawn bow and locate the jagged neck by touch.

His fingers were all thumbs and the simplest task seemed beyond him. Every four-letter word in every language he was familiar with came flooding to his mind, fuelling his rage. Eventually he found the rim, took a firm grip on the neck and fiddled around with it until the jagged edge was pointing upward, then he began to saw the rope. It occurred to him that all it needed was one slip and there was a real chance he would sever the arteries in his wrists. On the other hand, that would be the least of his problems if he was still trussed up like a chicken when the Russian returned.

A strand parted, then another, and suddenly his hands were free. He laid the implement down and flexed his fingers to restore the circulation before attacking the cord around the elbows. He worked both arms as though shrugging alternate shoulders while at the same time forcing them outwards to loosen the knot and bring the rope close enough to hack at it with the jagged glass. It took him less than five minutes to cut through what he later discovered was a length of clothesline. After that, it didn't take him any time at all to free his ankles.

Ashton scrambled to his feet and zipped up his pants. For some moments, his legs felt as if they didn't belong to him and he found it necessary to hang on to the wine rack until the sensation had passed. The temptation to get out of there as fast as he could was almost irresistible but deep down he knew that stealth rather than speed was the only safe course to take. As silently as he could, Ashton climbed the long flight of steps and tried the cellar door only to find it had been locked from the outside.

Stealth was out, brute force allied to surprise was in. He retraced his steps and picked up one of the few remaining bottles of wine. He weighed it in his hand, thought about breaking off the bottom, then decided the bottle would be a more effective weapon if he used it like a club. He had to put the bottle down to remove the light bulb from the socket. Then, his eyes quickly accustomed to the dark, he held the bottle by the neck in his right hand, and positioned himself near the top of the steps, adopting the almost horizontal stance of a world-class sprinter leaving the starting blocks in a 100-metre dash. The time spent in waiting for something to happen was always a nerve-racking business. Butterflies in his stomach, a tight band around his chest, heart pounding like a runaway steam engine, mouth dry as dust; Ashton was familiar with the symptoms of inner tension and experienced all of them before he heard footsteps outside the door.

The key turned in the lock and the door opened outwards to reveal the two Bulgarians, one standing behind the other. The light switch was on the inside; as the 'Squeaker' reached for it with his left hand, Ashton came out of the crouch like a coiled spring asserting itself. Grabbing hold of the Bulgarian by his jacket, he pulled him off balance and at the same time turned sideways to flatten himself against the wall. As the 'Squeaker' stumbled past, a raised foot did the rest, catching the Bulgarian below the knee to send him cartwheeling to the bottom of the flight of steps. The 'Smoker' decided to go for the pistol on his right hip but was slow to raise his free hand to ward off Ashton when he came at him with the bottle.

Ashton caught the Bulgarian with a glancing blow on the side of the skull which sent him reeling back, then delivered the clincher at the second attempt with a poleaxing club over the head. One man dead in the cellar with a broken neck, the other in bad shape with a depressed cranium. Ashton didn't wait to see where the Russian was hiding himself, and running to the door, he yanked it open and plunged out of the house into the grey light of dawn. To his right, the Volkswagen was parked off the pathway on a level piece of ground amongst the fir trees.

He started towards the vehicle with the intention of stealing it, then abruptly changed direction when the driver appeared from behind the blind side wheeling the flat he had just changed. By the time the driver recovered his wits and thought to do something about stopping him, Ashton had covered almost thirty yards and was well into the forest. The crack thump of two rounds from a high-velocity weapon cleaving the air above his head spurred him to even greater efforts, as did the third which clipped a tree to add the whine of a ricochet to the reverberating crash of gunfire echoing in the mountains. The warning shout was very much an afterthought, then Ashton realised the voice was somewhere over to his left. Peering in that direction, he caught a glimpse between the trees of the fourth man moving purposefully to cut him off.

The Russian, he thought; noted too that his adversary was carrying a large man-pack radio on his back while holding a satellite dish aerial in his right hand. Loaded down with something like forty pounds of equipment, Ashton knew there was no way the Russian was going to catch him. He ran on down the hillside, eyes searching the ground ahead as he followed a trail made by a mountain goat, the pain from the burns on his stomach forgotten in the need to lose his pursuers.

Pearman had a premonition that this particular Friday was going to be quite unlike any other he had known since joining the embassy when he walked into his office and found the local morning papers had been marked up for his attention by the Second Secretary

(Chancery and Cultural). When the Communist Party had been in power, Sofia had had eight daily newspapers serving a population of a little over a million; in the present political climate, it was difficult to keep track of the number of titles from one week to another. The *People's Army* and the *People's Youth* had ceased publication along with the *Worker's Cause* and *Fatherland Front*, but *Labour*, *Co-operative Village* and *Agrarian Banner* were still being printed. So too were the *New Socialist*, *Liberal Democrat* and the *Independent Clarion*, survivors of a host of titles which had mushroomed to represent the new political thinking in the country. The one story common to all six newspapers that morning was the murder of Henry de Vries and his housekeeper, but only the *Independent Clarion* carried it on the front page.

He read all six accounts, then placed the newspapers in the out-tray and lit a King Size Silk Cut. The government health warning on the side of the packet had absolutely no effect on him, and never would have; he enjoyed smoking and firmly believed a cigarette helped him to see the issues more clearly when he had to put his thinking cap on. Ashton had asked him for a blow-by-blow account of the police investigation once it had got underway and the sooner he informed the authorities of HMG's interest in the case, the better it would be for all concerned.

He opened the top drawer in his desk and took out the copy of British Airways worldwide timetable. If Ashton had been unable to get a seat on the Austrian Airways flight to Vienna yesterday afternoon, he would certainly be on the Balkan Airways 737 departing for Heathrow at five minutes to nine, which meant the Foreign Office would hear what had happened to de Vries by 14.00 hours at the latest. All the same, it would be as well to send them a cable for the sake of appearances. The diplomatic bag was supposed to be sacrosanct but even in this enlightened climate, you couldn't be sure the Bulgarian Intelligence Service would be above taking a peek. And some analyst might just wonder why the Ambassador was taking such an interest in the conduct of the murder investigation when he hadn't bothered to inform the Foreign Office about de Vries when his body had been found. But the cable would have to wait until he had prepared the ground with the Ministry of the Interior.

Fortunately, he knew who to call; the diplomatic round of official parties and receptions was frequently derided in the British tabloids but there was an inherent advantage in being able to put a face to a name, never mind the favours that were sometimes gained by presuming on a brief social acquaintance. Lifting the receiver, Pearman rang the Second Deputy Minister of the Interior. After exchanging the usual pleasantries, he explained why the embassy was interested in the case, let it be known that de Vries's next of kin in the UK might wish to have the body flown home for burial, and asked who was in charge of the murder investigation. He also asked if he could meet the officer concerned. The case officer, he learned in double-quick time, was Captain Ivan Khristov. However, it took the Second Deputy Minister of the Interior considerably longer to arrange a meeting for 12.00 hours at Militia Headquarters in the Central District.

Captain Ivan Khristov was a short man built like a prize fighter with broad shoulders, a well-muscled chest and slim hips. He was in his late forties, had black hair liberally flecked with grey, and the makings of a pot belly. He had not received the best training in the world to lead a murder investigation; before the Communist Party had been toppled from power in the free elections of 1989, he, like other officers of his ilk in the militia, had devoted most of his energy to keeping the student body in line, rousting down-and-outs and those penniless tourists who tried to save money by sleeping rough in the central railway station. Fraud, graft, corruption, embezzlement and even murder had not been unknown crimes in the old days, but now when he charged someone with an offence, he was required to prove it in a court of law where the verdict was not going to be a foregone conclusion, and that was a new and unwelcome experience for him. He had never had to explain what he was doing to a foreigner before, and that was another aggravation. Worse still from his point of view, he was up against an Englishman who could speak his native tongue so he couldn't pretend he hadn't understood the question.

'It's very good of you to spare me the time, Captain Khristov,' Pearman said, ever the diplomat.

The militia captain nodded as if to confirm that he agreed with the sentiment. 'The Second Deputy Minister has instructed me to give you every assistance.' Khristov smiled and spread his hands. 'So what can I tell you, Mr Pearman? A woman made an anonymous call to the local police station late yesterday afternoon to report a disturbance at 23 Car Simeon. When the militia officers arrived at the address, they could see that someone had forced their way into the house. So they went inside to investigate and discovered the bodies of Mr de Vries and the housekeeper who looked after him.'

'Do we know when they were murdered?'

'We are still awaiting the results of the post-mortem but I expect the pathologist to confirm they were killed sometime during the early hours of yesterday morning. An eye witness gave us a description of the probable killer who was seen leaving the house shortly after eleven o'clock. We expect to apprehend him very soon.'

'Really?'

'Oh yes, we have a very good description – a youngish man, middle thirties, very fit looking, dark hair, about one point eight metres tall, approximately eighty kilos.'

Pearman did a quick piece of mental arithmetic and came to the conclusion that the suspect was an inch under six feet and weighed about a hundred and seventy pounds. The description matched Ashton, and he had certainly been in the area of Car Simeon at eleven o'clock.

'He is also a foreigner.'

Pearman raised both eyebrows. 'How do you know that?' he asked.

'By the clothes he was wearing. Black shoes, dark blue trousers, jacket a shade lighter – very good quality – well cut – very expensive.'

It was Ashton to a T. Pearman was thankful he had left the country.

'He will not get away,' Khristov said confidently. 'We are watching the airport, the bus terminal and railway stations. We have also circulated his description outside Sofia.'

'Do you have a motive for the crime?'

'Robbery. Mr de Vries was obviously a very rich man.'

'Why do you say that?'

'He could afford to employ a servant to look after his needs. And the Second Deputy Minister told me his family wanted his body flown to England for burial. That will be a very expensive business.'

'Well, it's not definite yet,' Pearman said.

'I see.' Khristov stood up. 'You will of course let me know what the family decide?'

It was not the most polite dismissal Pearman had known but he consoled himself with the thought that he had learned everything there was to know at this stage.

'You can count on it,' he said, shaking hands with the militia captain. 'And I hope you will also keep the embassy fully informed regarding the investigation.'

The monastery formed a rough triangle enclosing a large courtyard and appeared to consist of a number of Italian-style villas joined together but of varying height, some having three upper floors, others four. The massive rear-facing walls, coupled with the uniformly small windows, reminded Ashton of a fortress. The monastery church was in the centre of the flagstone courtyard, its undulating shape emphasised by the diversity of the cupolas and the bold façade of horizontal stripes of red and white bricks. From his position high up on the hillside, he could see the wooden balconies fronting the monks' cells in the far side of the triangle and the stairways leading to the upper tiers above the graceful arches on the ground floor.

Ashton had no idea where he was and only knew the Colditz-type castle below was a monastery because he had spotted a priest crossing the courtyard. Judging by the number of people taking photographs, it was also a major tourist attraction, but not having read a guidebook, he was still none the wiser. After escaping from the house where he was being held, he had marched in a south-easterly direction for over two hours, using the sun's position and his wristwatch as navigational aids. When satisfied that he had left his pursuers far behind, he had started to backtrack. Eventually, he had picked up a stream which he had then followed down the mountainside knowing it would ultimately lead him to the plain, but that was the sum total of his knowledge.

Ashton moved to the left, looking for the road which led to the monastery. There had to be one because the tourists he could see in the courtyard didn't look as if they were dressed to go hiking. He saw the bus first, then a group of five cars parked higgledy-piggledy outside the entrance to the monastery. Salvation: he could walk down the hillside and ask one of the tourists to give him a lift back to Sofia. He could imagine the reaction if he did; he hadn't washed or shaved, there was dried vomit on his shirt front, his jacket stank of sour red wine and the elbow was out of one sleeve. As for the rest of his appearance, there was a lump on the back of his head, both palms were skinned and the index finger of his left hand had bled profusely from the slit. Even if he walked to the nearest town, he couldn't hire a taxi, catch a bus or take a train because the bastards had lifted his wallet while he had been unconscious. They had also taken his passport but had left him with his Omega which was a strange oversight on their part.

Ashton continued circling to the left to get a better view of the approach road. After covering roughly four hundred yards, he caught sight of another building lower down the mountain from the monastery. At first, he thought it was an isolated house, then he spotted a couple of Lada saloons parked round the side of the building and realised he was looking at a small hotel. If the owners were staying overnight, he would wait until dark and steal one of the cars; if they had gone by that time, he would just have to lift a bicycle from somewhere. It wasn't much of a plan but it was the best he could come up with. Meanwhile, he would retrace his steps to the stream and freshen up. He was tired, hungry and not a little despondent, but he had overcome worse situations and could do so again if he started thinking positively.

Commander (Retired) Reginald James Osbourne, OBE, DSC was fifty-nine and single, which Pearman thought was just as well considering the nature of his job. Born in 1934, Reggie Osbourne had become a Queen's Messenger after twenty-eight years in the Royal Navy. During his service, he had seen action in the Korean War as a midshipman on the cruiser *Belfast*, as a carrier pilot on the *Albion* in the Suez invasion and on detached duty with 3 Commando Brigade in Borneo where he had been awarded his DSC. Queen's Messengers covered the globe delivering and collecting the diplomatic bag to British embassies the world over and the constant upheaval this entailed was not conducive to family life.

Osbourne had a flat in Holland Park and a cottage in the Cotswolds near Stowe where he liked to spend every free weekend. Unfortunately, there hadn't been too many of those lately and it looked as if this coming one was also going to be taken up. The requirement to be available at a moment's notice was one of the reasons why he had been given an OBE in the 1990 New Year Honours List. It was also a fact that he had been a Queen's Messenger longer than anyone else in the organisation.

Pearman read the letter he'd delivered a second time. Like the envelope, it was addressed personally to him by name rather than appointment. It carried a security classification of Secret but there was no originator's file number or even a subject heading, which made registration of the document somewhat difficult. The handwriting was, however, familiar and Victor Hazelwood, the Deputy Director General of the SIS was nothing if not brief and to the point. The meeting with the 'Insider' from Moscow had been cancelled and he was required to contact Ashton and instruct him to return home forthwith.

'When were you told that you would be going to Sofia, Reggie?' Pearman asked, looking up.

'Last night,' Osbourne said with feeling. 'Phoned me at home at about seven thirty. Said it was urgent and I was being routed via Munich and would need to be at the airport by 06.15 at the latest.'

Osbourne had received the news roughly an hour before the connecting flight from Vienna arrived at Heathrow, assuming Ashton had managed to get a seat on the Austrian Airlines plane yesterday afternoon. If he had done so, Ashton would have got in touch with his Deputy DG soon after his flight had landed, which would have given both Century House and the Foreign Office plenty of time to tell Osbourne to stand down.

'I'd like you to do something for me, Reggie.'

'That sounds ominous.'

'The risks are minimal . . .'

'I can't tell you how many times I've heard that.'

'Well, now you are hearing it again from me, Reggie,' Pearman said with a smile. It was not the first time Osbourne had been to Sofia and they were almost old friends. 'I don't think you will be at risk,' he continued, 'but the embassy can't afford to be involved.'

'You certainly know how to instil confidence into a man, Michael.'

'This letter concerns a man called Ashton . . .'

'There's a Peter Ashton on the list of Queen's Messengers. Never met him though.'

'Hopefully, you aren't about to do so now. He was staying at the Sheraton Hotel and I'd like you to do the same. Tell the desk clerk he's an old friend and ask for his room number. If he has checked out, all well and good; if he hasn't, don't go near him.'

'This gets more interesting by the minute,' Osbourne said cheerfully.

'Jean is giving one of her dinner parties this evening,' Pearman told him. 'Seven thirty for eight. You're invited.'

'Is Jean expecting me?'

'Not yet.' Pearman smiled. 'But she will be. Get there a few minutes early. We'll take a stroll round the garden before the other guests arrive and you can tell me what happened at the Sheraton.'

Chapter 4

Reggie Osbourne arrived at five minutes to seven, a good half-hour before the first guests were expected and while Jean was still clad only in her underwear. That Osbourne was a last-minute addition and had upset her carefully arranged seating plan was bad enough, that he should arrive before she had finished changing for dinner was doubly annoying.

'You can bloody well look after him,' she told Pearman in no uncertain terms after their live-in maid had tapped on the bedroom door to announce that the Commander was waiting downstairs in the hall. 'He's your guest, you invited him to dinner.'

'I really didn't have much choice,' Pearman reminded her before leaving.

It was, he knew, a very minor spat and when Jean eventually joined them, no one, least of all Reggie, would be aware that they'd just had words.

'I'm not too early, am I, Michael?' Osbourne asked him breezily.

'Not at all.' Pearman ushered the former navy commander into the drawing room, fixed him a large gin and tonic and mixed a smaller one for himself, then suggested they took their drinks out into the garden.

'Good idea, it's a nice evening.' Osbourne followed him outside on to the patio and stood there admiring the display of hardy annuals in the flowerbeds – white, pink and purple alyssum, begonias, cornflowers, godetia, stock and phlox were some of the plants he could recognise. 'Jean's handiwork?' he asked.

'Yes, she's the gardener round here.'

33

'Another of her many talents. You're a lucky fellow, Michael.'

No one had to tell Pearman that but he enjoyed hearing it from other people, especially as Jean had not always met with universal approval. They had married on the seventeenth of May 1976 shortly before her twenty-second birthday. Eleven months later she had presented him with a son and heir to be followed by a daughter barely a year after. Although there was no rule as such, the Diplomatic Service preferred its younger officers to be single and unattached and in the eyes of his superiors, he had committed a number of sins. He had acquired a family before completing his first overseas posting as a Third Secretary with the embassy in Brussels and he had married someone who was unsuitable. When Pearman had met her, Jean had been the PA to Her Majesty's Consul General, which as everyone in the Diplomatic knew, was the Foreign Office description for a shorthand typist. "A career-minded officer does not allow himself to become entangled with a young woman who left school at sixteen with five O levels and completed her education at a secretarial college." The officer who had taken him aside to impart those few words of advice had subsequently been invited to leave the Service after being cited in a particularly messy divorce.

'I envy you,' Osbourne said.

'Yes, Sofia isn't a bad posting – can be a little dull though.'

'I was referring to Jean.'

'I know you were.' Pearman smiled. 'Let's talk about Ashton.'

'He's still at the Sheraton, leastways he hasn't checked out.' Osbourne contemplated the slice of lemon in his gin and tonic. 'On the other hand, no one has seen him since lunchtime yesterday.'

'You asked around?' Pearman said, hoping he had done no such thing.

'Didn't have to, the desk clerk volunteered the information after I'd asked him for Ashton's room number. Apparently, some young woman from a travel agency had been waiting for him and they went off together shortly after he returned to the hotel.'

'Did the desk clerk say who she was?'

'No. And I didn't enquire. I mean, you did tell me to be discreet.'

London had aborted the mission, Ashton had gone missing and

the militia were looking for a man answering to his description. Pearman wondered how much worse things could get.

'The desk clerk reckoned this girl couldn't have been more than eighteen.'

'What are you hinting at, Reggie?'

'Well, he gave me a knowing smile when he said she was from the Interbalkan tourist agency. I got the impression that perhaps she was on the game.'

'Nonsense.'

'It isn't nonsense; believe me, it's happening all over Eastern Europe. The State Enterprise Boards provide bilingual secretaries to assist foreign businessmen. I'm not saying the young women don't know their job and are indifferent interpreters, but they are quite willing to provide sexual gratification for the weary traveller in return for a not-so-small consideration. I've no idea what the going rate is in Sofia, but I'm told an eighteen-year-old high school graduate with a passable figure commands fifty dollars in Moscow and that's only for a quickie.'

'I wasn't referring to the girl,' Pearman told him. 'I was talking about Ashton. He's not stupid, he wouldn't take off with a hooker.'

'Well, you should know. As I said, I've never met him. But according to the desk clerk, they spent some time chatting over a drink and when they did leave, she didn't have to drag him out of the hotel.'

Pearman didn't doubt it. As he saw it, the girl had given Ashton a message of some kind and he had believed her. It was possible that he had been persuaded that she could lead him to where the mysterious 'Insider' from Moscow was hiding.

'Ashton is in trouble, I'm sure of it.' Pearman downed the remains of his gin and tonic. 'That's the message I want you to take back to London tomorrow, Reggie.'

'Tomorrow's Saturday.'

'I know it is, but there will be a resident clerk on duty at the Foreign Office who's cleared for access to Top Secret. Tell him the information must be passed to the Deputy DG of the Secret Intelligence Service as soon as possible.'

'Am I allowed to know what sort of trouble he's in?'

There were no security grounds for holding anything back from

Osbourne; Pearman only hesitated because much of his assessment was based on guesswork.

'I believe Ashton has been abducted by the Russians,' he said reluctantly.

'A bit old hat, isn't it? I thought that sort of unpleasantness had died a natural death with Brezhnev?'

'So did I, but it seems to be enjoying a new lease of life.' Pearman heard the muted sound of voices coming from the hall and realised that the first guests had arrived. 'Something else you should know. The militia are also looking for him, they believe he killed Henry de Vries and his housekeeper. Of course, they don't know it yet but Ashton was seen leaving the house shortly before the bodies were found. One of the neighbours gave the investigating officers a very good description of him.'

'Christ, he really is in trouble.'

'He won't be the only one if we stay out here much longer,' Pearman said quietly. Placing a hand under Osbourne's elbow, he steered him towards the French windows.

The night had started to draw in at 18.30 hours; three-quarters of an hour later with the new moon partially hidden by cloud, Ashton judged it dark enough to check out the hotel below. The last of the tourists had left the monastery shortly before dusk, gone too were all the vehicles that at one time or another had been parked outside the main entrance. Old habits die hard and the lessons learned in the SAS and on the streets of Belfast stood him in good stead as he moved in a series of tactical bounds through the fir and beech trees, stopping every thirty yards or so to observe and listen intently.

He reached the hotel without incident. A faded sign in the Cyrillic alphabet above the front door told him he was looking at The Rilets. The name left him none the wiser and he still had no idea where he was. There were no lights showing anywhere on the ground floor at the front but he could see a chink between the drawn curtains in one of the rooms upstairs. He had spent the whole afternoon watching the inn, observing the comings and goings, and had reached the conclusion that the proprietors were doing very little business in the way of the passing carriage trade. When one of the two Lada saloons parked round the side of the building had moved off down the road shortly after six, he had convinced himself that only the innkeeper and his wife, if he had one, and perhaps one or two members of the staff were on the premises. But now he had a nasty feeling that he had been guilty of wishful thinking.

Ashton moved back into the treeline and sat down. He wondered if the proprietors kept a dog. Coming face to face with an Alsatian, a Doberman or a Rottweiler was one of those nasty surprises he wished to avoid. Some country people relied on a flock of geese to raise the alarm; in London's more expensive residential neighbourhoods, householders spent hundreds of pounds installing infra-red intruder systems. But this was Bulgaria and he had seen nothing to suggest there was even a simple burglar alarm in place. As for a guard dog, there was only one way to find out; getting to his feet again, he crept towards the hotel.

There was no dog, no flock of geese and the one audible noise came from his stomach, growling with hunger. He approached the Lada saloon and tried the nearest door. His pleasure in finding it unlocked died when, having quietly released the bonnet, he went to hotwire the ignition and discovered the car was up on blocks and minus both front wheels.

His morale took a bit of a nosedive until he noticed the bicycle propped against the wall near the rear entrance. Hardly daring to believe his luck, Ashton took a closer look at the machine. There was nothing wrong with the bike, the tyres felt firm enough, it had brakes on both wheels and there was even a lamp of sorts, but no rear light. It didn't have any gears either but who was he to complain? The owner hadn't bothered to secure the bike with a padlock and chain and he thanked God there were still some trusting people left in the world. Lifting it by the frame, he carried the bike away and didn't attempt to mount it until he was some considerable distance from the hotel.

He hadn't been on a bicycle since leaving Nottingham University but some skills you didn't forget and riding a two-wheeler was one of them. At first, he wobbled from side to side, but eventually he got the hang of it and became confident enough to take one hand off the handlebars to switch on the lamp. He needn't have bothered; the dry cell battery was on its last legs and a couple of glow-worms could have produced a more powerful beam.

The road twisted and turned following the contours of the mountainside. While not particularly steep, the gradient was more than a gentle incline and for the most part he was able to freewheel. It was only when he reached the outskirts of a small village called Rila that Ashton realised he had been riding on the wrong side of the road.

Approximately half an hour after stealing the bicycle, the mountain road ended at a T-junction with a major highway where a signpost indicated he was 125 kilometres from Sofia. It still seemed a dauntingly long way even after he had converted the distance into miles.

The dinner party had been a big success and no one had wanted to leave, which Pearman accepted was about par for the course because he couldn't recall a single occasion in the past when something Jean had organised had not gone with a swing. The last guest, who had also happened to be the first, had departed at 1.15 a.m., or to be more accurate, he had bundled Reggie into his Ford Granada and delivered him to the Sheraton. Bulgaria might have embraced the market economy along with free elections, but night life in Sofia was as dead as a doornail after eleven o'clock and you couldn't find a cab for love nor money.

Pearman made a right turn off the Boulevard Vladimir Zaimov into San Stefano and pulled up outside his residence which overlooked a small park. Locking the car, he let himself into the house, switched off the hall light and went upstairs. Instead of being fast asleep, he found Jean sitting up in bed reading a novel.

'You were quick, darling,' she said without looking up from her book. 'I'm surprised Reggie didn't insist on giving you a nightcap.'

'He wanted to but there was no way I was going to set foot inside the hotel.' Pearman removed his dinner jacket and hung it up, then undid his bow tie. 'Couldn't afford to,' he added, 'much too risky.'

'Why so?'

Pearman kicked off his slip-on shoes, unzipped his trousers and stepped out of them. 'Because of official business,' he said vaguely.

'Now you're being enigmatic and it doesn't suit you.'

'You could say the same about my present appointment, at least as far as one particular facet is concerned. I don't like working for two government departments. I'm a Foreign Office man, not an Intelligence officer.'

'What are you trying to say, Michael?'

'There have been some very worrying developments and there could be some unfortunate repercussions for us if I put a foot wrong.'

'How unfortunate?'

'Like it was in '77.'

He didn't have to enlarge. That was the year Hugo had been born, to confirm the worst fears of Pearman's superiors who sincerely believed his chosen career would come a poor second now that he had acquired a family. When it had counted most, he had never again been considered for a high-profile appointment after Brussels. Instead, maximum use had been made of his second-string qualification with the result that two back-to-back postings to South America, where Spanish was practically the lingua franca, had followed, first to Santiago, then Buenos Aires. The latter posting had been short-toured when diplomatic relations with the Argentine were broken off following the invasion of the Falklands. Rehabilitation had been a long time coming and while he had no illusions about going on to higher things, by and large he liked his present appointment and certainly didn't want to leave it under a cloud.

'Would it help if we talked about it?' Jean asked.

Pearman hesitated. Strictly speaking, it would constitute a breach of security if he confided in Jean; on the other hand, there was precious little to be secret about with one agent dead, the other missing and the people at Century House washing their hands of the whole business. Havering no longer, he told her about de Vries, Ashton and the mysterious young woman who had been waiting for him at the Sheraton, and what he personally had learned after meeting Captain Ivan Khristov at Militia Headquarters. He held nothing back because once started, there was no point in trying to minimise the potential damage.

'I feel so damned inadequate. I mean, we are faced with a crisis out here and what remedial action do I take? Why, I send a message back to London with Reggie Osbourne to the effect that their man has disappeared and I am powerless to do anything about it. Furthermore, if by any chance he should surface again, please tell me what to do because the militia have his description and are hellbent on charging him with murder.'

'That's over the top,' Jean told him calmly. 'In the first place, the Ambassador will support you if there are any recriminations from London because he has confidence in you and knows that no one could have handled the situation better. And secondly I don't believe the militia would recognise Ashton if he walked into their headquarters tomorrow. Take away the distinctive clothing and the description could fit almost anybody.'

He hoped Jean was right but if something bad had happened to Ashton, he was unlikely to survive the inevitable post-mortem. There was a good chance he would end up carrying the can for the SIS. Although Bulgaria had been a member of the Warsaw Pact since its inception, it had never been a primary target for Intelligence gathering and Century House had saved money and manpower by relying on the Foreign Office to do the job for them. The fact that he was only a part-time Intelligence officer with no practical experience in the field would be conveniently ignored in the need to find a suitable scapegoat.

'When are you coming to bed, Michael?'

'After I've brushed my teeth,' Pearman said and went into the bathroom.

When he returned to the bedroom a few minutes later, the light was out and Jean was breathing deeply as if asleep. Taking care not to disturb her, Pearman got into bed and lay there flat on his back, hands clasped behind his head, staring blankly up at the ceiling.

'It's no use lying there worrying yourself sick,' Jean said presently. 'There is nothing you can do at this hour of the morning.'

'That's true.'

'And in the full light of day, things won't seem half as bad as they do now.'

He wanted to believe that also was true.

The bicycle had never been Ashton's favourite means of transport even when he had been a penniless student, and the one he had stolen happened to be a particularly cumbersome machine. It had a rock-hard saddle, a slack chain and weighed a ton; riding it was sheer torture. After nine hours on the road, his calf muscles were like lumps of iron and he ached in every bone. In that time he had clocked up just seventy miles.

The need to exercise caution, rather than the dilapidated condition of the bicycle, accounted for the indifferent performance. He looked dishevelled, had a two-day growth of beard on his face, had no money and no identity papers. He couldn't speak the language and should anyone stop him, he would be unable to explain what he was doing in the middle of the night riding a bicycle. Given those handicaps, the militia were the last people Ashton wished to encounter. To avoid them in a town like Stanke Dimirov, he had given the main thoroughfare a miss and had kept to the back streets. In the open country, he had dismounted and gone to ground off the highway whenever headlights had appeared in the distance or he'd heard a vehicle coming up behind him.

It had been a long, slow and exhausting process; fortunately, things had improved after midnight when the traffic had thinned out and from then on he'd practically had the road to himself. Now it was five thirty in the morning, Mount Vitosha, the wooded mass of granite on the outskirts of Sofia was behind him and the first trucks from the outlying farms were heading into the city with fruit and fresh vegetables for the market. Ashton waited until the road was clear in both directions, then dismounted and wheeled the bicycle into the adjoining field the other side of a straggly hedgerow. He removed his jacket, hid it in the undergrowth and rolled both shirtsleeves above the elbows, then picked up the bike and returned to the road. It wasn't much of a disguise but at least he didn't now look quite so conspicuous riding a bicycle and there was a reasonable chance that the casual observer would take him for a workman on early shift.

By 6.15, Ashton had reached the Knyazhevo District of Sofia without incident. The fact that the British Embassy would not be open on a Saturday morning wasn't a problem. Before leaving London, he had memorised Pearman's address; before leaving the Sheraton Hotel the day before yesterday, he had looked up San Stefano Road on the street map of Sofia and knew how to find it from the city centre. The map however didn't cover the outer suburbs and it wasn't until the approach road became the Boulevard Vitosha that Ashton knew where he was. Turning right off the boulevard, he abandoned the cycle near the university and walked the rest of the way. When he rang the doorbell of the house in San Stefano, the English-speaking live-in maid refused to allow him across the threshhold and was unwilling to call her employer until Ashton gave his name and claimed he was related to Pearman. The door closed in his face; when it reopened a few minutes later, a very surprised-looking Pearman was standing there in his silk pyjamas and dressing gown.

'Well, this is a pleasant surprise, Peter,' he said for the benefit of the maid who was standing behind him, then added, 'Come in, come in. Jean will be delighted to see you.' The serious business began once they were alone in the study. 'Where did you spring from?' he asked.

'About eighty miles from here,' Ashton told him, 'some place near Rila up in the mountains.'

'Is that where the kidnappers were holding you?'

'You heard from Denista then?'

'No one reported you missing. Was Denista the girl who was waiting for you at the hotel?'

'We seem to be talking at cross purposes. The people who grabbed me outside the hotel might have been in uniform but they weren't militia.'

'I have news for you,' Pearman said calmly. 'The police are looking for you.'

They started again from the beginning. Ashton described what had happened to him and Pearman gave a word-for-word account of his conversation with Captain Ivan Khristov. By the time they had finished comparing notes, Ashton had a clearer idea of what he was up against.

'Doesn't look too good, does it?' he observed.

'We'll do everything we can to help you,' Pearman assured him.

'I need a new passport, they stole the old one.'

'We can fix that.'

'They also took my wallet containing all my credit cards. I've got two hundred dollars in traveller's cheques and my plane ticket in the hotel safe but I needed the Gold Card to pay the bill at the Sheraton.'

'How much do you need?'

'Depends when I can get a flight back to London, but four hundred pounds should cover it if I have to stay over until Monday.'

'You're going back to the hotel?'

'It's going to look a lot worse if I don't.' Ashton smiled. 'Of course I'll need to shave and freshen up first. I could also use a clean shirt and need to borrow a pair of slacks.'

'You can have one of my sports shirts; it'll be a loose fit but I don't suppose that will matter. The trousers are out; they won't even reach your ankles. However, we can get the maid to clean and press yours.'

'It's best if I do it.'

'As you wish. I imagine you must be hungry?'

'Starving would be a more accurate description.'

'Well, we can certainly do something about that.' Pearman glanced at his wristwatch. 'Shall we say breakfast at 8.30? That will give you plenty of time for a bath.'

It also gave them plenty of time to discuss other matters. Pearman wanted him to give the airport a miss and get out by road or rail but the other exits weren't exactly promising. Yugoslavia was definitely out and a long-standing feud with Greece and Turkey dating back to the Ottoman Empire and the Balkan Wars at the turn of the century meant that customs officials tended to give travellers a hard time at the border crossing points.

'Listen,' Ashton told him finally, 'the description the militia have of me is so vague that it could fit almost anyone. Now, if the Russian Intelligence Service is calling the shots, it's a different matter. They've had my photograph on their files for the past two years and there's nothing to stop them running off several hundred copies for the Bulgarians, and if that is the case, they will pick me up wherever I try to cross the border. So we behave as if nothing is amiss. I flew in, so I'll fly out.'

'And if you are arrested at the airport?'

Ashton smiled. 'I guess the ball is then in your court. But I'm willing to bet nothing will happen.'

Ashton was right, but he had to wait forty-eight hours to prove it. The last plane out of Sofia had already departed before the replacement passport was ready, there were no international flights on the Sunday and he had to settle for the Balkan Airways 737 on the Monday morning. Pearman sent his deputy to the airport to keep a discreet watch on him but there were no unpleasant surprises. Those came later when Ashton phoned Century House from Heathrow to report that he had arrived safely and was informed that Victor Hazelwood, the Deputy DG wanted to see him urgently.

Chapter 5

In a little over eighteen months, Victor Hazelwood had been promoted from Head of the Russian Desk to Assistant Director, Eastern Bloc to Deputy Director General of 'The Firm'. Two years ago he had bought his suits off the peg, nowadays they were made to measure by Gieves and Hawkes. In an otherwise smoke-free zone, his office on the top floor of Century House was known as the Cancer Ward due to his addiction to Burma cheroots. According to popular rumour, Rowan Garfield, the newly appointed Assistant Director, Eastern Bloc had demanded to have his predecessor's office fumigated before he consented to move into it. Whatever the truth of the matter, one particular works service had been carried out by the Property Services Agency. Despite the difficult financial climate and the fact that the SIS were in the process of moving into their new premises at Vauxhall Cross, the DG had authorised the installation of an extractor fan in the Deputy DG's office before Hazelwood moved up the corridor.

He was, of course, smoking a Burma cheroot when Ashton reported to him. They had first met in September '82 when Ashton had been attending the induction course at the training school outside Petersfield and Hazelwood had delivered the standard lecture on the KGB to the new entrants. Their friendship dated from 1988 when Ashton had been assigned to the Russian Desk to work under Hazelwood's direction. This was after Ashton had spent two years learning the ropes in London followed by a three-year stint with Government Communications Headquarters in Cheltenham and a posting to South West Africa when he had been charged with assessing the extent of Soviet military involvement in Angola.

'Welcome home, Peter,' Hazelwood said with a broad smile. 'You had us pretty worried for a while.'

'I was pretty worried myself,' Ashton told him wryly.

'I imagine you were. The story we got from Commander Osbourne via the Foreign Office was both ambiguous and confusing.'

Ashton had been around long enough to recognise an invitation to give his side of the story no matter how obliquely it had been put to him. Leaving his suitcase inside the door, he pulled up a chair and sat down. 'Where would you like me to begin?' he asked.

'From the moment you got off the plane in Sofia.'

'I think everything had gone sour before that, Victor. I reckon de Vries was already being questioned by the men who would eventually kill him while I was waiting in the departure lounge at Heathrow.'

'I'd still like to hear what happened to you,' Hazelwood said mildly.

Ashton kept it brief. There was, he decided, no point in going over the same ground that Osbourne had already covered in his report. Instead, he talked about the interrogation and how the Russian had eventually broken him, and exactly what he had disclosed under duress.

'He nearly drowned me, Victor, not once, not twice, but four times.' Ashton undid his shirt and bared his stomach. The cigarette burns were still livid and a couple of them were weeping. 'This is how they revived me and why I didn't hold anything back,' he said, then buttoned up his shirt.

'You shouldn't feel guilty; in your shoes, once would have been enough for me. Matter of fact, I know I would have been ready to crack after seeing that film of Leven's execution.'

'Was he Valentin, the 'Insider' from Moscow?'

'No, what made you think he was?'

'It's what the Russian told me.'

'He was lying.' Hazelwood crushed the stub of his cheroot in a heavy glass ashtray. 'Alexei Leven was a lieutenant colonel in the GRU, he wouldn't have had access to the level of strategic information Valentin has, even when he was going places. And he was never going to make a comeback after you blighted his career.'

'That's virtually what my not-so-friendly interrogator told me. Seems we did for each other.'

Ashton had hoped for a reprieve after Stuart Dunglass became the Director General, but twelve months later, he was still vegetating at Benbow House. He had been plucked from obscurity and sent off to Sofia only because Valentin had asked for him by name.

'Could they have faked Leven's execution?'

It was the last question Ashton had expected and it threw him for a moment. 'I don't think so,' he said slowly, 'it looked real enough to me.'

Hazelwood opened the ornately carved box on his desk which he had bought on a trip to India and helped himself to another cheroot. 'It was just a thought,' he said with a shrug.

'Suppose you're right and it was an illusion? What would they hope to gain from the charade?'

'Maybe they suspected Leven was the 'Insider' and hoped you would confirm it.'

'Yes – well, they obviously had prior knowledge that I was the man Valentin had asked for. I mean, they didn't produce that movie at the drop of a hat. They also knew de Vries was going to put me in touch with him.'

'Are you implying there was a leak here in London?'

'No, I'm saying they broke Leven first, then went after me because they wanted to know what titbits he'd already fed us in order to capture our interest.'

'In other words, you are still convinced that Leven is the "Insider"?'

'I can't think of a better candidate.'

'In 1967 when you were still running around in knee pants, this country was hit by an epidemic of foot-and-mouth disease, the like of which had never been seen before. The Ministry of Ag and Fish imposed the most stringent regulations; infected herds were slaughtered on the spot and the carcases burned in situ, farmers in contaminated areas were not allowed to transport their cattle to market and anyone visiting a farm had to dip their boots in a trough of disinfectant before passing through the gate. The most rigorous measures were taken to prevent the disease spreading, but apparently to no avail. I was still a probationer in those days and I suddenly got landed with the job of plotting the outbreaks on a large ordnance survey map of the United Kingdom.' Hazelwood struck a match and lit the cheroot he had been rolling between his fingers. 'I tell you,' he said between puffs, 'there were that many spots on the map, the whole country looked as if it had a bad case of measles. But it didn't stop there; no sooner had the health inspectors declared an area free from infection, than there was a fresh outbreak. The Ag and Fish experts couldn't account for it, which is why we were invited to take a look at the phenomenon assisted by a working party from the Ministry of Defence and the Nuclear, Bacteriological and Chemical Warfare Establishment at Porton Down.'

The NBC team had produced a study they had done some years back assessing the vulnerability of the UK to a chemical strike using nerve agents. They had demonstrated that with the prevailing wind blowing in the right direction, twenty tons of liquid agent discharged off the east coast of Scotland by a Tupolev Tu95 four-engine turboprop bomber at forty thousand feet would achieve a scatter effect across the whole country from Newcastle-upon-Tyne to Falmouth in Cornwall. The template they had produced for that study had, to a very large degree, corresponded with the pattern of the foot-and-mouth epidemic. The RAF had then furnished a consolidated log listing the dates and times radar had locked on to a Tu95 violating British airspace. The Meteorological Office at Bracknell had subsequently compared their weather records with the intrusion dates and times.

'They matched,' Hazelwood continued. 'The prevailing winds were blowing in the right direction to achieve maximum scatter with a liquid agent. There was only one logical conclusion to be drawn: from bases in the Murmansk area, the Soviet Maritime Air Force was testing its bacteriological capability against this country in what amounted to a large-scale field trial. Anthrax would have been a little too obvious so they settled for foot-and-mouth, which is more or less an endemic disease.'

'So what happened?'

'Nothing much. The report was described as "imaginative" by the Cabinet Secretary before being quietly buried. On a more positive note, Lightnings from RAF Leuchars began to intercept and shadow the Tupolevs before they got anywhere near our airspace and the outbreak of foot-and-mouth was finally brought under control. The politicians maintained there was no connection between the two events and that it was merely a coincidence.'

'But twenty-six years later you know different?' Ashton suggested.

'Yes, our theory was confirmed by Valentin. It was one of the titbits he gave us.' Hazelwood reached out to tap the cheroot over the ashtray and missed the target, depositing ash on his desk. 'I think you will agree Leven was not in a position to access that kind of information,' he said.

'Okay, I'm convinced, Victor. The only thing that puzzles me is why you cancelled the mission at the last moment?'

'Valentin called it off, not me. GCHQ Cheltenham received a high-speed transmission to the effect that the timing was all wrong and he couldn't get out.'

There were a number of things which didn't make sense to Ashton, but most of all, he couldn't understand why Valentin had insisted on meeting him face to face in Sofia when it was apparent the Russian had access to a clandestine radio station operating direct to GCHQ Cheltenham. And judging by what Victor had just told him about the foot-and-mouth episode, it looked as if the 'Insider' had passed the information to the SIS via some kind of dead letterbox. There was, Ashton knew, no point in looking to Victor for an explanation; he was outside the magic circle and wouldn't get a straight answer. It was the old 'need-to-know' principle and it worked against him.

'So, it's a case of better luck next time, is it, Victor?'

'We'll have to wait and see.'

'And in the meantime?'

'You get on with your job, Peter.'

So it was back to Security, Vetting and Technical Services and Roy Kelso, the small-minded and embittered Assistant Director in charge of the Administrative Wing at Benbow House. Harriet Egan had been the one joy to come from Ashton's move to Southwark though it was true to say he had been less than fond of her when she had first arrived on attachment from MI5.

'Cheer up,' Hazelwood told him, 'it won't last for ever.'

'What won't?'

'Being out in the cold.'

'I wish I could be sure of that.' Ashton stood up, put the chair back where he had found it and collected his suitcase, then had one last thought and turned about. 'Henry de Vries,' he said, 'is it okay if I do some homework on him?'

'He's not a taboo subject as far as I'm concerned.'

'I'll need your authorisation to see his personal dossier.'

'Make out a request slip and I'll sign it.'

'I'd also like to see all the wartime files of the Special Operations Executive which deal with the Bulgarian Resistance movement.'

'Why the interest in ancient history, Peter?'

'Henry de Vries was born an Englishman and died as one. Bulgaria was allied to Nazi Germany in World War Two; if de Vries wasn't interned, I'd like to know why.'

'Okay.' Hazelwood buried the cheroot he'd been smoking amongst the other stub ends in the ashtray. 'But check with Harriet first; an assignment is about to land on her desk and she'll need a little help from you.'

Harriet Egan was half an inch under six feet, a fact of life which at one time she had tried to disguise by wearing low heels and walking with a slight stoop. Since meeting Ashton, she had become less self-conscious about her height and had even been known to wear court shoes on occasions. She had long tapering fingers and took a size seven and a half shoe. With her bone structure, there was no way she could slim down to under ten stone without looking seriously ill. Although Harriet refused to believe it, she was exactly the right weight for her height and frame and had a well-proportioned figure into the bargain. But it was the perfect symmetry of her face that claimed everyone's attention and remained firmly imprinted in their minds thereafter. Harriet was, in fact, quite beautiful though she herself was unaware of it.

Born in Lincoln on the sixteenth of February 1964, she had joined the civil service as a graduate entrant after obtaining a good upper second in Geography at Birmingham University. Harriet had originally opted for the Home Office but while still on probation, she had caught the eye of a talent spotter for MI5 who had persuaded her that she would find greater job satisfaction with the Security Service. After her induction course at the training school, she had been attached to the Armed Forces Desk in Bolton Street for eighteen months before moving to K2, the section which dealt with subversives. A posting to the British Services Security Organisation in Germany should have followed the stint at Gower Street, but this had been cancelled at the last moment and she had been seconded to the SIS instead. Single and unattached when she had reported to Benbow House, south of the river in Southwark, she now wore a sapphire and diamond ring on the third finger of her left hand, put there by Peter Ashton.

Ashton had telephoned from Heathrow shortly after one o'clock to let her know he was back but had to call into head office, meaning Century House. When her phone had rung again, after what had been a remarkably quiet afternoon, she had assumed it was Peter calling to say the meeting was going on longer than he'd expected. To her disappointment, she had found herself talking to Roy Kelso, the Assistant Director in charge of the Administrative Wing, who had wanted to know if she could spare him a few minutes. As Harriet had discovered to her cost, his idea of what constituted a few minutes differed from hers. Once summoned to his office on the top floor, she was lucky to escape in under half an hour. The moment he invited her to draw up a chair to his desk in order to make some notes, she had known that this particular afternoon was not going to be an exception.

'These are for you, Harriet,' he said, pointing to a collection of box files arranged in two equal stacks on a small table next to his desk. 'Each box contains approximately half a dozen folders of varying size, many of them incorrectly classified. The documents are at least forty years old and, at one time, belonged to the now defunct branch of Military Intelligence known as MI11 which came under the aegis of the War Office. MI11 was the recipient of all interrogations of returned deserters carried out by Field Security Sections in BAOR during the years 1948 to 1953. And believe me, there was no shortage of absentees and deserters in those days.'

Harriet cupped a hand over her mouth to conceal a smile. Roy Kelso was fifty-two years old, which meant that he wouldn't have reached puberty when the last of the deserters had returned in '53, yet he spoke of them as if they belonged to the same age group.

'National Service was not the be-all and end-all people like to pretend it was nowadays. As a result of conscription, there were a lot of young, unwilling soldiers in the army, some of whom held extreme left-wing views. Their fathers had lived through the great depression of the thirties and had known real poverty and despair.'

Although the desk was within easy reach, Harriet preferred to distance herself; crossing one leg over the other, she balanced the millboard on her thigh and made a few squiggles on the wad of scrap paper. She had developed her own version of shorthand but in this instance, she was merely going through the motions of taking notes. Roy Kelso wasn't telling her anything she hadn't heard before at the training school and when she had joined K2 Section in Gower Street.

'The attitudes of the fathers rubbed off on the sons; Uncle Joe Stalin was a good egg, the Soviet Union was the cradle of democracy and Communism the road to Utopia for the working class.' Kelso was enjoying himself and nodded approvingly at Harriet's apparent interest before continuing with his homily. 'A disgruntled soldier was called Bolshie, meaning he was uncooperative, rebellious and awkward. When NCOs tried to get a grip of him, the Bolshie soldier usually absented himself without leave and went on the run. Those serving with the British Army of the Rhine would nip over the border into the East Zone. Very easy thing to do in those far-off days – no wall, no minefields, no electrified fences, no guard towers to speak of. In Berlin, you simply hopped on the U-Bahn.'

Harriet dutifully made a few more squiggles on her notepad; when she looked up again, Kelso hastily averted his gaze. She was wearing a tailored skirt with kick pleats which he had seen before but this time around, the skirt didn't give him anything like the same amount of vicarious pleasure because she seemed to have sewn up the kick pleats, thereby denying him a tantalising glimpse of her legs.

'You were saying?' she murmured.

'Yes.' Kelso cleared his throat. 'Well, those who went across in uniform were quickly picked up by the East German police or the Red Army and were put in a detention camp near Leipzig. A deserter who took off in civilian clothes was likely to remain at large a lot longer, especially if he had a German girlfriend, but was treated much more harshly when eventually he was arrested. He was accused of being a spy and rigorously interrogated for weeks on end, which means he was knocked about. Of course, once the Russians were satisfied he wasn't a spy, the suspect was given the same asylum rights as any other deserter.'

In effect, this meant he was given a job consistent with the skills he'd acquired in civilian life or had learned since being called up. In this respect, a fitter in the Royal Electrical and Mechanical Engineers usually fared much better than an ordinary rifleman who had been a labourer before putting on a uniform.

'Sooner or later the vast majority of them got fed up with life behind the Iron Curtain and wanted out.' Kelso indicated the box files on the small table. 'They contain the dossiers of the prodigal sons who came home to face the music. However, five men never did return even when the wall came down and Germany was officially reunited on the third of October 1990. You will find their names listed separately in a letter our Armed Forces Desk obtained from the army's Personnel Staff branch at Empress State.'

Harriet was beginning to wonder if Kelso would ever get to the point when he suddenly removed a hardback folder from his pending tray and passed it across the desk. 'What's this, Roy?' she asked, straight-faced. 'Some more light reading?'

'Yes. It comes with the compliments of the *Bundesnachrichtendienst* and is the file the East German Security Service kept on an unidentified long-term deserter. The Stasi referred to him as "The Englishman".'

'That's not very original.'

'Neither were the KGB when he went to work for them as a hired killer. Anyway, the DG has asked us to identify him. When you read the MI11 interrogation reports, you will see that all returned deserters were asked if they had met any other British service personnel when they were living in the Russian Zone and it's possible that one of them might be able to throw a little light on the mysterious killer. But first, you have to read this Stasi file to see what clues they may have inadvertently offered. Okay?'

Harriet undid the tapes securing the hardback folder and looked inside. 'There's a small problem,' she told him. 'I don't understand German.'

'That's all right, Ashton does. He'll translate the contents for you.' Kelso smiled at her, a hollow gesture lacking both in warmth and spontaneity. 'No need to bother with the box files now, Harriet. I'll have one of the clerks bring them down to your office.'

'Thank you, Roy.' Harriet stood up, moved her chair back and hurriedly left the office.

Apart from the occasional ogle when he thought she wasn't looking, Kelso had never given her any cause for complaint. It was simply that his personality grated on her like chalk squeaking on a blackboard and she couldn't bear to be in the same room with him a moment longer than was strictly necessary.

The asthmatic lifts were as old as Benbow House itself and had a mind of their own. When they did respond to the call button it was always with extreme reluctance and after a considerable pause. Occasionally, they would ignore the summons altogether for no good reason other than downright contrariness. Eager to escape from Kelso before he thought of some excuse to detain her, Harriet ignored them and ran down the stairs to her office to find Ashton waiting for her outside the door.

'Hello, Peter,' she said, delighted to see him. 'I thought you would have gone straight to the flat from Century House.'

'I couldn't wait.'

'For what?'

'Unlock the door to your office and I'll show you,' he said and grinned.

Among the SIS fraternity, Sir Stuart Dunglass was referred to as The Chief; when summoned to his office, subordinates addressed him formally as Director; behind his back, he enjoyed the nickname of Jungle Jim in recognition of the fact that he had spent the greater part of his service in the Far East. He had been appointed to the post of Director General on Monday, the first of June 1992 and the knighthood had swiftly followed.

Victor Hazelwood, who had become his deputy on the same day, could have looked forward to a similar accolade before he retired if the goal posts hadn't been moved by the government's desire to reform the whole system of honours and awards. It was not something that exercised Hazelwood who considered himself fortunate to have got where he was. Baubles were not important to him; he enjoyed his work and got on well with Dunglass. His only complaint was that the Director had a habit of asking him to drop by his office just as he was about to go home.

'I thought you'd want to see these two intercepts, Victor,' he said by way of explanation. 'The first was transmitted by a station in the Rila Mountains of Bulgaria and was captured by a detachment of 9 Signal Regiment in Cyprus. It was not possible to get a precise fix on the other station but it seems likely it was operating somewhere within a twenty-mile radius of Moscow.'

The encoded messages had been broken by the cryptographers at GCHQ Cheltenham. To Hazelwood, the transmission from Rila struck a particularly chilling note and the reply from Moscow, though less menacing, was hardly reassuring.

'Tell me something, Victor, why do you suppose they called him Mercury?'

'By him, I assume you mean Ashton?'

'I don't see who else it could be,' Dunglass said tersely.

'Well, I suppose you could say he was a messenger of sorts.'

'Whom the man at Rila wanted to terminate. Right?'

'I think we can assume that's what he meant when he asked for disposal instructions.'

'Only to be told by Moscow that Ashton is far too valuable.'

'Yes.'

'So what are we to make of it?' Dunglass asked.

Ashton had been under a cloud ever since he had cultivated Lieutenant Colonel Alexei Leven of the GRU, and there were some Intelligence officers, particularly the Head of Station, Berlin, who believed he had been turned. Hazelwood thought he had dispelled that notion but it seemed this latest incident had renewed doubts in the DG's mind.

'Ashton is a known face,' Hazelwood said, choosing his words carefully. 'The KGB identified him roughly two years ago and his mugshot is on their files. I believe the Russian Intelligence Service want him alive because they think that even if he doesn't eventually lead them to Valentin, they will learn a lot about us simply by watching him.'

'And perhaps listening to him.'

'Ashton didn't tell them anything which could hurt us or put Valentin in jeopardy. He only talked under extreme duress; I know because I have seen what they did to him and you haven't. And let's not forget, he killed two agents of the Bulgarian DS security organisation.'

'We've only his word for it, Victor. There have been no reports about it from that embassy fellow in Sofia.'

'His name's Pearman, and he hasn't mentioned the incident because the Bulgarian authorities have kept it under wraps.'

'You're guessing.'

'What was it the Duke of Wellington said? All the business of war, and indeed all the business of life is to endeavour to find out what you don't know by what you do; that's what I called "guessing what was the other side of the hill".'

'I still think Ashton is a liability.'

Dunglass left his desk, walked over to the window and stood there, hands clasped behind his back as he gazed down at the maze of tracks leading into Waterloo station. It was not a view he would be able to admire for much longer since, in a week's time, they would move to Vauxhall Cross, close by the river. Hazelwood supposed the DG would then be able to contemplate the Thames.

'I think we should let him go, Victor.'

'You mean, make him redundant?' Hazelwood said incredulously.

'Why not? We've had to shed twenty per cent of our establishment in the interests of the peace dividend the politicians are always on about.'

'He's too good to throw away.'

'What can we do with him? I know he is fluent in German but Head of Station, Berlin, won't have him in his bailiwick.'

'You could send him to the Joint Services Intelligence Staff in Hong Kong.'

'Don't you think the Governor has enough problems with Peking as it is without our adding to them?' Dunglass turned about. 'I'm sorry, Victor, I know how you feel about Ashton but I don't see how we can employ him.'

'We could always use him as a decoy,' Hazelwood said grimly. 'But he deserves better than that.'

Chapter 6

It took the chief archivist three days to locate and then gather together all the documents that Ashton had asked for. The file on Henry de Vries should have been easy enough to find; it was still active and was held by the Eastern Bloc. Unfortunately, the department was in the process of moving to Vauxhall Cross and no one was quite sure exactly where the file was.

But the most difficult of all to trace were the wartime files of the Special Operations Executive, which had been dispersed all over the place. Some had landed up in the Public Records Office, others had been consigned to the historical repository at Hayes, Middlesex, near Heathrow. All had been downgraded from Top Secret or Secret to Unclassified. However, certain individual folios, which were still considered to be highly sensitive even fifty years after the event, had been removed. Worse still, the historical repository at Hayes had been unable to supply any classified registers to go with the files which made it almost impossible to track down the missing folios.

The World War Two material on Bulgaria turned out to be pretty thin, which didn't altogether surprise Ashton. Although Nazi troops had entered Bulgaria in 1941 to rescue Mussolini's disastrous campaign against the Greeks, and had subsequently made use of the country's Black Sea ports when invading the USSR, King Boris and his government had balked at the idea of declaring war on the Soviet Union.

In August 1944, the Bulgarians had taken more positive steps to disassociate themselves from the Axis powers. With Red Army formations from Marshal Tolbukhin's Third Ukrainian Front approaching their northern border with Romania, they had declared themselves neutral in the Russo-German war. The Soviet Union however had refused to recognise their declaration of neutrality and had called on the Bulgarians to declare war on Germany. On the ninth of September, the Chavdar partisan brigade had come down from the mountains and entered the capital to consolidate the coup d'état launched by the Fatherland Front the previous day. Hostilities with the Soviet Union had then ended on Sunday, the tenth of September. According to his security file, Henry de Vries had been a platoon commander in the Chavdar partisan brigade.

Ashton returned the wartime SOE files to the chief clerk of the Eastern Bloc Department who was still located at Century House, then rang Victor Hazelwood to check when he might be free to see him. The Deputy DG, it transpired, had a blank page in his appointments diary for that morning and would be happy to see him anytime.

From the day Ashton had joined, Century House had been synonymous with the SIS; now the twenty-storey building in Westminster Bridge Road was rapidly becoming an empty shell as the various departments moved to their new home in Vauxhall Cross. The Mid East Department and the Rest of the World, which now included the Pacific Basin, had already gone, together with most of the satellite communications staff. The rest of the East European and the odds and sods would follow on Saturday. Every room between the first and eighteenth floors had been stripped of furniture, leaving only the telltale marks on the haircord carpets to show where the desks and filing cabinets had once stood. It was something of a relief to step out of the lift and find it was almost business as usual on the top floor.

'So what's your verdict on Henry de Vries?' Hazelwood asked as soon as he walked into his office.

'If he wasn't a Communist, he had to be a fellow traveller long before he joined the partisans in the mountains. Of course, the way de Vries tells it, he had to convince the political commissars of the Chavdar brigade that he was a Communist before they would let him join the Resistance.'

'And you're saying he stretched the truth?'

'De Vries did more than that,' Ashton told him. 'He lied in his teeth to us. The Fatherland Front might have been a coalition of Social Democrats, Agrarians and Republicans, but it was the Communists who were the driving force and backbone of the partisan movement. You think their political commissars would have accepted a simple declaration from him? No, he would have needed a proven track record before they let him in. Besides, who do you suppose sheltered de Vries from the Gestapo when the *Wehrmacht* moved into Bulgaria in March '41? Hell, it had to be the Communists, there was no resistance movement to speak of before 1943.'

'Didn't SOE have a liaison team with the partisan brigade?'

'From March to September 1944.'

'So what did the team leader think of him?' Hazelwood asked.

'Henry de Vries could do no wrong in Alec Lister's eyes.'

A twenty-six-year-old major in the South Staffordshire Regiment, Alec Lister had been in charge of the five-man liaison team which had been parachuted into Kubratovo to provide material support for the partisans. De Vries had acted as his interpreter after they had established contact with the guerrillas.

'Well, there you are then,' Hazelwood said airily. 'If you live cheek by jowl with a man for six months, you get to know him pretty well.'

'Oh, come on, Victor, Lister didn't know a word of Bulgarian; he was dependent on him. Besides, he was too busy fighting a war to bother about the colour of his politics.'

In any event, Uncle Joe Stalin and the Red Army had been on the side of the angels at that time and could do no wrong. Furthermore, Henry de Vries had wanted to kill Germans and that was all that had counted in wartime.

'When did you last take a good look at de Vries's personal file?'

Hazelwood smiled. 'I skimmed through the dossier before the chief clerk passed it on to you.'

'Do you think we would have taken him on after the war if Lister hadn't given us such a glowing testimonial?'

'I don't know. There was a civil war raging in Greece between ELAS, the Communist underground army, and the government forces, and Bulgaria was being used as a safe haven by the insurgents. We needed to find out how much support they were getting from Sofia and we didn't have too many people behind the Iron Curtain who were prepared to work for us. I don't believe my predecessors could afford to be choosy when de Vries offered his services.'

'Right up to the moment of his death, he was classified as an A1 source,' Ashton said. 'And you can't get any higher than that.'

'So?'

'So "A" means the source is totally reliable and the numeral grading signifies that his information is in all probability true. Now, I've been through his file and I can't see why we had such faith in him. Oh, he gave us a few titbits every now and then but nothing startling. My question is, who chose him to be the link between Valentin and myself?'

'We did,' Hazelwood said promptly.

'And Valentin went along with it because he knew he could trust de Vries.'

'Are you implying he was a double agent?'

'Yes. I think he worked for the Durzhavna Sigurnost, the Bulgarian State Security Force, during the Cold War, and they being good lap dogs of the KGB passed his stuff on to Moscow.'

'Can you prove it?'

'It's unlikely there will ever be sufficient evidence to convince a judge and jury, but that's not the point, is it? De Vries is dead.'

'Exactly.' Hazelwood opened the ornately carved box on his desk, took out a Burma cheroot and lit it. 'I mean, just what do you hope to achieve by going down memory lane, Peter?'

'It might give you a different slant on the man you call Valentin and help to assess his true worth. Of course, that would be a pretty futile exercise if you already know his real identity.'

'Yes, it would.'

Ashton smiled. Hazelwood might not have said so outright but it was pretty obvious that Valentin was just a name. The SIS couldn't put a face to him and had no idea of his true standing in the Russian Intelligence Service.

'How's Harriet getting on with that assignment Kelso gave her?' Hazelwood asked, suddenly changing tack.

'The Stasi file isn't holding her up. I translated the whole caboodle into English while I was waiting for the Eastern Bloc Department to produce the material I'd asked for. That said, Harriet's no closer to identifying your mysterious long-term deserter.' Ashton paused, then said, 'Would I be right in thinking Valentin put up that particular hare?'

'You make it sound as though he has deliberately sent us off on a wild-goose chase.'

'I wouldn't go as far as to say that, but you've got to admit he could have saved us a lot of time and trouble if he had put a name to this sixty-one-year-old renegade.'

'Well, he didn't, and the Director keeps asking me for a progress report. So, the question is, what do I tell him?'

'We were hoping that one of the deserters might have said something to his interrogator which would give us a pointer, but no such luck. Now Harriet is trying a different angle and is looking into the personal background of all thirty-one men. Or she will be when the necessary dossiers arrive from the record office.'

'And that's it?'

'The impossible we can do at once,' Ashton quoted at him. 'Miracles take a little longer.'

'Quite.' As if suddenly tired of smoking, Hazelwood left his cheroot to smoulder away in the ashtray, wedged a knee against the desk and tilted his chair back to balance on the rear legs. 'How many men were there in this SOE team?' he asked, reverting to the original subject.

'Five. Two junior NCOs from the Royal Signals, a sergeant on secondment from the Royal Welch Fusiliers who was the weapons training instructor, plus a demolition king in the shape of a warrant officer in the Royal Engineers. And, of course, Major Alec Lister, the team leader.'

'And you want to trace and interview these men?'

'Those who are still alive.'

'You mind telling me why, Peter?'

'I think you already know the answer to that question. A number of folios have been removed from the wartime SOE files and it's possible that Lister, or one of his former subordinates may be able to fill in some of the blank spaces.'

There was a long silence while Hazelwood gave it some thought.

While he meditated, the cheroot burned down and finally went out, leaving a grey log of ash.

'I suppose you had better give it a whirl,' he said eventually. 'But only after you have identified the KGB's hired killer.'

'Harriet doesn't need my help to do that.'

'I think she does,' Hazelwood said firmly.

The box files contained thirty-one separate interrogations, each comprising one handwritten copy and one duplicate printed on coarse foolscap sheets of typing paper that looked as if they had been recycled more than once. Some interrogations ran to over twenty pages, others as few as four; the mean average was roughly twelve. The MI11 files all referred to army personnel, and it had occurred to Harriet that the hired killer she was looking for could have been serving in the Royal Navy or the Royal Air Force before he'd deserted. In answer to her query, the Admiralty had been extremely happy, and not a little smug, to inform Harriet that no officer or naval rating had ever defected to the Communist Bloc. From the Provost Marshal's Personnel and Security Branch, she learned that, as a matter of course, the RAF Police destroyed all files relating to deserters twenty-five years after the individual concerned had either surrendered himself to the appropriate authorities or had been apprehended. They had however retained the Board of Inquiry proceedings of three deserters who were still unaccounted for, which were hers for the asking, an offer she had gratefully accepted. Since the army also had five men who had never come home, it was reasonable to believe the killer had to be one of the eight missing personnel. But Harriet knew from experience that things were never that simple.

The Stasi file on 'The Englishman' offered few clues to his identity. There were, of course, no photographs of the assassin and such physical characteristics as were recorded, fell into the category of average height, average weight, no visible distinguishing marks, mouse-coloured hair and grey eyes, a description which could fit a multitude of men. But as the Stasi so quaintly put it, he had liquidated seventeen enemies of the people between 1955 and 1978 and that made him very different.

The East German Ministry of State Security had not been coy

about documenting the identity of his victims or how, when and where they had been murdered. In pursuit of his chosen career, 'The Englishman' had travelled far and wide, leaving his calling card in Spain, Switzerland, the Federal Republic, West Berlin, Sweden, Denmark and Italy. As a deserter, his description would have been circulated to every RMP, RAF Police and Field Security detachment in BAOR, yet most of the murders he had committed had been perpetrated in the Federal Republic and West Berlin. Apart from being ruthless, Harriet had also concluded that the man she was looking for had to be a remarkably cool customer.

There was, however, one enclosure on the Stasi file which, though it had been heavily censored, was nevertheless revealing. It had been referred to the Ministry of State Security by the *Kriminalpolizei* because the complainant, a civil servant referred to only as Fräulein X, had demanded that her assailant should be arrested and prosecuted with the utmost severity. The facts of the case were simple enough; Fräulein X had been to the opera in East Berlin with 'The Englishman' on a number of occasions before he had invited her back to his house in the Weissensee District of the city. In her words, he had always behaved like a perfect gentleman before, and she therefore had no reason to suspect he would not continue to do so. And that had been her big mistake because bondage, rape, sodomy and oral intercourse had been on his agenda for that particular night. The following morning, an elderly man out walking his dog in the woods by the Malchower See had found her stark naked and unconscious. There had been no prosecution and under considerable pressure from the Ministry of State Security, Fräulein X had agreed to withdraw her complaint. There was also a further notation on the file to the effect that 'The Englishman' had previously raped and indecently assaulted two other women, both of whom were coyly described as promiscuous, the East German euphemism for prostitutes.

The man Harriet was looking for liked going to the opera and was a sadomasochist with a penchant for kinky sex. It wasn't a lot to go on and the personal documents of the eight missing men which the Armed Forces Desk had obtained for her from the Records Office at Hayes were of no help. Each folder simply contained a spare set of identity discs, medical documents, dental charts, Record of

Service and, in the case of army personnel, their Regimental and Company conduct sheets. Some of these revealed a history of petty offences before the soldier had deserted, as did the equivalent crime sheets for the RAF personnel, but not one of the eight men had been charged with rape, indecent assault or buggery.

All thirty-one files that had been retained by MI11 proved to be a distraction. Although not one soldier had said anything which might have enabled Harriet to identify the killer, she had found herself spending more time on each interrogation report than was strictly justified. What had fascinated her was the wide variety of reasons that had prompted the thirty-one men to desert. Slightly more than fifty per cent had never been amenable to any kind of discipline whether in the home, at school, the workplace or in the army. A handful had gone over the hill because they had girlfriends living in the Russian Zone, while two men from the King's Liverpool Irish had broken out of the unit guardroom where they were being held under close arrest pending trial by court martial for causing grievous bodily harm to their platoon commander. A pay clerk from Berlin Infantry Brigade Headquarters had legged it after being gang-raped by four drivers from the transport section in the attic above the barrack block, and a signaller had sought political asylum to escape the attentions of a bullying NCO. Only one man had crossed over because of his political convictions. It had then occurred to Harriet that if the killer was not one of the eight men who were still missing, there was a faint chance he might be among the thirty-one soldiers who had returned from behind the Iron Curtain.

It was only after she had read the Stasi file for the umpteenth time that a pattern had emerged which tended to support the possibility. Between 1955 and 1978, 'The Englishman' had murdered seventeen people, three before 1957, the remainder after 1962. The five-year gap between the deaths of the third and fourth victims suggested he had been otherwise engaged during the intervening years. After conferring with Ashton, she had asked the Armed Forces Desk at Century House to obtain the personal documents of the former deserters from Hayes. All thirty-one dossiers had arrived that morning and she was still working her way through them when Ashton tapped on the open door and walked into the office.

'You were quick,' Harriet said, looking up with a smile. 'Does that mean Victor gave you the green light?'

'In a manner of speaking.' Ashton moved round the desk and looked over her shoulder. 'I see the files you asked for have finally arrived.'

'Yes. So far, they're not very interesting.' She pointed to the in-tray. 'I should think I've got about a dozen left.'

'I'll give you a hand.'

'Well, that's very decent of you, Peter, but I can manage . . .'

'No buts. Victor more or less insisted on it.' Ashton drew up a chair and sat down beside her. 'He's looking for a result and we have to come up with a name before I can do any further research on Henry de Vries. Okay?'

'All right then.' Harriet smiled apologetically. 'Don't think I'm teaching my grandmother to suck eggs but I've been paying particular attention to the medical records of these men.'

'Makes sense to me,' he said and helped himself to a wad of folders.

The Stasi file on 'The Englishman' indicated that he frequently consorted with prostitutes. It was therefore likely he had done the same thing while serving in the army and perhaps had been treated for VD. In the event, however, it was a regimental conduct sheet which pointed the way.

'Gunner Martin Nicholson, Royal Artillery,' he said aloud.

'What about him?'

'He was court-martialled and sentenced to six months' detention for indecently assaulting one of the girls who worked in the NAAFI canteen. This was when he was undergoing recruit training at Watchet Camp in Somerset.'

'Can we see his Record of Service?'

Ashton plucked the card from the folder and quickly read the document before passing it to Harriet. The Army Form B2763 filled in some of the blanks. Released from the Military Correction Centre at Colchester after serving four months of his sentence, Nicholson had been posted to Rhyl where he had been trained as a driver. Following seven days' embarkation leave, he had then joined 49 Field Regiment stationed at Fellinbostel on the eighteenth of June 1951. Eight months later, he had deserted and had spent the next six years behind the Iron Curtain before surrendering himself to the RMP post at the Helmstedt checkpoint on the autobahn to Berlin.

'There's also a photocopy of the proceedings of a Court of Inquiry and a report from the Special Investigation Branch of the Royal Military Police in his dossier.' Ashton passed the documents to Harriet for her perusal. 'Seems Nicholson managed to run down his troop sergeant during the autumn manoeuvres of 1st British Corps. The battery was moving into position under cover of darkness, driving without lights as they would do in wartime.'

There had been no moon and visibility had been extremely poor due to a thick ground mist. Like every other unit taking part in the manoeuvres, 49 Field Regiment had been on the move for eight days and nights and the men had been dog tired. In his statement to both the SIB and the Court of Inquiry, Nicholson had claimed he had been too exhausted to react swiftly when his troop sergeant had suddenly loomed up in front of his vehicle. As a result, the tractor, limber and trail legs of the 25-pounder gun/howitzer had already passed over the body before he had succeeded in bringing the vehicle and gun carriage to a halt.

'There had been bad blood between Nicholson and the troop sergeant and he had been heard to utter threats about getting even with him. That's why there was an SIB investigation.'

'Then Nicholson is our man,' Harriet said positively. 'He must be "The Englishman".'

'Let's not jump to any conclusions. The Court of Inquiry cleared him of all blame as did the SIB investigation. Two members of the gun crew were awake when the accident happened and they supported Nicholson's account.'

'The SIB were wrong, so was the Court of Inquiry. It wasn't an accident.'

'I think you should read the opinion of the brigadier who convened the Court of Inquiry first, Harriet. It's certainly a bit of an eye-opener. I'd no idea how many soldiers lost their lives during a large-scale exercise in those days.'

Some men had been killed as a result of tampering with discarded ammunition from World War Two that had been left lying around, others had blundered into uncharted minefields or had been drowned during an assault river crossing. With four divisions in the field, a dozen fatal accidents was not uncommon.

'You see what I mean?'

'Oh yes.' Harriet got up, walked across the room and leaned against the far wall, arms folded across her chest. 'Even so, I still think Nicholson is our man and that he killed that troop sergeant in cold blood, then was cool enough to sit it out for five months before he deserted in February 1952. "The Englishman" committed his first three murders before 1957 and then there was a further gap of five years before he started up again. And what was Martin Nicholson up to at the time? Why, he had surrendered to the MPs and told the army authorities he had run away because he had accidentally killed the star player of the regimental soccer team and everybody was picking on him and making his life hell. The President and members of the court martial who eventually tried Nicholson gave him twenty-eight days for the sake of appearances and he was out in three weeks, discharged, "Services no longer required".'

'All right, all right.' Ashton raised a hand to stop her. 'Now tell me why Nicholson came home?'

'The German Democratic Republic wanted to make better use of his talents so they sent him back to face the music and to apply for a British passport. That made it easier for him to travel around when he returned to East Germany. If you find that hard to swallow, take another look at the Stasi file and see how "The Englishman" branched out after '62. Spain, Switzerland, Denmark, Sweden and Italy; he went on a regular Cook's tour of Europe.'

'You can be very persuasive,' Ashton told her, then lost the thread of what he was about to say. Harriet was wearing a pin-stripe double-breasted wool jacket with matching high-waisted trousers over a sleeveless blouse with a ruffled front, an outfit he found very distracting.

'Does that mean you agree with me?' she asked.

'Nicholson is the most likely candidate, but proving it is another matter. Right now, we don't even know what he looks like.'

'I'll get you a photograph.'

'How?'

'I'll trace his family. It shouldn't be difficult; his date and place of

birth and national insurance number are shown on Army Form
B2763.'

'And if you draw a blank?'

'Then I'll go to the Passport Office, the Department of Social
Security and the Office of Population Censuses and Surveys at St
Catherine's House. There is no way Martin Nicholson can hide from
me.'

'Well, while you're at it,' said Ashton, 'you'd better trace those
two gunners who supported his statement. Maybe he bullied them
into it?'

'Right.' Harriet straightened up and moved back to her desk.
'Any other instructions?' she asked.

'Yes. Don't tell Kelso any more than you have to at this stage.'

Chapter 7

Nicholson was waiting at Berlin-Tegel Airport when Herr Joachim Wolff, Party Secretary of the New National Socialist Movement flew in from Hamburg. Even if he hadn't studied thoroughly every photograph of the Nazi orator that had appeared in the West German press, Nicholson would have had no difficulty in recognising him. On hand to meet the thirty-eight-year-old lawyer were four skinhead bodyguards, all well over six feet and whose presence seemed to worry not only the official reception committee but most other people in the immediate vicinity. They were dressed in the standard gear of the football hooligan – Doc Marten boots, disruptive pattern combat trousers and black T-shirts. All were tattooed, had rings on every finger and either wore an earring or a nose stud.

Their leader spared Nicholson no more than a passing glance as they shepherded Wolff towards the exit and the waiting limousines provided by the Berlin chapter of the movement. Nicholson fancied he knew what had passed through his mind when he had hurriedly looked away after their eyes had briefly made contact. 'A grey-haired old man in his sixties with failing eyesight behind steel-framed glasses, no taller than his shoulder and a scared rabbit.' If those had been his thoughts, the skinhead could not have been more mistaken; the spectacles were merely a prop and it had suited him to appear nervous in their presence. When strangers instantly dismissed you as a harmless nonentity, they were unlikely to remember your face.

Nicholson allowed the lawyer and his cohorts a slight head start before following them out of the terminal. When he signalled the cab driver whom he had retained on standby, the motorcade of three black Mercedes 180s had already reached the first underpass en route to the inner ring motorway. Although the tail end vehicle was almost half a mile ahead of them, Nicholson wasn't perturbed. As soon as they left the slip road to the airport, the cab driver, an Armenian deserter from 6 Guards Tank Army, would put his foot down and close the gap. Furthermore, he already knew where the Party Secretary intended to make his rabble-rousing speech that evening. A man who had modelled himself on Hitler, it was typical of Joachim Wolff that the venue he had chosen should be a *Bierkeller* on the fringe of the Kreuzberg District where the Turkish immigrants lived. In his philosophy, the guest workers from the orient were the Jews of yesteryear and served the same purpose.

'You are newsperson?' the Armenian said, bastardising the German language to the point where it was virtually unrecognisable.

'Freelance journalist,' Nicholson told him.

'What is this freelance, Herr Raucher?'

'It means I don't work for a particular newspaper. I write an article and then I sell it to some paper or a magazine. Sometimes I suggest a story line and they pay me to write it.'

'Like with this Fascist from Hamburg?'

'Right. Only this time it's *Stern* magazine who have asked me to do a piece on him.'

The Armenian wasn't the brightest of men; his passenger had already told him this once, but he didn't mind repeating the tale. If the cab driver did subsequently recall his face, Nicholson wanted the cretin to remember him as a distinguished correspondent. The very word 'distinguished' conjured up a physical appearance wholly at odds with reality. It added several inches to his height and a good thirty pounds in weight. Instead of his unimpressive five feet seven and a half and bantamweight physique, the authorities would be looking for a man who was close on six feet and looked every inch an athlete, assuming of course that they suspected he was the assassin in the first place.

'Looks like the Mercs are leaving the autobahn. You want me to follow them, Herr Raucher?'

'Yes, someone on the reception committee must be putting him up for the night.'

No hotel room for Herr Joachim Wolff; he was going to stay with one of his acolytes of the Berlin chapter and save on expenses. There was, of course, another consideration; no self-respecting hotel manager in the city would tolerate a bunch of skinheads standing guard over the would-be Führer. Politics would have nothing to do with it; the objections would be purely commercial and made in the knowledge that letters of complaint from offended guests to head office of the hotel chain would undoubtedly blight his career.

'The people who live in this neighbourhood must be worth a fortune, Herr Raucher.'

'They are,' Nicholson said tersely. 'We could not hope to earn a tenth of their wealth if we lived to be a hundred.'

The head of the Berlin chapter owned a large detached house on Witzleben Platz in the Charlottenburg District with enough land surrounding the property to keep two gardeners fully employed the year round. Traffic indicators winking, the convoy wheeled right, swept through the huge wrought-iron gates and went on up the drive towards a villa even the President of the Bundesrepublik might well covet.

'Don't stop,' Nicholson ordered him curtly.

'You have seen enough?' the Armenian said and laughed.

'More than enough. You can drop me at the Zoo Bahnhof.'

The house on Witzleben Platz was too well protected. The television cameras mounted above the gates and in the grounds were, he suspected, merely the first line of defence. It had looked the sort of place where the owners would hire a security firm to guard their property and it was likely the burglar alarm was wired to the nearest police station. Following Joachim Wolff to this palatial residence in the Charlottenburg District had at least proved one thing: for all the *Bierkeller* posed considerable difficulties for him, it was still the best location.

'You are liking ABBA, Herr Raucher?'

The Armenian didn't wait for an answer; taking one hand off the steering wheel and both eyes off the road, he rummaged through the junk on the shelf below the dashboard. Narrowly missing an elderly Volkswagen in the near lane, he eventually found the tape he wanted and shoved it into the cassette player. The first track was

'Waterloo' and Nicholson hoped it wasn't an omen. Although he didn't come close to hitting anything else on the way to the Zoo Bahnhof, it was still a considerable relief to pay the driver off across the road from the station and watch his cab disappear from view.

Before returning to the poky little hotel off the Alexanderplatz in East Berlin, Nicholson had one more chore to perform. Crossing the road, he ducked into one of the pay phones on the sidewalk outside the Bahnhof and rang Kommissar Heinrich Voigt, chief of the *Kriminalpolizei* for West Berlin and the man strongly tipped to be the next Police President of the united city. Although an ordinary member of the public would have had to go through the exchange, Nicholson had been given Voigt's unlisted number and was able to ring him direct.

'I have just one question for you,' he said in English. 'When the fuck are you going to do something about that Nazi piece of dog shit, Joachim Wolff?'

Of the five-strong SOE team which had parachuted into Kubratovo, Alec Lister was the only man Ashton had been able to contact. One of the two Royal Signals junior NCOs had succumbed to bronchial pneumonia in the harsh winter of '62, while the other had seemingly disappeared from the face of the earth. The warrant officer in the Royal Engineers had emigrated to Canada in 1948, and the weapons training instructor from the Royal Welch Fusiliers had been killed in action during the Korean War at the battle of the Imjin after re-enlisting in the Gloucesters.

Lister was seventy-five and bore only the most superficial resemblance to the young officer in the South Staffordshire Regiment whose photograph was attached to the file Ashton had recovered from the 'dead sack'. Apart from a monk's fringe of white hair, he was completely bald and a once lean face had rounded out and become a patchwork of tiny blue veins, the hallmark of a seasoned drinker. He lived in the shadow of Lichfield Cathedral, a mere four hundred yards from the office in Beacon Street where he had practised law as a solicitor in partnership with his wife and brother-in-law, both of whom had died within ten months of one another in 1987. Since then, he had been looked after by a forty-three-year-old divorcee whose demeanour suggested to Ashton that her duties were not confined to those usually associated with a housekeeper. She had also been reluctant to leave the two men on their own after showing him into the study where Lister spent the mornings reading the *Daily Telegraph* and the *Financial Times* before working on his autobiography from two to five every afternoon.

'A well-meaning woman,' Lister observed once they were alone, 'but Elaine is inclined to be overprotective which sometimes can be very irritating.'

'I can imagine,' Ashton murmured sympathetically.

'Palestine,' Lister said abruptly.

'What?'

'Saw you looking at the photographs on my desk. Most of them were taken in the Tiberias-Nazareth area where the 1st Battalion was stationed in 1939. The end two were taken in November 1940 when we formed part of the blocking force at Maktilla while the 4th Indian Division attacked the main Italian position at Sidi Barrani. After that show, I lost my camera and never got around to acquiring another one.'

'Why not?'

'Couldn't be bothered. You come up by train?'

In his old age, it seemed that Lister had acquired the mind of a grasshopper and the sudden change of subject between one sentence and the next took a bit of getting used to.

'It's quicker than driving,' Ashton told him.

'And you want to know what I made of Henry de Vries?'

'Yes.'

'May one ask why?'

'He was supposed to be one of ours and someone killed him.'

'I'm sorry to hear that. But for de Vries, I wouldn't be here now.'

'He saved your life?'

'And the others. I think it's likely the whole SOE team would have disappeared if he hadn't intervened. The Russians didn't regard us as allies, at least the NKVD who arrived with the Red Army didn't – to them, we were the enemy. There were more Communists in the Fatherland Front than there were Social Democrats, Agrarians and Republicans, and they had us arrested and thrown into jail the day after the Chavdar partisan brigade entered Sofia.'

All five members of the SOE team had been held in solitary confinement at the central prison where they had been interrogated at length by the NKVD officers attached to Marshal Tolbulkin's Third Ukrainian Front. Except for one of the wireless operators from the Royal Signals who had been forced to drink several quarts of castor oil, no one had been physically tortured. They had, however, been deprived of sleep and given very little to eat.

'The NKVD wanted us to confess that, on Churchill's orders, we had been parachuted into Bulgaria specifically to destroy the Communist Party. Since we were in solitary confinement, it was impossible for us to decide amongst ourselves what line we should take with our interrogators. Fortunately, common sense prevailed, even though we were all told at one time or another that so-and-so had already confessed. All of us sensed we would never see England again if we did make a statement admitting our guilt.'

Ashton knew the old man wasn't exaggerating. Several thousand British prisoners of war had fallen into Russian hands as the Red Army advanced on Berlin. The majority had been speedily repatriated via the Black Sea ports, some had been detained on the spurious grounds that they were unfit to travel and a few had never been accounted for. Almost without exception, the latter had included officers and men who had been taken prisoner since the D-Day landings in June 1944. All had been specialists of one kind or another – radar technicians, communicators, SAS personnel and commandos. As far as the army, navy and air force were concerned, these missing servicemen were eventually presumed to have been killed in action. However, rumours that some of them were being held at various camps in the Gulag Archipelago had continued to reach the Secret Intelligence Service well into the mid-sixties.

'Of course there were times when one had been tempted to confess,' Lister said with a wan smile. 'I mean, the Russians did have a point. In briefing me, SOE Headquarters in Cairo made it very clear that with our assistance, they hoped the partisans would liberate Bulgaria before the Red Army arrived on the scene.'

'How long were you in Soviet hands?'

'We were released on the sixteenth of October, a little over five weeks from the day we were arrested. I remember thinking it seemed more like five years.'

'I can understand why you thought so highly of de Vries. What puzzles me is how he managed to secure your release from the NKVD.'

'I made a very full report to SOE after I was repatriated. I'm surprised you haven't seen it.'

'The file has been weeded,' Ashton said bluntly. 'Your statement must be one of the missing folios.'

'I see.' Lister rubbed both kneecaps simultaneously. 'Rheumatism,' he grunted, 'one of the many curses of old age.' He struggled to his feet. 'Time I took some exercise. You want to come with me?'

Lister's idea of exercise was a short stroll around the Minster Pool in the grounds of the Cathedral Close, taking in the Bird Street Garden of Remembrance dedicated to the fallen of the 1914–1918 conflict on the north side as well as the similar one in memory of the victims of World War Two south of the pond. Their conversation was sporadic, conducted only when the old SOE man was satisfied they couldn't be overheard.

'Does the name Georgi Dimitrov mean anything to you, Mr Ashton?' he asked.

'Sounds familiar.'

'He was an apprenticed printer when he became a Communist. Apart from organising party cells and conducting a sustained propaganda campaign, he had won his spurs masterminding a series of damaging strikes throughout Bulgaria. Dimitrov subsequently left his native country to further his political career in fresh pastures and was for a time Secretary of the Comintern. He was arrested by the Nazis in 1933 and charged with others for setting fire to the *Reichstag*. He defended himself with great skill, with the result that the judges found him not guilty in spite of intense pressure from Goebbels and Goering to arrive at a totally different verdict. He went to the USSR, survived the great purge initiated by Stalin and while still based in Moscow, directed the activities of the Communist Party in Bulgaria. He was the man who became the first president of the People's Republic immediately after the war. I'm telling you all this because Henry de Vries claimed he was on first name terms with Georgi Dimitrov.'

'And he used his friendship with the Bulgarian leader to get you out?'

'That was what he inferred.'

'Did you believe him?'

'At first I did. Later on, I revised my opinion. This was after I had asked him where he had met Georgi Dimitrov. De Vries was very evasive, never did give me a satisfactory answer to my question. Still, what did it matter if he was a bullshitter?'

'Was he a good liaison officer in the field?'

'He was reliable.' Lister moved over to a bench seat and sat down to massage his kneecaps again. 'Had a bit of a chip on his shoulder though. Reckoned his mother would never have died from blood poisoning if they had been living in a society that was halfway decent. His parents had been as poor as church mice and had had no money to pay for a doctor, or so he reckoned. Given his attitude, I imagine he found it easy enough to adapt to the Communist way of life in Bulgaria.'

'That isn't the impression you gave SOE when you were debriefed,' Ashton said quietly. 'You gave de Vries a glowing testimonial. That's why we took him on.'

'Excuse me, I did nothing of the kind.' Lister got to his feet, his face suffused with a rush of blood, his mouth tight-lipped. 'I merely indicated that he might be worth cultivating.'

There was no mistaking his anger and it certainly wasn't contrived. Lister was genuinely convinced he hadn't gone overboard in his assessment of de Vries and had been misquoted. Whether his recollection was correct was however open to question. He had been debriefed at SOE Headquarters located at St Michael's House off Oxford Street in January 1945, and who could remember precisely what had been said over forty-eight years later?

'Are you coming, Ashton?' Lister asked impatiently.

Ashton followed on. 'Listen,' he said, 'it's almost twelve; what say we have a drink?'

'That would be nice.'

Ashton fell into step beside the old man. 'So where do you suggest we go?'

'The George,' Lister said promptly.

'Lead on then.'

'Am I allowed to ask a question?'

76

'Depends what it is,' Ashton said.

'Was Henry de Vries of any use to you people in the Cold War?'

'Not a lot. Matter of fact, I think he got more out of us than we did from him.'

It suddenly occurred to Ashton that de Vries had been an NKVD plant all along. They had released the SOE team in order to make him look good, hoping that eventually the British would regard Henry as their man behind the Iron Curtain. He wondered just how much duff information de Vries had fed the SIS over the years.

Neil Franklin was the twelfth Head of Station, Berlin, the SIS had had since the end of World War Two and had been continually in post since June 1986. He was also likely to be the last, which was why he had not been relieved at the normal five-year point. When the city eventually became the official capital and seat of government, the British Embassy would move house from Bonn and he would become redundant. No more masquerading as the owner of the English Bookshop on Budapesterstrasse opposite the *Zoologischer Garten*; whoever he was, the next SIS chief would be locked into the embassy supposedly as a First Secretary where he would be about as effective as a neutered tomcat.

Franklin was fifty-two, the same age as Hazelwood, but apart from that, they had nothing in common. A native of Newcastle-upon-Tyne, he had a reputation for being abrasive and until a year ago, had been pretty much a law unto himself. Under the old régime, he'd had the right to communicate directly with the DG in London, but that cosy arrangement had been terminated the day Stuart Dunglass had been installed in the hot seat. Since that unhappy event, he had found himself answering to Victor Hazelwood, a man he couldn't stand at any price for reasons entirely due to a mutual and sometimes explosive antipathy.

At odds with the new management, he longed to make the grand gesture, but second thoughts always prevailed whenever he started to compose a letter of resignation. First and foremost was the practical consideration that there weren't too many openings for a senior Intelligence officer outside the service. Franklin was also aware that his chances of obtaining a sinecure with the Institute of

Strategic Studies were less than hopeful. In the circumstances, he found it easy to persuade himself that it would be silly to throw up his job in Berlin which still had so much going for it, not least the rent-free house on the corner of Grunerweg and Alsenstrasse in the Wannsee District.

On the other hand, he was no longer quite the king of the castle he'd been before the wall had come down. In the old days, Berlin had virtually been an occupied city and no German police officer would have had the temerity to demand an audience with him in his own home at 2 p.m. sharp. But Heinrich Voigt of the *Kriminalpolizei* had, and to accommodate the Kommissar, he'd had to pack his wife, Ella, off to the golf club for the afternoon, an indignity she hadn't appreciated one bit.

Franklin heard a car turn into the driveway of his house and moved to the study window in time to see Voigt alighting from the unmarked BMW. A year ago, there would have been a live-in maid to answer the door but the domestic staff had been reduced to a cook/housekeeper, one of the many cuts Her Majesty's Government had imposed under their so-called peace dividend. It angered him every time he thought about the cheese-paring economy but somehow he managed not to show it when greeting Voigt on the doorstep.

'It's good to see you, Heinrich,' he said with feigned affability.

'And you, Neil,' the German told him with about the same amount of enthusiasm.

'I thought we'd use my study.'

'Whatever suits you best. Is Ella at home?'

'Her afternoon at the golf club.' Franklin pointed to the Cona gently simmering on the electric ring which stood on a small table next to his desk. 'Will you have a cup of coffee?' he asked.

'Thank you. Black, please, no sugar.'

'How about a brandy to go with it?'

'I do not think so, it is too early in the day for me.'

'For a moment there, I thought you were going to say you were on duty.'

'Oh, but I am,' Voigt said without the faintest suspicion of a smile.

Franklin poured him a coffee, added milk and two spoonfuls of sugar to his own, then filled a balloon glass with a generous measure of Courvoisier for himself. 'So what's the nature of your business, Heinrich?'

'A lunatic Englishman,' Voigt told him curtly. 'He asked me when the fuck I was going to do something about that Nazi piece of dog shit, Joachim Wolff.'

'And?'

'That's it.'

'Really?' Franklin sniffed the brandy, then took a draught and gradually swallowed it, revelling in the burning afterglow it gave him. 'Well, I don't imagine it was the first obscene phone call you've received,' he added flippantly.

'This man was serious, Herr Franklin.'

So was Voigt when he wanted to be and the formal mode of address wasn't lost on Franklin. 'I believe Wolff is making a speech at some beer hall tonight,' he said in a cumbersome attempt to pour oil on troubled waters.

'Yes, the location is within spitting distance of the Kreuzberg District.'

'And you think there will be trouble?'

'There is always trouble when Herr Wolff harangues a crowd,' Voigt said wearily. 'I don't want an outsider making things worse.'

'Outsider?'

'Some dangerous left-wing activist or perhaps an *agent provocateur* posing as such.'

'Now what exactly do you mean by that?' Franklin asked.

'The English have long memories. Some of you may feel we are doing very little to curb the various neo-Nazi groups in this country. Is it possible you wish to shame us into taking action?'

Voigt was being paranoic – or was he? Franklin liked to think he knew what was going on in his bailiwick, but two years ago he had been kept pretty much in the dark when Ashton had played fast and loose in Berlin. And it could happen again with Hazelwood sitting in the Deputy DG's chair. Hazelwood was one of those aggressive operators who believed in making things happen.

'I presume your MI5 keeps a watching eye on the movements of all known extremists?'

'That's what they are there for, Heinrich.'

'And you would be informed if one of them decided to pay us a visit?'

'Absolutely, and rest assured, you would be the first to know.'

Voigt finished the rest of his coffee and left the cup and saucer on the desk. 'Does that mean you haven't heard anything?' he asked.

'Yes. But don't worry, I'll check with London to make absolutely sure.'

A year ago he could have picked up the phone and talked it over with the DG on the secure link, but he didn't have that kind of special relationship with Dunglass. He would have to signal London instead with a copy to the FCO and the embassy in Bonn to ensure Hazelwood wasn't tempted to sit on it.

Chapter 8

Nicholson checked the contents of the zipper grip one more time to make sure he hadn't forgotten anything. The baggy corduroys, sleeveless sweater, check shirt, purple socks and scuffed shoes had been bought at the flea market located on the upper platform of the disused Nollendorf station, while the wig had been purchased from the hairdressing salon of the Kaufhaus des Westens department store in West Berlin. The contact lenses, which would change the colour of his eyes from grey to brown, had come from an optician on the Ku'damm whereas the false moustache had been stolen from a theatrical costumier's in the Charlottenburg District when the sales assistant hadn't been looking. Finally, the two hanks of rope had been purchased from a hardware store in the outer suburbs.

Satisfied he had packed everything he needed, Nicholson zipped up the bag, hefted his overnight suitcase off the bed and left the room. The desk clerk had his nose deep in a porno magazine and didn't look up when he dropped the room key on the counter and walked out of the hotel. The Volkswagen Polo was parked round the corner from the hotel Kleine Eisenhut; unlocking the door on the driver's side, he tossed the zipper bag and suitcase onto the back seat, then got in behind the wheel. From Alexanderplatz, he made his way to Holzmarkenstrasse and drove on out to the Berliner Stadtforst.

The rendezvous was a derelict farmhouse in what had once been a local training area for Soviet forces stationed on the periphery of East Berlin. Although no unit had used the facility for at least eighteen months, the scars had not yet healed and the surrounding heathland still resembled a lunar landscape crisscrossed with track-marks left by tanks, armoured personnel carriers and self-propelled artillery. The farmhouse stood back from the road at the end of a cinder lane. It was enclosed on three sides by a narrow belt of trees and there was no other dwelling place in the vicinity.

Like most German farms, the house was tacked on to the side of a large barn, but there the similarity ended. The agricultural machinery had been seized for reparations at the end of the war when the owners had been evicted by the Red Army and since then, the property had been neglected. The barn itself was a wreck; one door had rotted away while what little remained of the other hung askew, held upright only by the bottom hinge. The roof sagged in the middle where some of the rafters had collapsed, and most of the tiles were missing. Bypassing the barn, Nicholson parked the Volkswagen behind the house where it wouldn't be seen from the road. The man with the Strawberry birthmark on his face whom he knew as Ilya had had the same idea and had left his old BMW 320 outside the kitchen door.

Nicholson went inside the house and found the Russian waiting for him in what had once been the family parlour. Of the original furniture, only two items now remained – a battered armchair with two missing castors which was clearly unsafe, and a worm-eaten kitchen table covered in cigarette burns. The Russian was perched on the windowsill, right buttock on the ledge, left foot planted firmly on the floor close to a large canvas holdall.

'How long have you been waiting for me?' Nicholson asked him.

'Only a few minutes.' Ilya bent down, picked up the holdall and placed it on the kitchen table, then undid the webbing straps. 'Well, here it is,' he said, 'all the way from the small arms assessment centre at Maloyaroslavets, one Vaime sniper's rifle Mark III designed and manufactured by Oy Vaimennimetalli of Finland. Plus one of Mr Makarov's specials. You want to satisfy yourself that nothing is missing before you take delivery?'

Nicholson took the Vaime Mark III out of the holdall and stripped the weapon down as far as he could without recourse to an armourer's toolkit. The old Soviet Army had possessed a fine sniper's rifle in the 7.62mm Dragunov, which was intended to produce a first round hit at various ranges up to and including eight hundred metres but it was long, cumbersome and not too easy to handle in the field. The overall length of the Finnish rifle was less than forty-three inches and was a good three pounds lighter. The manufacturers had furnished the bolt-operated weapon with a bipod to give a sniper greater stability when taking aim but, for Nicholson, the integral Varminter silencer was the best feature. Most silencers were no more than noise suppressors which muffled the discharge; the one manufactured by Oy Vaimennimetalli completely eliminated both the muzzle flash and the sound of a .22 long rifle rim-fire cartridge.

'Time is running on,' Ilya said impatiently. 'You hang around here much longer and you are going to miss the target.'

Nicholson ignored the Russian. Mr Makarov's special was a 5.45mm PSM, a semi-automatic pistol about the size of a man's hand. Breaking the sealed box of cartridges, he loaded the magazine with eight rounds and inserted it into the butt, then cocked the pistol and applied the safety catch.

'Are you satisfied with the merchandise now?'

'I've no complaints.'

'Then sign this,' Ilya told him and thrust a receipt voucher under his nose.

'Anything to oblige.' Nicholson took out a biro and put a cross in the signature box. 'Only thing is, I never leave my name on any piece of paper.'

'I've got news for you, this time you do.'

Ilya had been trying to discover his identity ever since Moscow had paired them off. The arms chit was merely his latest ploy.

'It's not necessary. All you have to do is send that blank voucher to Moscow and they'll know who signed it.'

'How?'

'I picked it up, didn't I? That means they've got my thumbprint on one side, the index and first finger on the other. Now get the hell out of here, I've got work to do.'

Nicholson grabbed hold of Ilya, seizing his left arm above the elbow in a grip of iron. He had learned a thing or two in his time with the Stasi and the KGB, who had taught him how to hurt people. He knew how to displace a tendon and the agony it could inflict on a man. Exerting pressure where it would produce the most pain, Nicholson had the much bigger Russian dancing on tiptoe as he waltzed him out of the house and into the BMW.

After Ilya had driven off, Nicholson collected his zipper bag from the Volkswagen and returned to the parlour. He changed swiftly, discarding the sports jacket and slacks in favour of the baggy cords, check shirt, gaudy socks and sleeveless sweater. He applied the bushy moustache to his upper lip and with some difficulty, inserted the pair of contact lenses he had obtained on the Ku'damm. The dark brown wig, which matched the colour of his eyes, completed the transformation, changing one sallow-looking, sixty-one-year-old Englishman into a middle-aged Turkish guest worker.

Nicholson packed the sniper's rifle into the canvas holdall with the exception of the bipod which he discarded to make the weapon lighter as well as easier to handle in a confined space. That done, he cleared out the zipper bag, transferring the two hanks of rope to the holdall to leave plenty of room for the sports jacket and flannels and the rest of the clothes he had been wearing. Loose change, wallet, clasp knife, car keys; he checked his pockets to make sure he had them. Then, picking up the small Makarov automatic, he reached behind his back, tucked the pistol barrel first into the waistband of the corduroys and pulled the sleeveless sweater down to conceal the butt and trigger guard.

'That's it,' he said aloud, 'let's go.'

He carried the holdall and grip out to the car, dumped them on the back seat and got in behind the wheel. It occurred to him that before the day was much older, he would be numbered amongst the very few people who had been given an opportunity to change the course of history. Elated by the thought, he started the car and drove back to the city.

'There is no way Martin Nicholson can hide from me.' Harriet Egan wished she hadn't made that confident prediction because it was beginning to look as if she would have to eat her words. St Catherine's House had been unable to find any record of a Martin Nicholson born in the London borough of Wanstead on the fourth of October 1931 in the census return for 1961. The Department of Social Security had his national insurance number on their computer at Newcastle-upon-Tyne, but it seemed he had never drawn unemployment benefit even though he had been entitled to do so after his firm, Dover Metal Castings, had gone to the wall. Furthermore, according to the Inland Revenue, Nicholson had not paid any tax after forwarding the P1954 issued by his erstwhile employer.

Although the passport office at Clive House had been able to produce an application submitted in 1960, it did not represent the breakthrough Harriet needed. The original form had been microfilmed for record purposes, with the result that the photograph attached to the application had suffered in the process. She had tried enhancing the likeness with the aid of a computer but had failed to improve the quality of the head and shoulders polyfoto Nicholson had taken of himself. No matter which way Harriet held the enlargement up to the light, the impression remained that she was seeing his face through a veil.

'Who's the pin-up?' Ashton asked.

She had not heard him enter the room and until that moment had assumed he was still up in Lichfield. Taken completely unawares, Harriet reacted like most people would have done, and flinched.

'I wish you wouldn't creep up on me like that,' she gasped.

'I'm sorry.'

'You're forgiven.' Harriet put the blow-up on one side. 'How did you get on with Alec Lister?'

'He was very helpful. Trouble is, I don't know just how far one can rely on his memory. I'm very clear in my own mind that Henry de Vries became a Communist and Soviet agent long before the war and never renounced his allegiance to the USSR. Lister claims he told the SOE all this when he was being debriefed, but there's no record of this on his file, or any other one come to that.'

'Are you saying the debriefing officer doctored the interview?'

'That's one possibility.' Ashton reached across the desk and picked up the enlargement. 'There are others,' he said while studying the photograph. 'Lister may be convinced he told the Special Operations Executive that de Vries was a Soviet agent but that could be something he unconsciously brainwashed himself into believing over the years. Then again, you have to remember the debrief took place after the Balkans had ceased to be an active theatre of war. You've only to read the transcript of the interview to realise it was a pretty light-hearted affair for both men.'

'Have you traced the conducting officer?'

'Yes, he went to Palestine after the war and was killed in July 1946 when the King David Hotel in Jerusalem was blown up by the Irgun Zvai Leumi.' Ashton frowned. 'Is this a photograph of the mysterious Englishman?' he asked.

'Yes, that's Gunner Martin Nicholson.'

'You can hardly see his features.'

'There's usually some deterioration when you reduce the original to microfilm.'

'I doubt if anyone will recognise him from this likeness.'

'You think you're telling me something I don't know?' Harriet snapped, then instantly regretted her outburst. 'Have you seen Victor Hazelwood since you returned from Lichfield?' she asked, hurriedly changing the subject.

'No, I wanted to sound you out first before I did anything. I mean, there are a number of folios missing from the SOE file and Lister claims the debrief isn't a true reflection of what he said at the time. It's possible we could be looking at a conspiracy.'

'And you are wondering if you should come right out and say it?'

'Yes.'

Harriet supposed she ought to be flattered that Peter had asked for her advice albeit in a roundabout fashion, but instead she felt only anger at the way he had been treated. The man she was going to marry had been left to stagnate in the backwaters of the Administrative Wing for far too long and he was beginning to lose confidence in himself. She knew all about Lieutenant Colonel Alexei Leven of the GRU and why the SIS had viewed Peter with suspicion because he had got a little too close to the Russian for their liking. But goddamnit all, that had happened two years ago and Hazelwood was forever assuring him that everything would come right in the end but doing nothing about his rehabilitation. In the meantime, however, the SIS were not above sending him in harm's way; she had only to see the burns on his stomach to know the truth of that. She did not trust the Deputy DG but of course it was no use her saying so to Peter; he believed the sun shone out of Victor's backside.

'You want to know what I would do in your position? I'd give the DG and his Deputy a blow-by-blow account of my talk with Alec Lister and leave them to draw their own conclusions.' Harriet stacked the in-, pending- and out-trays on top of one another then locked them away in the safe. 'Look at it this way: they are both paid a very handsome salary so why should you do their work for them?'

'You're right.'

'Good. Now let's go home, we've got things to discuss. I had another letter from my mother this morning.'

She didn't have to say any more; Ashton would know the letter was merely the latest round in what was a contest of wills. Although a June wedding was no longer feasible, her mother had not yet abandoned all hope. Provided the ceremony was held before autumn made the weather too uncertain for a large marquee on the lawn, there would be no need to prune the guest list. Harriet wanted a much quieter wedding and as close to Christmas as possible.

'So what's the latest argument for a summer wedding?'

'My younger brother, Richard – the RAF navigator. He's being posted to a Tornado squadron stationed at Gütersloh, joins them at the end of August.'

'Germany isn't the other side of the world,' Ashton said. 'The RAF will give him leave over a weekend.'

'As of now, part of the squadron is deployed in Italy to enforce the no-fly zone over Bosnia. If I insist on December, Richard could well be doing his stint down there.'

'In that case, your mother has a point.'

'It's still blackmail.' Harriet ushered him towards the door, then took one last look round the office to make sure her desk had been completely cleared. 'And I don't like having my arm twisted,' she added.

'Who does?'

'So I want you to put your thinking cap on and come up with an excuse which will leave mother and daughter still speaking to one another.'

The phone started ringing in her office before they had taken more than a few paces towards the lifts and she instinctively attempted to turn back in order to answer it.

'You didn't hear that,' Ashton said firmly and grasping her hand, led her on down the corridor.

Hazelwood gazed out of the window. The view was different from the new premises, the Thames instead of the hustle and bustle of Waterloo station, but nothing else had changed. A crisis of one sort or another always seemed to break whenever he thought of leaving the office on time for once. This evening was no exception and he had Neil Franklin, that proverbial pain in the arse who also doubled as Head of Station, Berlin, to thank for this latest embuggerance. The cable he had sent after his meeting with Kommissar Heinrich Voigt of the *Kriminalpolizei* had been short on hard facts but long on inference. However, the implied threat to Anglo-German relations had been sufficiently alarming to put the Foreign Office in a tizzy and was the reason why Dunglass had asked him and Rowan Garfield to drop by his office.

Rowan Garfield was in charge of the recently formed European Department which had sprung from the old Eastern Bloc. The change of name served a threefold purpose: it sounded both innovative and progressive and at the same time, created enough new appointments to save every officer in Hazelwood's old department from being made redundant. It also gave the SIS a legitimate excuse to target member states of the European Community, something it had been doing from the year dot anyway.

The activities of the various neo-Nazi parties in both the former DDR as well as West Germany therefore fell within Garfield's remit. His department did not, however, keep a watching eye on home-grown extremists of whatever political persuasion; that was down to MI5, the security service, whose liaison officer at Benbow House happened to be Harriet Egan. It was part of her job to obtain whatever information the SIS needed from her parent organisation.

'It would seem Miss Egan is not in her office,' Dunglass said plaintively and put the phone down.

'Wise girl,' Hazelwood observed, 'she's gone home.'

'How much credence should we give the threat to Joachim Wolff?'

Hazelwood fancied he knew what lay behind the question. Dunglass was thinking of approaching his opposite number in MI5 and wanted someone to convince him he had every reason to do so before he picked up the phone and spoke to Mrs Stella Rimington.

'We don't have much to go on, Director,' Garfield said diffidently. 'One abusive phone call from an Englishman.'

'Neil Franklin was sufficiently impressed to inform the Foreign

Office as well as ourselves,' Dunglass pointed out.

'He was simply covering himself.' Hazelwood turned back from the window. 'Look at the date/time group of his cable if you doubt it. He dispatched the signal almost three hours after Voigt had been to see him. Giving it an Op Immediate precedence doesn't cancel out the original delay.'

'Are you suggesting we put off doing anything until tomorrow morning?' Dunglass enquired softly.

'No, I'm just trying to keep things in perspective. If you contacted Mrs Rimington right now, you couldn't expect to get an answer from MI5 before Joachim Wolff arrives at the *Bierkeller* to address the party faithful.'

'What about the Stasi file on "The Englishman"? Have we managed to put a name to him yet?'

Garfield cleared his throat. 'I understand Miss Egan has made a tentative identification,' he said and looked to Hazelwood for confirmation.

'Well, Victor, has she or hasn't she?' Dunglass demanded when he failed to respond.

'Harriet thinks he could be a former gunner in the Royal Artillery called Martin Nicholson,' Hazelwood said reluctantly. 'If he had stayed in this country, he would be drawing his old age pension in four years' time.'

'Does she have a photograph of the suspect?'

'Last I heard from Roy Kelso she was hoping to obtain one from the passport office.'

'But Nicholson's height, weight, colour of hair and eyes and any other distinguishing features would be recorded in his army medical documents, wouldn't they?'

'Yes, but they'll be forty years out of date.'

'Doesn't matter, it's better than nothing.' Dunglass turned to Garfield. 'Your duty officer can ring Miss Egan at home, get his description and pass it on to Head of Station, Berlin, by encrypted radio telephone.' A faint but decidedly mischievous smile touched his lips. 'Of course, it means that poor old Neil Franklin will have to go downtown and open up the bookshop to take the call.'

'My heart really bleeds for him,' Hazelwood said with feeling.

★　★　★

The Drei Löwen was on Katzbach Strasse, a stone's throw from Viktoria Park. The apartment blocks across the road from the *Bierkeller* belonged to pre-war Berlin and had survived countless air raids, including the total destruction of the nearby Anhalter terminus. The buildings however had not emerged entirely unscathed; almost fifty years on, a keen-eyed observer could still pick out beneath the accumulated grime the pockmarks which had been caused by shell, mortar and small-arms fire when General Chuikov's 8th Guards Army had tangled with the 28th Panzer Division as they fought their way towards the Potsdamer Platz. Tonight, this street in the working-class district of Kreuzberg was about to become a battleground once again. And knowing that he was the man who was going to make it happen gave Nicholson a feeling of enormous power.

The possibility of failure did not enter his head. Before leaving the Volkswagen Polo in a backstreet five hundred metres west of Katzbach Strasse, he had phoned his source in the *Polizeipräsidium*, the Central Police Station on Tempelhofer Damm, and knew precisely what preventative measures were being taken by Kommissar Voigt. One patrol car on Katzbach Strasse down the road from the Drei Löwen as a visible deterrent, a couple of plainclothes men inside the *Bierkeller* itself and a riot squad on standby ready to intervene at the first sign of trouble when the rally began to disperse. It wasn't anything to get worried about.

Nicholson crossed the footbridge spanning the derelict S-Bahn line below Yorckstrasse station and walked straight on towards Viktoria Park. As he neared the T-junction with Katzbach Strasse, he could hear the um-pah-pah sound of a band. There was, he thought, nothing like a bellyful of beer and a few rousing drinking songs to fire up an audience before the arrival of the star attraction. Turning left at the top of the road, he was greeted with catcalls and abuse by a group of skinheads outside the entrance to the Drei Löwen. Their cries of 'Foreigners Out', 'Germany for the Teutons' and 'Mother-fucking Turkish scumbag' were music to his ears.

The Jurgen family occupied a flat overlooking Katzbach Strasse on the fifth floor of the apartment block fifty yards up the street from the *Bierkeller*. Nicholson had never met, never even heard of them until the moment he chose to knock on their door. It was opened by a thin, poorly dressed woman in her late forties who looked as if she was all set to tell him what she thought of guest workers until he produced the Makarov automatic and shoved the pistol in her face.

'Thank you for inviting me into your home, Frau Jurgen,' he told her in German, then stepped across the threshold and used a heel to close the door behind him.

Chapter 9

There were five doors off the hall, one on the left, two at the bottom end of the passageway and a further two on his right, the nearest of which was ajar. The sound of a quiz game on television told Nicholson it opened into the living room.

'Is your whole family in there, Frau Jurgen?' he asked.

'Yes.' She was mesmerised by the small-calibre Makarov, incapable of movement, like a rabbit caught in the headlights of an oncoming vehicle. Her voice was barely audible.

'How many are there?'

'Three.' She swallowed, gulping for air, then added, 'My husband, mother and daughter.'

'Let's go then,' Nicholson said and waved the semi-automatic pistol towards the living room.

The studio audience watching the game show were becoming increasingly excited. So it seemed was Herr Jurgen who felt moved to offer some words of advice to one of the contestants. With the old lady and her granddaughter equally engrossed in what was happening on the small screen, Nicholson could not have chosen a more opportune moment to move in.

'Don't let me disturb you,' he said almost casually, then dropped the canvas holdall onto the floor.

They were sitting round the dining table, chairs angled to face the colour TV in the corner at the far end of the room, their backs to the door. Jurgen looked over his shoulder, half rose from the chair, then saw the pistol Nicholson was holding to his wife's head and promptly sat down again. The old woman called him a dirty,

Turkish bastard and started yelling for help. Double-glazed windows and the noise from the television made it unlikely that her cries would be heard by the neighbours let alone anybody on the street below, but that was not the point. Her defiance could ignite a spark of resistance in the other members of the family. Reacting swiftly, Nicholson shoved Frau Jurgen into the wall and grabbing a handful of hair, yanked her daughter out of the chair and held the pistol under her jaw. The grandmother had already got the message before he told them what would happen if she didn't shut up.

'Nobody hurt if you all behave. Okay?' He tightened his grip on the girl's hair and tugged it hard enough to make her cry out. 'You have name?' he asked.

'Renate,' she gasped, then whimpering like a puppy, begged him not to hurt her.

Nicholson thought she could be as young as thirteen or maybe as old as sixteen; it was hard to tell a girl's age these days. One minute they were skinny twelve-year-olds running around in ankle socks, the next they were either dolled up like hookers or else their clothes looked as if they had been scavenged from a rubbish tip. Had the miniskirt Renate was wearing been a fraction shorter, the police would have had grounds for charging her with indecent exposure.

'Your mother,' he demanded in a guttural voice, 'she has a first name too?'

'It's Monika,' Frau Jurgen told him before her daughter had a chance to answer.

Nicholson repeated her name and scowled as if he somehow found it offensive, then told Monika exactly what she had to do. He deliberately spoke to her in poor, uneducated German, pausing frequently to give Monika and the other members of her family the impression that he was groping for the right word. The grandmother had already shown that she believed he was a Turkish guest worker and it was essential the other three shared her opinion. Under his direction, Monika Jurgen trussed her husband up like a chicken, then did the same to her mother, using the hanks of rope in the holdall. Once she had completed the task to his satisfaction, he compelled Renate to subject her to the same kind of treatment. After that, there was only Renate to worry about, and a thirteen-year-old girl was hardly a problem for someone like Nicholson.

DEATH THROES

★ ★ ★

The English Bookshop on Budapesterstrasse was open from nine in the morning until ten at night, except on Sundays when it was closed to the public until 5 p.m. It was a landmark for Berliners and tourists alike. The great attraction was the massive thirty-four per cent discount on all hardcovers and paperback reprints which no other bookseller was able to match without going out of business. No one knew that better than Helga von Schinkel who ran the enterprise for Neil Franklin. Despite the high volume of sales, the firm could not survive without the injection of capital. Making a profit was not however the object of the exercise; the bookshop existed solely as a front to cloak Franklin's activities as Head of Station, Berlin.

None of the other German employees was aware of this; as far as they were concerned, Herr Franklin was a typical English business-man, the kind who came and went as he pleased, spending more time on the golf course than he did in the office. In their opinion, he was lucky to have someone like Fräulein Helga von Schinkel to run the bookshop for him and make it pay.

Franklin too considered he was fortunate to have her, as had every one of his predecessors for whom she had worked since March 1947 when the SIS had poached her from AMGOT, the Allied Military Government Occupied Territories. Apart from being fluent in English, French and Italian, her political credentials had been beyond reproach. In 1944, when a nineteen-year-old university student, she had been a courier for the Bendlerstrasse conspirators. Arrested after the failure of the July Bomb Plot to kill Hitler, Helga von Schinkel had appeared before The People's Court in January 1945 charged with high treason and had been found guilty. Sen-tenced to death, she had been taken to the Lehrterstrasse prison to await execution and had still been there when the Red Army had stormed the city three months later.

In the days when she had worked for AMGOT, no one had been better qualified to root out the die-hard Nazi element within the ranks of the reconstituted civil service. Helga had thought she was doing much the same for the SIS until it had dawned on her that the Allies were busily organising a German national resistance move-ment to counter any possible Soviet aggression and that she had been helping the British to recruit former members of the *Waffen SS*. The discovery had led to a crisis of confidence and it had been on the understanding that henceforth she would only be employed on administrative duties that Helga had been persuaded to withdraw her resignation.

Thereafter, her work experience had been extensive. A car body repair shop, a small travel agency and an extremely modest hotel in the Wittenau District were among the many ventures she had managed on behalf of the SIS. As Franklin could personally vouch for, Helga was also a natural actress with a gift for ad-libbing whenever the unexpected happened. He wasn't surprised therefore when, in the hearing of a sales assistant, she apologised for dragging him down to the bookshop.

'That's all right,' he said gruffly, 'we didn't have anything planned for this evening. Let's go into my office.'

The office was next door to the stockroom at the back of the premises and was separated from the bookshop itself by a frosted glass partition. When the sales assistant could no longer see them, Helga von Schinkel went into the stockroom, leaving Franklin to open up his office.

The room was a minor fortress. In addition to a conventional burglar alarm, there was an infra-red intruder system and the door, walls and ceiling were lined with steel plates. Opening the bricked-in combination safe, Franklin took out the crypto-protected radio telephone and plugged it into the wall socket, then dialled the SIS communication centre at Vauxhall Cross and was patched through to the duty officer, European Department. He was more than a little surprised when a woman answered.

'You're not the person who rang me at home,' he said, then remembered to check that he had activated the secure speech facility. 'I assume you are guarded?' he added unthinkingly.

'Confirmed.'

He thought she sounded amused and cursed himself for being so crass. Had the link been unprotected, they simply wouldn't have been able to communicate with one another. 'So who am I speaking to?' he demanded, reacting defensively.

'My name's Harriet Egan. I have the information you asked for.'

Franklin grabbed a scratchpad, plucked a Biro from the cluster in the pewter mug on his desk, then told her to go ahead. Three minutes into the dissertation, he brought her up short. 'What's all this damned nonsense about a sixty-one-year-old deserter from the British Army? I'm interested in extreme left-wing agitators, not some geriatric in a wheelchair.'

'This man is a trained assassin. He worked for the Stasi first, then the KGB.'

'And now he's been pensioned off?'

'I honestly don't know.'

'Well, is he here in Berlin?'

'I can't say.'

'Let me make it easier for you, Miss Egan. Is it possible that Nicholson is somewhere in East or even West Germany?'

'I'm afraid we've no idea where he is. There are no entries on his file after September '78.'

'So he could be dead for all you people know.'

'I suppose that's possible,' she agreed reluctantly. 'However, according to the source, he is still very much alive and kicking.'

Franklin glanced at the physical characteristics he had jotted down on the notepad and wondered how anyone could be expected to recognise the renegade Englishman from such a vague description. 'Do you have a photograph of this man?' he asked.

'Only one that was taken a long time ago when he applied for a passport. It's not very good.'

'I assume it's better than nothing?'

The photograph, he learned, had been taken in 1960 and was therefore thirty-three years out of date. Furthermore, if the original lacked definition, the microfilm copy was fuzzy to the point of being unrecognisable.

'Jesus Christ,' Franklin exploded, 'is that the best you can do?'

'I did indicate he was a highly trained . . .'

'I wanted a list of known troublemakers in the ranks of the Anti Nazi League, and what do I get? The name and half-baked description of an army deserter in his dotage.'

'That isn't what I was told,' she protested.

'I wasn't told,' he repeated in a mocking tone of voice. 'What kind of an excuse is that, Miss Egan?'

'I'm not making one—'

'Good. In that case, I suggest you use your initiative and ask to see my cable, then hopefully you will understand what is required.'

'Look, I'm sorry if you think we have failed you in some way but—'

'I don't want an apology or an explanation. Just get me the information I've asked for and send it Op Immediate via the Berlin squadron of 13 Signal Regiment. All right?'

'Yes. May I ask you a question, Mr Franklin?'

'By all means.'

'Tell me, do you work at being rude and overbearing, or does it come naturally?' she asked, and then broke the radio telephone link while he was still speechless.

Some instinct prompted Ashton to glance to his right at the precise moment Harriet emerged from the Vauxhall Cross building. Without taking his eyes from her, he switched off the car radio just as Placido Domingo was declaring his love for Carmen. Even though Ashton couldn't see the expression on her face, the way Harriet stalked towards the car told him she was extremely angry about something. He knew the phone call she had received from the duty officer of the European Department couldn't be the cause because she had been even-tempered enough when he'd driven her to the expensive new home of the SIS. Leaning across the passenger's seat, he opened the nearside door for her.

'Don't ask,' Harriet warned him as she got into the Vauxhall Cavalier.

'As bad as that?' he murmured.

'If I never have to speak to Neil Franklin again, it'll be too soon,' she said vehemently. 'He's easily the most abrasive man I've ever had the misfortune to deal with.'

'Don't let Franklin get under your skin, he isn't worth it.' Ashton started the engine, shifted into reverse and backed out of the parking bay. 'I'll make you a stiff drink as soon as we're home.'

'The drink will have to wait. The information I've been asked to provide is held at Gower Street.'

'Yeah? What's going on?'

'Have you heard of a police officer called Heinrich Voigt?'

Ashton nodded. 'He's head of the *Kriminalpolizei* in Berlin. Our paths almost crossed two years ago. Good thing they didn't because if we had met, Voigt would have done his level best to put me inside. He's not exactly fond of the SIS, takes exception to us committing mayhem on his turf.'

'How about Joachim Wolff? Does his name ring a bell?'

'No, I can't say it does.'

'Wolff is the Party Secretary of the New National Socialist Movement. He is due to make a speech at some beer hall tonight and Voigt thinks there could be trouble. Seems he also has reason to believe that at least one of our left-wing agitators is likely to be involved. Anyway, Franklin wants to know if any members of the Anti Nazi League are in Berlin right now.'

Ashton drove across Westminster Bridge, went round Parliament Square and turned into Whitehall. Listening to Harriet, it was evident that Franklin had fired off a signal to London simply to cover himself against any eventuality. And London had pulled Nicholson out of the hat because he represented a lethal threat and was thought to be somewhere in Europe because there was certainly no trace of him in the UK.

'Of course, it would have been helpful if Franklin had made it clear in the first place that he was interested in the Anti Nazi League. Instead of which, he has the nerve to bawl me out for not using my initiative.'

Whitehall fed into the usual snarl-up around Trafalgar Square. The office workers might have long since departed, leaving the West End to the tourists, buskers, theatre-goers and the night people but the traffic seemed as heavy as it did in the rush hour. Rain was falling from a darkening sky but not heavily enough as yet to send the homeless scampering into the nearest shop doorway.

'This file on Nicholson,' Ashton said presently. 'What did Kelso tell you about it? I mean, did he say how we got hold of it?'

'He told me the *Bundesnachrichtendienst* had sent it with their compliments. Apparently, the West German Intelligence Service obtained the file from their opposite numbers after the Wall came down and the Stasi was disbanded.'

'We didn't ask for it?' Ashton queried.

'No. Roy Kelso definitely gave me the impression that the BND passed it to us when they realised "The Englishman" was a deserter from the British Army.'

The Wall had come down in 1989 and barely twelve months later, Germany had been reunited; it had then taken the BND another three years to turn up the file on Nicholson. Ashton supposed the time scale was not unreasonable considering the Stasi was reputed to have opened files on half the population of the former German Democratic Republic. Ordinary criminals, police informers, doctors, nurses, lawyers, judges, university lecturers, students, civil servants, dancers, athletes, gymnasts, servicemen and women; no one had escaped their notice. Then he remembered what the Deputy DG had said to him and he almost shot the lights at the intersection of Cranbourn Street with Charing Cross Road.

'Hazelwood told me it was the Russians who fingered Nicholson,' he said aloud.

'What?'

'The mysterious Valentin; the information allegedly came from him.'

'Does that make the file suspect?' Harriet asked.

'I don't know.' The lights changed from red through amber to green; shifting into gear, Ashton went on past Leicester Square Underground towards Cambridge Circus. 'However, all the entries on the file are in German and that does make me a little suspicious.'

'Because at some stage Nicholson went to work for the MVD and you would have expected his file to go with him?' Harriet asked.

'Right.'

'And therefore the later entries should have been in Russian.'

'Right again.'

'Unless the MVD, and subsequently the KGB, controlled him through the East German security service? They could have told the Stasi what they wanted from him and left the East Germans to brief Nicholson.'

'I think you've just cracked it,' Ashton told her and wondered why the possibility hadn't occurred to him.

There had been two files; one had been kept by the KGB's First Chief Directorate at Yasenevo on the Moscow ring road, the other by the East German Ministry of State Security in the Lichtenberg District of Berlin. It would explain why all the entries on the file

Kelso had given Harriet were in German and why the mysterious Valentin had known of its existence.

'Now that we've solved that problem, where does it get us, Peter?'

'I'm damned if I know,' he admitted.

The evening performance of *Les Miserables* at The Palace had already started but the solitary juggler was still performing where the queue for the gallery had been even though his once captive audience had vanished. The Phoenix, Astoria and Dominion; they left theatreland behind them as they entered Tottenham Court Road.

'I'll tell you one thing though,' Ashton said, having given the matter some thought, 'I can't understand why Valentin demanded that I should meet him in Sofia when he must have already established a pretty efficient means of communication with London.'

'Did you ask Hazelwood for an explanation?'

'No, Victor operates on the need-to-know principle.'

'And of course you always do as you are told,' Harriet observed drily.

'There was a time when I didn't, but I don't want to spend the rest of my service in the Admin Wing.'

The British Museum is at one end of Gower Street, University College at the other. Between these two well-known landmarks in the heart of Bloomsbury, there are a number of anonymous buildings, none more so than the one occupied by the security service. An armed police officer stopped the car in the entrance to the basement garage and asked to see their ID cards, which caused a small altercation because Ashton's was only good for Benbow House. Standing orders clearly laid down who could or could not be admitted to the MI5 building and nothing Harriet said could alter the fact that he did not have the requisite clearance. Furthermore, the police officer refused to issue him with a visitor's pass on the grounds that he didn't have any official business with the security service. The same rules applied to both Century House and Vauxhall Cross but to find himself barred from Gower Street was somehow infinitely more humiliating.

★ ★ ★

Both windowsills in the Jurgens' living room were a jungle of indoor plants. Ten minutes before Joachim Wolff was due to arrive at the Drei Löwen, Nicholson removed the African violets, mother-in-law's tongue, grape ivy and busy Lizzies from the farthermost ledge and placed them on the floor near the TV. Then he unlatched the double windows and opened them just far enough to give himself room for a clear shot at the target without shattering the glass. The skinheads he had seen earlier in the evening were still on guard outside the entrance to the *Bierkeller* and the band had not yet exhausted their repertoire of rousing marches. Between them, the um-pah-pah band and the Nazi thugs generated an air of malice on Katzbach Strasse but it was nothing like the naked hatred the Jurgen family directed at him. He had, of course, gagged all four of them – mother, father, daughter and grandmother, but their eyes told him what they would like to do to him to assuage their shame and humiliation. But, in their heart of hearts, they knew that even if they had been able to do so, they wouldn't have raised a hand against him. The 5.45 Makarov semi-automatic was a powerful deterrent and they would even have sat there and watched while he forced thirteen-year-old Renate to go down on him. That was the shame the whole family would take with them to their graves.

Nicholson opened the canvas holdall, took out the .22 calibre sniper rifle and donning a pair of cotton gloves, loaded the magazine with five rounds and closed the bolt. Then he rubbed the stock, butt, silencer, telescopic sight and all the working parts he had touched when taking delivery of the rifle from Ilya, thereby obliterating his fingerprints.

His stomach started knotting up the way it always did immediately before a kill, but fortunately, Joachim Wolff did not keep him waiting long. At twenty-seven minutes past eight and right on time, the same cavalcade of black Mercedes he'd seen at Berlin-Tegel that morning rolled down Katzbach Strasse and stopped outside the Drei Löwen.

The new generation of stormtroopers hurriedly formed two inward-facing ranks on the sidewalk moments before one of the entourage riding in the second limousine leaped out and opened the rear nearside door for Wolff. Standing back from the window in order to ensure that no one on the street below who happened to look up at the apartment house could see him, Nicholson pulled the butt into his right shoulder and took aim. Through the German-made ZF telescopic sight with its four power 24 mm optic lens, a mole on the left side of Wolff's face looked as big as a bottle top at a range of a hundred and fifty feet. He breathed in, held it, took up the slack on the trigger and squeezed off the first round. Opening the bolt to eject the spent case, he then closed it, feeding another .22 calibre long cartridge into the breech, and fired again. Two aimed shots in a fraction over three seconds; he might be sixty-one years old but his touch hadn't deserted him. He had seen the first .22 hit Wolff just above the left ear and knew it would continue on a downward trajectory to exit somewhere below the jaw on the right side of the face. He also knew it was a lethal hit. The second round, which had struck the German between the shoulder blades as he went down, had therefore been unnecessary but in Nicholson's philosophy, a way of making absolutely sure.

He shoved the rifle into the canvas holdall, carried it out into the hall and left the apartment, closing the door quietly behind him. He moved swiftly towards the emergency exit at the rear of the building and went down the external fire escape as silently as the iron rungs would allow. The hard beat of rap was coming from one apartment; in another on the second floor he could hear a man and a woman shouting at each other. He reached the bottom without incident and cut through the narrow passageway between the tenements facing the parallel road in rear of Katzbach Strasse. Walk – don't run – look natural; Nicholson reminded himself of the dictum as he stripped off the cotton gloves and shoved them into his jacket pockets. By the time he reached the parallel road, he had removed the wig, straggly moustache and, stopping for no more than seconds, disposed of the contact lenses.

He turned left on the road and made his way to the footbridge spanning the disused S-Bahn line below Yorckstrasse station. Witnesses to a violent incident resulting in sudden death were invariably gripped by a collective paralysis and he calculated that at least a full minute would elapse before anyone in Wolff's entourage thought to ring for an ambulance. In planning the assassination, Nicholson had made it his business to discover the location of the emergency services closest to the Drei Löwen and knew he could rely on a further four to five minutes before they arrived on the scene. Given that time span, he expected to reach the Volkswagen Polo five hundred metres west of Viktoria Park and get clear away before the police sealed off the neighbourhood. With a sympathiser in the *Polizeipräsidium* running interference for him, it was hardly a calculated risk.

The rioting started half an hour after Joachim Wolff was pronounced dead on arrival at St Thomas's hospital on Mittenhofstrasse. Gangs of youths roamed the Kreuzberg District looking for the *Untermenschen*. In an orgy of destruction, cars were overturned, shops looted and apartment buildings housing guest workers were fire-bombed. Three people were killed and forty-one injured before the riot police intervened in sufficient strength to restore order. It was not a good night for a foreigner to be out on the streets in that part of Berlin.

Chapter 10

As Assistant Director in charge of Administration, Roy Kelso was responsible for courses, clerical support, Boards of Inquiry, internal audits, claims, expenses, departmental budgets, control of expenditure and supervision of the Security Vetting and Technical Services Division. Of all the various sections lumped together under the umbrella of the Administrative Wing, finance was the one over which Kelso exercised the most control. It also happened to be the largest sub department and occupied the whole of the fourth floor directly below Kelso and immediately above Ashton's Security Vetting and Technical Services Division.

Being two floors below the Assistant Director suited Ashton; the lifts in Benbow House were inclined to be temperamental and since tearing the ligaments in his left knee twelve months ago, Kelso avoided the stairs whenever possible. He therefore rarely dropped in on Ashton hoping to catch him unawares, and usually the two men only saw one another at the weekly conference held every Monday morning at 09.00 hours sharp. However, every now and then he would summon Ashton to his office on the top floor. This morning was one such occasion.

'My office, please,' Kelso had told him cryptically when he had answered the phone, and had then added, 'Drop whatever you're doing; this is important.'

A hunch that perhaps the Assistant Director had found something wrong yesterday when he'd checked the controlled stores on charge to Technical Services was proved false when he walked into Kelso's office. Victor Hazelwood and Rowan Garfield of the European

Department were the last people he had expected to see. He was even more surprised to find Harriet there as well and wondered how long she had been conferring with the others and why.

'No need to panic,' Hazelwood told him cheerfully, 'you haven't missed anything important.' He waved a hand towards the only vacant chair in the room. 'Come in and sit down.'

As was his wont, Hazelwood had reorganised the office, seating himself behind the desk with Garfield on his right facing the displaced Kelso at the other end. Harriet had played it safe, choosing to sit next to the head of the European Department rather than her own Assistant Director. Ashton ended up between the two of them.

Hazelwood produced the inevitable Burma cheroot from the top pocket of his jacket and carefully pierced the end with a matchstick before lighting it. 'Better show him the latest from Berlin, Rowan,' he said between puffs.

The latest was a situation report from the Head of Station. Garfield was reluctant to part with it because the Sitrep had been transmitted by 13 Signal Regiment and he rightly suspected that Ashton was no longer cleared for Sigint. No great insight was needed to deduce this. Although the reason for his posting to the Admin Wing had never been made public, in most people's eyes, his transfer from the Russian Desk to Benbow House had certainly not been a career move. In this instance however, Garfield was interpreting the rules pedantically; although the information had been passed through Sigint channels, it had not been acquired by the intercept service eavesdropping on the host nation or any other country.

Ashton's knowledge of events in Berlin had been garnered from the newspapers. If Harriet knew more than he did, she had never divulged it. They might share the same bed but her pillow talk was confined to their relationship and plans for the future and not what had passed across her desk during office hours.

The Sitrep from Franklin two days after the rioting in the Kreuzberg District was very illuminating and much more detailed than anything Ashton had read in *The Times*, *Telegraph*, *Independent* and *Guardian*. It was classified Secret, and rightly so, because Franklin had been highly critical of the German authorities, which would definitely sour relations between the two countries if the communication fell into the wrong hands. In his opinion, the riot police had been slow to respond to the situation and even more reluctant to intervene. Petrol bombs had been thrown into a ground-floor flat of an apartment block and three people had died in the blaze because the firemen had refused to deal with the conflagration without police protection. To support his contention that there had been collusion between the neo-Nazis and the forces of law and order, Franklin cited the fact that the day after the riot, twenty-four members of the élite riot police had marched down Oranienstrasse in their green fatigues singing the Horst Wessel song.

'It's pretty damning,' Ashton said and returned the signal to Garfield.

'Well, Neil Franklin was never one to mince words,' Hazelwood said, 'and the *Kriminalpolizei* were expecting trouble that evening. Your old sparring partner, Heinrich Voigt—'

'I only know of him. We've never met and I doubt he's even aware of my existence.'

'I was only speaking metaphorically, Peter,' Hazelwood said in injured tones. 'Anyway, the Kommissar received a threatening phone call from an Englishman and took it seriously enough to call on our Head of Station.' He smiled. 'I expect Harriet told you the rest?'

Ashton wished he knew what was going on. There were enough senior officers present to form a Board of Inquiry and reading between the lines, it was evident that Franklin had a chip on his shoulder and was gunning for someone.

'That depends on what the rest is,' he said cautiously. 'If we are talking about the information Franklin asked for, then, sure, I know he was given everything we had on Nicholson.'

'Which he claimed was inappropriate before Herr Wolff was shot dead, whereas, after the event, he thought it was all too relevant.' Hazelwood looked in vain for an ashtray on Kelso's desk and tapped his cheroot over the metal wastebin instead. 'So he sat on the information and informed Voigt that all the leading lights of the Anti Nazi League had stayed at home.'

'What Mr Franklin told him wasn't strictly correct,' Harriet said quietly. 'None of the membership is under surveillance; all MI5 could say is that to the best of their knowledge, the Anti Nazi League hadn't sent any representatives to Berlin.'

'Well, to give Neil his due, I think he was merely being positive. He wanted Voigt to believe he was being completely open with him. The question we have to answer now is whether our esteemed Head of Station is justified in thinking Nicholson could be the killer? I don't know enough about him to make a judgement. Neither does Rowan.' He turned to Ashton. 'Only you – and Harriet of course – have studied his file in depth and are equipped to do that.'

So now we know what this is all about, Ashton told himself. He also knew that although Kelso had read Harriet's report, he was unlikely to give a lead. The Assistant Director liked to gauge which way the wind was blowing before he committed himself.

'I'm not saying Franklin's wrong,' Ashton said, offering his opinion, 'but I think he's guessing. We gave him the name of an assassin, Wolff gets shot and suddenly it's all down to our geriatric army deserter, as he once described him. The fact is that we have been told precious little about the mechanics of Wolff's assassination other than it involved the use of a firearm.'

'We lack a signature,' Harriet added, 'something we can point to and say, yes, that's Nicholson's trademark – and there's the problem, because he really doesn't have one.'

Of the seventeen murders attributed to Nicholson, less than two-thirds of his victims had died from gunshot wounds. Among the exceptions, one woman had been electrocuted, a man had apparently committed suicide by placing his head on a railroad track, another had been poisoned with ricin, while on separate occasions a further two had suffered fatal coronaries after he had discharged cyanide gas pistols in their faces.

'It would seem variety is the spice of life and death where he is concerned,' Garfield observed.

'In more ways than one. Nicholson has a taste for abnormal forms of sexual activity.'

'Such as?' Kelso asked slyly and looked everywhere but at Harriet when she turned to face him.

'He's a sadomasochist; it's on record that he whipped and sodomised one young woman after he had forced her to give him oral sex. There is a note from his case officer on the file to the effect that he was invariably sexually aroused just before and immediately after an operation. Following the incident with the young woman, the Stasi used to hire a prostitute to keep him happy whenever he was about to come on heat.'

Ashton watched Kelso turn a delicate shade of pink. If he had intended to embarrass Harriet, the boot was now on the other foot. It wasn't so much what she said as the way it came out. In giving him the salacious details, she had sounded as though she was reluctantly satisfying the curiosity of a dirty old man.

'I don't see where this gets us,' Garfield said, breaking an awkward silence. 'If these aberrations only occur before or after a murder, they can hardly be called his signature or modus operandi.'

'I agree with you,' Harriet told him. 'All I'm saying is that we should keep these proclivities in mind.'

'That's all very well but it doesn't solve the problem.'

'Problem?' Ashton echoed. 'What problem is this?'

Hazelwood leaned over the side of his chair, picked up the wastebin and used it to stub out his cheroot, then put the receptacle back where it belonged on the floor. For some moments, a thin, interrupted plume continued to rise towards the ceiling like an Indian smoke signal. 'The one Franklin inadvertently created,' he growled, reappearing above the desk.

The riot had already started when the Berlin squadron of 13 Signal Regiment had rung Franklin at home to inform him they had received an Op Immediate communication from London addressed for his eyes only. By that time, he was also aware that Joachim Wolff had been shot and killed by a sniper. From being dismissed as a geriatric army deserter, Nicholson had now entered the frame as Europe's most deadly hit man. Whether he had actually killed the Party Secretary of the New National Socialist Movement was beside the point in Franklin's opinion. What counted were the political repercussions that would surely follow should the German authorities suspect that Wolff had been murdered by an Englishman.

'There's an old maxim,' Hazelwood continued. 'When in doubt, do nothing, and basically, this is precisely what Head of Station, Berlin did. Uppermost in his mind was the conviction that Voigt might well conclude we believed Nicholson had done it if he gave him the information he had received from Harriet. Unfortunately, Neil wasn't aware it had been gleaned from a Stasi file.'

Nor, it transpired, had he known that the BND had only passed the file to London after considerable pressure had been brought to bear on Bonn at ministerial level. The day after the Kreuzberg riot, he had unintentionally exacerbated the situation by briefing the Foreign Office representative at Headquarters British Forces, Berlin. Within a matter of hours, the embassy in Bonn and the mandarins in Whitehall had received a verbatim report of their conversation.

'You can probably guess the rest,' Hazelwood said in conclusion. 'We've been ordered to put matters right because it's even money that the BND retained a photocopy of the Stasi file, and naturally we don't want Bonn asking us if we have succeeded in identifying him yet.'

'In other words,' Kelso said disbelievingly, 'we let the Germans know we think Nicholson is the KGB's hired assassin?'

'Precisely. What we have to decide is how and when we feed it to them. Obviously the timing is critical. We mustn't appear either slothful or too eager. But above all, we don't want to give the Berlin authorities the impression that somehow we feel responsible for what happened in their city.' Hazelwood looked round the assembled company. 'Anyone got any bright ideas?' he asked. 'Peter?'

'Forget Voigt, give it to the BND and let them make the connection.'

'And if they don't, then it's their bad luck, and we still come up smelling like roses.' Hazelwood grinned happily. 'I like it, Peter.'

Rowan Garfield thought the suggestion had merit, which was enough for Kelso to add his endorsement. Only Harriet remained silent. Ashton didn't blame her; he wasn't exactly proud of himself either. A couple of years ago he would have played it straight down the line and urged Victor to ensure the information reached Voigt. But something had happened to him since the move to Benbow House and he'd become devious, willing to do whatever was expedient to further his rehabilitation. Preoccupied with these dark thoughts, he vaguely heard Garfield say something about despatching a senior desk officer to Bonn, then Kelso chipped in with a suggestion that it would look even better if the desk officer was accompanied by someone from MI5 and suddenly he realised the three wise men were looking at Harriet.

'I'll be happy to go,' she said quietly.

'Now, just a minute—' Ashton began.

'It's only a liaison visit, Peter,' she said, interrupting him.

'Quite so,' Hazelwood added in a breezy manner that was meant to dispel any lingering doubts. 'And it's not going to happen tomorrow either. These things can't be rushed, we have to pick the right moment.'

Hazelwood stood up and moved his chair back, then thanked everyone for being so helpful and said he thought it had been a very successful meeting.

Ashton was on the way out with the others when Victor called him back and asked Kelso if he would mind leaving them alone for a couple of minutes so that they could have a word in private. Kelso minded like hell but stretched his mouth into the semblance of a smile and invited Hazelwood to take as long as he liked.

'What's this all about, Victor?' Ashton asked once they were alone.

'This,' Hazelwood said and reached inside the breast pocket of his jacket for a slip of paper.

Although the signal had been topped and tailed to disguise its origin, the subject matter clearly indicated that it had been decoded at GCHQ Cheltenham, and it hadn't been intercepted yesterday either. The Russian who had interrogated him at Rila had asked Moscow for disposal instructions and had been told that a valuable asset should never be wasted.

'I'm "Mercury", am I, Victor?'

'It would seem an apposite codename for a courier.'

'So how long has this signal been kicking around then?'

'Long enough.'

'And the Director has seen it?'

'But of course; one could hardly withhold it from him.'

'So what are you trying to tell me, Victor? That there is no way back?'

'Not at all. You're going to the Ministry of Defence, Military Operations (Special Projects). It's a good job, one that should be right up your street since it involves working hand in glove with the army.'

Ashton stared at him blankly, unable to take it in at first. 'When does this happen?' he asked eventually.

'You report there tomorrow, 10.00 hours on the dot.'

'Who's going to take over from me?' he asked, still in a daze.

'Harriet.'

'Harriet?'

'What's the matter, Peter? Don't you think she's up to running your division?'

'She can do it standing on her head. But that's not the point; it happens to be one of our posts.'

'Not any more.'

The establishment was being cut again to reduce government spending under the guise of the peace dividend. Harriet's old appointment of Staff Assistant to Head of Security Vetting and Technical Services Division was to disappear. And in future, his job could be filled by an officer from either the SIS or MI5, depending on availability.

'We can't promote her, Peter, but she'll definitely get the pay.'

'Can I tell her the good news?' he asked.

'Better leave it to Roy. He is, after all, in charge of the Admin Wing.'

'Right. And thanks, Victor, I was beginning to think I was doomed to spend the rest of my service at Benbow House.'

'I wouldn't have allowed that to happen.' Hazelwood smiled. 'Can I have that signal you're holding?'

'Yes, of course. I'd completely forgotten all about it.' Ashton returned the flimsy and started towards the door, then turned about. 'Have you heard anything from Sofia about the de Vries investigation?'

'It's not getting anywhere.'

'The police haven't found Denista then?'

'Who?'

'The girl from the tourist bureau.'

'They are not even aware of her existence and Pearman can't enlighten them without implicating the embassy. Best thing you can do is forget about her.'

★　★　★

As the senior First Secretary and Head of Chancery, Pearman rarely lunched at home on a weekday. On those few occasions when he did, he usually walked both ways and told himself that he ought to make a habit of it because it certainly toned up the old muscles and helped to keep his weight down. And besides, there was nothing to beat a little gentle exercise on a warm sunny afternoon such as this. His appointment diary was also a complete blank, which made it an even nicer day.

In a thoroughly equable frame of mind, Pearman turned into Marshal Tolbuhin Boulevard and walked on towards the embassy. He had cleared his in-tray before lunch, and not by the simple expedient of transferring the more difficult files to the one marked pending. There was therefore every reason to suppose the day would end as uneventfully as it had begun, until the Third Secretary, Consular Affairs, walked into his office moments after he had arrived to ask if he could spare him a few minutes.

'My time is yours, Larry,' he said cheerfully. 'What's the problem?'

'A girl. She walked in off the street and asked for political asylum.'

Pearman gaped at the younger man. So far as he knew, no one had ever sought refuge in the British Embassy even at the height of the Cold War when the quality of life had been lousy and people had an incentive to leave the country. Of course, in those days there had been an armed militiaman on guard outside the embassy to deter any would-be escaper, never mind the plainclothes security men from the Durzhavna Sigurnost who kept an eye on the place from the park across the road. But now, when the guards had gone, the Communist Party was no longer in power, and conditions had improved beyond measure, they had their first refugee. It didn't make sense to Pearman.

'Who is she?' he asked.

'I don't know, Michael, she wouldn't give me her name. She mumbled something about how her grandmother had introduced her to Mr de Vries which was why her life was now in danger. I thought you'd –'

'Never mind that, Larry. What does she look like?'

113

'The girl's very young, no more than eighteen – quite tall and slender, in fact almost thin. She has shoulder-length dark hair – heart-shaped face – speaks quite good English.'

Denista. It had to be Denista; there couldn't be two young women in Sofia who matched the description Ashton had given him and had been acquainted with Henry de Vries.

'I'd better see her, Larry.'

'That's what I thought.'

No one could have been quicker off the mark or more eager to unload an awkward problem than the consular officer. In next to no time, he ushered the girl into Pearman's office and escaped to his own.

When Ashton had met her, Denista had been wearing a floral, three-quarter-length silk dress with a black crotcheted shawl around her shoulders. Today it was an equally modest skirt and blouse. Judging by their rather worn-down appearance, Pearman thought she only had the one pair of high-heeled shoes.

'Sit down, Denista,' he said and saw her eyes grow wider. 'You're a guide with Interbalkan, aren't you?'

She nodded dumbly, then found her voice. 'I used to be.'

'Oh? Why did you leave?'

'There were difficulties,' Denista said and looked down at her hands clasped loosely together on her lap.

'Over Mr de Vries?' Pearman suggested.

'He is dead.'

'He was murdered,' he told her flatly.

'Yes. It was very bad.' Her voice had all the personality of a synthesiser and she reacted like a robot.

'If you know anything, you should go and see Captain Khristov at Militia Headquarters in the Central District. He's in charge of the investigation.'

'No.' Denista looked up and shook her head vigorously. 'No, is too dangerous. There are bad men, they kill me.'

The more agitated she became, the more her command of English deteriorated. If it was an act, Pearman thought it was a fine performance, but he reminded himself that she was only eighteen and wasn't a student at a state-run drama school.

'Would it help if we conversed in Bulgarian?' he asked.

114

'My English is not good today.'

'It's only to be expected. When you are upset, it's not easy to express yourself in a foreign language.'

Pearman took out a packet of King Size Silk Cut, one from several cartons that had arrived with the diplomatic bag, and offered her a cigarette. When Denista told him she didn't smoke, he asked her if she minded if he did and promptly lit one.

'My colleague tells me you have asked for political asylum,' he said in Bulgarian. 'Why is that?'

'Because I am frightened.'

There was a brief pause before it all came tumbling out. Denista's account of what had happened followed no logical sequence and for that reason, he believed her story. She had gone to the Sheraton to meet Ashton on the instructions of State Security. The manager of Interbalkan had called her into his office earlier that morning and had left her alone with an officer of the Durzhavna Sigurnost. She had known he was a DS man because he had produced his ID card for her inspection. He did not however give her time to memorise his surname which, in any case, was partially obscured with a thumb. 'Call me Nikola,' he'd said, 'it's more friendly.' He had then shown her a photograph of Ashton and informed her that the dark-haired man was believed to be a drug baron.

'Nikola said the police wanted to search his hotel room when he wasn't there and that was where I came in. He insisted it was my duty as a good citizen to help the Militia.'

The DS man had also left Denista in no doubt that she could well lose her job with the government-funded tourist bureau should she refuse to co-operate. Anticipating the obvious question, Nikola had told her exactly what she had to do and just how she could lure the Englishman away from the Sheraton Hotel.

'I was to tell him that Mr de Vries had sent me and that I knew where his friend Valentin was staying.'

The DS man had led her to believe that both de Vries and Valentin were dealers, an allegation which had shocked Denista because the old Resistance hero was a friend of her grandmother's and she had known him since childhood. According to Nikola, Valentin had been an undersecretary in the Ministry of Cultural Affairs when the Communists had been in power and she had had no difficulty in accepting that the former government official was even more corrupt now that he was no longer in office.

'I was instructed to lead Mr Ashton towards St Nedelya Church when we left the Sheraton so that the police would know it was safe to search his hotel room. I did not know they were going to arrest him.'

Pearman left his cigarette to smoulder in the ashtray, completely oblivious to the acrid smell. 'What did you do when they bundled him into the van?' he asked.

'Nothing. The militiamen said he had murdered Mr de Vries. Later, I realised it couldn't be true, so I ran away.' Denista raised a hand to her mouth and chewed on the thumbnail. 'I have a cousin who lives in Varna on the Black Sea coast,' she said between nibbles. 'I stayed with her. Yesterday, while I was out of the house, two men came looking for me.'

'And that's why you are here now?'

'Yes, I caught the mail train to Sofia.'

His mind busy on other matters, Pearman paid little heed to her account of the trials and tribulations she had encountered along the way. Certain discreet enquiries would have to be made before the Ambassador could decide whether or not Denista should be granted asylum. A very detailed record of her interrogation would also have to be dispatched to the SIS as soon as possible, but he couldn't risk transmitting that over the embassy's wireless link. Nor was he keen to send it in writing via the diplomatic bag. It looked like a case of Hobson's choice until he suddenly remembered that Flight Sergeant Morley, RAF, staff clerk to the Defence Attaché, was due to return home on mid-tour leave on the eighteenth of June, a date which could easily be brought forward. As the Defence Attaché had once remarked in his hearing, 'Successful administration was often the wise manipulation of coincidence.'

There was, Pearman thought, a great deal of truth in that adage.

Chapter 11

Every government ministry in Whitehall had its own security organisation. The department which looked after the Foreign and Commonwealth Office and was responsible for the positive vetting of members of Her Majesty's Diplomatic Service was situated in a quiet backwater off Storey's Gate, a bare ten-minute walk from Downing Street. Located in what resembled a four-storey Edwardian house fronted by an impressive wrought-iron gate and railings, the property deserved a better name than number 4 Central Buildings.

It was not the first time Flight Sergeant Morley had visited the establishment. After the long language course at Beaconsfield, he had been required to attend a special briefing by the FCO Security Department prior to taking up the appointment of staff clerk to the Defence, Naval, Military and Air Attaché, Sofia.

Ashton had been a frequent visitor back in the days when he had been on the Russian Desk and had played a leading role in the debriefing of officers in the Diplomatic Service, Defence Attachés and support staff on their return from Moscow. Since then, he hadn't been near the place and didn't expect to do so now that he had been posted to Military Operations (Special Projects) at the Ministry of Defence. A phone call from Hazelwood on what was only the second day in his new appointment had made nonsense of that assumption and sent him scurrying over to number 4 Central Buildings.

The fact that Flight Sergeant Morley was waiting for him in the interview room on the second floor when he arrived suggested to

117

Ashton that someone else had originally been slated to meet the RAF NCO. Fortunately, one of the clerks had thought to give Morley a cup of coffee.

'I'm Peter Ashton,' he said, shaking hands with him. 'Sorry I'm late but things are rather hectic this morning and we are a bit short-handed.'

'That's okay, sir.'

'Peter,' Ashton told him with an easy smile.

'Oh, right.' Morley cleared his throat. 'I'm Ted.' He cleared his throat a second time. 'Would you be the same Mr Ashton who had a run-in with the Durzhavna Sigurnost?'

'That's me. I hear Denista has asked for political asylum?'

'Yes, she walked into the embassy bold as brass.'

'And you were present when Mr Pearman questioned her?'

'Well, not at the first session, but I did sit in on the subsequent interrogation.'

'So tell me about it. What's Denista's version?'

'From the beginning?'

'That's as good a place as any to start.'

Morley nodded, took a deep breath as though preparing himself for some kind of physical ordeal, then began by recounting what Denista claimed had happened before she went to the Sheraton Hotel. He told her story lucidly, was rarely lost for a word, and never once had to backtrack to cover a point of detail he had omitted.

'Did you believe her?' Ashton asked when he had finished.

'Yes. She was scared all right, kept biting her fingernails.'

'Denista was cool enough the morning we met in the hotel lobby.'

'So I understand from Mike,' Morley said and shifted in his chair.

With his ginger hair, and face and neck a mass of freckles, it was difficult to tell whether he had coloured up, but Ashton got the impression that the flight sergeant wasn't entirely at ease with the camaraderie senior diplomats like to foster with members of the support staff during office hours. It was unusual for the bonhomie and first name terms to extend beyond the embassy. Although Pearman was hardly conventional, it was doubtful if even he had socialised with the Morleys during their leisure time.

'He said we had to remember that Denista had been brainwashed into believing you were a drug trafficker.'

'What's your opinion, Ted?'

'I think Denista knows what's what. She's a bit old-fashioned compared to girls of her age in this country and has a highly developed sense of right and wrong. All her formative years were spent under a Communist régime and she was brought up to respect authority. I doubt if she would question what a police officer told her.'

Recalling his own impressions of the young Bulgarian, Ashton thought Morley had got her character about right. She was young, naïve and altogether far too trusting. Her eyes had been opened when the DS security men had snatched him off the street outside St Nedelya church and from that moment on, she had feared for her own safety.

'When did she take off for her cousin's place in Varna?' he asked.

'The day after you were lifted. She claims that one of the militiamen who bundled you into the van told her de Vries had been murdered before it was reported in the newspapers. After work that day, Denista went to see her grandmother whose house is only a stone's throw from where de Vries lived because she thought the old lady would be upset after hearing that he had been killed. Apparently, the militia had only just found the bodies when she arrived at her grandmother's place.'

And that had scared the hell out of Denista because she couldn't understand how the DS men could possibly have known that de Vries was dead before the militia did. When she saw the manager of the travel bureau the following morning and tackled him about it, he had said he didn't know what she was talking about. He had also flatly denied introducing her to a police officer and subsequently leaving them alone together in his office. In a complete daze, she had taken an English couple on a guided tour of the city which had finished at lunchtime and after delivering them back to their hotel, she had returned home, packed a bag and fled to Varna.

'And a week later the police came looking for her?'

Morley nodded. 'That's her story.'

'She makes it sound as though the bad old days are back again.'

'Well, I wouldn't know what they were like because I was only posted to Sofia nine months ago. But old hands tell me life now is comparatively good for the Bulgarians. There's freedom of speech, the militia don't throw their weight about like they used to, and the Security Service is practically invisible these days.'

'But you wouldn't be able to convince Denista it was all sweetness and light?' Ashton suggested.

'You're right there.'

'What about her parents, do they think she is in danger?'

'Denista hasn't been near them since she ran off to Varna; she came straight to the embassy from the Central Station.'

And seemingly, no one from the embassy had been to see her parents either which was pretty bad because someone should have let them know how their daughter was and where she was. Ashton made a mental note to have a word with Hazelwood on the subject. He didn't see why Pearman or the consular affairs officer shouldn't do it; ten to one the embassy had already been compromised thanks to Denista and they could scarcely make things worse. If the Security Service or the Militia were hellbent on finding her, they might well conclude she had sought asylum in one of the Western embassies in Sofia. And since locally employed personnel outnumbered the diplomatic staff in every case, it wouldn't take the DS long to learn where she was hiding out.

'What's going to happen to Denista?' Morley asked. 'Will the Foreign Office get her out of Bulgaria? And if so, will she be allowed to enter this country and remain here?'

Three questions and all of them impossible to answer. 'I don't know,' Ashton told him. 'It's not up to me, the decision will be taken at ministerial level and of course the Home Office will also have to be consulted.'

'I see.' Morley cleared his throat noisily. 'Mike Pearman was wondering what your attitude might be?' he said, looking deeply embarrassed.

'I'm not a friend of Denista's, but you can tell him I won't do anything to block her application.'

'He'll be pleased to hear it.'

'When is that likely to be?'

'Not before I return from mid-tour leave.'

'How long have you got?'

Ashton felt obliged to ask even though he already knew it was four weeks from the day of arrival in the UK. What did surprise him was the fact that the flight sergeant had had an extra three days tagged on so that he shouldn't lose out when he came up from Plymouth for the interview at number 4 Central Buildings. It was also evident that Morley had known the date and time the Foreign Office wanted to see him some forty-eight hours before Hazelwood had phoned the Ministry of Defence, a further indication to Ashton that he had been a last-minute substitute.

'Is there anything else I can tell you?' Morley enquired.

'I don't think so, Ted. You've been very helpful.'

'My pleasure.'

'Where are you off to now?'

'Back to Plymouth soon as I can get a train.'

'Well, enjoy the rest of your leave.'

'I intend to,' the flight sergeant told him.

Ashton signed off the visitor's pass, returned it to Morley, then walked him downstairs where they shook hands and went their separate ways. Returning to the interview room, Ashton tried ringing Hazelwood, only to be informed by his PA that the Deputy DG was in conference and couldn't be disturbed. Five minutes after the flight sergeant had departed, he left the Foreign Office Security Department and walked back to his office in the Ministry of Defence via Storey's Gate and Horse Guards.

He believed Pearman should visit Denista's parents as soon as possible and rehearsed in his mind the arguments he would put to Hazelwood. It was important to gauge the extent to which the Bulgarian Security Service had been involved in the de Vries affair. The demeanour of the parents would be a useful indicator; if they seemed ill at ease and reluctant to say anything about their daughter, there was a strong possibility they had been visited and threatened by the Durzhavna Sigurnost. Should that be the case, then the Russian who had interrogated him at the house near the Rila Monastery had been able to count on more than just token support from the Bulgarian Security Service.

Ashton turned on to Horse Guards Parade, went through the archway and continued on past the mounted sentries from the Blues and Royals into Whitehall. Side-stepping the camera-clicking Japanese tourists on the pavement, he waited for a break in the traffic, then crossed the road to enter the main building of the Ministry of Defence by the side door in Whitehall Place.

He called Hazelwood again from his office and this time managed to catch him during a free moment. It was not a wholly productive conversation; although conceding there was some merit in Pearman seeing Denista's parents, Hazelwood didn't see it as a matter of some urgency.

'We need to catch them while they are still jittery,' Ashton told him. 'The longer we leave it, the calmer they will become and we'll never know whether the DS gave them a rousting.'

The argument fell on deaf ears. As far as Hazelwood was concerned, if the Bulgarian Security Service had really gone to town on behalf of the Russians, Ashton would never have escaped from Sofia.

'Think about it and you'll know I'm right,' he said and put the phone down.

The rest of the morning was fairly quiet. Director Military Operations was required to have a contingency plan for every potential trouble spot the world over and there were enough of them on the shelf to keep Ashton in reading material for several weeks on end. Harriet Egan rang just as he was thinking of getting a bite to eat from one of the pubs in the neighbourhood.

'I've not caught you at a bad moment, have I?' she asked.

'Absolutely not,' he assured her.

'Good. I've managed to find one of the gunners who was awake when Nicholson ran over his troop sergeant. His name is George Bennett and he lives in Queensbury.'

'And you will be home late this evening because you're going to see him?'

'Wrong, we are both going to be late home,' Harriet corrected him. 'I want you to come with me and do most of the talking.'

'Why?'

'Because he is not going to admit to me, a mere woman, that he was scared stiff of Nicholson.'

'I think you are selling yourself short . . .'

'Charing Cross station, Jubilee Line, six o'clock.' Harriet paused, then said, 'Be there, Peter, I'm counting on you.'

★ ★ ★

His name was Leonid Nikolaevich Zelenov. He was an old Red Army man, gone sixty-eight and a former major general of paratroops. He had been old enough to see action at Riga, Vilnius and Königsberg in World War Two and had been one of the few senior officers to come out of Afghanistan with his reputation enhanced. He had retired in 1986 and had elected to live in Tallinn, exercising a privilege enjoyed by every ranking general in the Soviet Armed Forces. He had got to know Estonia in 1950 when engaged on counter insurgency operations against the Forest Brethren, the survivors of the forty thousand Estonians who had fought alongside the *Wehrmacht* in a vain attempt to hold back the Red Army in 1944.

He therefore had had no reason to like the Estonians but even in the immediate postwar years, the Baltic States had enjoyed a better standard of living than the remaining Soviet republics. That was even more true when Leonid Nikolaevich had left the army seven years ago and was the reason why he had chosen to settle in Tallinn.

Before the break-up of the USSR, the Estonian government had been required to provide him with rent-free accommodation appropriate to his rank and service. Before Gorbachev, his life savings had been worth something; now, thanks to that balding arsehole, the money he had on deposit with the State Bank wouldn't buy a week's groceries for his wife, Vera Vorontsova, and himself and inflation had eroded his pension to the point where it had become a sick joke. And what the hell had that drunken Siberian Fascist Yeltsin done to improve matters? A great big fuck-all. Those shitheads in Moscow had made paupers of them and that was something he could never forget or forgive.

There had been other gross betrayals, like the time he and other retired senior officers from the army, navy, air force and KGB had seized the parliament building of Toompea Castle when the Estonians had declared independence. Damn nearly forty per cent of the population was either Russian, Belorussian or Ukrainian and the Estonians were planning to make second-class citizens of them with no voting rights for at least three years. He had figured Moscow would send in the *Spetsnaz* or the Black Berets to support them, but those shithead politicians had looked the other way and they had found themselves isolated in the parliament building, surrounded by a hostile crowd of Estonians. The inevitable had happened and they'd been forced to surrender and walk out of Toompea Castle one at a time through a narrow lane in the crowd who'd jeered and spat at them.

After that débâcle, he had definitely become a second-class citizen in an alien country, which had been pretty hard to swallow for a former major general who was a Hero of the Soviet Union and had also been awarded the Order of Lenin. Fortunately, life had taken a turn for the better since April when his pension had been supplemented by the local mafia who paid him a retainer of ten American dollars a month to place his flat at their disposal whenever they needed it for some nefarious deal. He never knew from one day to the next when he and Vera Vorontsova would have to vacate their apartment for several hours. So, at ten thirty every morning he went to a certain shelter in Tammsaare Park and spent an hour there reading a newspaper.

The man who came and sat next to him on the bench a few minutes after he had arrived was simply known as Boris. He was a tall, slender young man with blond curly hair and a boyish smile. He was, however, a bastard in anyone's language.

'Two tickets for the Youth Dance Festival at the Kalevi Central Stadium,' he said and pressed them on Zelenov with a five-dollar bill. 'Fifteen thousand school kids in national costume; should be quite a sight. Be there at 7 p.m. and give your old trout a treat.'

It was not the most gracious invitation Leonid Nikolaevich Zelenov had ever received but the hard currency did a lot to assuage his anger.

Although born in the same year, George Bennett was in fact a fortnight older than Nicholson. Demobbed from the army on the twenty-sixth of January 1953, he had started work on the London Underground a week later, simultaneously becoming a fully paid up member of the Transport and Salaried Staffs Association. He had retired at sixty after nearly forty years on the railway, during which time he had risen to be chief booking clerk at Neasden, three stops up the Jubilee Line from where he lived.

The semi-detached in Collingwood Avenue where he had spent his entire life, except when he'd been called up for National Service, had been inherited from his parents. An only child, Bennett had married late in life and despite his commanding height and well-built physique, Ashton immediately formed the opinion that he was still a bit of a mother's boy and soft with it. His wife, Eileen, a stolid woman in her late forties, confirmed his supposition by the way she treated her husband. For all that she appeared to hang on his every word, there was no doubting who wore the pants in the family. She would start him off on one topic of conversation, then subtly change the whole thrust and direction when she felt he was becoming too loquacious.

'George is a very keen gardener,' she told Harriet, only to cut the ground from under his feet when he began to explain why his dahlias always took first prize at the local horticultural show. 'Likes everything to be neat and tidy,' she confided to Ashton. 'Even does the Council's job for them.' She turned to her husband. 'Couldn't stand the sight of that unruly verge any longer, could you, dear?'

'It was getting to look like a ruddy hayfield,' Bennett agreed dutifully.

Ashton now knew why the patch of grass between the pavement and the kerb outside number 108 was not only shorter than the rest of Collingwood Avenue but was also entirely weed free. He also knew that if they waited all night for Eileen Bennett to make a move, she would never leave them alone in the sitting room with her husband.

'We'd like to ask you a few questions about a man called Martin Nicholson,' Ashton said, taking the plunge. 'I can't tell you why we are interested in him but I can assure you that whatever you tell us won't go beyond these four walls. Okay?'

'You mean you are not even going to pass it on to your own superiors?' Eileen said before her husband had a chance to open his mouth.

'No, I mean he wouldn't have to give evidence in court or anything like that.'

Bennett exchanged glances with his wife and got a faint nod of approval. 'Sounds fair enough to me,' he said.

'Good. Well, suppose we start at the beginning and you tell me how well you knew Martin Nicholson. Am I right in thinking you were close friends?'

'No way.'

'But you were in the same gun crew?'

'Yeah.' Bennett shifted uncomfortably in his armchair. 'We got on all right, but we weren't mates, if you know what I mean.'

'What about Sergeant Ormskirk? How did you get on with him?'

'I was only a gunner; senior NCOs didn't fraternise with the likes of me. Only time I got to see the inside of the sergeants' mess was when they held the annual ball in celebration of Waterloo and they needed extra waiters.'

'That's not what I asked you,' Ashton said quietly. 'I want to know how you rated him. Was he good at his job or did you have to carry him?'

'Ormskirk was a real toper, used to put away eight or nine pints on a pay day.' Bennett avoided their gaze and looked down at the carpet as though fascinated by the floral design. 'I shouldn't have said that,' he mumbled, 'the bloke's not here to defend himself.'

'You don't owe him anything, George,' Eileen told him firmly. 'You forgotten all the money he borrowed from you and never repaid?'

'I wasn't the only one,' Bennett said defensively. 'He tapped all the blokes one time or another.'

'Including Nicholson?' Harriet asked.

'Him too, but only the once. Nick – that was his nickname by the way – Nick was smart. Next time Ormskirk asked him for a loan, he looked the sergeant in the eye and said he was hoping he could touch him for a few BAFS.' Bennett smiled. 'Know what they are?'

Ashton shook his head. 'Haven't the faintest.'

'British Armed Forces Script – Monopoly money specially printed for Rhine Army and RAF Germany. Anyway, Nick as good as told him to get stuffed.'

'Don't tell me Ormskirk allowed him to get away with that?'

'Well, all I can say is he never put him on extra duties like he did the other blokes who asked for their money back.'

Bennett was becoming more and more confident by the minute and no longer looked to his wife for guidance. He obviously felt himself on safe ground with Ormskirk, and Ashton was content to let him ramble on.

'Eighteen years' service and still only a sergeant when he copped it. No Long Service and Good Conduct Medal either which should tell you something.'

Ashton nodded. He could always ask the record office at Hayes for his personal documents but he was prepared to bet here and now that Ormskirk had been up and down the ranks like a yo-yo. Then Bennett told him that for a small consideration Ormskirk would take a man off guard duty and he knew damned well that the sergeant had had a crime sheet as long as his arm.

'Got the '39–'45 African and Italy Stars. 'Course I didn't believe half the war stories Ormskirk used to spin us. The lads all reckoned he'd spent most of the time back in "B" echelon and had rarely been up at the sharp end. Still, he wasn't the only one on the fiddle. The German economic miracle was hardly underway in the early fifties and there was nothing the Krauts wouldn't give for a jar of coffee or a carton of cigarettes. Everybody was into the black market.'

'Not everybody,' Eileen reminded him tartly. 'You weren't for a start.'

'No, I didn't approve of it,' Bennett said hastily.

'What about Nick?' Harriet asked.

'Oh, he was into a few rackets, had a couple of regimental bikes working for him.'

'What?'

'Tarts, miss; they were known as regimental bikes because everybody rode them.'

'Don't be so disgusting,' Eileen told him in a sharp voice that was guaranteed to bring one particular man to heel.

Ashton ignored her. No thin-lipped, small-minded shrew was going to stop him asking Bennett a few pertinent questions.

'Nicholson was chancing his arm, wasn't he? How come he got away with it?'

'He had a set of keys to the accommodation stores and greased a few palms whenever he smuggled the girls into the barracks.'

Before turning the stores into a brothel, Nicholson would have had to square the guard commander, the orderly sergeant, the storeman and possibly the battery quartermaster sergeant. Furthermore, Nicholson would have had to know the persons involved rather well before he attempted to bribe them, otherwise he would find himself in deep shit.

'And the girls only performed when your lot were the duty battery and found all the guards and fatigues. Right?'

'Yes.'

'I thought as much,' Ashton said. 'Didn't anyone ever try to muscle in on his racket?'

And that too was almost an unnecessary question because Ashton had a pretty shrewd idea of the likely answer even before Bennett told him that Nicholson had had thirty bouts under his belt as an amateur and had been the losing bantamweight finalist of the BAOR championships. Bennett also recounted the time when three privates in the Highland Light Infantry had picked a fight with him in some *Gasthof* and how he had pulverised them.

'Used a broken bottle on one, cut him up something dreadful . . .'

Eileen clucked her tongue. 'I'm sure Mr Ashton doesn't want to hear all the gory details, George.'

'Oh, but I do,' Ashton assured her.

'Really? Well, I am surprised.' A loud sniff underlined what she thought of him.

'Did you ever cross swords with him, George?' Ashton enquired when Bennett least expected it.

'Me?' A furred tongue appeared between his nicotine-stained teeth and nervously explored the bottom lip. 'Good Lord, no.'

'And you were wide awake when Sergeant Ormskirk was run over and killed?'

'Yes.' His eyes darted from Ashton to Harriet and then to Eileen. 'I said so at the Court of Inquiry, didn't I?'

'And you are satisfied it was an accident?'

'Yes. Like I told the President of the Court, it was a foggy night and Ormskirk loomed up out of the mist.'

'Did Nicholson lean on you in any way?'

'What is this?'

'Did he perhaps suggest what he wanted you to say at the Court of Inquiry?'

Bennett stared at him, mouth open. 'I wasn't the only one who gave evidence. What's Ron Perry been telling you?' he asked in a voice full of bluster.

Ashton didn't answer, gazed instead at the garden outside the French window and admired the lupins, roses and the prize-winning dahlias, leaving Bennett to sweat it out.

'Are you accusing my husband of lying?' Eileen demanded. 'Because if you are, you'd better come right out and say so.' An even more disturbing thought suddenly occurred to her. 'Are you saying George was an accessory to murder?'

'Mr Ashton's saying nothing of the kind,' Harriet told her soothingly.

'Sounds suspiciously like it to me. I don't know what makes you people think you've got the right to come into our home and browbeat George and me, but we've had enough of it.'

Eileen Bennett was going to report them to their MP, and the editor of the *Sun* was also going to hear about it, and how did they like that? Furthermore, didn't they know when they had outstayed their welcome? Ashton thanked them both for being so helpful and apologised for taking up so much of their time but it didn't make a jot of difference. The door still slammed behind them with a resounding crash before they reached the front gate.

'So what do you think?' Harriet asked as they walked towards Queensbury station.

'Bennett lied to the Court of Inquiry and the Special Investigation Branch of the Military Police. He may look as if he could stand up to Nicholson but essentially he is a windy barrel of lard. It's unfortunate the Inquiry was held before the SIB investigation because Bennett was too frightened to change his story by the time the police questioned him. Same goes for Gunner Ron Perry.'

Time spent in a military corrective establishment didn't count as National Service and Nicholson only had to convince both men that they would get at least six months' detention for Bennett and Perry to toe the line. Neither man would have wanted to be in the army a day longer than he had to.

'What about a motive, Peter?'

'For killing Ormskirk? Maybe he was taking hush money and threatened to pull the plug on Nicholson if he didn't give him a bigger cut? What does it matter anyway? I mean, you and I are trying to make sense of a lot of ancient history that some sleazeball of a Russian is passing to our superiors, and no one will tell us what the hell is going on. Is there a crock of gold at the end of the rainbow, or what?'

'Maybe we don't need to know,' Harriet said quietly.

'I killed two Bulgarians, I think I'm entitled—'

'Promise me something,' Harriet said, hugging his arm.

'Like what?'

'That you'll stop kicking over the traces. Let's just do the job we are paid to do and get on with the rest of our lives. Okay?'

'I think that's a damned good idea.'

Harriet hoped it wasn't wishful thinking on her part but she thought Ashton sounded as if he meant it.

The communicator was a twenty-eight-year-old Starshii Serzhant from the Signal Corps on secondment to the Russian Intelligence Service as the First Chief Directorate of the KGB was now called. The message he was required to send had been prerecorded in code and would be transmitted in a half-minute burst once contact had been established on the fixed frequency.

It was not the first time he had been to the flat on Vana Viru and he knew the key would be on top of the door frame. Reaching for it, he unlocked the door and let himself into the tiny hallway.

The transmitter was built into an executive briefcase and had an operating range in excess of one thousand five hundred kilometres. With four fixed frequencies to choose from, the Starshii Serzhant had been instructed to use Channel Delta. Plugging the unit into the nearest power point in the living room, he switched on the set and began tapping out his call sign with the morse key at forty-second intervals from 20.00 hours local time.

The receiving station answered up at the first natural break. One minute later, having squirted the prerecorded message, he left the apartment, locked the door behind him and placed the key on top of the frame where he had found it.

The message was from Valentin; it stated where and when he wanted to meet Mercury, the codename for Ashton.

Chapter 12

The mail that morning had included a specimen wedding invitation. It read: *Mr and Mrs Frederick Egan request the pleasure of the company of . . . . . . at the marriage of their daughter, Harriet, to Mr Peter Ashton at All Saints Church, Lincoln, on Saturday, 18 December 1993 at 3 p.m. and afterwards at the White Hart Hotel, Bellgate.*

The postman had popped it through the letterbox together with a wad of circulars just as Harriet and Peter had been about to leave the flat in Churchill Gardens for their respective offices. Harriet had recognised the handwriting on the envelope and hadn't bothered to open it before catching a District Line train from Victoria. Even then, she had only given the invitation a casual glance, noting the gilt copperplate script and thinking it was typical of her mother that, despite having lost the argument, she should still be determined to take charge of all the arrangements.

No late-summer wedding, no marquee on the lawn, and a much reduced guest list; it seemed too good to be true because Margaret Egan didn't know the meaning of defeat. Still not quite able to believe it, Harriet took a much longer and harder look at the invitation when she arrived at Benbow House. She turned the card over, read the brief pencilled note on the back and bit her lip. No last-minute appeal for an August wedding before younger brother Richard, was posted to RAF Gütersloh, merely a cheerful request that she okay the proof and return same in due course. Reading the note again, Harriet wondered why she should feel guilty; it was after all the bride's prerogative to choose the date.

'Morning, Harriet.'

The familiar voice grated on her and she hoped the smile on her mouth didn't resemble a grimace. 'Morning, Roy,' she said, looking up at Kelso.

'How did you and Ashton get on with Mr Bennett?' he asked and pulled up a chair. 'Or to be more accurate, what exactly did he have to say for himself?'

This was her third day as Head of the Security Vetting and Technical Services Division. On day one, Kelso had made a point of looking in on her to make sure she was happy with her new office. Yesterday, he had spent an hour over two cups of coffee explaining why he couldn't take her off the duty officers' roster even though she now enjoyed the same status as the Head of Finance who was exempt. This morning, Harriet was determined to get rid of him before he became too comfortably ensconced even though Kelso had a genuine reason for visiting her. In as few sentences as possible, she gave him the salient points and the conclusions they'd drawn after talking to the ex-gunner and his wife, Eileen.

'Soldiers always take snapshots of their tank, or squad or gun crew. Did you happen to ask Bennett if he had one with Nicholson in it?'

Harriet shook her head. 'I did think about it, but George Bennett was demobbed in January '53 and we already have the passport photograph taken at least seven years later than anything he could have given us.'

'Granted, but he might have produced a much clearer picture.'

Harriet reluctantly agreed that this was indeed a possibility, then mentally scolded herself for being so churlish. Kelso might be a pain in the neck but that didn't mean he was a complete clown.

'Perhaps if you went back again this evening . . .?'

'I don't think that would do any good, Roy. We were hardly the flavour of the month when they showed us the door. Even if Bennett had one, Eileen wouldn't let him part with it.'

'What about Nicholson's parents?'

'Mother died when he was eight, father married a much younger woman a year later who refused to have anything to do with her stepson, so he ended up in care. The couple then split up in 1951 because Nicholson senior had started drinking heavily. A bad case of hepatitis coupled with cirrhosis of the liver finished him off less than twelve months later. His son had deserted before the army had a chance to ask him to nominate an alternative next of kin.'

'What a pity.' Kelso pulled a face as if to convey his extreme disappointment. 'This whole business is grinding to a halt for want of a recognisable photograph.'

Although Harriet's contention that ex-Gunner Nicholson was the assassin whose professional services the KGB and the Stasi had used on seventeen occasions between 1955 and 1978 was not in dispute, the Foreign Office appeared to be having second thoughts. At one stage they had been in favour of passing the information to Bonn when, in their opinion, the time was ripe. But now, from what Kelso was saying, they were holding back for want of a decent photograph that was going to be at least thirty-odd years out of date, even supposing she was lucky enough to find one.

'What about this Gunner Perry who also gave evidence at the Court of Inquiry? Have you traced him yet, Harriet?'

'No, and I don't think I'm likely to either.'

Every year thousands of people went missing. A lot of them disappeared without trace and were never seen or heard of again. Ron Perry was one such statistic.

'I don't think we should throw in the towel just yet,' Kelso told her primly. 'If we really put our minds to it, I'm sure there must be some avenue we haven't explored.'

Instead of 'we' read 'you'. For all his encouraging noises and assumption of joint responsibility, Kelso would stop short of actually doing any of the spadework.

'Perry was dragooned into a shotgun marriage by the parents of the girl he had made pregnant while home on leave from Rhine Army. He walked out on his wife and baby daughter a year after he had been demobbed. No one has seen or heard from him since then.'

'Have you tried—?' Kelso began.

Harriet raised a hand and using her fingers, ticked off the various agencies she had involved in the hunt for Ron Perry. The Ministry of Defence, in case he had re-enlisted, the Departments of Health and Social Security, the Inland Revenue, the Registrar of Births, Marriages and Deaths, the Home Office, the National Identification

Bureau, the Director of Public Prosecutions et cetera, et cetera. 'Now you tell me who else we can ask?' she demanded.

'Family and friends?' Kelso suggested tentatively.

'Both parents are dead, we don't know if either one had any brothers or sisters. As for friends – well, Perry was born and brought up in the Handsworth district of Birmingham and I don't have to tell you how much that neighbourhood has changed over the years.'

'I don't fancy telling the Director we're beaten.'

'You don't have to,' Harriet said.

'I don't see how I can avoid it. We want a good likeness and all we have is a blurred photo taken in 1960 when Nicholson applied for a passport. You've already told me that we have enhanced that as far as it will go.'

'That's right. Now we hand the end result over to a portrait artist.'

'A portrait artist?' Kelso repeated as though his ears had deceived him.

'And we ask him or her to age the face by thirty years. A few tramlines on the forehead, crow's feet around the eyes, scrawny neck, hollow cheeks, that sort of thing.'

'Brilliant. Why didn't we think of this before?'

Harriet didn't have the heart to tell him that she had been toying with the idea for some time and was still unconvinced of its merit. After thirty years, Nicholson could now be bald and have a face like a cadaver; alternatively, he might have a full head of hair and a visage as round as a football with several chins to go with it. There was also the possibility that a plastic surgeon had altered his features beyond recognition after his British passport had expired in 1970.

'Do you have a portrait artist in mind?' Kelso asked.

'I know of one.'

'Is he expensive?'

'I don't know.' Harriet smiled. 'I've never commissioned him.'

'You can go up to two hundred pounds. If he wants more, check with me first.' Kelso stood up and moved his chair back. 'Okay?' he asked with a dazzling smile.

'Yes.'

'Good. Let me know how you get on.'

Harriet said she would do that, waited until Kelso had left her office, then picked up the phone and rang Ashton to let him know about the wedding invitation, only to be informed that he was out. No one in Military Operations (Special Projects) had the faintest idea where he had gone or when he would be back.

Ashton was beginning to wonder why he had been posted to the Ministry of Defence, and so was Lieutenant Colonel Yeomans, the grade one staff officer and joint leader of the Military Operations (Special Projects) branch. Yesterday morning, Hazelwood had dispatched Ashton to 4 Central Buildings; this morning, his presence had been required at Vauxhall Cross. In both instances he had received no prior warning from the Deputy DG.

Rowan Garfield was present when Ashton walked into the Deputy DG's office overlooking the river. Hazelwood had removed his jacket and was displaying pillar-box red braces over a blue and white striped shirt that was rapidly losing its freshness. For once, flaming June was a reality instead of a myth and his office was nicely placed to catch the sun from first thing in the morning to last thing at night. Although it was only 9.30, the atmosphere was already like a hothouse. Only Garfield seemed to be unaffected by the heat.

'Better run your eyes over this, Peter,' Hazelwood said and gave him a flimsy to read. 'Then you'll understand why I've sent for you.'

There was no need for either the date/time group or originator's reference; the content and nature of the signal made such niceties superfluous. The text merited the Top Secret security classification it had been accorded.

'This has got to be a joke,' Ashton said. 'After what happened in Sofia, Valentin wants to set up another meet, this time in Tallinn? The man must be hellbent on committing suicide.'

'I don't think so,' Garfield said, intervening decisively. 'He would probably feel relatively safe in Tallinn.'

The Head of the European Department listed a number of reasons to support his contention. First Lenin and then Stalin had given the Estonians good cause to hate their Russian neighbours. Eager to get out of the First World War, Lenin had ceded the Baltic States to Germany under the Treaty of Brest-Litovsk in March 1918 and had then tried to grab them back again eight months later. Garfield seemed to forget that Ashton had spent four years on the

Russian Desk before his banishment to Benbow House and knew that when Soviet troops had moved into the country following the non-aggression pact with Nazi Germany, thousands of prominent Estonians and their families had been deported to Siberia. Ashton was also aware that there had been a repeat performance when the Red Army had liberated the country in 1944.

'The Russians literally colonised Estonia – moved in settlers by the hundreds of thousands and altered the school curriculum, restricting the native language to just two periods a week.'

'You're not telling me anything I don't already know,' Ashton said quietly. 'It's only two years since I had access to all this background stuff.'

'The policemen are very young,' Garfield continued, unabashed. 'Before independence, no Estonian could be a ranking officer in the militia. Now that they've kicked out all the Russians, promotion prospects have never been so good and they have had to recruit eighteen-year-olds straight from school to fill the establishment. Same goes for Customs and Immigration. They are so inexperienced, half of them don't know what they're doing.'

'You've been there, have you?'

'No need to, we've got an embassy in Tallinn these days.'

With an ambassador based in Helsinki, Ashton added silently. Benbow House might be far removed from Whitehall but the Foreign and Commonwealth staff list occasionally found its way there and passed across his desk. But that was beside the point.

'Maybe the Estonians wouldn't lift a finger to help the Russians and perhaps the police force was so inefficient it couldn't even catch a cold, but my face is too well known and there are too many Russians living in Tallinn.'

'I can understand your concern,' Garfield assured him, 'but we wouldn't dream of sending you in harm's way.'

'Well, that's nice to hear but I'm not about to volunteer.' Ashton pursed his lips. 'I don't know how this Valentin has survived as long as he has because his personal security is non-existent. I mean, let's face it, Russian Intelligence knew I was going to meet him in Sofia before I was even briefed for the job.'

'I think Henry de Vries had a lot to do with that,' Hazelwood said. 'When we informed him he was to be the link man between you and Valentin, he checked with Moscow and let the cat out of the bag.'

Ashton thought Victor was right. After reading the wartime SOE files and talking to Lister, he had come to the conclusion that de Vries had been a double agent ever since the SIS had recruited him. Always the loyal Communist, it was ironic that he should have inadvertently signed his own death warrant by communicating with the wrong people in Moscow.

'They tortured him because they believed he knew where Valentin was staying in Sofia.'

'You are referring to Henry de Vries?' Hazelwood said.

'Yes. Why else would they have whipped the soles of his bare feet?'

And Valentin had cancelled his trip to Sofia at the last minute because he had somehow learned that de Vries had blown the whistle on him. There was a time when Ashton had thought the 'Insider' was an archivist in the Historical Department of the Russian Intelligence Service. Certainly, the out-of-date information he had passed to the SIS thus far had supported this supposition, but now there were grounds for believing otherwise. The control officer who had handled de Vries would have discussed the query he'd received from his agent in Sofia with a very senior officer. Nothing would have been circulated in writing and only those at the very heart of the organisation would have been briefed. If, as seemed likely, Valentin was a member of the inner circle, then he had to be one of the eight deputies who ran the Intelligence Service, which would make him at least a major general.

'Tell me something,' said Ashton. 'What has Valentin given us so far, apart from the unnamed deserter and an explanation for the massive outbreak of foot-and-mouth in 1967?'

'Nothing.' Hazelwood opened the carved box on his desk, took out a cheroot and lit it, enjoying the long-suffering expression on Garfield's face as much as he did the aroma of the cigar. 'And we haven't paid him anything on account either. He gave us a couple of freebies to prove he had access.'

'So what do you hope to get from him in Tallinn?'

'High-grade, bang up-to-date information.'

Valentin was expected to disclose the objectives of the Russian

Intelligence Service in order of priority and the resources allocated to each one. There were high hopes that he would also provide the SIS with the names of illegals operating in the UK, the Commonwealth and the United States. The latter, it was felt, would go some way to re-establishing the special relationship with Washington that had been soured by the Conservative Government's efforts to help Bush get re-elected. Finally, the 'Insider' had indicated he was in a position to assess the effectiveness of the Russian Sigint Intercept Service.

'I don't have to tell you how valuable that would be,' Hazelwood said. 'Apart from telling us just how secure our own communications are, the Sigint material will enable us to gauge the value of the other information we receive from him.'

'Not necessarily. Just because the intercepts are genuine, it doesn't follow that everything else we get from Valentin will be kosher.'

'I only said it would assist us to assess the value of his information,' Hazelwood observed in a mildly reproving tone. 'I didn't claim it would be as good as a seal of approval. In our line of business, a certain amount of scepticism is essential. One should never accept anything on trust.'

'Like the security of this latest communication from him?' Ashton suggested.

'Oh, that's absolutely watertight,' Garfield assured him eagerly.

'Convince me.'

'We provided him with the communications equipment as well as the requisite keying material.'

The Sigint people at Cheltenham hadn't liked the idea but their objections had been brushed aside by the Joint Intelligence Committee who met once a week under the chairmanship of the Cabinet Secretary. As a result of this decision, Valentin was able to prerecord a message using a crypto-protected transmitter before the tape was squirted through in a twenty-second burst.

'I'd say the chances of a hostile station intercepting such a high-speed communication are about zero.' The smoke-laden atmosphere began to have an effect on Garfield; cupping a hand over his mouth, he coughed delicately and cleared his throat before continuing. 'But even if the Russian Sigint Service did happen to pick up the message, they wouldn't be able to read the playback unless they possessed one of our fill guns charged with the correct electronic keying material.'

Ashton had checked the fill guns on charge to Benbow House often enough to know just what a complicated gadget it was. Resembling the type of laser weapon favoured in science fiction epics, it was loaded with electronic ciphers from the master grid and then used to transfer those key variables to an infinite number of compatible radio sets. It occurred to him that if by chance the Russian Intelligence Service had swept Valentin into the bag, they would have the fill gun which the SIS had provided for his use.

'I don't like the way Valentin is calling the tune either,' Hazelwood said, as if reading Ashton's thoughts. 'But we are going to change all that with your help.'

'Are you asking me to go to Tallinn?'

'I want to discover the real identity of Valentin. When we know who he is, we can apply a little pressure and make him supply the kind of information which will enable us to be several moves ahead in the game.'

'You haven't answered my question, Victor.'

'All right, I'd like you to go to Estonia with a view to meeting our Russian friend.' Hazelwood crushed the Burma cheroot in the ashtray. 'Now are you satisfied?'

'Yes.'

'So how do you feel about it?'

He could refuse to go, and that would be the end of it. Nobody would be sent in his place because Valentin had made it clear he would only deal with him. 'I'm not wildly enthusiastic,' Ashton said.

'I think I would have put it a little stronger in your shoes,' Hazelwood told him cheerfully.

'What do you suppose Valentin will do if I don't show up?'

'I don't know. It depends whether or not he has already been turned down by the CIA before he approached us. If that was the case, then he's either got to find another buyer or adopt a more reasonable attitude. We can only wait and see what happens.'

'You're beginning to sound like Mr Micawber,' Ashton said with a smile.

'Well, I don't have much choice.'

'I hope you weren't planning to send me in alone.'

There was no audible sigh of relief from Garfield. On the other hand, he was extremely eager to tell Ashton just how they intended to support him in the field in the not unjustified assumption that somehow Hazelwood had talked him into going.

Werner Immelmann was proud of his surname. Although not related to the World War One fighter ace, he liked to give the impression that Max Immelmann was family. A native of Berlin, he had joined the *Schutzpolizei* after graduating from high school in 1986. Five years later, he had been transferred from the uniformed force to the Kripo on accelerated promotion and was regarded by Kommissar Voigt as one of the brightest detectives in the division. Of the team assigned to the Wolff case, he had been the natural choice to run the crime index of the investigation.

The task involved long and irregular hours; no one was therefore surprised when, towards mid-afternoon, he left the Central Police Station on Tempelhofer Damm to grab a late lunch. However, instead of going to the nearest corner bar, Immelmann made his way to the apartment house on Schiller Strasse where Fräulein Birgit Simon, senior lecturer in computer studies at the nearby University of Technology, resided.

Birgit Simon was thirty-seven, twelve years older than Detective Immelmann. She was tall, slender, wore her straight blonde hair in a bun and liked to dress severely. Her skirts always came well below the knee, she was never seen in anything other than low-heeled shoes and every blouse she possessed buttoned to the neck. Her jackets were either black or dark brown. Her sexuality was the subject of much speculation amongst the student body. The men all thought she was a butch lesbian while the women undergraduates saw her as a sour old maid. As far as the neighbours were concerned, she was a rather introspective person who preferred her own company.

Immelmann was one of the few people who knew her for what she really was. When Birgit let him into her apartment that afternoon, she was wearing a pair of frayed denim shorts, a cotton singlet and open-toed sandals. There was a heavy metal bracelet around her left wrist.

'You look all hot and bothered,' she told him. 'I've got a bottle of hock chilling in the fridge. Care for a glass?'

'That would be nice.' Immelmann followed her into the sitting room and sank down in his favourite armchair. 'Have you got anything to eat?' he asked. 'I'm starving.'

'Some cheese and a piece of sausage. Will that do?'

'Fine.'

'Help yourself to a cigarette. I won't be a minute.'

Immelmann preferred his own brand. Birgit had nothing but Turkish and as he had frequently told her, they tasted like camel dung. He did however make use of her Zippo lighter.

'How's the murder investigation coming along?' Birgit asked from the kitchen.

'There's been an interesting development. A couple of patrolmen have found the wig the killer had been wearing.'

'I don't understand.'

'The patrolmen were investigating a complaint by some sixteen-year-old slut who'd alleged she had been raped by two buck niggers with American accents.'

Birgit returned from the kitchen bearing a tray with two glasses of white wine and a plate of black bread, cheese and cold sausage which she placed on the low coffee table in front of him. 'I presume they were air force personnel from Tempelhof,' she said calmly.

'That's her story.' Immelmann stubbed out the cigarette he'd been smoking. 'Anyway, she led the patrolmen to the waste ground by the disused S-Bahn below Yorckstrasse where the alleged offence was committed.' Immelmann broke off to plonk the cheese and cold sausage between two slices of black bread which he then proceeded to devour. 'They came across the wig in the long grass while looking for evidence to support the girl's complaint,' he added between mouthfuls.

'How do you know it belonged to the killer?' Birgit asked, still ice cool.

'Well, Forensic said the wig had been lying there about a week which was several days before the niggers were supposed to have shafted the girl, and some bright spark decided Kommissar Voigt ought to be informed. Old man Jurgen had given us a very detailed description of the gunman who had terrorised his family and that wig matched to a T the colour of the guy's hair and the way it was styled.' Immelmann wiped his mouth on a handkerchief, then reached for a glass of wine and drank it. 'The Jurgens recognised the wig the moment they saw it. Now we are looking for a man with grey hair.'

'Why?'

'Forensic again. They found a couple of thin strands on the underside of the wig. The killer must have thrown his disguise away as he crossed the footbridge spanning the old railroad tracks. So Voigt has now got the uniforms combing the whole area searching for what else might be there.'

Birgit leaned forward in the chair, legs pressed together, shorts riding even higher than they had before. 'Is this what the police call a major breakthrough?' she asked in a slightly husky voice.

'Absolutely not,' Immelmann assured her. 'Voigt is clutching at straws because he knows the whole investigation is steadily grinding to a halt. Nothing is going to come of this latest development; you see if I'm not right.' He put his empty wine glass down on the coffee table and glanced pointedly at his wristwatch. 'Time I was leaving,' he announced.

'So soon, Werner?'

'Well, if there is any other way I can be of service . . .'

'You know there is,' Birgit said and led him into the bedroom.

As always, she was very businesslike. Removing the singlet, Birgit unzipped her denim shorts and pulled them down, then kicked them aside. Immelmann was the first to admit that she was no great beauty. Her body was all angles rather than gentle curves and the lemon-size breasts tended to droop, but she excited him as no other woman could hope to emulate.

She waited for him on the bed, legs spread wide apart, eyes narrowing in anticipation at the size of his erection. As he entered Birgit, he looked up at the oil painting of Adolf Hitler on the wall above the bed and wondered what the Führer would have made of his latter-day disciples. Then Birgit reached for the riding crop she kept beside the divan and struck him across the rump and he forgot about such philosophical questions in his desire to please her.

Chapter 13

Ashton left the train at Petersfield and walked through the booking hall to the car park where a Rover 800 from the training school was waiting to take him on to Amberley Lodge. Everything was happening fast, perhaps too fast. Hazelwood had never been one for allowing the grass to grow under his feet, but that morning he had really surpassed himself. Before Ashton could have second thoughts about going to Tallinn, the Deputy DG had whisked him next door to have his photograph taken in the PA's office. By the time the photographer had finished, Garfield had been ready to outline the new identity his department had prepared for him.

'You won't have any difficulty mastering the brief,' he said breezily. 'It's based on your work experience as a technical author with British Aerospace before you joined us.'

The brief had been decidedly thin but they were working on that. At this very moment, Kelso was ringing a number of firms who owed the Foreign Office the odd favour in an attempt to get him accredited as one of their sales representatives. If Roy was successful, there would be time to visit whichever firm had agreed to sponsor him before he flew out to Estonia. Right now however he was about to meet the decoy duck who was going to draw any fire which might have been intended for him.

Crawford, John, known as Jack, born Malton, North Yorkshire on the eighth of March 1962. Formerly corporal of horse, Household Cavalry, now acting warrant officer 22 Special Air Service Regiment on secondment to the SIS. The biographical details furnished by Hazelwood had also been decidedly sketchy, but

Ashton could read between the lines and knew a man didn't get to be an acting warrant officer in an élite unit at the age of thirty-one unless he was mustard. And an élite regiment proud of its reputation would never wish a duff number on to the SIS when required to provide a specialist instructor.

All the permanent staff of the training school were known to Ashton. The man who came forward to meet him as the Rover drew up outside Amberley Lodge was a new face and could only be Crawford. Give or take the odd half-inch, he was about the same height, but there the similarity ended. He had fair hair and a rounded face to go with the snub nose and mouth that seemed to be hovering on the brink of a smile.

'I'm Peter,' Ashton told him as they shook hands.

'And I'm Jack. You fancy a spot of lunch?'

'No, thanks, I'm not hungry. I bought a sandwich from a snack bar at Waterloo and ate it on the train. But don't let me stop you.'

'I've already eaten,' Crawford told him.

They strolled round the house, Ashton leading the way past a lawn tennis court turning brown under the sun. 'What have they told you about this jaunt?' he asked.

'Not a lot. I know we're going to Tallinn and I'm to be issued with a passport identifying me as Peter Ashton. You'll be travelling under the name of Walter Quick and Admin is hoping to book us into the same hotel. If they can't manage to fix it, we've got problems because I'm supposed to stand between you and the agent in place who calls himself Valentin. I'm his point of contact. After I've checked out the rendezvous, you keep the appointment and I watch your back while you are head to head with him.'

'Did they tell you what happened in Sofia?'

'They said there was a foul-up and the opposition gave you a hard time.'

'Who told you all this?'

'Some guy from the European Department called Gervase who turned up here shortly before noon. Of course, they rang the Commandant first to warn us he was coming, so the old sales patter didn't come as a complete surprise.'

'And this Gervase talked you into volunteering?' Ashton said in a flat voice.

'I didn't need much persuading.'

Crawford had begun to question what he was doing at Amberley Lodge. Since joining the training school five months ago, he had spent three weeks teaching a mixed bag of counter-terrorist agents how to remain undetected in IRA territory and had run a survival exercise in the Brecon Beacons for desk-bound officers of the SIS. In between time, he had played bodyguard to an Assistant Under-secretary of the Foreign and Commonwealth Office on a brief fact-finding mission to Mogadishu. Now he had virtually nothing to do until the new entrants assembled for their induction course in September.

'I don't think Gervase was entirely frank with you,' Ashton told him. 'Oh, you'll be watching my back all right and the rest of it but the truth is you'll be a decoy. And you could draw fire that was intended for me. How do you feel about that?'

Crawford shrugged. 'I can look after myself.'

The indoor firing range was in the old stable block on the north side of the house. It wasn't until the SAS man produced a key from his jacket pocket and unlocked the door that Ashton realised he had been led there by the nose without knowing it. Crawford flicked on a low-wattage overhead light just inside the entrance and pointed to a control box standing on an old kitchen table behind the firing point.

'Do you recognise that box of tricks?' he asked.

'Yes, it's a video target rear projection system.'

'Then I guess you know how to operate it.'

'This is all a bit childish, isn't it? I mean, you are going to demonstrate what a hot shot you are with a handgun and I am supposed to leave this place feeling quietly confident.'

'I just do what I'm told, Peter. Now, why don't we get on with it? You'll find a pair of ear defenders in the centre drawer of that kitchen table.'

The defenders were nothing more than the headset of a field radio that had been tarted up with earmuffs to fit snugly over the lobes. They were intended to reduce the number of decibels emitted by a firearm discharged in a confined area like an indoor range.

'Ready when you are,' Crawford said, then added, 'choose whatever mode you like.'

The video system could present a target in a green image as if the firer was using a passive night sight. Alternatively, it could fake an infra-red device or simulate varying degrees of visibility ranging from poor to good at any time of the day or night. Ashton selected a variable light input, set the freeze-frame at minimum pause, then ran the tape forward before hitting the "vision on" button.

Dusk: a car moving slowly from left to right up a quiet street. The passenger turning sideways to aim an Uzi sub-machine-gun in the direction of the firing point. Reacting with almost incredible speed, Crawford snatched a revolver from the shoulder holster under his jacket and holding the pistol in a double-handed grip, squeezed off two shots before the freeze-frame automatically stopped the video. The first round had struck the gunman high up in the chest a few inches below the throat, the other had drilled a neat round hole between the eyes.

The tape started running again ten seconds from the moment it had been held by the freeze-frame. No matter what Ashton did with the control unit, he could not throw the SAS warrant officer. Crawford continued to hit each target with infallible accuracy. Forced to reload in the middle of a simulated fire fight, he released the cylinder, pushed it clear of the frame, ejected the spent cases and filled all six chambers by the time Ashton had counted up to five.

'I'm glad you're on my side,' Ashton told him.

'Thanks, but you do have a head start with a precision engineered firearm.' Crawford broke the weapon open. 'This is a .357 Ruger Speed Six revolver,' he said and gave Ashton the handgun to examine while he picked up the empty cases on the firepoint. 'US Army issue specially designed for clandestine security operations. Weighs just under two pounds and has a two-and-three-quarter-inch barrel.'

'Very neat.'

'I think so.' Crawford retrieved the Ruger .357 and slipped it into the shoulder holster.

Ashton followed the younger man out of the range, waited for him to lock the door, then moved on towards the house. It was one thing to fire a kill shot at an image on a flickering screen, quite another to aim the revolver at a human being and squeeze the trigger.

'You ever done it for real?' he asked, pursuing the train of thought.

'Once,' Crawford admitted reluctantly.

'Where was that?'

'Somalia. The Assistant Undersecretary I was looking after wanted to see for himself what was going on in Mogadishu, and we were motoring along this deserted backstreet when these three gunmen appeared from nowhere and held us up. Normally, I wouldn't argue with a Kalashnikov, but these Somalis were getting very uptight because we weren't carrying too many valuables. So, one of the bastards shot our Pakistani driver for the sheer hell of it and the other two grabbed the girl—'

'What girl?'

'Oh, didn't I mention her? She was in the Red Cross, came from Dublin, about twenty-four and very pretty. Anyway, they pulled her out of the Land Rover and you didn't need a Mensa IQ to know what they had in mind. That's when I went for broke. First I took out the guy who was still holding a gun on us when his attention wandered, then I shot the other two who were busy stripping the girl to the waist.' Crawford paused, then said, 'The eldest gunman was about seventeen, the two who had the girl on the ground were fourteen or fifteen. The Foreign Office man thought it was a bad show, reckoned there was no need to kill the two boys when I had the drop on them. I didn't hear any complaints from the pretty Dubliner though; must have been the first time the SAS were good news south of the border.'

'How did you get the revolver through the security checks at Heathrow?'

'Trade secret.'

'Not if you are planning to export it to Estonia. I'm not having the roof fall in on me because of a cock-up on your part. Now, either you come clean or I call the whole thing off.'

'Well, if that's the way it is, I don't have much choice.' Crawford frowned as if not sure how or where to begin. 'There are no direct flights to Tallinn from Heathrow,' he said presently. 'So whether you go by Finnair or British Airways you are routed via Helsinki.

And if you use the Finnish national carrier, you still check in at one of the BA desks. The revolver will be in my suitcase. The girl on the desk will go through the usual rigmarole of asking who packed it, then after the suitcase has been labelled, it goes on down the conveyer belt to the baggage handling area where a colleague will be waiting to make sure it doesn't go through the X-ray machine or any other security check.'

'And that's it?'

'Yeah. The Finns don't examine the baggage of passengers in transit at Helsinki, so you're home and dry.'

The suitcase would obviously have to be marked in some way so that the colleague in the baggage handling area could instantly recognise it, but that was a minor point of detail and Ashton didn't bother to pursue it. That would be like teaching your grandmother to suck eggs and there were more important things to be ironed out between them.

'Let's talk about contact procedures,' he said abruptly and started on another circuit of the grounds.

The Gasthof Adler was only a few minutes' walk from the U-Bahn station on Rohrdamm in the Siemensstadt District of Berlin. In need of a good facelift on the outside, the interior looked equally run down and was impregnated with the smell of flat beer and stale tobacco smoke. The Adler was off the beaten track for tourists and wasn't featured in any of the guidebooks to the city, which was another reason why the passing trade, such as it was, kept on passing it by. Neil Franklin wouldn't have been seen dead in the place but for a phone call from Willie.

His surname was Baumgart but he was Willie to family, friends and even the most casual of acquaintances. He was the sort of man who, once seen, remained firmly imprinted in the mind. Baumgart was five feet nine, weighed a hundred and thirty five pounds and had light brown hair. When a young man, his left eye had been gouged out in a fracas with a drug pusher and he had worn a black patch over the empty socket ever since. His left leg was almost totally rigid following injuries sustained in a traffic accident two years ago which had resulted in the loss of the kneecap and had left the foot at ninety degrees to the shin. Although the surgeons had done their best for him, it still remained at a curious angle. The other visible reminder of the accident was a broad white scar across the forehead where he had nearly been scalped.

If he wasn't already conspicuous enough, his sartorial tastes ensured he would not go unnoticed in the most crowded of public places. When he limped into the Adler that evening, Willie was wearing a royal-blue silk shirt with dark brown slacks and suede loafers. Fortunately, the *Gasthof* was three parts empty and Franklin was spared the embarrassment of finding himself the centre of attention.

'Good evening, Herr Franklin,' Willie said quietly and sat down at the corner table, his left leg outstretched ramrod straight. 'Is that for me?' he asked, eyeing the beer and schnapps.

'Would you prefer something else?'

'No, it's just what I need on a sultry evening like this.' He tossed back the schnapps, then reached for the beer and downed it in one draught. 'That's better,' he added and burped to show his appreciation.

Taking the hint, Franklin signalled the waiter to bring him the same again.

'I think you said you had something for me, Willie?' he said.

'Yes. I spent an interesting afternoon parked outside a certain apartment house in Schiller Strasse where Fräulein Birgit Simon lives. You have heard of her?'

'No, I can't say I have.'

'She is a senior lecturer in computer studies at the Tech University.'

'Still doesn't ring a bell,' Franklin said.

'She is a Nazi. I'm surprised Fräulein von Schinkel hasn't informed you.'

After the rioting in the Kreuzberg District which had been triggered by the assassination of Joachim Wolff, Franklin had decided on his own initiative to compile a list of prominent neo-Nazis. London had shown little interest in the activities of the various right-wing groups, but that could change overnight and he wanted to be prepared. He had discussed the matter with Helga von Schinkel because, while working for the Allied Military Government, she had taken an active part in the denazification of the civil service in the immediate postwar years. Much to his surprise, he had discovered that she had continued to keep an eye out for potential Nazis ever since and had immediately been able to present him with a list of suspects.

'Did Helga tell you to watch Fräulein Simon?' he asked.

'Well, she pointed me in her direction. Turns out she was right to do so. The lady keeps a portrait of Adolf Hitler above her bed.'

'How do you know that?'

'Don't ask,' Willie told him with a grin. Unbuttoning his hip pocket, he took out a battered-looking wallet and extracted a couple of snapshots which were still damp. 'I think this guy called on her this afternoon.'

'Why do you say that?'

'Because of the way he behaved.'

Willie had observed the blond man approach the apartment house on foot. Before pressing the buzzer and speaking to the occupant on the intercom, he had looked back down the street as if to make sure no one was following him. When he left the apartment house approximately forty minutes later, Willie had watched him in the rear-view mirror and had then made a U-turn when he disappeared round a bend in the road.

'His Volkswagen was parked about four hundred metres from the block of flats. Soon as he turned on to the Tempelhofer Damm, I knew he was returning to the *Polizeipräsidium*. I had him tagged for a member of the Kripo the moment I laid an eye on him.'

Franklin believed him. Before his left eye had been gouged out, Willie had been a detective sergeant and could recognise a plain-clothes officer when he saw one. Nowadays, he was officially employed as a dispatcher for Blitz Taxis in Theodor-Heussplatz. Off the record, he moonlighted for the SIS and was the best contract agent Franklin had on the payroll.

'Should I try to discover his name?' Willie asked.

'Can you do that?'

'I still have one or two friends on the force but they may ask me why I want to know.'

'Better forget it then. Anyway, just because he called on a Nazi, it doesn't follow that he is tarred with the same brush.'

There was, however, a far more cogent reason for backing off.

Voigt already suspected the former detective sergeant was one of his agents and he had no desire to provide him with the requisite proof. Furthermore, Voigt would take exceptional umbrage if he thought British Intelligence was spying on one of his officers. It could lead to a major diplomatic row and his replacement as Head of Station, Berlin.

'Do you have any instructions for me, Herr Franklin?'

'Maybe. One thing puzzles me – how were you able to recognise Fräulein Simon?'

'Your assistant pointed her out to me.'

'When was this?'

'A couple of weeks ago, before the end of the last semester.'

Before Wolff was assassinated, before he had decided to compile a list of prominent Nazis. Sometimes Franklin wondered who was running the show, himself or Helga von Schinkel.

'I want to keep Fräulein Simon under twenty-four-hour surveillance. Can you arrange that, Willie?'

'It'll cost you. I'm going to need at least three men on eight-hour shifts plus a swinger, in addition to my own services as the co-ordinator.'

'What's the daily rate for the whole team?'

'Twelve hundred and fifty D-marks,' Willie said after a quick piece of mental arithmetic.

The pound was running at two forty-nine. Rounding it up a whole pfennig, Franklin calculated the operation was going to cost him five hundred a day. Although it was going to make a dent in his budget, he reckoned he could afford to let it run for a fortnight. If the surveillance team came up with anything worthwhile, he could always go cap in hand to London for a sub from the Foreign Office contingency fund.

'You've got yourself a deal,' he told the German. 'Now, when can you start?'

'Let's say 08.00 hours tomorrow, that will give me time to recruit a team.'

'Good.'

'Meantime, could I have something on account? Say two, maybe three days up front?'

'I'm not carrying that much cash on me.' Franklin took out his wallet and looked inside. 'Is two hundred any good to you?'

'It'll have to do for now. When do I get the rest?'

'Give Fräulein von Schinkel a ring tomorrow morning. Arrange a time and a place that suits you and she will deliver the balance of the thirty-seven hundred.'

'And fifty,' said Willie whose mind worked like a cash register.

'And fifty,' Franklin repeated with a sigh. 'Just be sure you are as quick off the mark with Fräulein Simon. I want to know where she goes, who she sees.'

'Throw in another two thousand as a one-time payment and I'll tell you what she says behind closed doors.'

'Are we talking about bugging her apartment?'

'You have some objection?'

'It's too risky.'

'I know a man who could do it standing on his head. He would supply the necessary equipment too.'

'And if he should be caught red-handed?'

'The trail stops at me, Herr Franklin. You wouldn't be implicated.'

'I wonder.'

'Hey, when have I ever let you down?'

It was true. There was no one more loyal than Willie Baumgart. He had been watching Ashton's back the night a truck driver had deliberately side-swiped his Audi off the road. He had ended up in hospital with the most appalling injuries but the girl who had been with him had been decapitated. Voigt had been convinced that there had been nothing accidental about the collision but Willie had stuck to his story that torrential rain had made it impossible for the unknown truck driver to see his vehicle in the rear-view mirror when he'd pulled out to overtake him, and Voigt had been unable to prove otherwise. So he had charged Willie with reckless driving and the court had imposed a stiff fine and banned him from driving for a year. But for the wily German lawyer Franklin had covertly hired, he might have gone to prison.

'I'm sorry, Willie,' he apologised. 'You are right, you've never let me down.'

'Thank you. And the other little matter? Do we do it?'

'Do what?'

'Bug the lady's apartment.'

Franklin looked round to make sure no one was within earshot, then leaned forward to make doubly certain he couldn't be overheard. 'Go ahead and do it,' he muttered.

'That's what I like about you English,' Willie said with a chuckle. 'You're always so open and above board.'

Ashton could feel the chilly atmosphere as soon as he opened the door to the flat in Churchill Gardens. The contact procedures he'd needed to arrange with Crawford had taken far longer than he had anticipated and it was after seven when the staff car had dropped him off at Petersfield station. A ripple of laughter told him that Harriet was in the lounge-diner watching a comedy show on television. Full of intended apologies, he walked into the room and found her curled up on the settee, legs tucked under her rump.

'You're late,' she said coldly.

'I'm sorry,' he began and was cut short.

'Don't they have any telephones at Amberley Lodge?'

'You heard that I had to go down there?'

'Roy Kelso told me.'

'Oh,' he said inadequately.

'I've already eaten. Your dinner's in the oven, though it's probably a burnt offering by now.'

'Look, I really am sorry and you're right, I should have phoned.'

'I'd like to see the rest of this programme, Peter,' she told him, her voice even colder, if that were possible.

Well, up you too, he thought, and went into the kitchen.

The veal escalopes were turned up around the edges, the anchovies wrapped around the olives looked singularly unappetising and the duchess potatoes resembled burned pine cones. Fortunately however, there was nothing wrong with the green salad in the cut-glass bowl on the kitchen table. Pouring himself a glass of chilled Muscadet, he began to chomp his way through the escalopes, determined to look as though he was enjoying them even if it choked him. The charade was wasted on Harriet when she walked into the kitchen a few minutes later.

'Your new passport, Mr Quick,' she said and slapped it down on the table.

Ashton closed his eyes. He should have told her, goddammit. Blank passports to meet just such an emergency were held by the Security Vetting and Technical Services Division and she was sitting in the chair now. How could he have been such an idiot to overlook this?

'You are on Finnair flight AY 836 to Helsinki departing Heathrow 07.05 hours the day after tomorrow. Check in time is 05.00.'

'I should have told you . . .'

'You are booked into the Viru Hotel in Tallinn, as is the friend who's using your name,' Harriet said and placed the address in front of him. 'You're a sales representative for Stilson Manufacturing in Acton. They make machine tools and metal castings.' Another slip of paper appeared under his nose. 'Their MD will brief you ten o'clock sharp tomorrow morning.'

'Right . . .'

'And this,' she continued remorselessly, 'is the proof copy of the proposed wedding invitation, though why it should interest you is beyond me.'

'What can I say?' Ashton moved his plate aside. 'I shouldn't have volunteered without first consulting you.'

'That isn't the reason I'm angry.'

'It isn't?'

'No, I'm angry because you can't see that Victor Hazelwood is using you.'

'You don't understand . . .'

'No, it's you who doesn't understand,' Harriet told him. 'But I'm warning you, you'd better come back to me from Tallinn in one piece or you'll have my mother to deal with as well as me, and she is much more formidable.'

He searched her face hoping to see the glimmer of a smile, but her mouth was set.

Chapter 14

Same time, same bench in the same covered shelter in the same park. Leonid Nikolaevich Zelenov, ex-major general, Hero of the Soviet Union and holder of the Order of Lenin, looked up at the cloudless sky and took some comfort from the thought that at least it was unlikely to rain this morning. Yesterday, the heavens had emptied and a strong wind had turned Vera Vorontsova's umbrella inside out, which hadn't pleased her. It hadn't pleased him either because his old army trenchcoat was no longer waterproof and he had been soaked, especially across the shoulders. And all for nothing; Boris, that son of a bitch with the blond curly hair and little boy smile, hadn't put in an appearance. In fact, he hadn't seen him since the Youth Dance Festival, three, or was it four days ago? That was the trouble with getting old, your memory played tricks with you.

Zelenov sat down on the park bench and opened his newspaper. Before Estonia broke away from the Soviet Union he had been able to buy the first edition of *Pravda* every morning from his local kiosk, courtesy of Aeroflot. Unfortunately, nowadays he had to make do with the *Daily Citizen*, the only Russian-language newspaper printed in Tallinn. He didn't know why he bothered with the rag; the editor was always toadying to the Estonians and bad-mouthing Lenin, Stalin, Moscow, the army and everything Russian. Hardly a day went by that he didn't read something which made him angry and raised his blood pressure to the point where he was courting a heart attack.

This morning was no exception. 'If we wish to enjoy life to the

155

full in our adopted country, we must identify with our Estonian neighbours. Those who are not willing to do this and think of themselves only as Russians living in an alien land should return to Moscow, St Petersburg or whatever place it is they think of as home.' Well, he had news for the arse-creeping, sanctimonious hypocrite who had written the leader; if it were possible, he would be off home like a shot. But thanks to Gorbachev and that other scumbag Yeltsin, inflation had wiped out his life's savings and he couldn't scrape up enough money to buy a ticket to the border, let alone the air fare to Moscow. And if by some miracle he did manage to put it together, where would he and Vera Vorontsova live? As sure as there was a tomorrow, the municipal authorities in Moscow wouldn't allocate them a flat. If he wrote to them first, they would simply point out that he had chosen to settle in Estonia and wash their hands of him.

'Nice enough morning for you, Leonid Nikolaevich?'

Zelenov flinched as if he had been physically struck, then barely raising his voice above a harsh whisper, he reeled off a litany of foul language acquired during a lifetime spent in the army. 'What the hell do you want to creep up on me like that for?' he demanded.

'You must be getting deaf in your old age,' Boris said and sat down beside him on the bench.

'Fuck your mother, arsehole.'

'Now, you listen to me, Leonid Nikolaevich, you're not a general any more, you're a peasant with a begging bowl and you would do well to remember that.'

The desire to lash out, to maim this despicable streak of piss was almost ungovernable. Thirty years ago, he could have snapped Boris in two like a matchstick. But time had caught up with him. The arteries had hardened, the joints had stiffened up and he ran out of breath all too easily. Apart from the physical limitations imposed by a worn-out body, Zelenov also recognised that he and Vera Vorontsova would find life unbelievably hard without the occasional back-hander from the local *Mafiozniki*.

'What do you want?' he asked testily.

'A favour,' Boris told him and pressed a twenty-dollar bill into his hand.

Zelenov stared at the portrait of Andrew Jackson. 'Is this a forgery?'

'No, it's genuine all right.'

'So who do I have to kill for it?'

'No one.' Boris laughed as if he had just cracked a huge joke. 'I simply want you to deliver a letter for me,' he added, wiping the smile from his face.

'Where to?'

'The Hotel Viru at three o'clock this afternoon.' Boris took an envelope out of his pocket and gave it to him. 'You will approach one of the desk clerks in the lobby and say that you understand a Mr Ashton from England will be staying at their hotel when he arrives in Tallinn later today. Then you ask the girl on the counter to make sure he gets this letter.'

Zelenov looked at the name printed on the envelope. 'Aak . . . sh . . . ton,' he said, trying to get his tongue round it. 'Is that the correct pronunciation?'

'It'll do. Soon as you've delivered the letter, make your way to the Town Hall Square and wait for me outside the pharmacy.'

'That's a long walk.'

'Hire a cab, you've got the money for it.'

'Supposing the Englishman isn't staying at the Viru?'

'Then I'll have to think again, but you still meet me outside the pharmacy no matter what. Otherwise you will be in serious trouble.' Boris drew a finger across his throat. 'You take my point?'

'I could hardly miss it,' Zelenov growled.

Had he been keeping an eye out for him, Ashton would have had a hard time spotting Jack Crawford at Heathrow. Even at six o'clock in the morning, Terminal 1 was busier than most municipal airports at their peak hour. By the time he had checked in his suitcase at one of the BA desks, got himself a window seat in the non-smoking section and passed through Immigration and security, there were precious few seats to be had in the departure lounge. He had bought a paperback from Menzies and had buried his nose in it until he heard the last call for Finnair Flight AY 832 over the public address system. There had been a dozen or so other latecomers at Gate 14 but Crawford had not been one of them.

But, once in Helsinki, Ashton discovered it was a different story. The terminal building was on a much smaller scale and it was difficult for passengers in transit to avoid bumping into one another. After queueing at the Finnair desk to confirm his onward flight to Tallinn, he turned away from the counter and came face to face with the SAS warrant officer. Crawford looked right through him as if he weren't there and did so again a quarter of an hour later when Ashton was killing time over a coffee. No one could have given a better or more natural performance, but there was a limit to the number of times they could eyeball each other without a glimmer of recognition passing between them. Leaving the cafeteria, Ashton checked the gate number and latest information on the Tallinn flight on the visual display unit, then found a seat in the waiting area.

He looked at the bank of telephones in the concourse and wished he had rung Harriet from Heathrow when he had been waiting in the departure lounge. The cold front had really set in after she had discovered that he had agreed to go to Estonia at Hazelwood's behest; thirty-six hours later it had still not thawed. Last night he had slept on the couch in the living room, the excuse being that he didn't want to disturb her when he got up at the unearthly hour of 4 a.m. Every couple had a spat now and then but to quarrel over what Harriet had called his subservient attitude towards the Deputy DG had been the height of stupidity and he should never have allowed it to happen.

Ashton glanced at the clock suspended from the ceiling; 14.45 hours local time meant that it was a quarter to one in London. It was possible to raise Harriet's number at Benbow House without going through the switchboard. If he rang now there was a good chance he would catch her before she went to lunch. It was risky, as well as a gross breach of security, but he wanted to put things right between them. Suddenly making up his mind, he walked over to the bank of pay phones and had actually got as far as dialling the international code for London when he heard his flight being called forward. He hung up with a guilty feeling of relief that at the last moment he had been prevented from doing something really stupid.

Ashton returned to the departure gate, showed his boarding pass to the Finnair rep on the desk and went on down the staircase to the waiting bus. Although the twin-engined Aerospatiale ATR42 turboprop was less than three hundred yards away, the driver took a circuitous route to reach it which, if nothing else, gave him the chance to change out of first into second gear.

At 15.20 hours Flight AY 736 to Tallinn thundered down the runway and took off exactly on schedule. In the twenty minutes it took to cross the Gulf of Finland, he just had enough time to brush up his knowledge of machine tools and metal castings from the brochure he'd collected yesterday from Stilson Manufacturing in Acton.

Compared to Moscow's Sheremetyevo 2, Tallinn airport was a model of efficiency. No entry visa was required, nor was he requested to fill out a customs declaration form listing the amount of hard currency, jewellery and other valuables he was bringing into the country. The Estonian Immigration officers certainly looked absurdly young but contrary to what Rowan Garfield had led him to believe, they knew what they were about. The officer who dealt with him took rather less than a minute to examine his passport before stamping it on the penultimate page. Finally, his suitcase ended up on the right carousel in the baggage hall, something which did not always happen in Moscow.

Crawford had to arrive at the hotel first. To make sure he did, Ashton left his suitcase on the carousel until he saw him pass through the Nothing to Declare channel on his way out. By the time Ashton reached the cab rank, the SAS warrant officer had gone.

There was no mistaking the Hotel Viru. Once the proud flagship of Intourist, its twenty-two storeys dominated the city's skyline and the flat surrounding countryside. Not surprisingly, it could be seen from the airport which was only two miles from the town centre on the Tartu Road. Anxious to pick up another hard currency fare, the taxi driver dropped Ashton off at the bus station below the hotel and left him to carry his suitcase up the flight of steps and into the lobby.

Crawford was still questioning one of the girls on reception when Ashton approached the desk. While the concièrge was dealing with him, the SAS man went over to the Bureau de Change to buy some Estonian kroons. Timing it to perfection, he then returned to ask yet another question as Ashton completed the registration slip and collected his room key.

'Sixteen forty-one,' Ashton said in a voice loud enough for Crawford to hear, then asked the concièrge to confirm that it was on the sixteenth floor.

Ashton went up to his room and unpacked. Observing the contact procedures they had discussed at Amberley Lodge, Crawford allowed a good half-hour to pass before he called on him. No one saw the SAS man enter the room; key ladies on each floor were past history in the age of the market economy and the corridor in that wing of the hotel had been deserted when Crawford had stepped out of the lift.

'This letter is for you,' Crawford told him. 'One of the girls on the desk gave it to me when I booked in. I thought it best to open it in front of her. The only thing which made any sense to me was your name on the envelope.'

The letter was in Russian and had been composed in longhand by a man who knew how to express himself clearly and concisely. There was no signature at the bottom of the page, Valentin had simply printed his name.

'We've been given a rendezvous for tonight,' Ashton said. 'Eight o'clock outside the pharmacy on the north side of the Town Hall Square.'

'Which way are we going to play it?' Crawford asked. 'Do you want me up front or do I watch your back?'

'There's no way you can stand in for me. My face is known to the Russian Intelligence Service and it's even money Valentin will have read my dossier. Besides, it's still broad daylight at eight.'

'I'll cover you then.'

'That might be more difficult than you think.' Ashton fetched a couple of glasses from the bathroom, opened the bottle of Glenfiddich he had bought in the Duty Free shop at Heathrow and poured a tot of malt whisky into each tumbler, then gave one to Crawford. 'I get the feeling tonight's show is merely a dress rehearsal,' he continued. 'Valentin is sending a guide to meet me, a sixty-eight-year-old veteran of the Red Army by the name of Leonid Nikolaevich Zelenov. He has described his physical appearance in some detail to ensure I'll have no difficulty recognising him.'

'So where's the problem?'

'I think Valentin will be observing me from somewhere in that square to see if I am being followed.'

'Then I will have to be very careful, won't I?' Crawford said drily. 'Tell you what, I'll get there an hour ahead of you. That should give me plenty of time to blend into the background.'

'You will also need to be mobile in case Zelenov has a taxi waiting to take me on to the actual meeting place. Better rent yourself a car; there's a self-drive agency at the airport.'

'Yeah, I noticed it in the concourse.'

'It might be advisable to get a road map while you're at it.'

Although Rowan Garfield's department had provided both of them with a guide book to Tallinn which included a street map, the eventual meeting place could well be outside the city limits.

'Right.' Crawford finished his whisky and left the glass on the coffee table. 'Anything else?' he asked.

'What have you done with the Ruger pistol?'

'I'm wearing it.'

'I'm not expecting any trouble tonight. Oh, I know it could be a case of famous last words, but Valentin would be cutting his own throat if he turned hostile at this stage. So far, he has given us a couple of freebies as a come-on. Now he wants cash up front. If he does intend to play dirty, I think he will hold off until he's sure we have fulfilled our side of the bargain, and the money man doesn't arrive until tomorrow.'

'Does he know that?'

'I'm told he does,' Ashton said.

'Are you telling me to leave the hardware behind?'

It was the last thing Ashton had in mind. If his own room was anything to go by, there was nowhere Crawford could leave the .357 magnum and be utterly confident that the chambermaid wouldn't accidentally come across it.

'No, I'm just saying be careful. Don't run foul of the law by leaving the car in a No Parking zone or anything like that. We don't want the police feeling your collar while you are tooled up.'

Ashton reflected how easy it was to slip into the vernacular of the underworld and how apposite the language happened to be on this particular occasion.

It was not the first time Reggie Osbourne had been to Helsinki, nor

161

was it likely to be the last by a long chalk. But of all the papers, documents and secret briefings he had carried over the years, the contents of this particular bag were like no other and a great deal heavier than most. Furthermore, he could not recall a previous occasion when he had felt quite so nervous. He was therefore very relieved to find that the embassy had sent the Third Secretary with a chauffeur-driven limousine to meet him at the airport.

Although Osbourne had packed an overnight bag, there was now a good chance that he wouldn't have to stop over in Helsinki. The British Airways flight from London had arrived at 15.45 hours, five minutes ahead of schedule. This meant he had an hour and a quarter in which to deliver the bag and get back to the airport in time to catch the last plane to Heathrow departing at 17.00. No problem, he thought, and congratulated himself on having had the foresight to make a provisional reservation on Flight BA 797. The rude awakening came when he reported to McKenzie, the First Secretary and Head of Chancery.

'Got a little present for you, Gordon,' he said cheerfully. 'One hundred thousand US dollars in denominations of hundreds, fifties and twenties. Don't spend it all at once.'

'Oh, very droll,' McKenzie said without a glimmer of a smile. 'How many bundles are there?'

'A hell of a lot.' Osbourne unlocked the pouch which was slightly larger than a Gladstone bag and began to stack the bundles on McKenzie's desk. 'The hundred-dollar bills are done up in packets of five thousand, so are the fifties. The twenties are sealed in wads of two thousand. All told, there are twenty-three packets and I can tell you they weigh a ton.'

'I can imagine.' McKenzie counted the bundles on his desk, tapping each one with a pencil. 'Seems to be all there,' he said. 'I'll give you a temporary receipt for the money after I've locked it away in my safe. You can return it to me when you pick up the bag tomorrow morning.'

'You've got some stuff for London then?' Osbourne said, unable to conceal his disappointment.

'Not as far as I know.'

'Then I don't understand . . .'

'Oh, didn't they tell you, Reggie? You are going to deliver the

162

money to the consular affairs officer in Tallinn. Your plane leaves at 07.40 hours.'

'Have you any more good news for me?'

'You'll be met at the airport.'

'How very considerate of the Foreign Office.'

'Well, we can't have you being mugged on the way into town.'

'Julius Caesar,' Osbourne said in what for him amounted to blasphemy.

'No, you're wrong, his name is Ashton,' McKenzie said and this time permitted himself the semblance of a smile.

A pleasantly warm day had been superseded by a chilly evening with a grey sky offering the prospect of rain before too long. But the possibility of inclement weather had not affected the night life of Tallinn. Every café, restaurant and bar around the Raekoja Plats was crowded, as was the ice cream parlour, one of the joint enterprises run in conjunction with the Swiss and located on the south side of the square facing the Town Hall.

But not everyone was enjoying a night out; as he walked towards the pharmacy, Ashton was accosted half a dozen times by youngsters wanting to sell him postcard-size pictures of the city. And there was no mistaking the identity of the old man who approached the pharmacy from the direction of the Holy Spirit Church on the north side of the square. 'Looks like a gorilla,' Valentin had written, 'broad shoulders, round head, no neck to speak of, thickset, short legs. Arms appear out of proportion to the rest of his body. Suffers from curvature of the spine and walks with a slight stoop.' As he drew close, Ashton noted the cleft chin and sunken eyes which clinched it for him.

'Good evening, Leonid Nikolaevich,' he said in Russian.

'Who the hell are you?' Zelenov growled.

'I'm Ashton, the man Boris sent you to meet.'

'You'd better come with me then, my vehicle's parked round the corner.'

The vehicle was an elderly, ochre-coloured Volvo 244. The chrome beading on the nearside was missing leaving just the protruding studs on the wings and door panels. Where the offside headlight should have been, there was a gaping hole.

Zelenov walked round the car, unlocked the door and got in behind the wheel, then leaned across and raised the catch on the nearside so that Ashton could join him. He started the engine, released the handbrake and shifting into gear, let the clutch out. The Volvo took off like a kangaroo under his heavy foot on the accelerator. It wasn't easy to crash the gears but the Russian managed it.

'Where are we going?' Ashton asked.

'You'll find out soon enough,' Zelenov told him.

He wondered if the Russian was as much in the dark as he was.

After driving around the backstreets for roughly five minutes, they ended up where they had started. Had Zelenov looked in the rear-view mirror now and again, Ashton would have said he had doubled back on his tracks to make sure they weren't being followed. His audible sigh of relief when he turned left into Dunkri Viru suggested he had missed it the first time.

'Too many one-way streets, that's the trouble with this place.'

'I hadn't noticed,' Ashton told him.

'Probably got your mind on other things. What are you selling?'

'Industrial tools.'

'I bet they don't belong to you. This poxy dump is full of pickpockets, thieves and racketeers.'

The road took them past the Post, Telegraph and Telephone Office opposite the Hotel Viru and on out of town in a north-easterly direction to pick up the motorway to St Petersburg. It started raining shortly after they joined the M11. There was very little traffic on the road and absolutely no sign of Crawford. Ashton supposed he might be driving without lights but with the night drawing in fast, he doubted it.

'You'll find a blindfold in the glove compartment,' Zelenov said. 'You have to put it on now.'

'You're joking.'

'Those are my instructions. If you refuse to do it, I am to turn the car around and drive back to Tallinn. It's up to you whether we go on or not.'

Ashton opened the glove compartment. The blindfold consisted of two large circular pads with an elastic headband to keep them in place over the eyes. Once he had put it on, Ashton couldn't see a damned thing.

His other faculties however were not impaired. They had been doing a steady fifty the last time he had glanced at the speedometer; roughly five minutes after voluntarily blindfolding himself and some three miles farther on, Zelenov left the motorway for a secondary road. At the same time, he eased his foot on the accelerator so that their speed rapidly fell off to a little over twenty miles an hour. They began to hit one pothole after another, forcing the Russian to change down to a lower gear, something he should have done earlier. A little farther on, he made a right turn onto a road that was in an even worse state of repair; then, when Ashton least expected it, he came to a halt and switched off the engine.

'You wait here,' Zelenov told him and got out of the Volvo.

The seconds ticked away, each one seeming more like a minute. The rain continued to fall, drumming on the roof loud enough to deaden any other sound. Presently, someone opened the nearside rear door and got in.

'Don't look round,' the newcomer told him and he felt the barrel of a revolver pressing against the base of his skull.

Chapter 15

Ashton took a deep breath and let it out slowly. 'Are you Valentin?' he asked and was conscious of a nervous edge to his voice.

'But of course. Who else were you expecting?'

'Damned if I know.'

'You have the money?'

'No.'

'No? What do you mean, no?' Valentin asked and gave his head a dig with the pistol. 'Are you playing games with me?'

'I think the shoe's on the other foot,' Ashton said, keeping a tight rein on himself. 'You know damn well this evening is only a dress rehearsal, a sign of good faith on our part.'

'And what are you expecting from me?'

'Something that will prove we'll be getting value for money this time instead of the crap you've been feeding us so far.'

'Crap?' Valentin echoed, his voice rising indignantly. 'What the hell are you talking about?'

'The geriatric English assassin without a name, the foot-and-mouth epidemic of 1967 courtesy of the Soviet Maritime Air Force. We're not in the market for ancient history.'

Ashton hoped he sounded a lot more confident than he actually was. Apprehension knotted his stomach and made him want to empty his bladder.

'Put this on over your head,' Valentin said and pressed a square of cloth into his hand.

Like a blind man, Ashton identified the object with his fingertips. A bag, drawstring at the neck; Jesus Christ, the bastard meant to hood him. And suddenly the memory of an incident long suppressed surfaced to haunt him again.

'What do I need this for?' he said desperately. 'Goddammit, I'm already blindfolded.'

'Shut your mouth and do it.'

Another time, another place. The tenth of February 1980, the semi-detached in Waverley Crescent, part of a large council estate on the periphery of Catholic West Belfast. He and Corporal Sally Drew, WRAC, had almost completed their tour of duty with the army's Special Patrol Unit. Seven nerve-racking months of under-cover work posing as IRA sympathisers were behind them when it had happened.

A black night, rain falling steadily like it was now. He had been sitting in the dark observing the street from the front bedroom and had watched the black taxi draw up opposite the alleyway between their house and the neighbouring one on the left. Three men and a woman had got out of the cab, two of the men had been masked, the other had his wrists tied behind his back and had to be supported because his legs kept buckling under him. The woman's hands had also been lashed together behind her back but unlike her compan-ion, she had still had some fight left in her. Somehow, she had broken free and had run off down the road, screaming for help. The taxi driver had leaped out of the cab and had caught up with her in a matter of a few yards. He had dragged her back to the alleyway, kicking and screaming, and the whole fucking neighbourhood had ignored her terrified cries. And so had he, but not from choice. He had wanted to go out there and blow them away with his twelve-shot Browning High Power 9mm automatic but Sally Drew had stopped him and he liked to think she had been right to do so. If he had intervened, their cover would have been blown, seven months of hard and dangerous graft would have gone down the sewer and the lives of many of the sources they had cultivated would have been put at risk. So he had radioed for help while the IRA men had hooded their victims and executed them in cold blood.

And now, seemingly, it was his turn. He was even more helpless than the husband and wife the Provos had murdered because they were informers. At least the twenty-eight-year-old brunette had been presented with a fleeting opportunity to escape, but what chance did he have with Valentin holding a gun to his head? His hands shaking, Ashton slipped the bag over his head and pulled the drawstring.

'That's more like it,' Valentin said briskly. 'Now give me your left hand.'

Ashton reached over the back of his seat. Whatever the Russian had in mind for him, he wanted it over and done with quickly. He had passed the stage of being frightened and considered himself already dead; then Valentin folded Ashton's hand around something which felt like a filmstrip and he wondered if his ears were deceiving him because, from what he was being told, it seemed that everything was going to be all right after all.

'That piece of celluloid you're holding is as good as a blue chip investment. You understand what I am saying?'

'Yes. And if it's okay, you'll be paid in full.'

'Good. Leonid Nikolaevich will tell you where and when you are to meet him tomorrow night.' Valentin opened the rear door, then said, 'Don't remove the hood until you reach the motorway.'

The door closed with a solid clunk. Sitting there in the dark, Ashton strained his ears to catch the sound of movement but could hear nothing above the rain drumming on the roof of the Volvo. Some moments later, Zelenov returned; grumbling to himself, he cranked the engine into life and shunted the car backwards and forwards until he finally managed to complete what should have been a three-point turn. As he drove off and started to change up through the gearbox, Ashton removed the hood and blindfold, then lowered the window on his side.

'Don't throw them away,' Zelenov told him sharply. 'You'll need them again tomorrow night.'

'Like hell I will.'

'I am to pick you up from the car park opposite the Baltic railway station eight o'clock sharp.'

'What makes you think I will be there?'

'Market forces,' Zelenov said and laughed uproariously. 'He has something you want and he is willing to sell.'

Ashton hoped that was the case. Certainly it was the reason why he had come to Tallinn but on tonight's showing, Valentin's business methods left a lot to be desired. He was still trying to fathom what the Russian had hoped to achieve with his intimidatory tactics when Zelenov pulled into the kerb and stopped.

'All right if I drop you here?' he asked.

'Where are we?'

'Outside the Estonian National Theatre. Go through the park behind it and you'll come to your hotel.'

Ashton tossed the hood and blindfold onto the back seat of the car, alighted from the Volvo and just had time to close the door before Zelenov took off like a Formula One driver on the starting grid. The rain had eased considerably and was now little more than a fine drizzle; turning the collar up on his jacket, he set off for the Hotel Viru. It was, he rapidly discovered, a lot farther away than the Russian had led him to believe.

There was no sign of Crawford in the hotel lobby, but that didn't really surprise him; apart from the reception desk and the Bureau de Change, there was no gift shop or hard currency bar to attract a hotel guest. Ashton collected his room key from the concièrge, then took the lift up to the sixteenth floor. The phone rang as he was pouring himself a large and well-deserved malt whisky. When he answered it, the caller apologised for dialling the wrong number and hung up on him. It was not one of the drills they had arranged in the event they were separated and he wondered what Crawford was up to. He didn't have to wait very long for an explanation; less than five minutes after he had put the phone down, the SAS man was in his room telling him they had a problem.

'You want a drink first?' Ashton asked.

'Wouldn't mind,' Crawford said.

Ashton fetched another tumbler from the bathroom and poured him a large tot from the bottle of Glenfiddich. 'Mud in your eye,' he said automatically.

'Yeah, well somebody's certainly throwing dust in them.' Crawford swallowed some of the whisky, then wiped his mouth on the back of his other wrist. 'Were you expecting me to watch your back tonight or was I supposed to be a decoy?'

'You were followed?'

'Yes – they must have picked me up when I left the hotel.'

'They?'

'I'm only guessing but I don't see how one man could have tagged me. Hell, I lost track of you soon after you left the Town Hall Square with the old guy and got into the battered Volvo. By the time I'd collected the Lada from where I'd parked it, you were long gone.'

Crawford had quartered the neighbourhood looking in vain for the ochre-coloured vehicle. Before giving it up as a bad job, he had widened the search to include the area bounded by the Church of the Holy Spirit to the north and the Niguliste Church in the south. He had started from the museum and travelled in an anticlockwise direction and had almost reached the halfway point when he had realised that he was being followed.

'I gave them the old run around,' Crawford continued. 'Nothing dramatic that would tell them I knew they were tailing me but enough twists and turns to prove it wasn't just my imagination working overtime. Then I led them out of town on the main trunk road to the border with Latvia. I stopped at the first roadside café I came to, went inside and ordered a bowl of soup.'

Fortunately for Crawford, the café had not been deserted. At one end of the tavern, four truck drivers had been drinking at the bar and most of the booths at the other end had been occupied. Much to their surprise, Crawford had joined a young couple in one of the booths.

'The guy knew a few words of English and could understand some of my god-awful German. We were having quite an animated conversation when the bird-dog walked into the café. He looked the wrong side of forty and was about twenty pounds overweight for his height. He was dressed casually, black cotton roll-neck sweater under a windcheater, pale grey slacks, good quality shoes. He had to be a foreigner or a member of the local mafia, he was too affluent to be anything else.'

The way Crawford saw it, the bird dog had entered the café with a two-fold purpose in mind: to see who he was meeting and to flush him out into the open. When eventually Crawford had decided to leave, he had solemnly shaken hands with the young couple.

'I thought the gesture would give him something to think about. Anyway, I headed back to Tallinn, keeping an eye out for the bird-dog and his driver in my rear-view mirror. It was pretty dark by then and I figured they would have to use their headlights. There were precious few vehicles on the road and I don't know how many miles I covered before I saw anything behind me.' Crawford shook his head in disgust. 'I should have looked at the map. The moment I made that U-turn outside the café, they knew I couldn't leave the trunk road before Tallinn because there are no minor roads feeding into it. They could afford to give me a head start.'

'And they were on your tail when you reached the outskirts of the city?' Ashton suggested.

'I'm not sure. By that time, I had begun to encounter a fair amount of local traffic and a number of vehicles overtook me before I reached the Hotel Viru. One of them looked like the same dark blue BMW I had seen outside the café.'

The two men who had followed the SAS warrant officer were an unknown quantity. Whether they were in business on their own account or were working for Valentin was immaterial as far as Ashton was concerned. In either event, they represented a threat.

'A courier will arrive from Helsinki tomorrow morning with a hundred thousand dollars in the diplomatic bag,' he said, voicing his thoughts. 'The consular affairs officer will meet him at the airport with a car, but I think we had better ride shotgun. I'll take a cab out to the airport straight after breakfast and rent a car from the self-drive agency. Meantime, you will shadow the consular affairs officer from the moment he leaves the embassy on Kentmanni.'

'And if I see the BMW again?'

'Take no action unless they show hostile intent. If they are after the money, they won't do anything before the courier arrives.

'And if they try any funny business on the way back to the embassy?'

Ashton smiled. 'Then I'll ram them,' he said.

'And that's it?'

'For now.'

'Right.' Crawford emptied his glass and set it down on the table. 'Thanks for the drink,' he said and let himself out of the room.

Ashton locked the door after him and slipped the security chain into the slot. Then he stripped off and took a long hot bath before examining the film strip Valentin had given him as a sweetener. It was about the size of a business card and was an incomplete transcript of a distress call from the *Katya Zellko* which was under attack by a Mi-24 Hind helicopter somewhere off the Crimean coast. The call was acknowledged by the frigate *Leningradsky Komsomoletz* and the Black Sea Command of the Russian Navy. The date/time group indicated that the incident had occurred exactly sixteen days ago. It gave Ashton plenty to think about as he lay in bed waiting for sleep to come.

Ashton slept badly, plagued by an old nightmare that had been dormant for more than a decade. It was always Waverley Crescent and he was standing in the alleyway carefully loading a revolver the size of a cannon which could stop an elephant in its tracks. The informer was lying flat on his stomach and couldn't move because one of the boys had a foot planted firmly between his shoulder blades. The revolver now fully loaded, he saw himself walk up to the informer and aim the huge .455 Webley at the sandbag enveloping his head. His index finger took up the first pressure, then squeezed the trigger, releasing the hammer. The cannon roared, bursting the over-ripe melon in the sandbag and then the woman came running at him hate in her eyes, mouth gagged, hands behind her. He shot the woman twice in quick succession at point-blank range, the double impact from the soft nose huge-calibre rounds lifting her bodily into the air. And suddenly her features changed dramatically and it was Harriet who was lying dead at his feet.

He woke up sweating, kicked the sheet and thin blanket aside and swinging his feet out onto the floor, sat up on the edge of the bed. Heart still pounding, he stared at the dust motes swirling in the shaft of sunlight which entered the room through a chink in the curtains. A psychiatrist, he thought, would have a fine old time explaining the significance of that particular nightmare, but he did not need to lie on a couch to understand why it still had the power to disturb him. He was racked with guilt because he had watched the Provos execute their two prisoners and he had been too numb with fear to do anything about it. Maybe he could justify his inaction on the grounds that an undercover agent had no business to get himself involved in a firefight if it could be avoided, but it haunted him that the reality had been otherwise no matter what Corporal Sally Drew might have said at the time.

Ashton got to his feet, went over to the window and drew back the curtains. He had a job to do and there was no point dwelling on the past. He felt better after he had washed and shaved, better still after breakfasting in the rooftop restaurant. Leaving the hotel a good hour before the Finnair flight from Helsinki was due to arrive, he hailed a cab and went out to the airport. From Ideal Cars Limited in the terminal building, he rented a Toyota Corolla for thirty-five US dollars a day plus thirty-five cents per kilometre, then parked the vehicle in a vacant slot outside the Arrivals Hall.

Hazelwood had been unable to give him the name of the courier but that wasn't a problem; the man charged with bringing a hundred thousand dollars into the country would be one of the thirty-four official Queen's Messengers. Ashton had been the unofficial thirty-fifth, a cover that had been meant to disguise his real activities when visiting one of Her Majesty's embassies for the purpose of carrying out a security inspection. In fleshing out his legend, he had studied the photographs of his supposed colleagues so that he could describe any one of them should he be interrogated by a hostile security service who refused to believe he was a Queen's Messenger. That was why he was confident he would recognise the courier the moment the man emerged from Customs.

Crawford was somewhere amongst the crowd waiting in the Arrivals Hall. So was the Consular Affairs Officer, but he couldn't spot him either. He checked the flight information screen to see whether Finnair AY 836 was on time and saw the plane had already landed. With no other arrivals scheduled immediately after the flight, there were no delays at either Passport Control or Customs.

Commander (Retired) Reginald James Osbourne, OBE, DSC was the first person to come through Customs. Even if he hadn't seen his photograph, Ashton would have recognised him. Not all Queen's Messengers were retired officers but whether they were former members of the Diplomatic Corps, the Civil Service or the Armed Forces, they all dressed alike. With his immaculate appearance and ultraconservative, slightly dated style of dress, Osbourne was hardly the contemporary businessman or average tourist. He moved purposefully towards the exit, his eyes scanning the waiting crowd in search of a familiar face. Beyond the barrier, he suddenly veered to the left. As the crowd parted to let him through, Ashton saw he was making for the embassy chauffeur who was holding a small placard across his chest with Osbourne's name on it.

He watched Osbourne and the consular affairs officer leave the building with the chauffeur, then looked round for Crawford and spotted the SAS warrant officer moving towards the automatic doors. When Ashton followed him out of the concourse, Osbourne was just getting into a Ford Sierra displaying CD plates. As the embassy party moved off with Crawford close on their tail in the Lada, he crossed the approach road to collect the Toyota. However, before he could pull out of the parking slot, a dark blue BMW had tagged on to the other two vehicles.

Ashton expected trouble, but nothing happened. The motorcade cruised on towards the city at a sedate forty and then made a left turn onto the outer ring road. A mile farther on, the Ford Sierra turned right, then left at the next road junction and left again into Kentmanni to halt outside the embassy. Crawford went on past the Sierra before he pulled into the kerb, the BMW stopped thirty feet behind the embassy car. Ashton did the only thing open to him and overtook all three vehicles to park under a lime tree down the street. Using the wing and rear-view mirrors, he watched Osbourne and the consular affairs officer enter the embassy, their backs protected without their being aware of it by Crawford, who waited until they had disappeared into the building before he got out of the Lada and followed them inside. A few moments later, the occupants of the BMW did the same thing.

Ashton wondered if he were watching a re-run of an old Mack Sennett comedy, then the penny suddenly dropped. Number 20 Kentmanni was also the address of the American Embassy and the Estonian Youth Hostel Office. Alighting from the Toyota, he walked up the road to where the Ford Sierra was parked.

The British Embassy was on the second floor, below the Youth Hostel office and above the United States Embassy. When he entered the modest building and started up the staircase, the two men from the BMW had just reached the first landing where they found themselves confronted by Crawford.

'Well now,' said Ashton, 'are you guys off hostelling or are you thinking of applying for a UK passport?'

The driver of the BMW was on the short side and had a swarthy complexion, but his most notable feature was a pockmarked face which suggested he had suffered from acne in his formative years. Ashton thought his companion was about the same height as himself but a good deal heavier and some ten years older if the amount of grey in his black hair was anything to go by.

'I don't understand what you are saying,' the older man told him in Russian.

'I think you do. My name's Ashton and you've been following the wrong man.' He smiled. 'And since we're all in the same line of business, why don't we sit round a table and come to some kind of arrangement before we step on each other's toes?'

There was just the briefest pause before the older man returned his smile. 'Why not? I'm Hal Reindekker, this here is Frank Agostini.'

'Jack Crawford,' Ashton said, introducing the SAS warrant officer. 'Now, whose embassy are we going to use?'

'Ours, I guess,' said Reindekker, 'but just you and me. Two's company, four's a crowd. Right?'

'Whatever you say.'

'So let's go.'

Telling Crawford to wait for him by the car, Ashton followed the American downstairs, past the Marine guard in dress uniform and into an office at the back of the building. Reindekker waved him to a chair, asked his PA next door if they could have two cups of coffee, then made small talk while they waited for her to appear.

'Have you got any means of identification?' Reindekker asked him after the coffee had arrived.

Ashton thought it was a little late in the day for such formalities but let it pass. 'Only a passport belonging to a Mr Walter Quick,' he said.

'Terrific.'

'I'm in Tallinn to buy information from a senior Russian Intelligence Officer who calls himself Valentin. I imagine you are also doing business with him?'

'That's a pretty big assumption.'

'Is it?' Ashton smiled. 'Then what were you doing following my partner under the mistaken impression that you were tailing me?'

'Well, okay, we've heard of Valentin. He approached our people in Moscow and indicated he had access to top-grade material.'

'And he gave you the lowdown on what the Colorado beetle did to the potato crop in Idaho in '64.'

'I don't get it.'

'He gave us a free sample,' Ashton said and told Reindekker about the germ warfare trial conducted by the Soviet Maritime Air Force against the UK. 'What did he give you?'

'The KGB's relationship with Lee Harvey Oswald.'

'That's interesting.'

'We thought so.'

'But if you want something that isn't ancient history, you have to pay for it?'

'That's about the size of it,' Reindekker agreed.

'And he named you as the contact man?'

'Wrong. My job is to find out who this Valentin really is. He sent word to our front man that he had a deal going with the Brits and would cut us out of it if the money wasn't right. We thought maybe you could lead us to him.'

'Maybe I can, but we'll have to play it carefully.'

'I'm sure we can work something out,' Reindekker said.

For the next twenty minutes or so they discussed the mechanics of the surveillance operation from the stake-out of the car park opposite the Baltic station to the method of tailing the Volvo after Leonid Nikolaevich Zelenov had picked him up from the RV. They also examined the pros and cons of shadowing Valentin when he and Ashton went their separate ways after the exchange.

'Are you going to share the information you get from Valentin with us?' Reindekker asked.

'I think that's something which would have to be agreed at director level.'

'Sure, I understand.'

'Don't worry, I expect they will come to some kind of agreement.' Ashton stood up. 'Right now, I'd better make my number with our people upstairs. Thanks for the coffee.'

'You're welcome.'

Ashton started towards the door, then stopped as if he had suddenly thought of another point. 'Did Valentin give you my name?'

'He certainly did.'

Reindekker was stretching the truth. The National Security Agency at Fort Meade in Maryland had undoubtedly intercepted every message from Valentin and passed it on to the CIA. The thing that bothered Ashton was the fact that the Russian had always referred to him as 'Mercury'.

Chapter 16

Although Osbourne wasn't pressed for time, he was impatient to finish his business in Tallinn and resented having to wait for Ashton to put in an appearance. He didn't see why he couldn't hand the money over to the consular affairs officer, but apparently Her Majesty's representative in Tallinn had received contrary instructions from the embassy in Helsinki. One reason he chafed at the delay was the fact that he and the consular affairs officer had run out of small talk long ago. It was, he thought, hardly surprising in view of their respective ages; the Foreign Office man was under thirty, which made Osbourne old enough to be his father. Small wonder then that they had precious little in common.

He had done his best to keep the conversation going but the younger man had not been following the Wimbledon fortnight and thought the Test series between England and Australia a complete bore. It transpired he was an opera buff and enjoyed the ballet, both of which had failed to strike a responsive chord with Osbourne. It was therefore questionable who was the more relieved, the consular affairs officer or himself, when Ashton finally arrived.

'Sorry I'm late,' Ashton said in a cheerful voice which tended to negate the apology, 'but there was a small problem I had to sort out with our friends downstairs.'

'Have you some means of identification?' the consular affairs officer asked him.

Ashton seemed genuinely surprised. 'I thought you were going to vouch for me, Reggie.'

'Me?' Osbourne said in a strangled voice. 'How can I when I've never seen you before?'

'Didn't the Foreign Office give you a photograph of me?'

'Of course they didn't. Surely you've got a passport?'

'For a man called Walter Quick. There's a Peter Ashton sitting in a Lada outside this embassy but his real name is Crawford.'

'This is ridiculous,' Osbourne said and was conscious of sounding peevish.

'You were in Sofia a few weeks ago,' Ashton said, cutting him short. 'Mike Pearman, the First Secretary and Head of Chancery, wanted to know whether I had left the country and he asked you to check with the Sheraton.'

Osbourne found himself listening to what had happened that evening, how he had learned that Ashton had left the hotel with a young woman from the Interbalkan tourist agency who had been waiting for him. And, more importantly, what he had said to Pearman as they took a stroll round the garden before the other dinner guests arrived, something which no outsider could have possibly discovered. Satisfied that he was dealing with Ashton, he asked the consular affairs officer whether he objected to him using his desk and promptly emptied the diplomatic bag on it before he had a chance to demur.

'One hundred thousand US dollars,' he said. 'Perhaps you would like to count it?'

Ashton picked up each bundle in turn and rippled the notes. 'Just want to make sure there are no blank sheets of paper in amongst the bills,' he said.

'I'm not sure I care for the implication,' Osbourne told him indignantly.

'It's nothing personal. If you were acquainted with our dirty tricks department you wouldn't put anything past them either. I presume you'd like a signature for this little lot?'

Osbourne produced the receipt voucher from his wallet and placed it in front of him. 'I certainly do, then I can get off.'

'Off?' Ashton echoed. 'You mean you are returning to Helsinki this afternoon?'

'Is there any reason why I shouldn't?'

'Your task here isn't finished yet. Her Majesty's Government is buying one hundred thousand dollars worth of highly classified information and it's going home in the diplomatic bag.'

It seemed Ashton didn't trust the source who was supplying the material and couldn't ignore the possibility that Valentin might take the money and then attempt to recover the material. The Russian had already demonstrated how resourceful he was and a bogus story about currency speculators from England might be enough to persuade Estonian Customs to search the personal belongings of all UK citizens departing from Tallinn.

'One thing they won't do is stop and search a Queen's Messenger.'

'Quite so, but—'

'The Foreign Office neglected to mention that there was more to this job than delivering a bundle of money?'

Osbourne frowned. No one had said he could expect to spend at least two nights away from London; on the other hand, he hadn't been told he would be returning the same day. In the absence of a firm timetable, he had simply assumed that was the intention. He had learned this was not the case on arrival in Helsinki and apart from the fact that he had neglected to bring a change of clothes, there was no reason why he shouldn't stay over in Tallinn. Thirty-four years as a naval officer and, more recently, his experiences as a Queen's Messenger had conditioned him to be flexible.

'Where and when am I likely to receive this material?' he asked.

'Here at the embassy tomorrow morning, say nine o'clock.' Ashton opened the executive briefcase he had brought with him and removed some illustrated brochures published by the Stilson Manufacturing Company, then began to fill the available space with bundles of US dollars. 'There is one other thing – my backup is carrying a .357 revolver. Bringing the weapon into Estonia wasn't a problem, getting it out again is a different matter.'

Osbourne fancied he knew what was coming and decided to forestall it. 'You can forget that idea. The Libyans, Iraqis and Syrians might have used the diplomatic bag to smuggle weapons in and out of the host country but we are not about to follow their example.'

'That's what I thought you would say.'

Ashton closed the briefcase and locked it, told the consular affairs officer to keep the brochures because he would need them again and then wished them both a cheery good morning. Osbourne nodded curtly, privately thinking Ashton had the cheek of Old Nick.

Franklin left the U-Bahn and walked up Olympic Way towards the athletics stadium and a much depleted Headquarters British Troops Berlin the other side of the Maifeld. Following the break-up of the Warsaw Pact and the steady withdrawal of the Russian Army, he rarely attended the weekly conference held by the General Officer Commanding. Nowadays the threat, if it existed at all, was of an internal nature and was therefore a matter for the British Services Security Organisation. He was only here now because Willie Baumgart had rung Helga von Schinkel that morning before she left her apartment in the Mariendorf District for the bookshop.

Willie had borrowed one of the Mercedes belonging to Blitz Taxis and was parked in the square facing the hockey stadium. In an effort to make himself less conspicuous, he had discarded the black patch over the left eye in favour of a pair of dark sunglasses. He had also taken to dressing like a cab driver in blue jeans and a black sweatshirt. As Franklin approached the Mercedes Willie leaned across and opened the front nearside door.

'I hope you haven't dragged me out here under false pretences,' Franklin said and clicked the seat belt into the housing.

'Absolutely not.' Willie started the Mercedes, shifted into drive and touched the accelerator. Turning right, he went on down the Olympic Way and then headed out to Spandau. 'I know you will be interested to hear what's on this tape.' He reached down between the seats, picked up a cassette and inserted it into the stereo. 'The man was calling from a pay phone,' he added and set the track running.

The number rang out briefly before a woman lifted the receiver and said hello.

'Birgit? It's me, Werner.'

'Werner. Well, this is a pleasant surprise, darling.'

'Are you alone?'

Birgit laughed throatily. 'Yes, but you will have to hurry, my other lover will be here any minute.'

'Cut it out, this is serious,' Werner told her and sounded angry and not a little worried.

'What's the matter?'

'I think you'd better take that picture down and hide it. The heat's on.'

'What do you mean?'

'I am talking about the painting above your bed,' Werner said heatedly.

'I know you are. Now calm down and tell me what has happened.'

'My flat was raided this morning by the uniformed branch.'

'What?' Birgit's voice rose a full octave.

'Don't be too alarmed, I wasn't the only one they called on. The bastards descended on the whole damned squad. Kommissar Voigt has got it into his head that the killer had inside help from the Kripo.'

'I see.'

'They took away my personal telephone directory; your number is listed under your first name . . .'

'What possible consolation is that? It won't take them long to discover who I am—'

The phone started bleeping before Birgit could finish. Reacting swiftly, Werner fed several coins into the box to keep the line open.

'Did you hear what I said?' she asked.

'Yes, but I don't think they were all that interested in the directory.'

'Then why did they take it away?'

'I don't know.' Werner cleared his throat. 'There's something else you should be aware of. The Political Intelligence Division of the BND has been in touch with Voigt; apparently they have reason to believe that the man who assassinated Joachim Wolff was hired by members of his own political party.'

'That's nonsense.'

'I'm only repeating what Voigt told me yesterday evening. Seems Wolff was opposed to merging the National Socialists with the Deutsche Alternative, the Deutsche Volksunion and the National Offensive to bring all the neo-Nazi movements under one banner, so he had to go.'

'I don't believe it, Werner.'

'Neither do I. I think the Political Intelligence Division of the BND must be staffed with a bunch of idiots, but they are saying the National Socialists needed a latterday Horst Wessel to unite the party and Joachim Wolff filled the bill. For what it's worth, Voigt is now working on a hunch that the Berlin chapter of the movement hired an Englishman to shoot Wolff. He bases this on a phone call he received shortly before the assassination.'

'Then he also is mad.'

'I'm beginning to think so too, but we need to get our stories straight. If I am questioned about our friendship, I am going to say that we met by chance one evening three months ago at the Gasthof Leica.'

'Where's that?'

'In Lenne Strasse off the Tiergarten. The place was packed and you accidentally bumped into me and I spilt a lot of beer all down my shirtfront.'

'And are we lovers?'

'You bet your sweet life we are—'

The bleeps started up again, Werner said he had run out of loose change and moments later the connection was automatically terminated.

Ejecting the cassette from the stereo, Willie gave it to Franklin. 'Pretty sensational, huh?'

'When did that conversation take place?'

'Yesterday, around noon.'

Franklin could visualise the sequence of events that would occur should Voigt obtain a court order only to discover that somebody had already bugged Fräulein Simon's apartment. As he knew to his cost, Heinrich was very good at putting two and two together and arriving at the right answer. The fur would really begin to fly if word of the incident reached Bonn. He had only been extended in post because his appointment was likely to disappear when the German seat of government moved to Berlin. Since that had recently been postponed for several years on financial grounds, his fiefdom was becoming shakier by the day and London wouldn't need much persuading to move him on.

'We've got to remove that bug from her apartment, Willie.'

'My thoughts exactly, Herr Franklin. In fact, the matter is already in hand. The instant Fräulein Simon leaves her apartment, we'll be in there.'

'Good. Soon as you've recovered the transmitter, I want the operation closed down. No one is to follow her or keep the lady under surveillance in any way. Naturally, I shan't expect you to refund any of the money you received from Fräulein von Schinkel the other day.'

'That's a relief,' Willie said with feeling. 'The hired help wouldn't have taken it too kindly.'

Franklin grunted non-committally. Baumgart had taken the ring road around Spandau Altstadt and was now heading back through the Siemensstadt District.

'Where are you planning to drop me off?' he asked.

'Wherever you wish, Herr Franklin.'

'Then let's make it the nearest S-Bahn station.'

'Very good.' Willie pursed his lips. 'This business of the English assassin,' he said, 'do you think there is any truth in it?'

'I doubt it.'

'They do say the Stasi used him on a number of occasions.'

'Where did you hear that?' Franklin asked him sharply.

'From a former colleague in the Kripo.'

He wondered if Willie was lying in order to protect someone. Helga had been working late at the bookshop the evening the Egan woman had phoned him about Nicholson. The line had been crypto protected, making it impossible for Helga to eavesdrop on their conversation, but it was possible that he had been a little indiscreet after he'd put the phone down and had said something out of turn. But whoever's fault it had been was irrelevant; what he had to do now was square things with Heinrich Voigt. He would call the Kommissar from the bookshop and tell him what he knew about Martin Nicholson. Then he would call London and ask Kelso to dispatch his passport photograph.

At five minutes to eight, Ashton drove into the car park opposite the Baltic railway station and reversed the Toyota into a vacant slot. Grabbing the briefcase on the adjoining seat, he got out of the vehicle, locked the doors behind him, then walked back to the entrance where Zelenov would expect to find him. There was no sign of the dark blue BMW Agostini had been driving earlier in the day, nor could he spot Crawford's Lada in the immediate area. Only Reindekker, who had borrowed the Volkswagen belonging to his PA was visible, parked down the road with the offside wheels up on the sidewalk.

Zelenov arrived dead on time driving the same ochre-coloured Volvo 244 which was rapidly going downhill thanks to his less than tender loving care. In addition to all the other faults, it was now afflicted with a deep-throated snarl from a blown silencer. Stamping on the brakes, Leonid Nikolaevich brought the vehicle to a shuddering halt opposite Ashton, then threw open the nearside door.

'Move your arse,' he growled. 'I haven't got all night.'

Ashton got in beside him, closed the door with one hand and at the same time placed the briefcase on the floor under his legs. Before he could fasten the seat belt, the Russian took off, tyres screaming in protest as he flattened the accelerator and his other foot suddenly leaped off the clutch as though it had been scalded. Reindekker was facing the wrong way and they shot past him, their tail end fishtailing before Zelenov eased up and brought the Volvo under control some fifty yards beyond the Volkswagen. They went on down the avenue, past the lake in Toompark and the castle up on the hill, then slowed down to make a left turn at the crossroads by the Hotel Tallinn.

Ashton couldn't see if anyone was following them; there was no wing mirror on the nearside and the rear-view was tilted to suit the driver. However, Reindekker had covered the avenue top and bottom and at least one car had to be facing in the right direction. He had also obtained three hand-held synthesised radios to enable him to keep in contact with Crawford and Agostini.

Zelenov made a right turn down the hill from the Alexander Nevsky Cathedral and headed south on a tree-lined avenue which separated the Hirvepark from the Hierjumagi park. The city map in the guidebook supplied by Garfield's department ended at that point and Ashton was unable to identify any of the landmarks thereafter.

'Lost your bearings, Englishman?'

'It's not surprising considering this is the first time I've been in Tallinn. Where are we going?'

'You'll find out soon enough.'

They continued to head south through the outer suburbs, then picked up a major road signposted to Pärnu.

'Whereabouts is that?' Ashton enquired.

'On the Gulf of Riga,' the Russian told him curtly.

A yellow Lada saloon overtook them and steadily drew away from the Volvo. Even from the back, there was no mistaking the driver. Ashton watched the vehicle disappear into the distance and assumed that Agostini was now sitting on their tail.

The highway ran nearly arrow straight through the sprawling forests of pine and silver birch interspersed with fields of rye, oats, barley, flax and potatoes. The plain was as flat as a pancake. Over fifty years ago, von Leeb's Army Group North, spearheaded by three panzer and three mechanised divisions, had come this way brushing the Russian infantry and cavalry units aside with almost contemptuous ease. The advance guard had averaged a spectacular forty miles a day but the panzers hadn't ventured too far into the forests. Ashton could understand now how large numbers of Red Army men had managed to evade the enemy and why the partisans operating behind the lines had been able to survive for so long.

'We're almost there, Englishman. Time to put your hood on.'

Ashton undid the seat belt and leaning forward, picked up the briefcase before opening the glove compartment. With a hundred thousand dollars at stake, he wanted freedom of movement in case Zelenov tried to grab the briefcase and chuck it out of the window. He took out the blindfold and the hood fashioned from part of an old Red Army blanket and put them on. Soon afterwards, the Russian turned off the highway and bumped along an uneven track.

The deeper Zelenov went into the forest, the more he had to slow down until finally the Volvo was barely making ten miles an hour. The track jinked left and right and at one stage appeared to double back on itself. Calculating time and space, Ashton reckoned they had covered roughly two miles when Zelenov missed a turning and had to back up. It was only the first of several errors which left Ashton disorientated when the old man finally stopped the Volvo and switched off the engine.

'I'm going to leave you now,' Zelenov told him, 'same as I did last night.'

Ashton listened to his footsteps as he moved away from the car and heard him curse as he tripped over an exposed tree root. He did not hear Valentin approach the Volvo and could not help flinching when the rear nearside door opened and the Russian got in behind him. Convinced no one could have been so light on his feet, he concluded that Zelenov must have pulled up alongside him.

'You have the money?' Valentin asked in a low voice.

'Yes, in the briefcase on my lap. You want to tell me what I am getting in return?'

'Microfilm copies of Top Secret Operation Orders which will make your politicians become white-haired old men overnight.'

'That's got to be worth at least a hundred thousand dollars,' Ashton said drily.

'So let's have the briefcase. Pass it slowly over your head.'

Ashton hesitated. It was odds on that Valentin hadn't made his way to the RV on foot. The Russian could take the money and run; by the time he removed the hood and blindfold, Valentin would have a head start and there would be little hope of catching him before he reached his vehicle.

'What are you waiting for?'

'Nothing.' Ashton unlocked the briefcase and passed it back. If Valentin double-crossed him, there would be no further payments and from what Hazelwood had said, the exchange of information for hard cash was destined to be an on-going arrangement. It was a comforting thought to hang on to while he sat there listening to the Russian counting the money.

'Satisfied?' he asked when he heard him close the briefcase.

'Perfectly.'

'Well, I'm not.'

'You are a very impatient man, Mr Ashton,' the Russian said. 'This envelope I am about to give you contains the microfilm I spoke about. Put it away in your jacket and don't attempt to remove the blindfold until you hear me drive off.'

'You must think I was born yesterday.'

'Unless you are very tired of life, I strongly advise you to do as you're told.'

Ashton felt the envelope. There was something inside it that could be a few strips of microfilm but he was taking an awful lot on

188

trust. 'Whet my appetite,' he said.

'What?'

'Tell me something about the material I've just bought.'

'Last night I gave you an incomplete transcript of an incident involving a Mi-24 helicopter, a frigate and a ro-ro transport. Both vessels were Russian, the helicopter gunship belonged to the Ukrainian Air Force. It attacked and sank the ro-ro with a salvo of rockets, then engaged the frigate with a 12.7mm Gatling gun killing among others the navigating officer, first lieutenant, helmsman and two look-outs on the bridge. The rest of the material refers to contingency plans dating from 1991 which were subsequently updated as a result of this unprovoked clash. Are you satisfied now?'

'Yes.'

'Good. It's been a pleasure doing business with you.'

The fire fight started when Valentin opened the door and was about to get out of the Volvo. It began with a single shot close at hand and was answered by a fusillade. It was enough to upset the most even-tempered man, let alone Valentin who had an extremely short fuse. Screaming obscenities, he stunned Ashton with a rabbit punch to the nape and pushed him out of the Volvo. Barely conscious, he could hear the agonised cries of someone in pain, and then Valentin started the engine and took off like a scalded cat.

Chapter 17

Still dazed, he thought how unreasonable it was of Harriet to be angry with him when he was very much in one piece; then he realised there was more than one voice and all of them were several notes lower than her normal tone. He also realised that both the hood and blindfold had been removed and he was lying on the ground with Crawford hunkered down beside him.

'Peter, are you okay?' he asked.

'I think so.' Ashton sat up and gingerly moved his head from side to side while massaging the nape with his free hand. 'Got a bit of a stiff neck though,' he added in what was something of an understatement.

The Volvo had gone, so had his briefcase. Ashton went through his jacket and sighed with relief when he discovered the envelope containing the microfilm was still tucked away inside the breast pocket. Slowly, like an old man bent with arthritis, he got to his feet and straightened up. Somewhere over to his left, a man obviously in pain kept repeating, 'Shit, shit, shit.'

'Who's that?'

'Agostini – he got hit high up on the left shoulder. Reindekker's with him, doing what he can to stop the bleeding.'

'And where's Zelenov?'

'With the dead man on the other side of the clearing,' Crawford said laconically.

There were any number of questions Ashton wanted to ask but they would have to wait until later. The important thing right now was to get away before some brave soul arrived on the scene intent on finding out what had been going on. Telling Crawford to come with him, he walked over to the two Americans.

Agostini didn't look too good. The whole of the left side of his shirt front from the entry wound near the collarbone to the waist was bloodstained. In a state of shock, he was shivering, while his face, wet with sweat, was the colour of old parchment. Reindekker had removed his own jacket and was endeavouring to drape it around Agostini's shoulders in an attempt to keep him warm.

'What can we do to help?' Ashton asked.

'I need to get Frank to a doctor and fast.'

'So where's the BMW?'

'Back near the main road about a mile plus from here.'

'Give me the keys and we'll fetch it.'

'We?' Reindekker frowned. 'Why does it have to be the two of you?'

'There's more than one vehicle involved.'

'Yeah? How do I know you guys aren't planning to run out on Frank and me?'

'Oh, for Christ's sake,' Ashton said impatiently, 'if that's the way you feel, I'll stay here and hold your hand.'

Reindekker glared at him, then, taking care not to hurt Agostini, went through his pockets until he found the keys. 'I guess I have to trust you,' he said as he handed them over. 'Just try to be as quick as you can, Frank's hurt real bad.'

At Nottingham University, Ashton had once managed to do the mile in a fraction under four minutes, but that was back in 1979 when he had been a member of the athletics team and had spent weeks training for the event. Fourteen years on, it was a different story and he found it difficult to keep up with Crawford. The track was uneven and full of spine-jarring hazards that taxed his strength and reminded him that he now spent the greater part of his life in a desk-bound job. Lungs bursting and with a stitch lancing into his side, he followed the SAS man into a clearing where all three cars were parked.

'No lights, you lead,' he told Crawford.

He aimed the command module at the BMW and pressed it to switch off the security alarm and release the central locking. Then he got into the car, started the engine and shifting the automatic gear into drive, released the handbrake and applied minimum pressure on the accelerator. Although Crawford's Lada was noisy, he was certain Valentin and the dead bodyguard could not have heard it coming above the deep-throated snarl from the blown silencer on the Volvo. It was also a fact that when he reached the rendezvous where Agostini had been wounded, the odometer on the BMW showed that Crawford and the two Americans had walked a mile and a quarter after leaving their vehicles behind.

Agostini was still conscious when they came to lift him into the car. There was no easy way of doing it and although they tried to handle him gently, the pain got to him and provoked an agonised scream.

'Frank will be okay once I get him to a hospital,' Reindekker said optimistically.

'What about the police?' Ashton asked.

'They won't bother us.' The American rubbed his thumb and index finger together. 'Like they say, money talks.'

'Let's hope you're right. Better give me the keys to the Volkswagen so that I can drive it back to your embassy.'

'You're a pal,' Reindekker told him and got into the BMW.

'Have you left anything behind?'

'Frank dropped his infra-red camera somewhere and he also had a revolver.'

'Okay, we'll find them.'

Ashton wished the American luck, then turned to Crawford and asked him how the fire fight had started. He already had a pretty shrewd idea; hearing it first-hand merely confirmed his supposition. After leaving their vehicles in the clearing, the three men had advanced in line like a row of beaters. Reindekker had been in the centre with Agostini on his left and Crawford on the right flank. They had heard the Volvo stop and had figured the RV Valentin had chosen was about a mile from where they had started walking.

'For civilians they weren't too bad,' Crawford went on. 'They moved silently enough even though they were in a hurry. Unfortunately for them, there are several intertwining tracks in this forest and they couldn't read the signs and were unable to tell which one had just been used. Consequently, they drifted away from me and took longer to locate and then home in on the Volvo. I don't really know how the fire fight started but for what it's worth, I think Agostini must have blundered into the bodyguard when he was trying to find a spot where he could be sure of a good close-up. Anyway, there's no doubt in my mind but what the Russian got the first round off and missed. Agostini must have dropped the camera, drawn his pistol and returned the fire. The muzzle flash obviously pinpointed his position and gave the Russian something to aim at because he was promptly hit and went down. Of course, by this time Reindekker had joined in and he went on shooting until his magazine was empty.'

'What about you?'

'I didn't open fire.' Crawford continued to move slowly forward, scouring the ground in front of him for the infra-red camera. 'The three of us were strung out in a crescent which meant I was practically opposite Agostini on the other flank. If I'd opened up, Reindekker might have thought he was confronting two gunmen and there's nothing worse than coming under friendly fire.'

'You'll have to dump your revolver in the sea or the nearest lake,' Ashton told him. 'We can't send it home in the diplomatic bag; Osbourne won't hear of it.'

'I'm not surprised.' Crawford suddenly bent down, scrabbled around in the bracken, then straightened up. 'Looks like we've hit the jackpot,' he announced triumphantly. 'I've got Agostini's revolver as well as his camera. I'll get rid of this gun too.'

'Check the cylinder.'

'Right.' There was a brief pause before Crawford announced that the American had only fired the one round.

'Okay, see if you can find any of the empty shells from Reindekker's automatic while I have a word with Zelenov.'

Leonid Nikolaevich was sitting on the ground, his back resting against a tree trunk. He was smoking a pungent cigarette and seemed completely oblivious of the body lying in the grass a few feet away.

Ashton thought the dead man was in his late twenties or early thirties. He had blond, curly hair, a snub nose and a round face. He was curled up in a ball on his right side, knees pressed against the abdomen, one hand clutching his stomach as if in the moment of death he had tried to close the gaping wound.

'A *Mafiozniki*,' Zelenov growled. 'No one is going to miss that piece of dog shit.'

'Do you know him?'

'He said his name was Boris, at least that's what he told me to call him. We did a little business now and then.'

'Well, now you have a new business associate,' Ashton told him.

'Meaning you, I suppose?'

'I don't see anyone else queueing up for your services. Now get up off your backside and wait for me by the Lada.'

Ashton left him and walked back across the clearing to see how Crawford was getting on. The warrant officer had found three empty 9mm cases in the grass and believed there were probably another five lying around somewhere. The lot and batch numbers indicated that the ammunition had been manufactured in East Germany for the Warsaw Pact forces which Ashton thought was just as well because they couldn't afford to waste any more time looking for the missing rounds.

Zelenov couldn't see why they had to transfer to the Volkswagen a mile and a bit down the track when the dead man had a perfectly good Mercedes that was going begging. Ashton had already figured that Boris had arrived in his own transport and it suited his purpose to leave the car behind. When eventually the body was discovered, there was a good chance the police would conclude they were looking at another *Mafiozniki* killing, especially if Boris had been a known racketeer. The dead man had come to a lonely place well off the beaten track. There was a pistol lying near him that had been recently fired and his prints would be on the butt. All the evidence would point to a deal that had gone sour. However, the fact that he had deliberately abandoned the Mercedes continued to rankle Zelenov.

'Stop bellyaching,' Ashton told him. 'You couldn't have kept the damned vehicle and it's your fault you lost the Volvo. Valentin could never have driven off in it if you hadn't left the keys in the ignition.'

'It's what Boris told me to do. Did the same thing last night but your friend didn't run off with the car then, did he?'

'Was Boris there yesterday evening?'

'Yes, why wouldn't he be?'

What Valentin had done suddenly made sense to Ashton. He'd wanted the keys left in the Volvo in case something happened which Boris couldn't handle and he was forced to make a quick getaway.

'Tell me something, Leonid Nikolaevich,' he said, 'have you ever met this Valentin person face to face?'

'I don't mix with *Mafiozniki* scum,' Zelenov growled.

'No, you just take their money and look the other way.'

'Fuck you, Englishman. What do you know about me?'

'Plenty. You're an old Red Army man, retired as a major general after a distinguished record in the Great Patriotic War of '41 to '45 and in Afghanistan.'

'Who told you that?'

'Valentin. It was in the letter you left for me at the Hotel Viru. It was you who gave it to one of the receptionists, wasn't it?'

'I've already told you, I've never met Valentin. Boris gave me that letter.'

'Was it his handwriting on the envelope?'

'How would I know? He never put anything in writing before, we always communicated by word of mouth.'

Ashton checked the rear-view mirror to make sure the road behind was clear of traffic, then tripped the indicator and pulled off the highway onto the grass verge and stopped. Reaching into his jacket, he took out a worn leather wallet and extracted five ten-dollar bills.

'What are you waving that money under my nose for, Englishman? Do you think I can be bought?'

Ashton was tempted to inform Zelenov that they'd already established that, but he was a proud man and humiliating him would only be counterproductive. If he was to get anywhere he would have to massage the Russian's ego. An apology cost nothing and it was easy enough to tell Leonid Nikolaevich that he hadn't meant to insult him by inferring he could be bribed.

'You're an expatriate Russian war hero,' Ashton said, laying it on with a trowel, 'the Estonians are giving you a hard time and Moscow is doing nothing to help you out.'

'Well, that's Yeltsin for you.'

'So do me a favour and take the money.' Ashton pressed the fifty dollars into his hand. 'I was once a soldier too.'

'Yes? What were you in? Intendance and Administrative Corps? Plenty of opportunities to make a bit on the side in one of those outfits.'

'I was SAS.' Ashton tripped the offside indicator and pulled out on to the road. 'The same as your Spetsnaz,' he added.

'I guess that makes you a better man than those two *Mafiozniki*,' Zelenov said after due reflection. 'But I'm still not happy about taking a hand-out from someone like you.'

'Then earn it, tell me how you came to meet Boris.'

Zelenov didn't need much urging. Once he started talking he couldn't stop and it was almost as if a dam had suddenly given way under enormous pressure. He told Ashton exactly how, when and where he had first met Boris. With a little encouragement, he was also prepared to reminisce about his latter years as a major general in the old Red Army. The only time he digressed from the subject was to direct Ashton to his small flat on the Vana Viru. When they eventually parted company, a stranger could have been forgiven for thinking they were the closest of friends.

From Vanu Viru, Ashton drove across town to the American Embassy on Kentmanni. There was no sign of the dark blue BMW, much less of Reindekker. Locking the Volkswagen, he walked up the road apiece, then turned right into Kauka and strolled round the block. When he returned to the car, the American was waiting for him.

'So how is Frank?' Ashton asked.

'He's going to be okay. He's in a good clinic and getting the best medical attention money can buy in this country.'

'I'm glad to hear it.' Ashton gave him the keys to the Volkswagen. 'Can you run me over to the Baltic station so that I can pick up the Toyota?' he asked.

'It's the least I can do.' Reindekker unlocked the doors and told him to get in, then started the engine.

'We found Frank's revolver. Crawford's going to dump it in the sea. I hope that's okay?'

'Sure, no problem.'

'His camera is on the back seat.'

'So I noticed,' Reindekker said and pulled away from the kerb.

'We also recovered some of your empty cases, 9mm stuff manufactured in East Germany. What were you using? A Makarov?'

'Yeah, that's why I wasn't too concerned about the empty cases.'

'Very smart.'

'No, just a routine precaution. Did you get what you came for?'

'Valentin gave me some microfilmed copies of various contingency plans in the event of hostilities between Russia and the Ukraine.'

'I know we would like to see that material.'

'Well, like I said this morning, I'm sure it can be arranged. Can you give me some idea what we might expect in return?'

'The appetisers he gave us before getting down to the hard sell. What we know about Valentin.'

Ashton nodded gravely and managed not to smile. Privately, he thought Reindekker wasn't giving much away. What the CIA knew about Valentin could probably be written on the reverse side of a business card. Why else would the Americans have been so keen to muscle in on tonight's operation if there weren't huge gaps in their knowledge of the source they were dealing with?

'You get much out of the old Russian guy?' Reindekker asked casually.

'Nothing to get excited about. Zelenov said the man you shot was a *Mafiozniki* called Boris. He didn't know his other names. And he's never met Valentin, not tonight or any other time.'

'You believe him?'

'Yes. He's an old army man down on his luck who has to run errands for the local racketeers to make ends meet.'

'Great minds think alike. We're not going to bother with him either.'

As soon as Reindekker said that, Ashton knew he intended to cultivate Zelenov. The fact that he hadn't asked for his address didn't mean a thing. Once he put his mind to it, Reindekker would find ways and means of running the Russian to ground. And when it came to offering financial inducements, the Secret Intelligence Service couldn't begin to compete with the CIA. Their only hope was to get in first.

Ashton parted company with the American outside the car park, collected the Toyota and drove back to the hotel. The lobby was deserted and he had the lift to himself all the way up to the sixteenth floor. He let himself into his room, locked the door and hooked in the security chain, then stripped off and took a long hot bath. It was only 23.00 but the last three hours seemed more like twenty-four and he went out like a light moments after hitting the pillow.

He had forgotten to put in for a wake-up call and slept right through until 8.30. It was well known that Osbourne set great store by punctuality and that he always had, from the days when he had been a naval cadet at Dartmouth. It was said of him that one of the reasons why he had remained a bachelor was the fact that he had never met a woman who shared his fetish for time-keeping. To Osbourne, nine o'clock meant nine o'clock, not a minute before or a minute after.

Osbourne therefore was extremely irked that Ashton should be late for their appointment, especially as it was he who had stipulated where and when they should meet. Although he fancied he was too much of a gentleman to show his annoyance, he couldn't resist a small dig when Ashton did arrive.

'Thought I was going to miss my plane to Helsinki,' he said and laughed heartily.

'You still could,' Ashton told him. 'We had a spot of bother last night. Valentin's bodyguard was trigger happy, one of our friends downstairs was wounded and the Russian was killed.'

The consular affairs officer closed his eyes, muttered some imprecation to himself, then recovered sufficiently to ask whether any of the subsequent fall-out was likely to hit the embassy.

'The bodyguard was a local racketeer,' Ashton told him, 'and there is a pretty good chance the police will think it was another gangland killing. But there is a witness who knows it was nothing of the kind. His name is Leonid Nikolaevich Zelenov and he's a former major general who is smart enough to realise I am not an English businessman on the make. That's the bad news; the good news is that he hates the Estonians and won't lift a finger to help them.'

Osbourne also gathered that yesterday's war hero couldn't make ends meet and was open to financial inducements. The way Ashton saw it, they could do more than just buy his silence; with careful handling, Zelenov could be turned round and put to work for British Intelligence without his realising it. Osbourne couldn't see how this was possible, neither could the consular affairs officer, but Ashton wasn't saying any more than he had to.

'Leonid Nikolaevich would like to go home to Moscow; it's in our interests to make his dream come true because he's no use to us here in Tallinn.'

'I'm not sure what all this has to do with me,' Osbourne pointed out.

'You will be home before I will.'

'Are you expecting trouble?'

Ashton ignored his question. 'I'm going to offer the old man a job and pay him a retainer until we can get things properly organised.' He turned to the consular officer. 'I've got a feeling our friends may try to poach Zelenov so you will have to keep him sweet while he's in your bailiwick.'

'I take my instructions from the Ambassador,' the consular officer said huffily.

'And he gets his from London and I'm just telling you what needs to be done if we get the green light. Okay?'

'I suppose so.'

'Good. For the record, Zelenov occupies one of the flats at 21 Vana Viru.' Ashton reached into his jacket and took out an envelope. 'This is what I want you to put in the diplomatic bag, Reggie.'

The atmosphere following the exchange between Ashton and the consular affairs officer was still electric and it was some moments before Osbourne realised he was expected to say something.

'Oh, right,' he said and picked up the envelope.

'It's microfilm,' Ashton said by way of explanation when he saw him weighing the envelope in his hand.

'And is it worth a life?' Osbourne enquired.

'Better one man should die than millions, especially if we got sucked into the maelstrom.'

There was nothing of the politician in Ashton, expressing regret and going on to talk about the greater good; for better or worse, he said what he meant and meant what he said.

'What plane are you catching, Reggie?'

'I've made a provisional booking on Estonian Air to Helsinki departing at 11.05 hours,' Osbourne told him. 'Gives me a choice of onward flights to Heathrow. What about you?'

Ashton shrugged. 'Depends on how things go. I'm not making any firm arrangements until I've seen Crawford off on the hydrofoil early this afternoon.'

'You are expecting trouble then?'

'I wouldn't put it as strongly as that,' Ashton said, 'but the fire fight wasn't the only piece of bad luck we had last night. Crawford bumped into a couple of police officers at just the wrong moment.'

The SAS warrant officer had consulted his road map looking for a suitable location where he could dump his Ruger pistol and the revolver belonging to Agostini. Lake Ulemiste due south of Tallinn had seemed the ideal spot; it was close to the trunk route back to town and a long way from the nearest village.

'Getting to the lake wasn't as easy as he had thought it would be,' Ashton continued. 'And it was only after several false starts that he eventually found a track going in the right direction which didn't peter out. The police must have been watching that particular track for some reason. Anyway, they stopped him before he rejoined the main road after dumping the firearms.'

Neither police officer had known much English and Crawford had played the idiot foreigner, eager to help but unable fully to understand what they wanted from him. In the end, they had thrown in the towel and let him go.

'Crawford said it had all been very amicable but they checked his passport and he thinks they took the registration number of the Lada. There was precious little traffic on the road last night and when those two officers hear about the dead Russian, it's possible they might make a connection. That's why I want to make sure Crawford gets out of Tallinn.'

'Because, according to his passport, he is Peter Ashton?'

'Well, he was always meant to be a decoy but I don't think anyone in London envisaged this particular situation.'

There was a long silence. The consular affairs officer started playing a five-finger exercise on his desk which Osbourne supposed was his way of remaining aloof. In the end, he felt compelled to say something.

'Is there anything I can do to help?' he asked.

Ashton hesitated as if he wasn't sure of him, then said, 'Would you get in touch with my Deputy DG and tell him I think there is more than one Valentin?'

Chapter 18

Breakfast for Harriet was never more than orange juice, a cup of coffee and one thin slice of lightly buttered toast with a smidgen of marmalade. This morning even that meagre repast was too much for her and she moved her plate aside, unable to finish more than half a slice of toast. The last forty-eight hours had been the longest she could ever remember. On reflection, it was actually more than seventy-two hours because the whole stupid business had started the evening Peter had returned from Amberley Lodge.

So what if he had been thoughtless and the damned dinner had burned to a cinder, it wasn't the end of the world, was it? He had said he was sorry and if his apology had sounded a touch perfunctory that evening, he had certainly tried to make amends the next day. A huge bunch of roses and a porcelain figure of a flower girl to go with the other pieces of Lladro she had collected over the years. And how had she received his peace offering? With something like contempt. 'Don't think you can get round me with a few presents,' she had told him and his tentative smile had vanished quicker than she could snap her fingers. And so Peter sleeps on the couch in the living room the night before he leaves for Estonia and she is lying awake in the double bed wishing like hell he would come to her but too proud to make the first move. Stupid, stupid, stupid.

Harriet cleared the table, scraped the half-slice of toast into the pedal bin, then stacked the glass, sideplate, cup and saucer into the dishwasher. Using the telephone in the kitchen, she rang for a minicab, then went into the bedroom to finish dressing. A cream blazer over a silk shirt and matching dark skirt; she didn't look too bad in the mirror except for the dark circles under her eyes. She opened the executive briefcase lying on the bed and for the umpteenth time since yesterday, checked to make sure she hadn't forgotten anything. Artist's impression of subject, colour photographs of same, computer enhancement of snapshot on passport application – everything was there.

She closed the briefcase, picked up her overnight bag and carried both items out into the hall. On a sudden impulse, Harriet returned to the living room where she had left a note for Peter. Rummaging through her handbag, she found the Parker fountain pen with the gold nib which her brother had given her as a present before she went up to university. On the envelope immediately below his name she printed I LOVE YOU in block capitals. Ignoring the strident summons from the doorbell, Harriet then added an exclamation mark and underlined the message several times to ensure he didn't miss it.

The minicab driver was an irrepressible north Londoner who ended each sentence with a rhetorical question and was prepared to offer his considered opinion on just about every subject under the sun. All the traffic was heading into town and they virtually had a clear run all the way out to Heathrow. For Harriet however, the seventeen-mile journey to the airport seemed to take for ever. Gervase, the general dogsbody of the European Department was waiting for her outside the Bureau de Change in Terminal 1 where they had arranged to meet.

'There's been a last-minute change of plan,' he told her. 'I'm not coming to Berlin with you.'

'Why is that?'

'The Deputy DG stuck his oar in, told Rowan it didn't need two of us to brief the Germans, especially as you had done all the donkey work.'

Harriet wasn't going to argue with him. What Hazelwood had said was essentially true; she had done most of the hard graft and she didn't need anyone to hold her hand when she eventually saw the BND in Bonn. However, meeting Franklin on her own might prove a little sticky; they hadn't exactly hit it off when she had talked to him over the phone the night Joachim Wolff had been assassinated.

'Are you worried about something, Harriet?'

'I was thinking about Head of Station, Berlin.'

'Yes, I've heard he can be difficult but I'm sure you'll have him eating out of your hand.'

'Thanks for the vote of confidence,' she said drily.

'Don't mention it. Here's your ticket to Berlin with an open one to Bonn and then back to Heathrow.'

'Fine.'

'Your flight will arrive in Berlin at 10.40 hours. Instead of meeting you at the airport, Franklin wants you to go to his private residence.'

'Noted,' Harriet said absently.

'His home address is 41 Alsenstrasse; that's on the corner of Grunerweg.'

'Good.'

'Are you listening to me, Harriet?'

'Of course I am. My plane arrives at ten forty and I take a cab to 41 Alsenstrasse.' She frowned. 'Whereabouts is that?'

'It's in the Wannsee District,' Gervase said. 'Are you sure there isn't something on your mind?'

'Someone,' Harriet said, putting him straight, 'and his name is Peter.'

'Ashton's okay.'

'How do you know? Has he been in touch?'

'No, but the consular affairs officer in Tallinn would have contacted the Foreign Office via the embassy in Helsinki had there been any trouble.'

It was what Harriet wanted to believe, what she wanted to hear, especially from someone who wasn't emotionally involved.

'How are you off for Deutschmarks?'

'I've got four hundred and fifty in small denominations.'

'You'd better have mine in case that's not enough.' Gervase took out his wallet and extracted a small wad of fifty D-mark notes bonded together with a narrow strip of adhesive brown paper. 'There's five hundred there,' he said.

'Thanks all the same but I don't think I am going to need it.'

'Better safe than sorry. The way things are going, you could end up doing a Cook's tour of Germany.'

There was always that possibility. How, when and to whom they were going to pass the information on Martin Nicholson had been the subject of endless debate. Until yesterday, Hazelwood had maintained that it was a question of choosing exactly the right moment. He had also said that when the identity of the English assassin was released, it should go to the BND. Now it was going to the *Kriminalpolizei* in Berlin and at a time not of their choosing thanks to Head of Station, Berlin.

'You're not listening to me again,' Gervase gently chided her.

'Yes, I am.' Harriet smiled. 'And thanks, I will take the money. I'll return it to you as soon as I'm back.'

'I drew it from the paymaster at Benbow House – you would be doing me a favour if you gave it straight back to him.'

Harriet said she would do that, shook hands with Gervase, then joined the shortest queue at one of the British Airways desks in the concourse. It took her less than twenty minutes to check in, clear Immigration and pass through security. Among the free newspapers offered on British Airways Flight BA 982 was the *Independent*. Tucked away at the foot of page three was a report from Berlin that Turkish guest workers in the city were organising themselves into a self-defence corps.

The apartment house at 21 Vana Viru was a five-storey building which appeared to have been heavily influenced by the German style of architecture at the turn of the century. In one sense, the building was right for the city; Tallinn had joined the Hanseatic League in 1285 and had been under German domination in one form or another since the arrival of the Knights of the Sword until the beginning of the twentieth century. In a more literal sense however, it was a complete fake. According to the guidebook provided by the European Department, much of the upper town and lower town dating back to the Middle Ages had survived the war intact. But Vana Viru lay outside the old city and had been virtually destroyed by the Russian Air Force in March 1944. Ashton wondered in passing why the Russians had allowed the apartment house to be rebuilt in the old style during the Stalinist era when they had been hellbent on colonising the city.

He pushed the swing door back and walked into a large gloomy hall. The list of tenants displayed on the notice board to the right of the entrance showed that the Zelenovs occupied one of the flats on the top floor. Either the architect had decided that a lift would not be in keeping with the character of the building or else the local party bosses had cut a few corners in order to line their own pockets. Whatever the reason, the tenants had to contend with a concrete spiral staircase which was already beginning to crumble.

The woman who opened the door to him on the fifth floor back was in her mid-sixties. She had a round, doughy face, small button eyes, a disjointed nose and a mouth that could only be described as grim. Her grey hair was parted in the middle and looked as if she had cut it herself with a pair of blunt scissors. Like her husband, Vera Vorontsova had the legs, thighs, chest and shoulders of an Olympic shot-putter.

'I have come to see the General,' Ashton told her. 'On business,' he added. 'I owe him some money.'

She smiled, opened the door wider and invited him to come in. If the living room was anything to go by, the flat was far larger than the vast majority of Russians in Moscow could expect to be allocated, but of course Leonid Nikolaevich had been a two-star general and a Hero of the Soviet Union to boot. Just how much longer he could afford to live in the apartment was something that had certainly bothered him yesterday evening.

Zelenov was sprawled in an armchair reading a Russian-language newspaper that had been printed in Tallinn. He was wearing a red and white striped shirt open at the neck, a grey sleeveless pullover, pale grey slacks, matching socks that hung in wrinkles about the ankles and a pair of black lace-up shoes. A cigarette smouldered in a cut-down brass shell case which balanced precariously on the right arm of his chair. Last night they had parted amicably, this morning Leonid Nikolaevich was barely civil to him.

'Well, if it isn't the Englishman,' he said, lowering the newspaper to nose level. 'What brings you here?'

'Something you said to me last night about wanting to settle in Moscow.'

'A pipe dream.'

'I can make it happen.'

'What are you going to do, give me the train fare?'

'More than that.'

Zelenov closed the newspaper, folded it in two and tossed it on to the dining table. 'How much more?'

'May I sit down?'

Zelenov grunted, waved a hand at the other chair, a floral pattern chintz-covered affair with lace antimacassars on the arms and back. 'You were saying?'

'I would pay you a regular salary in hard currency. I think you and Vera Vorontsova could live very comfortably on a hundred dollars a week.'

Zelenov tried to look disinterested but it was an unequal struggle and his eyes gave him away. His wife, Vera Vorontsova, had even less talent at disguising her instinctive reaction. The way she caught her breath said it all and guaranteed Leonid Nikolaevich would find some excuse to send her out of the room.

'You want some tea, Englishman?' he suddenly asked.

'That would be nice,' Ashton said, making it easy for him.

Zelenov waited until Vera Vorontsova had disappeared into the kitchen, then leaned forward in a confidential manner. 'Where would we live in Moscow?' he said. 'Do you think it will be easy to find an apartment? There are twenty million of us Russians scattered throughout what used to be the USSR. Now every fart-arsing pisspot republic wants to kick us out. How do you think a country which is going bankrupt can house that number of displaced persons?'

'There are ways and means of overcoming the housing shortage,' Ashton told him. 'For instance, you would receive a generous resettlement allowance from my company.'

'A resettlement allowance? What the fuck is that?'

'Hard cash; grease the right palm with it and the money will buy you the key to the door.'

'What is this company you work for, Englishman?'

'Stilson Manufacturing; we make industrial tools.'

'And you deal with the *Mafiozniki*.'

'Sometimes we have to bribe people in order to do business, especially when we've been invited to tender for a very lucrative contract. I understood Valentin was a government official with the Tallinn Joint Enterprise Board and was prepared to give us a little inside information about our competitors for a consideration. It seems he also undertook to do the same thing for our rivals; that's why things turned nasty last night.' Ashton shook his head. 'I was completely taken in by Valentin, I thought he could be trusted.'

'What has this got to do with me?'

'We expect to do a lot of business in Moscow and we'd like to hire you as a consultant.'

'Why would you do that? I don't know anything about industrial tools.'

Ashton assured him his lack of technical expertise was not a problem. Stilson Manufacturing didn't expect Zelenov to sell the product. He had been a major general in the élite airborne and would have had a wide-ranging number of contacts in and out of the army, people he could personally vouch for.

'We would come to you with a name, Leonid Nikolaevich, and if you knew the person, we would ask if he or she could be trusted.'

'What if I'd never heard of them?'

'Well, then we would have to use our own judgement.'

It was a pretty thin story and he doubted if Zelenov wholly believed it, but the Russian was interested and that was what counted. Encouraged by this, Ashton began to enlarge on the terms and conditions of employment, when he might expect to move house to Moscow and the interim salary he would receive while waiting to take up his appointment. Vera Vorontsova returned with their lemon tea in the middle of the sales talk and was promptly dispatched to the kitchen again for two glasses of vodka.

'This is your retainer,' Ashton said and gave him two hundred dollars while Vera Vorontsova was out of the room. 'You will receive a further payment in a fortnight's time from one of my associates.'

'I'll look forward to meeting him,' Zelenov said drily.

'A man like you could suddenly find himself in demand,' Ashton said. 'One of our competitors may approach you with what appears to be a better offer. Before you accept, just ask yourself whether it might not be better to do business with someone you already know.'

Zelenov said Mr Aak . . . sh . . . ton could rely on him to do the correct thing, then Vera Vorontsova returned from the kitchen and they toasted each other. It was a pepper vodka with a near-lethal delayed action that made a forty per cent single malt seem almost non-alcholic. They drank it the traditional way, straight down in one gulp, only for Leonid Nikolaevich to insist they had another because Vera Vorontsova had been a mite stingy with the measure. Ashton could have sworn he'd had the equivalent of a triple and knew he couldn't keep pace with the Russian who'd practically been weaned on the stuff. He also knew that it would not stop at two and would go on until he fell down in a drunken stupor unless he did something about it.

He took the second vodka without batting an eyelid and politely but firmly declined to have another, and managed to excuse himself on the grounds that he had an important business meeting, which wasn't too far from the truth. Crawford had checked out of the Hotel Viru after a late breakfast and had then driven out to the airfield to return the Lada to the Ideal Rental Agency. Right now he would be waiting at the ferry terminal for the 14.00 hours hydrofoil sailing to Helsinki and, while the SAS warrant officer didn't need anyone to nursemaid him, Ashton wanted to make sure there was no last-minute hindrance that went unobserved.

No police officer stopped Ashton on the way to the ferry terminal for the purpose of breathalysing him, which he thought was just as well because in all probability the bag would have turned all the colours of the rainbow. Crawford didn't have any problems with the police either. Without let or hindrance, he boarded the Luik of the Finnish-owned Helta Line and departed for Helsinki at a steady thirty knots.

One look at the house on Alsenstrasse and Harriet could understand why Neil Franklin was so desperate to hang on to his job. A secluded, rent-free, five-bedroom villa in a highly desirable neighbourhood was not to be sneezed at, nor was the salary commanded by a Head of Station, Berlin. Harriet paid off the taxi, then walked up the drive, overnight bag in one hand, briefcase in the other. The lawn fronting the house would not have disgraced Wimbledon and she wondered if a gardener or a general handyman was another of the perks Franklin still enjoyed. Considering his evident status, Head of Station, Berlin was the last person she expected to meet her at the door.

Franklin was some two inches shorter than herself. She had

formed a mental picture of a snappy terrier from their acerbic telephone conversation and for once the preconceived image was accurate.

'Welcome to Berlin, Miss Egan,' he said and greeted her with a thin smile. 'It's a pleasure to meet you.'

'And you,' Harriet said and wondered who was the bigger hypocrite.

'Better leave your overnight bag in the hall.'

'Oh, right.'

'I thought it would be helpful if we had a quiet talk before meeting the *Kriminalpolizei*.' Franklin opened a door off the hall and led her into his study. 'My den,' he said proudly.

Harriet looked round the room. The desk was positioned by the window facing the driveway, bookshelves took up the whole of one wall and there were a couple of easy chairs with a low table between them. A Cona bubbled away on an electric ring which rested on a second table near the desk.

'Very nice,' she murmured dutifully.

'I like it. The hardbacks come from the English Bookshop, and yes, I have read all of them – partly for pleasure but mainly because it would look pretty odd if, as the owner, I couldn't talk knowledgeably about the latest publications.'

'I imagine it would.' Her eyes drifted towards the desk again focused on a severe-looking woman in tartan trews, polo shirt and baseball cap who stared back at Harriet from the silver frame.

'That's Ella,' Franklin informed her, 'taken the day she won the ladies championship last year; went round the course in one under par. Now, can I get you a cup of my rather special coffee?'

'Thank you, that would be nice.' British Airways had filled her with coffee until the stuff was practically running out of her ears but it seemed churlish to refuse. After one sip, the bitter taste of Franklin's special brew made her wish she had declined.

'May I see the art work?' he asked.

Glad of an excuse to leave the coffee, Harriet placed the cup and saucer on the low table, picked up the briefcase and balancing it on her knees, took out the computer enhancement of the passport photograph and the artist's impression of Martin Nicholson thirty years on.

211

'He may look harmless,' Harriet said, 'but he is a very nasty piece of work.'

'Do you know of a hired killer who could be described as nice?' Franklin said bitingly.

'No,' she said, the angry colour rising in her cheeks.

'Then tell me what makes Nicholson so particularly nasty?'

That was easy, assuming the English assassin employed by the Stasi and the army deserter were the same man. Harriet began with the NAAFI girl at Watchet Camp he had sexually assaulted, then went on to describe how he had raped, whipped and sodomised a young East German woman who had been a civil servant with the Ministry of Economic Planning.

'He had beaten her up so badly that she damn near died.'

'Sounds a real bastard.' Franklin looked at the artist's impression again. 'When exactly did you identify Nicholson as the English assassin?'

'I wouldn't put it quite as definite as that.'

'No? How would you put it then?'

'I would prefer to say he was the most likely candidate.'

'All right then, when did he become Top of the Pops?'

The waspish tone stung Harriet. 'You already know that,' she retorted. 'I gave you his name the night Joachim Wolff was murdered – in fact, a few hours before he was shot.'

'That isn't what you are going to tell Kommissar Voigt. As far as the *Kriminalpolizei* are concerned, MI5 were as much in the dark as we were until the day before yesterday.'

'MI5?' Harriet repeated as if she hadn't heard him correctly.

'Yes. You are seconded from them, aren't you?'

'Well, of course I am, but I don't see—'

'The Stasi file was referred to the security service because it was agreed at Cabinet Office level that identifying the English assassin probably fell within the jurisdiction of Counter Intelligence. Naturally, the SIS were kept fully informed throughout.' Franklin paused. 'I hope you are remembering all this,' he added.

'I've got the general idea. Do you mind if I ask a question?'

'Feel free.'

'Why are you so convinced Nicholson is the man who broke into the Jurgens' flat?'

212

'I wasn't until just now when you told me about his history of sexual offences. You see, I already knew the intruder had compelled Renate, the thirteen-year-old daughter, to give him oral sex in front of the whole family.'

In Franklin's opinion, showing Nicholson's likeness to the Jurgens was a mere formality which would make a tricky situation even more difficult. Ever since receiving the anonymous phone call the day Wolff had been assassinated, Voigt had suspected the killer was an Englishman. If he now got the impression that the British had been sitting on the information, there was no telling what diplomatic repercussions might follow.

'Now perhaps you can understand why we have to do some fancy footwork,' he concluded.

'I'm beginning to.'

'Believe me, Miss Egan, Kommissar Voigt is a very prickly man to deal with.'

And not the only one, Harriet thought, then asked, 'What time are we going to see him?'

'Seventeen hundred hours.'

Harriet felt her jaw drop. 'We're not going to meet him this morning then?'

'No. He's had to stand in for the Police President at the last moment and is tied up all day with a visiting delegation from Bonn. It's not a problem, is it?'

'I am supposed to liaise with the BND . . . '

'No need to worry; they've already been warned not to expect you before tomorrow.'

'Oh. Well, in that case, I'd better check into a hotel.'

'Nonsense, you are staying with us,' Franklin told her firmly. 'Ella has prepared a room for you. There would have been one for Gervase too if he hadn't been withdrawn late yesterday.'

Harriet could understand now why the general dogsbody of the European Department hadn't been exactly heartbroken when he'd told her he wasn't going to Berlin.

Chapter 19

Heinrich Voigt was over six feet and looked in the peak of physical condition except perhaps around his waist where he was carrying a little too much weight. He had a full head of dark brown hair, eyes that were more blue than grey, and a generous mouth. He reminded Harriet of Chancellor Helmut Schmidt; she also discovered Voigt had that politician's charm, rising to his feet to shake her hand with a warm smile and a slight bow when Franklin introduced them to each other.

It had been Franklin's intention to do all the talking. Her job was to answer any questions Voigt might put to her, otherwise she was to keep quiet. Maybe Head of Station, Berlin hadn't put it quite as baldly as that before they had left for the *Polizeipräsidium* on Tempelhofer Damm, but that was the general thrust of what he had said to her.

It might have worked if, of necessity, German had been the lingua franca but Voigt happened to be reasonably fluent in English. Furthermore, he made it clear that if Fräulein Egan had identified the man who was known as the English assassin then he wanted to hear all about it from her. She wondered if this was what Franklin had really meant when he'd told her the German was prickly.

'How much do you already know about this man, Herr Kommissar?' she asked.

'Only what the BND told me was in the Stasi file. I understand he is a deserter from the British Army?'

'Not any more.'

'What?'

'Well, if I'm right and Nicholson is our man, then he is no longer a deserter. He surrendered to the military authorities in 1958, was court-martialled and sentenced to twenty-eight days detention before being discharged with ignominy.' Harriet smiled. 'I hope you don't think I am being pedantic but I believe the Stasi ordered Nicholson to give himself up to the British authorities.'

'Why would they do that, Fräulein Egan?'

'I think his case officer wanted him to acquire a British passport so that he could travel more freely. The KGB knew he would be an embarrassment as far as our army was concerned and they were banking on the Adjutant General's branch wanting to get rid of him as soon as possible.'

'I see. What are your other reasons for thinking Nicholson is the assassin?'

Harriet started with his court martial for indecent assault, went on to describe his career as a pimp while serving in BAOR and how, in all probability, he had murdered his troop sergeant in cold blood. And then, for the first time, she began to have doubts. Suddenly, the evidence which had led her to identify Nicholson as the English assassin looked thin. The former artilleryman was a bad number all right, but was it enough?

'I understand you have a photograph of this man, Fräulein Egan?'

Harriet opened her briefcase, took out the computer enhancement and the artist's impression and passed them to Voigt. 'The second one is pure guesswork, Kommissar. He may not have aged as much as we think.'

'Assuming he is still alive,' Franklin hastened to add.

'Natürlich,' Voigt said. 'We also have a picture of the killer drawn by a police artist from the description given by the Jurgens.'

'May I see it?' Harriet asked.

'But of course.' Voigt went to the bottom of his pending tray and pulled out a Wanted poster. 'I regret it doesn't bear much likeness to your Mr Nicholson.'

Franklin edged his chair nearer to Harriet and peered over her shoulder. 'Doesn't look like him at all,' he said in a manner which brooked no argument. 'Nicholson might be the English assassin but he didn't shoot Joachim Wolff. This man doesn't even resemble a European. I'd say he hailed from the Middle East.'

'The Orient,' Voigt said. 'The family were convinced the man who broke into their apartment was a Turkish guest worker.'

'Well, there you are then,' Franklin said.

'No. This man disguised himself. We found the wig he had been wearing.'

'Even so, it still doesn't prove that Nicholson is your killer, or any other Englishman for that matter. I mean, let's face it, Heinrich, if that nutter hadn't phoned you the day Wolff was shot you wouldn't be going down this particular road.'

'How many ordinary people in England had heard of Joachim Wolff before he was killed?' Voigt turned to Harriet. 'Fräulein Egan?'

'I recall reading about him in one of the Sunday supplements back in March.' She frowned. 'I can't remember which, but I do know he was only one of the neo-Nazis featured in the magazine and was regarded as a very minor figure.'

'So how many people read these – what do you call them? – quality newspapers?'

'Yes. All told, I suppose two and a half million copies are sold every Sunday, but not everyone in the household would necessarily have read or even seen the article.'

'I do not think the man who phoned my office would have read any of those newspapers. He was too coarse and ignorant.'

Franklin's snort of derision didn't put Voigt off. There was, he told Harriet, a serious split within the ranks of the New National Socialist Movement. A large faction wanted the party to merge with the Deutsche Alternative, the Volksunion and the National Offensive to form one strong Fascist Party, but Wolff had been bitterly opposed to the idea. Uncertain of their ability to remove the Party Secretary in a popular vote, the cabal who wanted to effect the merger had decided to murder him.

'Who told you that?' Franklin asked. 'The BND?'

The thoughtful way Voigt gazed at him before answering his question told Harriet that Franklin had hit the nail on the head. She also got the impression that the German didn't think it had been a lucky guess on his part.

'And the BfV, the *Bundesamt für Verfassungsschutz*,' he said, then explained to Harriet that the BfV was quite literally the Office for the Protection of the Constitution. 'It's their job to monitor the activities of extremist groups. Anyway, the people who wanted to remove Wolff decided to hire an outsider to do the job for them. They wished to keep their hands clean, you understand.'

'And then this highly trained assassin telephones you to ask what the fuck you intend to do about the Nazi piece of dog shit.' Franklin smiled mockingly. 'Why do you suppose he did that, Heinrich?'

'Perhaps it was part of his contract?' Harriet ventured. 'Perhaps the people who'd hired him were hoping that word of the anonymous phone call would reach the newspapers, the idea being to divert suspicion from themselves amongst the party faithful.'

She knew Franklin was angry with her. Right from the very outset he had believed irreparable harm would be done to Anglo-German relations if it transpired that Wolff had indeed been killed by an Englishman. Voigt had to be told that Nicholson had been tentatively identified as the English assassin but that was as far as he was prepared to go.

'Well, while you're at it, young lady, you might as well tell us why the killer disguised himself as a Turk?'

Harriet didn't like his patronising tone, especially the young lady bit, but she refused to let it rile her. Keeping her temper, she told Franklin it was an insurance in case there was no leak to the press. The people who had gathered in the *Bierkeller* to hear Wolff had been only too willing to believe the agitators who told them the Party Secretary had been murdered by the Turks.

'I think Fräulein Egan is right,' Voigt announced calmly.

'It still doesn't mean to say that Nicholson did it,' Franklin reaffirmed obstinately.

'Why don't we suspend judgement until the Jurgens have seen both the computer enhancement and the artist's impression?'

'That could be a long time, Fräulein Egan.' Voigt cleared his throat. 'The family has made it very clear that they are no longer prepared to co-operate with us. This man did things to their daughter you would not believe. You can imagine what it did to her. Ordinarily, we would never have asked Renate for a description of her assailant when there were three other witnesses but her mother was too traumatised by what had happened to be of any assistance. The grandmother wasn't much help; to her the intruder was just a dirty Turk. The father gave us a pretty good description of the man but it was essential to check the details with a second witness, so we had to question Renate. That was bad enough but it was ten times worse after the wig had been found and we had to go back and ask her if there were any other physical details she could remember. Renate became hysterical and Jurgens ordered my officers out of the house.'

'Was there a woman officer present at the time?' Harriet asked.

'Of course there was.'

'Was she in uniform?'

Voigt nodded. 'On reflection, I would have to say that was probably a mistake but there is not much we can do about it now. If we attempted to interview the family again, the newspapers would take up their cause and there would be a public outcry.'

'Supposing an outsider showed them a picture of Nicholson and asked if they had seen him before? No mention of the intruder or anything like that, just a simple enquiry.'

'Who is this outsider?'

'Me,' Harriet said.

'You can't speak the language,' Franklin said tersely.

'That wouldn't be a problem,' said Voigt. 'Detective Immelmann could accompany Fräulein Egan. He can speak English well enough to be her interpreter.'

The streets of Belfast and the windswept hills of the Falklands had taught Ashton that trouble usually occurred when you least expected it. He had also learned that the converse was equally true, a rule of thumb that had been proved to his entire satisfaction when, like Crawford, nothing untoward had happened to prevent him from leaving Tallinn. The short-haul turboprop of Estonian Airlines had arrived in Helsinki in time to connect with the British Airways Flight BA 797 to Heathrow departing at 16.45 hours. With Finland two hours ahead of the UK, his plane had touched down at ten minutes to six.

Before collecting the Vauxhall Cavalier from the long-stay car park, Ashton had phoned the flat to let Harriet know he was back. Unable to get an answer, he had tried her number at Benbow House and had drawn a blank there as well. He hadn't liked that at all, especially when he recalled how they had parted company. The possibility that Harriet had moved out of the flat and out of his life haunted him all the way into town. It didn't ease off when he turned into Churchill Gardens and pulled up outside the flat.

Ashton got out of the car and locked the doors. Churchill Gardens was up-market but street crimes happened even in the nicest of neighbourhoods and he was quite attached to the Vauxhall. Letting himself into the flat, he called out to Harriet. The ensuing silence finally destroyed a lingering hope that perhaps she was already on the way home when he'd phoned Benbow House. In a despondent frame of mind, he carried his overnight bag into the bedroom fully expecting to find her clothes had gone from the wardrobe. The sight of her old dressing gown hanging from the hook on the back of the door restored his morale. The letter she had left for him in the living room with the three magic words, 'I LOVE YOU!', on the envelope lifted it through the roof.

He read her note twice, savouring every word. When the phone rang, he assumed it was Harriet calling from Berlin. Answering it, he was disappointed to find himself talking to Hazelwood.

'How did you know I was back?' he asked.

'I didn't,' Hazelwood told him. 'I merely rang on the off chance. I was told Reggie Osbourne had arrived and I wondered if you had been on the same flight.'

'No, I think he must have been on an earlier one.' Ashton recalled that a McDonnell Douglas MD 80 of Finnair had been about to depart for London when his plane had landed at Helsinki.

'You doing anything special tonight?' Hazelwood asked.

'No, I've only just got in.'

'Well then, have supper with us. Nothing fancy, come as you are.'

Ashton hesitated. There was probably something in the fridge but he didn't feel like cooking a meal. 'Are you sure Alice won't mind?' he asked.

'Of course not, she'd love to see you,' Hazelwood said glibly, then cheerfully told him to make it sooner rather than later.

Hazelwood was one of the very few residents who referred to his house in Willow Walk as a maisonette, much to the distress of his wife, Alice, and the incomprehension of their neighbours. One of three identical properties, Willow Dene was part of a much larger Edwardian residence that had been built in 1900 from Mendip stone. Beneath the slate roof there had originally been six large bedrooms, two bathrooms, a study, library, games room, parlour, dining room, drawing room, conservatory, kitchen and scullery. Although the external fabric of the building had not changed, the interior no longer bore any resemblance to the original. Over the years, rooms had been skilfully subdivided or converted for other uses so that the parlour had become the kitchen in one residence while in another, the dining and drawing rooms had once been the library.

Before the bottom fell out of the property market, Hazelwood's three-bedroom maisonette would have commanded nearly four hundred thousand. Nowadays, it was unlikely to fetch more than a quarter of a million despite the fact that Willow Walk itself was only one street back from Hampstead Heath. Unlike some of the more recent owner-occupiers, Hazelwood would never be caught in a negative equity trap; for one thing, he had no intention of selling the property, for another, he had bought the maisonette in 1970 before house prices went sky high and the mortgage had long since been repaid.

Ashton parked the Vauxhall in a vacant space at the kerbside beyond Willow Dene, then walked back down the road. He pushed open the wrought-iron gate set in the hedge and followed the crazy paving to the front entrance on the left side of the house. Before he could ring the bell, Hazelwood opened the door to him.

'Welcome home, Peter,' he said warmly. 'Supper's nearly ready but I thought we would have a drink in my study first.'

It was, Ashton thought, almost a standard operational procedure with Victor. He had lost count of the number of times he had taken a whisky and soda off the Deputy DG in this room when Hazelwood had been Head of the Russian Desk and subsequently Assistant Director, Eastern Bloc.

'What's all this I hear from Osbourne about there being more than one Valentin?' Hazelwood asked and handed him a very stiff Johnnie Walker with a splash of soda.

'The Russian I met last night wasn't the same man I talked to the night before. His voice was totally different.'

'Are you sure he wasn't trying to disguise it?'

'Why would he do that?'

'I don't know,' Hazelwood confessed.

'I presume Osbourne also told you about the unpleasantness last night?'

'He did. I gather our friends were involved?'

Ashton nodded. 'There were two of them – Frank Agostini, who took one in the shoulder, and Hal Reindekker.'

'I hear you were in the wars too.'

'I collected a stiff neck but it's practically worn off now. Anyway, it appears Valentin is trying to do business with us and the Americans. Reindekker claims the Russian gave the CIA my name as a come-on.'

'Do you believe it?'

'Hell no, they've been eavesdropping on the air waves, intercepting every coded message London has received from Valentin and vice versa.' Ashton sipped a little whisky, rolled it appreciatively around his tongue. 'They would like to do business with us, Victor,' he added. 'Exchange of information, that kind of thing. I told Reindekker any such decision would have to be made at director level.'

'Quite. Any idea what they are offering?'

Ashton shook his head. 'We never got around to discussing it. All I learned from Reindekker is that he's been given the job of identifying Valentin.'

'He could have his work cut out if there is more than one Russian operating under that codename.'

'We're dealing with a cell, Victor.'

'Really?' Hazelwood opened the cigar box on his desk, a duplicate of the ornate one in his office. Almost reverently, he took out a Burma cheroot, trimmed the end and then pierced the leaf before lighting it. Except when they had people to dinner, his study was the only place in the house where he was allowed to smoke. You only had to smell the aroma on the curtains, the furniture and on the yellowing pages of the hardbacks on the bookshelves to know that Hazelwood spent a great deal of time in this room. 'And just how many people do you think there are in this cell?' he asked between puffs.

'Well, I don't believe the head man ever leaves Moscow. The bodyguard who was killed in the shoot-out was a real low-life *Mafiozniki* and I doubt Valentin would mix with the likes of him. Add the two different men I met in Tallinn and you're already up to three.'

There was also at least one radio operator. But one of the key figures was the man who knew ex-Major General Zelenov was down on his luck and would be willing to perform certain minor services for a consideration. Such a man would have to be a high-ranking officer in what was once the KGB's Third Directorate, the security organisation responsible for keeping an eye on past as well as present members of the armed forces.

'Zelenov would like to go home,' Ashton continued. 'I believe it's in our interest to help him realise that dream.'

'On the off chance that he could lead us to Valentin?'

'Well, I'm pretty certain he would be curious to know how Zelenov could afford to return to Moscow. Of course we would have to provide the old man with a cast-iron legend for his own protection.'

'If only that were all,' Hazelwood said with feeling.

'It's not going to cost us the earth, Victor. You should have seen the way his eyes lit up when I offered him a hundred dollars a week.'

'I wonder how long Zelenov will be content with that?'

'Who can say? But if we don't sign him up, you can bet your life Reindekker will, and then how are we going to restore the old special relationship? I mean, correct me if I'm wrong, but didn't you say that was one of our principal aims? Because, if it is, we won't have much to offer them unless we can control Valentin.'

Hazelwood thought it over out loud. If they did go ahead, palms would have to be greased in order to secure accommodation for the Zelenovs in Moscow. The operation would be run by the European Department through Head of Station, Moscow, who would be responsible for providing close protection. But that wasn't a problem. Hard currency could buy you the moon and the stars in Moscow, even the services of reliable police officers, part-time of course but working in shifts to provide cover round the clock.

He talked on, the Burma cheroot burning down between his fingers, ash spilling into his lap, the fall-out evident on the skirt of his jacket. Ashton had done a very good job and he couldn't thank him enough, but it was a different ball game now and he would have to sit this one out on the substitute's bench. In any event, it was doubtful if Valentin would want to use him again after what had happened in Tallinn. It was at this point that Alice walked into the study to inform her husband that supper had been on the table for the last ten minutes.

Within minutes of meeting Detective Immelmann, Harriet had learned that he had always wanted to be a policeman, an ambition which he evidently believed called for some sort of apology because it was not the politically correct thing to do. She thought he was good-looking in a blond Aryan sort of way and there was no denying that he had great charm, a quality that owed something to his quaint usage of English.

He was perhaps a little too apologetic; after all, it was scarcely his fault that she had had to kill time twiddling her thumbs until almost eight o'clock before he reported for duty at the Central Police Station. Immelmann was working a twelve-hour shift and was entitled to a rest break.

'I hope you were seen to?' he said as they drove off.

'What?'

'My *Kameraden* – they gave you coffee – yes?'

'Oh, they certainly did, my cup was never empty.'

'Good. It is a pity however that no one could talk with you.'

'I wasn't bored,' Harriet assured him. Franklin had offered to keep her company but she hadn't seen the point of that when he wasn't going to be present when she met the Jurgens.

'How many times have you been to Berlin, Fräulein Egan?'

'This is my first visit, Herr Immelmann.'

'Please to call me Werner.'

'Oh well, my name is Harriet,' she said and kept looking straight ahead.

'Berlin is a nice city.'

'Yes, it is.'

'But not where the Jurgen family is. Katzbach Strasse is too near the Kreuzberg District where the *Gastarbeiter* live.'

'Who?'

'Turkish people, Yugoslavs. It is not a good place. Always trouble there.'

'With the neo-Nazis?' Harriet suggested.

'Those also. Now they are forming gangs to fight.'

Harriet wasn't sure whether he was referring to the neo-Nazis or the Turkish workers.

'This is where it happened,' Immelmann said and pointed across Harriet. 'The *Bierkeller* to your right is where Joachim Wolff was shot.'

Immelmann went on up Katzbach Strasse and made a U-turn beyond the entrance to Viktoria Park. At little more than a walking pace, he then doubled back and stopped outside a grim-looking apartment house on her side of the road. Alighting from the Volkswagen, he walked round the car and opened the door for her.

'The Jurgens live at the top,' he said. 'We have to walk up. It is an old building, Harriet, and there are no lifts.'

She thought it was also a neglected one if the communal area was anything to go by. The entrance hall looked as if it hadn't been redecorated in years and some of the concrete steps in the staircase needed repointing. When eventually they reached the fifth floor, Immelmann suggested she might care to wait on the landing while he had a word with the family before introducing her.

'If you think that's best, Werner,' she said.

Harriet walked on past the door to the Jurgens' apartment to the landing window and stood there gazing down at the street. Presently, two skinheads and a butch-looking girl wearing leather trousers and a biker's jacket over a T-shirt emerged from the *Bierkeller* across the road and began arguing amongst themselves on the pavement outside the entrance. The elderly Turkish woman in her unfashionably long dress and yashmak could not have chosen a worse moment to be out on Katzbach Strasse. Suddenly, with one accord, the group turned on her and while the double-glazing made it impossible for Harriet to hear what they were saying, there was no mistaking their hostility. Panic-stricken, the woman started running, her fat bottom the target for the butch girl who kept on kicking her buttocks until she disappeared into a side street.

'Harriet.'

She spun round to face Werner. 'Did you see that?' she demanded angrily.

'*Bitte?*'

'What those animals were doing to that old woman.'

'No, I was inside the apartment talking to Herr Jurgen. You can come now, they are waiting for you.'

Harriet looked back. The two skinheads hadn't moved and the girl was almost bent double, convulsed with laughter, as she retraced her steps to rejoin them.

'Harriet, please.'

'All right,' she snapped, 'I'm coming.'

Thirteen-year-old Renate was absent from the family circle gathered round the table in the living room. To Harriet, it seemed their collective anger was directed at her rather than the man who had sexually abused the youngest member of the household. All she wanted to do was show them the impression of Nicholson and get the hell out of there as fast as she could.

The Jurgens were just as determined to see the back of her. Grandmother took one look at the likeness and nodded, but that didn't mean anything because the description she had originally given the police was totally at odds with Nicholson's portrait. There was no reaction from Monika, but her husband took one look at the artist's impression and deposited a great glob of saliva on the offending face.

'I take it Herr Jurgen has just made a positive identification?' Harriet said drily.

Immelmann said indeed he had and hustled her out of the flat and on down the staircase. Had he not been quite so anxious to leave, they might have avoided the riot on Katzbach Strasse. The butch girl wasn't laughing now; she was curled up in the foetus position on the sidewalk, trying to protect her head and stomach against the flying boots. One of her companions was already unconscious; the other was being held by two members of the Turkish Self-defence Corps while a third was using the German's face as a punchbag.

The first rock went through a window before they could reach the Volkswagen. The second came out of nowhere, crunched into Harriet's skull and put her down before she could run back inside the apartment house.

Chapter 20

Ashton returned to Military Operations (Special Projects) to the kind of welcome normally accorded to a conquering hero. Everyone seemed delighted to see him, especially Lieutenant Colonel Yeomans whom, it transpired, had a vested interest and feared he would have to forego a week's sailing in Lymington if a relief could not be found for him. The mini reception over, Ashton opened his safe, removed the filing trays and arranged them on his desk, then made two phone calls. The first was to Director Naval Intelligence for a run-down on the Krivak I Class of frigate and the ro-ro ship; the other was to the Ukrainian Desk at Vauxhall Cross for an update on the current political situation.

Naval Intelligence was the first to return his call with the information he had asked for. The 3100-ton *Leningradsky Komsomoletz* was classified as a missile frigate by NATO and packed a considerable punch with a quadruple surface-to-surface launcher in addition to its conventional main armament of four 76mm guns. Originally commissioned in 1972, the frigate in company with the roll-on/roll-off *Katya Zellko* had been transferred from the Baltic to Black Sea Command in September 1986. However, Naval Intelligence was not aware that both vessels had been attacked by a Hind Helicopter on the third of June and that the ro-ro had been set on fire and sunk.

The Ukrainian Desk was getting hot under the collar because President Leonid Kravchuk in Kiev was refusing to acknowledge the strategic arms limitation treaty Boris Yeltsin had negotiated unless the Ukraine received a cut of the US aid programme Russia had been promised. Since the Ukrainians had already grabbed a sizeable chunk of the Black Sea Fleet, this latest squabble might be seen as the last straw by Moscow.

'What about the attack on the two naval vessels?' Ashton asked.

'Better pray the gunship was Georgian. Mr Shevardnadze is having all kinds of problems with the breakaway Abkhazia region and his officials are claiming that the Russian Army has supplied the rebels with tanks and missile launchers. Maybe the ro-ro ship had been carrying further munitions for the insurgents and the Georgian Air Force took appropriate action.'

'And if the helicopter was Ukrainian?'

'What do you think?'

Ashton said he supposed he could think about digging his own personal fallout shelter and hung up.

The phone rang a third time and he picked it up thinking Naval Intelligence were calling back with additional information on the ro-ro ship. The moment he heard Hazelwood's voice, Ashton knew something was terribly wrong even before he told him that Harriet had been badly injured in a riot and was now in hospital. Like a stone man he sat there, unable to make any sense of it – fractured skull, pressure on the brain, still unconscious, condition serious but stable.

'When did this happen?' he asked in a dull voice.

'Last night, at approximately 20.30 hours.'

'And we've only just heard about it?'

'There was a cock-up. The police were slow to inform Franklin and even then they failed to tell him which hospital she had been taken to. It took him some time to find out and naturally he wanted the full facts about the extent of her injuries before he reported them to us.'

'For God's sake, that couldn't have taken him all night.'

'Harriet was on the operating table for over three hours.'

'Jesus.' Ashton pushed a hand through his hair. 'What about her parents? Have they been informed?'

'Roy Kelso is on the phone to them now. I know it would have been better coming from you but your line seemed to be permanently engaged.'

'Never mind that, Victor, what's the name of the hospital?'

'St Thomas's – it's on the Mittenhofstrasse.'

Ashton thought the name sounded familiar, then recalled that Joachim Wolff had been taken to the same hospital where he had been pronounced dead on arrival.

'Look, I realise it's no consolation, but Harriet couldn't be in better hands. The neurosurgeon at St Thomas's has a reputation second to none.'

'You won't mind if I see that for myself, will you?'

'What are you going to do?'

'Well, after I've spoken to Harriet's mother, I'm booking myself on to the first available flight to Berlin, and I don't want any arguments.'

'You won't be hearing any from this office,' Hazelwood told him. 'I'll get Roy Kelso's people to book you into a hotel.'

'Thanks, Victor.'

'If there's anything else I can do, let me know. And call me after you've seen Harriet.'

'I will.' Ashton put the phone down and looked across the room at Yeomans. 'I don't know whether you heard all that,' he said, 'but your week in Lymington is beginning to look a bit iffy.'

'It always was,' Yeomans said wryly. 'The number you want is 0345 222111.'

'What does that get me?'

'British Airways reservations, fares and advance travel information.'

Some numbers Ashton didn't need to look up. Lifting the receiver, he rang Harriet's mother in Lincoln. The next ten minutes were some of the most distressing he could remember. He had no idea what Kelso had said to her but Mrs Egan was very distraught and was convinced her daughter was dying. She didn't know what to do; she wanted to drop everything and fly out to Berlin but her husband was attending a two-day symposium in York and she hadn't broken the news to him yet. Ashton managed to calm her down, checked to make sure she knew how to get hold of her husband in York and promised to call back when his own plans were firm.

The girl at British Airways said she could get him on the flight departing at 12.45, which would arrive in Berlin at half-past three local time. Ashton confirmed the reservation, gave his Gold Card number and said he would pick up the ticket from the desk in Terminal 1. Then he returned to the flat in Churchill Gardens and packed a change of clothing in an overnight bag. Kelso rang shortly afterwards to say the travel section had booked him into the Excelsior Hotel and that Head of Station, Berlin had been requested to provide cash facilities when required.

He called Harriet's mother again, learned that she had contacted her husband who was now on his way back to Lincoln. As soon as he arrived home, they were going to see their local travel agent about a flight and hotel accommodation in Berlin. Although he doubted they would still be in Lincoln by then, Ashton promised he would ring again after he had seen the surgeon who had operated on Harriet. Then he phoned for a minicab to take him to Heathrow.

The strident jangle from the battery-powered alarm clock on the bedside table finally roused Werner Immelmann. Still half asleep, he reached out to stop the noise and groping for the clock managed to sweep it on to the floor where it continued to ring defiantly. With a good deal of reluctance, he threw the duvet aside and sat up on the edge of the bed, then slowly bending down, he picked up the clock and switched off the alarm. Eleven thirty on a bright summer morning and he felt dog tired, but so would any man who'd had less than four hours' sleep.

Immelmann shuffled into the bathroom, took one look at the haggard face in the mirror above the wash basin and couldn't believe he had aged that much in the space of twenty-four hours. It had been a rough old night; the incident report had not been good enough for Voigt, and the Kommissar had questioned him for hours on end like he would a prime suspect. Throughout the whole interrogation he'd had this nasty feeling that the Kripo Chief had tagged him as the source who had kept the assassin informed of the precautionary measures the police were taking the night Joachim Wolff had addressed the party faithful in the *Bierkeller*.

So, to protect himself, he had informed the Herr Kommissar that both Jurgen and the grandmother had recognised Nicholson and were prepared to swear he was the man who had fired the fatal shots. The irony was he'd got it wrong; there was no suspicion that he was a neo-Nazi sympathiser. Voigt had merely been concerned to make sure his account of the incident could be verified by neutral observers in case the Englishwoman gave him a different version when she regained consciousness. Far from being in a tight corner, he had done himself a power of good. The uniformed branch might still have his private telephone directory which listed Birgit's home number, but his personal file now contained a letter of commendation from the Kripo Chief himself.

Immelmann filled the wash basin with hot water, lathered his face with supercream foam and shaved. Fräulein Egan, the beautiful but unobtainable *Engländerin*, the concerned liberal occupying the moral high ground and ready to defend the rights of the *Untermenschen*. 'Did you see that?' she'd angrily demanded before referring to three young Germans as animals. He wondered how she would describe the Turks who had attacked her? Ten to one she no longer saw them as her downtrodden friends. The calm, self-assured beauty had rapidly become one panic-stricken lady when the rocks had begun to fly. If Fräulein Egan had not been struck down within a few strides, she would have shown the Olympic 100-metre sprint champion a clean pair of heels. Still, he should be grateful to the bitch, she had made a hero of him.

He finished shaving, took a quick shower and dressed even more quickly. A few minutes after twelve, he left his flat in the Marienfelde District and drove across town towards the Grosser Wannsee. Stopping at the first pay phone he came to, Immelmann rang Birgit Simon.

'It's a glorious day,' he said when she answered the phone, 'and I'm feeling particularly horny.'

'Really? So what do you expect me to do about it?'

'Take the U-Bahn out to Krumme Lanke and I'll pick you up from the station between 12.45 and 1.00. I know a quiet spot by the Wannsee.'

'I'm sure you do,' Birgit said archly.

'And I'm not on duty until four o'clock.'

'What are you telling me?'

'That we have time for a couple of quickies provided you get a move on.'

'You're not being exactly delicate, are you, *Liebchen*?'

'You won't have any reason to complain once we get together.'

'Promises, promises,' she murmured.

'And I always keep them,' Immelmann said and put the phone down.

It was vital he saw Birgit and the lewd telephone call was simply a means of protecting himself. If the uniformed branch had identified Birgit Simon from the number in his private directory, he wanted any eavesdropper on the line to believe their relationship was purely sexual.

Ashton thought hospitals were the same the world over – clean impersonal, antiseptic, well-ordered and ultimately depressing. There was a sepulchral hush on the surgical ward at St Thomas's, as if the nursing staff feared the worst and expected Harriet to die at any minute. She looked awful; there was no other word to describe her condition. Her face was the colour of marble and resembled a skull, the skin stretched tight as a drum, the cheeks sunken. The woman he loved was just a mess of tubes, drips and wires, her hair, or what was left of it, concealed under a white turban.

Contrary to his initial impression, the staff nurse let it be known that they were very pleased with Harriet, but that was as far as she was prepared to go. The Herr Professor who had performed the operation was however a little more forthcoming.

'Fräulein Egan is a very lucky young woman,' he said.

'How do you make that out?'

'She has a thin skull. Observe . . .'

Ashton found himself looking at an X-ray of the left side of the head and thinking it could be anyone. A pencil indicated the point of impact where the rock, stone or piece of brick had struck Harriet above and slightly behind the ear, then traced the extent of the fracture. The injury had necessitated an operation to relieve the pressure on the brain from a ruptured artery which could have resulted in permanent damage.

'You mean she could have become a vegetable?' Ashton said in a shaken voice.

'There was a distinct possibility that she would have been severely disabled, perhaps even comatose if we had delayed the operation. But as I said before, she is very fortunate . . .'

'The prognosis is pretty good then?'

'I don't think her speech will be affected, Herr Ashton, but only time will tell. Fräulein Egan will recover but we cannot guarantee that she will be as good as new. She may not be as confident of herself as she was before. Also, both her character and personality may change. These are things you should be prepared for.'

Hesitant instead of decisive, withdrawn as opposed to out-going, distant rather than loving; was that the interpretation he should put upon the friendly words of advice? Did it mean Harriet would treat him like a stranger? He closed his mind to the possibility and concentrated on the more pressing matter of her treatment.

'What's the immediate programme?' he asked.

'Your fiancée will remain in the recovery room for the next twenty-four hours. After that, she should be fit enough to be transferred to a general ward.'

'And how long before she can be moved?'

'Moved? Where to?'

'England, by air ambulance,' Ashton told him.

'A week, but I would not like to be held to it at this stage.'

Ashton knew that even if he pressured him all night, the Herr Professor wouldn't commit himself any further than he had already done. After thanking him for being so helpful, he looked in on Harriet again before collecting his overnight bag from the porter on duty at the enquiries desk in the entrance hall. The hospital was out on a limb, far removed from the bright lights and therefore way outside a cab driver's territory, but Ashton was lucky; one happened to be dropping off a fare as he walked out of the building.

He checked into the Excelsior, near the *Zoologischer Garten* U-Bahn station. Having failed to raise the Egans when he rang their number in Lincoln, he then left the hotel and walked to the English Bookshop half a mile away. Although it was after seven o'clock, Helga von Schinkel was still there, minding the shop. There was nothing unusual about that; old hands who had known her since joining the service swore they could not recall a single occasion when she had left the office on time. Ashton had met her only once and that had been some two years ago, but she recognised him the instant he walked into the bookshop. As he stopped by the table displaying the current ten best sellers in the UK, she moved in quickly before one of the sales girls had a chance to ask if she could

233

be of assistance. In nothing flat, Ashton found that he had made le Carré richer by one pound twenty-eight pence, the unofficial admission fee to Head of Station's office at the back.

'I want to know how it happened and why,' Ashton told her. 'You understand what I am talking about?'

'But of course. And Herr Franklin is expecting you, he will be here shortly.'

Ashton wasn't surprised to hear that Franklin would arrive at any minute. The Administrative Wing would have told the Berlin office that they had booked him into the Excelsior, but Head of Station wouldn't have left it at that. Franklin was a man who prided himself on knowing what was going on in his bailiwick and he would have covered the airport and hospital as well as the hotel. From the moment he had walked into the terminal building at Berlin-Tegel, Ashton's every movement had been observed and reported to Franklin.

'Can't you tell me?'

'I could, but he has spent most of today with the *Kriminalpolizei* and is much more conversant with the facts.'

Loyalty was one of Helga's strong suits and she would never do or say anything which might undermine or diminish Franklin's authority. Ashton recognised this as a fact of life and knew that no amount of cajoling would persuade her to unbend. So they sat around making small talk until Franklin arrived.

The two men had first met in what could only be described as inauspicious circumstances shortly after Gorbachev had been deposed, and the passage of time since then had done nothing to heal the rift between them. Had it been delivered by anyone else, Franklin's expression of regret for what had happened to Harriet might not have sounded quite so perfunctory.

'I asked Helga how it had happened,' Ashton said, cutting him short, 'and she told me it would be best if I heard it from you. I hope she's right.'

'I sent a full report of the incident to London last night,' Franklin said coldly. 'Didn't Hazelwood show you a copy of the signal?'

'We don't work in the same building. All I know is that Harriet went to see the Jurgens with some police officer and was caught up in a neo-Nazi riot when she left the apartment house.'

'She was stoned by a group of youths calling themselves the Turkish Self-defence Corps. It is of course true to say that a few Fascist thugs were responsible for provoking the incident.'

Franklin was nothing if not pedantic. Furthermore, while quick to pick up on other people's mistakes, he was always reluctant to admit to any of his own making. For a man who claimed to have a finger on the pulse of the city, it was inconceivable that he was unaware of the volatile situation in the Kreuzberg District. On that premise, he should never have allowed Harriet to get within a mile of Katzbach Strasse.

'What is the name of this German police officer who was supposed to be her guardian angel?' Ashton demanded.

'Werner Immelmann, and we can do without your snide observations. Detective Immelmann is a first-rate officer.'

'You know that for a fact, do you?'

There was a momentary hesitation before Franklin told him that Harriet would not be alive today if he hadn't been there to save her. As the mob had advanced towards her, Immelmann had drawn his pistol and fired a warning shot over their heads. Instead of stopping the crowd in their tracks as he had hoped, the show of force had only deterred them briefly. He had lacked the means to summon assistance because he had left his personal radio in the Volkswagen and at least six Turkish youths had been lurking behind the vehicle.

'If Immelmann had tried to get to the radio, the mob would have lynched him. So when the rocks started flying again, the only thing he could do was shoot the nearest Turk in the leg; then he warned the crowd that next time he would shoot to kill. Apparently, the young man Immelmann had wounded was screaming blue murder which had a salutary effect on the others who began to drift away in ones and twos. They moved a damned sight faster when they heard the riot police moving into the area.'

'And that's the whole story?'

'Story?' Franklin bridled. 'Are you implying that what I've just told you is a complete fabrication?'

'I just asked a simple question,' Ashton said mildly. 'Why can't you give me a simple answer?'

'I've given you a resumé of the report Immelmann submitted to Kommissar Voigt. I might add it was also corroborated by all the residents living in Katzbach Strasse who witnessed the incident. What more do you want?'

'The opportunity to thank Immelmann in person.'

Again Franklin hesitated. 'It might do him some good if you write to Kommissar Voigt instead.'

'Okay, if that's what you recommend.'

'Is there anything else?' Franklin asked and glanced pointedly at his wristwatch.

'We are going to need a medevac plane when the surgeon at St Thomas's confirms that Harriet is well enough to be moved,' Ashton said and found himself being ushered from the office into the bookshop.

'I'm sure we can arrange something with the RAF.'

'Her parents are on the way to Berlin and I've no idea where they are staying. I tried ringing them from the hotel but they'd already left.'

'I'll put Helga on to it; she'll run them to ground.'

'Thanks, Neil.'

'And I want you to know I'm really sorry about Harriet.'

'It wasn't your fault she was in the wrong place at the wrong time.'

Ashton still held him responsible but accusing Franklin of negligence couldn't undo what had happened.

'I just wish something good had come out of the whole lousy business.'

'You mean the Jurgens didn't identify Nicholson?'

'It's not that simple.'

It wasn't. Ashton couldn't recall when he had listened to such a convoluted story. At first, Immelmann had believed that both Renate's father and grandmother had recognised the artist's impression. However, on reflection, he had come to the conclusion they would have said the moon was made of green cheese to get the police off their backs. Jurgens may have spat on the likeness but the more he thought about it, the more Immelmann suspected the old man had done it purely to hoodwink him.

'You have to understand the whole family is pretty traumatised by what happened to Renate and they are prepared to put anyone in the frame if it'll stop the police harassing them.'

'But that is only Immelmann's opinion?'

'Yes, he made that very point with Voigt when I was there this afternoon. Indeed, he urged him to send another officer to reinterview the family.'

With a view to doing what, Ashton wondered. To confirm the identification or persuade the father and grandmother to retract? He sensed that, despite his earlier defence of Immelmann's integrity, Franklin had a number of reservations concerning the detective sergeant. As they parted company, it occurred to him that Head of Station, Berlin knew something about the German that others didn't.

Leopold Ultich was a quiet, softly-spoken man of forty-eight. He was five feet six in his stockinged feet and weighed a mere hundred and thirty pounds. A narrow pointed face was crowned by a few strands of mousey hairs which were carefully arranged to conceal his pink scalp. He exuded a slightly unworldly air and was a good listener, which of necessity he needed to be in his chosen profession. Leopold Ultich was in fact one of the city's foremost psychiatrists, an occupation that enabled him to purchase a large detached house on Witzleben Platz in the Charlottenburg District as well as a swanky office and consulting room on the Kurfürstendamm. He also happened to be the head of the Berlin chapter of the New National Socialist Movement.

Ultich was obliged to work long hours in order to provide the quality of life his wife and family had come to expect as their inalienable right. Consultations which started at a time when most Berliners who enjoyed a similar income were off to the theatre or a concert were not unusual.

Tonight, he had one extra patient, a last-minute appointment who arrived at 8 p.m., a good half-hour after his secretary had departed. The patient was Birgit Simon and she hadn't come to see him because she needed counselling. He did however treat her like any other patient and recalled in detail the problem they had supposedly confronted together in their last session. Then he put on a compact disc of *Swan Lake* to help her relax, a ploy that allowed them to conduct two quite separate conversations on different levels just in case the authorities had bugged his office and consulting room.

In her normal voice, Birgit told him that she had fallen in love with one of the students at the Technological Institute, a girl called Hedwig. 'I saw the policeman this afternoon,' she added quietly. 'He said two members of the family had identified the English assassin.'

'Did your friend give you a name?'

'Martin Nicholson.' Birgit raised her voice so that she could be heard above the music and told him of her desire to go to bed with Hedwig. 'There is more,' she continued in a lower tone. 'The policeman said he believed he could persuade the Jurgens to retract their evidence. He told me he was going to see Kommissar Voigt late this afternoon and suggest another police officer should reinterview the family. He said that should do the trick.'

'Perhaps it will,' Ultich murmured.

'If the police should find Nicholson . . .'

Ultich waved a hand to silence her. Their conversation on this particular subject had gone on long enough and in any event, he was quite capable of drawing his own conclusions. Nicholson knew who had hired him and why, something he would not hesitate to disclose if he thought the circumstances warranted it.

'I don't think your feelings towards Hedwig need cause you any concern,' Ultich said.

It was another way of telling Birgit Simon that steps would be taken immediately to ensure Nicholson would not be in a position to do them harm.

Chapter 21

Ashton walked into the English Bookshop barely a minute after it had opened at 9 a.m. If Fräulein von Schinkel was surprised to see him, she was remarkably good at hiding it. She had phoned the Excelsior twice yesterday evening, first to let him know that Harriet's parents had booked a double room at the Schweizerhof Hotel on Budapestertrasse, and then to confirm they were definitely on the British Airways flight scheduled to arrive at 21.40 hours. Helga therefore had good reason to suppose he was unlikely to require her services again in the foreseeable future.

The only other person in the bookshop was a young woman whom he took to be a university student employed on a part-time basis during the long vac. In a voice sufficiently loud for the girl to hear, he asked Helga if she had *The Times* or the *Daily Telegraph*, then went into a lengthy explanation concerning a need to consult the financial pages to gauge market trends. The UK newspapers wouldn't arrive before mid-afternoon but he reckoned Franklin's deputy had been in the game long enough to catch on.

'I have yesterday's editions in my office,' she said, justifying his faith in her. 'Would they be of any use?'

Ashton said they certainly would and followed Helga into her room at the back. 'How's the Imprest Account?' he said before she had a chance to ask what she could do for him.

'You need some money now?'

Ashton nodded. The hundred pounds which he'd drawn from one of the cashpoints at Heathrow and changed into Deutschmarks was looking a bit sick. 'How much can you let me have out of the petty cash?' he asked.

'Business was very poor yesterday,' she told him. 'The takings were down and all I have is 159 marks. Will that help?'

'It'll pay a few taxi fares to the hospital and back.'

Helga went over to the safe and unlocked it. 'How is Fräulein Egan?' she asked in a low voice, her back towards him.

'Not good.'

'I feel so ashamed . . .'

'Don't be,' Ashton said. 'You aren't responsible for what happened. Good Lord, everyone in London knows what appalling risks you took in the war. And you've done everything you can to prevent the resurgence of the Nazi movement. Right?'

Helga turned about to face him. 'If you say so.'

'No, that's what we've been told by Neil Franklin. He said you had been keeping tabs on the new generation of National Socialists.'

Helga stood there staring at him, her mouth slightly open, the small bundle of notes she had removed from the safe clutched in her right hand. Her expression suggested she didn't know whether to believe him or not.

'There's a buzz going the rounds that you and Willie Baumgart have discovered more about the assassination of Joachim Wolff than the Kommissar of the *Kriminalpolizei* and the entire detective force.' Ashton smiled. 'By the way, how is Willie?'

'He's as mobile as a man can be with a shattered leg.'

Her tone of voice left Ashton in no doubt that she held him responsible for the injuries Willie had sustained.

'Is he still working at Blitz Taxis?'

'There's your money, Mr Ashton,' she said and gave him the thin wad of Deutschmarks. 'Perhaps you would give me a receipt for the cash after you have checked it.'

'Oh, come on, we're on the same side, aren't we?'

'I hope so.'

'Well then?' Ashton said prompting her.

'All right, Willie is still with the firm.'

'I'd like to see him.'

'Ring him up, you'll find the number of Blitz Taxis in the book.'

'Unless you speak to Willie first, he's never going to be in when I phone his office. You know that.'

'We haven't used Willie in months. He doesn't know anything about the Wolff case other than what was reported in the papers.'

'No.' Ashton shook his head. 'No, I'm sorry, I don't believe it. Your boss is convinced the assassin was kept abreast of developments by an informer inside the *Polizeipräsidium*. He has actually put it in writing. Willie Baumgart is a former detective sergeant with a lot of contacts inside the force. Of course Neil used him, who else would he have turned to?'

It was what he would have done in Franklin's shoes but the question failed to draw any admission from Helga. Although the Chinese enjoyed a reputation for being inscrutable, they had nothing on Fräulein von Schinkel. In her youth, she had been questioned by the Gestapo at their headquarters on Prinz Albrecht Strasse and had learned the hard way how to keep her face blank.

'I'll tell you something for nothing,' Ashton continued. 'Long before Wolff was shot, I think you had compiled a list of neo-Nazis, some of whom were targeted for further investigation. The morning after the riot in the Kreuzberg District which followed the assassination, you put Willie on to the more prominent members of the New National Socialist Movement.'

'That's a very interesting theory, Mr Ashton, but that's all it is.'

Helga counted the money in front of him, arranging the notes on her desk in denominations of fives, tens and twenties, then gave him a Biro to sign the receipt voucher she had prepared while he had been talking.

'Willie is the foot soldier for this station; he's the man on the street who knows who can do what and how far they can be trusted when it comes to hiring people to do the dirty work. He gets results but sometimes his methods could be politically embarrassing if they ever came to light.'

Ashton took the pen. Helga wasn't saying anything; the interrogator had yet to be born who could outwit her. As he scrawled his signature on the docket, it suddenly occurred to him that she might lower her guard if he could make her feel guilty.

'I don't understand how you of all people could bring yourself to protect a Nazi,' he said quietly.

'What?' The accusation shocked her to the core, then her eyes flashed in anger. 'How dare you say that to me.'

Her anger was genuine, his was contrived because he felt no bitterness towards Helga. It was nevertheless a convincing performance by any standard. In a low, furious voice, Ashton told her he dared to say it because the woman he was going to marry was in hospital with a serious head injury. He dared to say it because he believed he knew the identity of the mole in police headquarters but needed Willie's help to prove it.

'And yours too,' he added in a softer tone as though regretting the outburst.

There was just the briefest pause before Helga gave him a hesitant smile. 'What time were you thinking of phoning Willie?' she asked.

'After I've taken Harriet's parents to the hospital. Let's say around midday to be on the safe side.'

'He'll be there when you call.'

'Thank you,' Ashton said, 'I appreciate it.'

With Boris dead and the offer of a job as the Moscow-based representative of Stilson Manufacturing, Leonid Nikolaevich Zelenov had no reason to go to Tammsaare Park. He kidded himself that he had done so purely out of curiosity to see whether the *Mafiozniki* still needed his services and had found someone to replace Boris. However, the truth was that Vera Vorontsova couldn't bear to have him under her feet when she was cleaning their flat and had shown him to the door.

For the first time in almost a month, the neighbourhood news vendor had managed to furnish him with a copy of yesterday's *Pravda* instead of one that was at least two days old. He read it avidly, especially the leader deploring the rift between Yeltsin and Vice President Aleksander Rutskoi. Anybody who got up the nose of that Siberian scumbag had his vote, and Rutskoi was a good egg, a hot shot fighter pilot with a record second to none in Afghanistan where he had met him a couple of times.

Suddenly conscious that he was being watched, Zelenov lowered his paper and found himself looking at Aak . . . sh . . . ton's business associate, the man who had shot and killed Boris.

'Mind if I join you, General?' he asked in fluent Russian.

'Have we been introduced?'

'No, but I know who you are. My name's Reindekker, Hal Reindekker. Is it okay if I use the bench?'

Zelenov shrugged. 'Please yourself, I don't own it.'

Reindekker sat down, took out a packet of cigarettes and offered him one. 'American,' he said.

'Should I be impressed?'

'They're a good smoke.'

'I prefer my own brand.'

'Vera Vorontsova told me I'd find you here,' Reindekker said, apparently completely unruffled by his rudeness.

'Did she now?' Zelenov wondered how long it had taken him to find out where he lived. The American was obviously a very pushy fellow and he didn't like the way Reindekker had referred to his wife as Vera Vorontsova as if they were old friends.

'I've got a proposition for you, Leonid Nikolaevich. How would you like to earn three hundred US dollars a week?'

That was three times what the Englishman had said he would be paid. He almost drooled at the thought of what he could do with the money. 'You want me to sell industrial tools like Mr Aak . . . sh . . . ton?' he asked feigning innocence.

Reindekker gazed at him thoughtfully. 'Has he made you an offer?' he said and looked down in the mouth when Zelenov nodded. 'Did he mention the name of this company?'

'Yes, it's Stilson Manufacturing.'

'Okay, whatever they've offered you, we'll double it.'

Zelenov got to his feet, walked over to the litterbin and dumped his copy of *Pravda*, then returned to the park bench. 'A man like you could suddenly find himself in demand' – the Englishman's words, and it seemed he had been right.

'What do you say?' Reindekker asked, pressing him for an answer.

'It's very tempting. Unfortunately I have already accepted a retainer.'

'Repay it, we'll give you the money.'

The American was eager to secure his services, which was flattering, but he hadn't indicated what he wanted from him yet. It was also a fact that Reindekker was inviting him to break his word and that was something he had never done before. On the other hand, he would do well to bear in mind that this man could turn nasty if his plans were thwarted. Boris might not have existed for all the notice the newspapers had taken of his death, and then there was the medical treatment the wounded foreigner must have received before he could be whisked out of the country. Reindekker obviously had powerful friends to get away with that kind of thing, people who could make life exceedingly difficult for him and Vera Vorontsova if he gave the word.

'I don't want to stay in Tallinn,' he told the American.

'Hell, I can understand that. The way the Estonians are treating you, it's only natural you should want to leave their country. Matter of fact, we were planning to relocate you and Vera Vorontsova anyway.'

'You also want me to be your representative in Moscow?'

Reindekker blinked. 'Moscow?' he repeated in a stunned voice. 'Is that part of the deal you've got with Ashton?'

'Yes. I am to receive a resettlement allowance from the company he works for. Stilson Manufacturing will also use their influence to persuade the municipal authorities to get us an apartment without having to spend months on a waiting list.'

'Now I know why you are reluctant to do business with us.'

'It is a question of honour,' Zelenov said primly.

'And this deal is already signed, sealed and delivered, is it?'

Zelenov hesitated. He liked to think it was but life had taught him there was no such thing as a stone-cold certainty. All he had was a promise that he would receive another two-hundred-dollar retainer in twelve days' time. 'Barring the unforeseen,' he said.

'Damn right.' The American pulled a billfold from his hip pocket and extracted several notes which he folded in two before pressing them into the General's hand. 'This is just option money in case there is a last-minute foul-up. You're not under any obligation and you don't have to return it if things work out for you. Okay?'

'This is crazy.'

'No, it's how we do business in my country.' Reindekker stood up. 'You'll get used to it,' he said and moved away.

Zelenov unfolded the dollar bills and discovered there were five in all, each one worth a hundred. He knew he could certainly get used to that kind of serious money.

For Willie Baumgart, variety was definitely the spice of life. There was the never-to-be-forgotten occasion when Ashton had met him for the first time in Diener's Place, the self-proclaimed Raffles of Berlin on Seybelstrasse where a third of a litre glass of beer had cost ten Marks, the cover charge two years ago for the lewd girlie cabaret and the non-stop selection of porno movies shown on four small video screens high up on the wall behind the long bar.

He had also watched him breakfast off ham, liver sausage, salami, cheese and pickled herrings with rye bread at two o'clock in the afternoon in Bertholt's, a backstreet *Frühstückskneipe*. And then there had been the Café Rosa in East Berlin, a drab ediface decorated in chocolate brown and dull cream paint. This afternoon, Willie had chosen the open-air café in the Zoological Garden, an altogether more salubrious rendezvous.

When Ashton arrived, Willie Baumgart was in the process of demolishing a large slice of Black Forest gâteau with a side helping of whipped cream. Two years ago when they first met, his flamboyant taste in dress had made him stand out like a sore thumb; this afternoon, his appearance was less provocative in black loafers, pale grey slacks and a white open-neck shirt under a brown, double-breasted leather jacket. With dark sunglasses instead of a black eye-patch, he was almost inconspicuous.

'Hello, Willie,' Ashton said extending his right hand. 'It's good to see you again.'

Baumgart put down the pastry fork and half rose from his chair to shake hands with him. 'And you, Peter.' His face clouded. 'How is Fräulein Egan? You have come from the hospital, yes?'

Ashton pulled out a chair and sat down. 'She is much improved, thank you.'

While Harriet might not be sitting up and taking notice, she was conscious and aware of her surroundings. Her speech was not impaired, although talking was an effort and she tired easily. She had recognised her parents immediately and had been overjoyed to see them. However, this afternoon when they had been alone together, she had seemed distant and withdrawn and had treated him as though he were a stranger. But that was something Ashton kept to himself.

'Can I get you another coffee?' he asked, pointing to Willie's empty cup.

'A cappuccino would be most welcome.'

Ashton signalled a passing waitress and ordered one cappuccino and one regular coffee, then said, 'Ever heard of a detective sergeant called Werner Immelmann?'

'Werner?' Baumgart frowned. 'Would he be a member of the team assigned to the Wolff case?'

'Yes. Do you know him?'

'I'm afraid not. He must have joined after I had left the *Kriminalpolizei*.' Willie picked up the pastry fork and resumed his attack on the gâteau. 'On the other hand, I doubt there are two Werners in the same squad.'

'Would you care to expand on that observation?'

'The skinheads you see on the streets are the asphalt foot soldiers of the New National Socialists. Like elsewhere, the Berlin chapter of the movement has its share of intellectuals. One of those we know of is Birgit Simon, a senior lecturer in computer studies at the Tech University. She has a boyfriend in the police, an officer called Werner who is close to Kommissar Voigt and tells her how the Wolff investigation is going.'

'How do you know all this?'

'It's a long story.'

'I'm not in a hurry,' Ashton told him. 'Hospital visiting hours in the evening are from six to eight.'

Willie chased the last piece of gâteau round the plate with his fork, killing time until the waitress had placed the cups of coffee in front of them and moved away from the table.

'I had Birgit Simon under surveillance for approximately three weeks during the semester which ended this June. Ever since I have known her, Fräulein von Schinkel has kept a little black book on right-wing extremists. I don't know what the lecturer in computer studies had done to deserve it, but she had a whole page to herself. I got the feeling it was my job to dig up enough dirt to justify the entry.'

With no one to help him with the surveillance, it had only been possible to keep Birgit Simon under observation eight hours in twenty-four. Ten days into the operation, he had felt compelled to ask Helga von Schinkel what she had on the thirty-seven-year-old university lecturer. The damning piece of evidence turned out to be an article Birgit Simon had written for a technical journal with a limited circulation. In it, she had argued that the day would come when computer technology would make even the most skilled manual workers redundant. Eventually it would mean there were too many people chasing too few jobs.

'She reckoned it would lead to social unrest, the like of which the German people hadn't seen since the days of the Weimar Republic in the twenties and thirties. The semi-skilled would be competing with the guest workers for the low-paid jobs and it was necessary to deal with this tumour while it was still operable. I couldn't see it myself but Helga said it was the most vicious, racist piece she had read since Hitler had committed suicide in the bunker.' Baumgart pressed a finger against his temple. 'Personally, I thought she was a bit unbalanced.'

He had changed his mind after breaking into Birgit Simon's flat on Schiller Strasse in broad daylight when she, along with most of the other residents in the apartment house, had been out. Apart from a portrait of the long-dead Führer above her bed, he had found an old photograph album underneath a pile of sweaters on the top shelf in the fitted wardrobe which had been even more revealing.

'From a family photograph on the dressing table, I knew the album had belonged to her mother. There were dozens of snapshots of her hanging on to the arm of a *Hauptsturmführer* in the *Das Reich SS* Panzer Division. He had the Knight's Cross with Oak Leaves and Swords as well as a chestful of campaign medals, and you could tell by the way she was looking up at him that the *Hauptsturmführer* must have been either her lover or first husband. Her brother had served in the same outfit and had evidently survived the war because Birgit had been photographed with him when she was a little girl.' Baumgart took out a packet of cigarettes and lit one. 'You could see the hero worship in her eyes.'

'And that was enough to convince Helga von Schinkel that she was right?'

'Well, Helga closed down the operation a few days later, but it could be she couldn't afford to finance it any longer.'

'You mean she was using her own money?'

'Must have been. I'm pretty sure Herr Franklin didn't know what I was up to because she insisted that what I discovered was for her ears only. Of course the investigation was reopened on an official basis after Joachim Wolff had been assassinated.'

From then on he had reported direct to Head of Station, Berlin. Franklin had wanted Birgit Simon watched all round the clock and to this end had authorised him to recruit a surveillance team. He had also agreed they should bug her flat.

'That's how I knew she was getting information from a police officer called Werner.'

'Did you give Mr Franklin a transcript of their conversation?' Ashton asked.

'I gave him the actual tape and he decided there and then to pull us out.'

'Why?'

'Because, according to Werner, the whole Kripo Division was under investigation and the uniformed branch had confiscated his private telephone directory and her number was in it. Although he hadn't named her, Herr Franklin believed it was only a question of time before the police discovered her identity.'

Ashton could guess the rest. Willie had been told to remove the bug because Franklin was afraid the police might find it if they searched Birgit's flat. He wondered if Franklin had destroyed the tape or locked it away in his safe. The one thing he wouldn't have done was hand it over to Kommissar Voigt.

'The recording was okay, was it, Willie? No background mush or anything like that which might degrade the voices?'

'It was as clear as a bell.'

An inclination to give Franklin the benefit of a lingering doubt receded even farther. By his own admission, he had been present yesterday when Immelmann had suggested the Jurgens would have said anything if it meant the police would stop bothering them. Unless there were two Werners assigned to the Wolff case, he should have recognised the voice.

'I don't suppose you happened to get a photograph of this man while you were watching Birgit Simon?' he asked hopefully.

Baumgart reached inside his jacket and brought out two snap-shots. 'Helga said you were bound to ask so I ran off a couple of prints. The originals were taken the day after it was decided to put the lady under surveillance again.'

'Did you see him enter her flat?'

'No. I can't be a hundred per cent sure that he is the mysterious Werner either, but my nose tells me he is a policeman. He was also heading in the right direction for the Central Police Station when I last saw him.'

'Thanks, Willie.' Ashton pocketed the snaps. 'You've been a great help.'

'Is there anything else I can do?'

'Not at the moment.'

Baumgart levered himself out of the chair and stood up. 'It's been a pleasure meeting you again, Herr Ashton,' he said formally and bowed his head as they shook hands.

For once it looked as if the English Bookshop really was a commercial enterprise. When Ashton walked through the door, five potential customers were hovering round the table where the current UK ten best sellers were on display and there were at least as many others elsewhere in the store. The smile he received from Helga could not have been friendlier; Franklin however was not best pleased to see him when he entered his office unannounced. His expression became even more sour the moment Ashton placed the two snapshots on his blotter.

'Would this be Werner Immelmann?' Ashton asked without preamble.

'You've been talking to Willie Baumgart.' Franklin placed the photographs on one side. 'And behind my back,' he added.

'Yes, that was remiss of me, but I didn't think you would object considering the circumstances.'

'I could have saved you a lot of time and effort if you had spoken to me first.'

'How's that?'

'Willie is inclined to be a little too enthusiastic at times; he's not above fabricating a result if it suits him. He gave me the same two snaps which he claimed had been taken outside the apartment house on Schiller Strasse where Birgit Simon lives. The man could be Immelmann but I've driven up and down that street and I have to say I don't believe those photos were taken on Schiller Strasse.'

'What about the tape?' Ashton said quietly. 'Is it also a fake?'

'No, it's genuine, but it wasn't Immelmann I heard. The voice belonged to someone else.'

Franklin was lying. Ashton was equally certain that he had wiped the tape. There was a time when Franklin would have picked up the phone and discussed the matter with the DG before taking such a drastic step. But Stuart Dunglass was in the chair now and Neil had never seen eye to eye with Victor Hazelwood who had the ear of the new chief.

'It would seem I have made a fool of myself by listening to Willie Baumgart.' Ashton smiled ruefully. 'You can be sure I shan't make that error again.'

'We all make mistakes,' Franklin told him magnanimously.

'No hard feelings then?'

'Of course not.'

Ashton thanked him for being so understanding and apologised yet again for contacting Willie without his prior knowledge. He made no attempt to recover the snapshots before he left; getting another set of prints wasn't a problem and it was important he did not alert Franklin to what he had in mind.

Chapter 22

Blitz Taxis was controlled from an office in Theodor-Heussplatz. A faded sign above the plate glass window showed that at one time in the distant past, the premises had been rented by a ladies' outfitters. Ashton thought it still resembled a small dress shop even though the floor space had been divided in two by a hardboard partition to separate the dispatchers from the purely clerical staff. On that Saturday morning, the front office was being run by a plump brunette in her mid-thirties who, in between answering the phone, was trying to type a letter. A Dymo name tag pinned to her silk blouse identified her simply as Karin.

'I'm here to see Herr Baumgart,' Ashton told her as if he were keeping a prearranged appointment with Willie.

'Your name please?'

'Ashton, Peter Ashton,' he said and saw her eyes flicker briefly.

'I'm sorry, Herr Baumgart is not here this morning. It's his day off.'

Her eyes were fixed on his in a conscious effort to refrain from glancing in the direction of the hardboard partition to her left. Willie had not returned any of his calls since they had parted company in the Zoological Garden and it looked as if he was still determined to avoid him. Although he couldn't distinguish Willie's voice in the general rhubarb, Ashton was sure the German was lurking in the dispatchers' office.

'Can I take a message?' Karin asked, her face assuming a concerned expression.

'Yes, you can tell Willie I'm waiting for him in Bertholt's round the corner in Pommerallee.'

'Bertholt's,' she repeated and wrote it down on a scrap of paper. 'In Pommerallee?'

'You've got it. You can also inform our mutual friend that if I don't see his happy smiling face in the next fifteen minutes, I'm going to have a quiet word with Heinrich Voigt, which will do him no good at all.'

'Heinrich Voigt?' Karin knitted her eyebrows in perplexity. 'The name sounds familiar,' she murmured.

'It certainly is to Willie.'

'But fifteen minutes . . .'

'What's the problem? I'm sure you have his phone number.'

'Yes, we have, but he may not be in.'

'I think you will find that he is,' Ashton told her.

He hoped Bertholt's still existed. Fads and fashions didn't last; yesterday's 'in' place was today's empty property and it was almost two years since he'd put foot inside the *Frühstückskneipe*. For a few bad moments, it looked as if he had picked a bum RV and it was a great relief to discover the café was farther down Pommerallee than he remembered. He had already breakfasted at the Excelsior and wasn't hungry, but you couldn't walk into Bertholt's and just order coffee, so he settled for a platter of cold ham and cheese with pumpernickel bread. Willie limped into the *Frühstückskneipe* with five minutes to spare before the deadline and joined him at the table.

'I'm not very pleased with you,' Baumgart announced. 'Why are you making trouble for me?'

'Suppose you tell me why you've ignored all my calls? I've left messages all over town for you.'

'You should address that question to Herr Franklin.'

'He warned you off?'

'What do you think?'

Franklin was obviously a good deal smarter than he'd allowed for. Leaving the snapshots behind hadn't fooled him one bit; he had read what was in his mind and had taken what he considered was appropriate action.

'He threatened me with Voigt, said the Kommissar would be only

252

too happy to get his hands on me.'

'Why don't you give your order, Willie? The waiter's beginning to take root.'

'What's that you're eating?'

'Ham, cheese and pumpernickel.'

'I'll have the same with a beer,' Baumgart told the waiter, then watched him until he was out of earshot before picking up from where he had left off. 'The Kommissar and I are like cat and dog. He can't forget I called him a cringing arsehole to his face.'

'That wasn't an altogether wise thing to do.'

'Yeah, well he tried to put the knife into me when the press started crusading.'

'The drug pusher who gouged your eye out,' Ashton said, recalling what the German had told him when they had first met. 'I believe in getting even,' Willie had said, 'so I threw him downstairs and he happened to break his neck.' The pusher had been a college kid from a good family with plenty of money and a lot of influence.

'Little shit ended up paralysed from the neck down. The family and their friends put it about that I had tried to kill him and because of the orchestrated wave of protest, I got kicked off the force.' Baumgart shrugged. 'But all that was before Voigt came on the scene. I got in bad with him the last time we teamed up. Remember what happened then?'

Ashton nodded. He was unlikely to forget that episode, even if Willie's injuries were not a visual reminder. Voigt had been convinced the police were dealing with something more than a traffic accident. But Willie had kept his mouth shut and hadn't said what he was doing on the road that night and had consequently spared the SIS a lot of embarrassment.

'My bad-mouthing him isn't the only grudge Kommissar Voigt has against me,' Baumgart continued. 'He doesn't like British Intelligence playing fast and loose on his patch and while he can't prove it, he suspects that I do quite a few odd jobs for you people. That was the other reason for him wanting to throw the book at me. The press making a song and dance about the accident and reminding their readers of the run-in I'd had with the drug pusher was only part of it.'

Voigt had tried to get Willie for manslaughter, had settled for reckless driving and had seen the former detective sergeant get away with careless driving thanks to the wily German lawyer covertly hired by Neil Franklin.

'The Kommissar bends with the wind – is that what you're saying, Willie?'

'He doesn't like bad publicity.'

'So rather than put the Kripo in a bad light he would turn a blind eye towards Nazis like Werner Immelmann?'

'Hey, I didn't say that.' Baumgart broke off while the waiter placed his order in front of him, then said, 'Voigt isn't bent, he's as straight as an arrow. Show him a bad number in his Division and he'll hang the man out to dry.'

'I'm glad to hear it,' Ashton said. 'Makes your phone call to the *Polizeipräsidium* worthwhile.'

Baumgart froze, the fork halfway to his mouth with a piece of ham dangling from the prongs. 'Come again?'

'I want you to ring the Kripo Division.'

'No way.' The fork wagged from side to side like a metronome, the piece of ham describing a gentle are before coming to rest on the floor.

'I want you to ask for the crime index officer, Detective Sergeant Immelmann . . .'

'Are you out of your mind?'

'You're the only man who can recognise his voice,' Ashton continued unperturbed. 'I've not heard the tape and it no longer exists.'

'What about Herr Franklin?'

'He says the voice on the tape is not Immelmann's.'

'Well, there you are then. What more do you want?'

'The truth, and I'm not going to get it from Herr Franklin. If Immelmann is the source, he won't pass it on to Voigt. Look at it from his point of view; in the process of spying on a German national, he broke every rule in the book – housebreaking, illegal phone taps, invasion of privacy – you name it, he sanctioned it. If those offences ever came to light, he would be lucky if he was just deported.' Ashton swallowed the rest of his coffee and placed the cup and saucer on top of the plate for the waiter to clear away. 'He likes the people of this country and wants to spend the rest of his service in Berlin. That's the top and bottom of it.'

'Are you expecting me to pull your chestnuts out of the fire?'

'No, I'm asking you to do it for yourself. We are talking about a potential high-flier in the Kripo who happens to be a neo-Nazi. Now, if this was my country, I wouldn't like to leave a guy like that in place. But of course, I can't answer for you.'

'You don't pull your punches, do you, Herr Ashton?'

'Not when I'm trying to prove a point.'

Baumgart toyed with his food. 'Let me think about it,' he said presently.

'I don't have the time. I'm going home on Tuesday.' Ashton smiled. 'The neurologist at St Thomas's has agreed that Harriet will be fit enough to travel by then.'

'That is good news.'

'Yes, it is, but I don't want to leave any unfinished business behind in Berlin. Immelmann may have saved Harriet from a Turkish mob but he was also the guy who helped to put her in jeopardy in the first place.'

'Oh, Jesus.' Baumgart sighed. 'Okay, I'll do it, but just bear in mind what could happen to me if things go wrong.'

'Don't worry your head about it, I'll stand between you and Voigt.'

'So what am I going to say to Immelmann?'

'Birgit Simon lives on Schiller Strasse – right?'

'Correct.'

'Okay, make up an address on the same street and tell him you believe you saw Joachim Wolff leaving an apartment house down the road from your place only a few hours before he was killed. That is the basic story; pad it out if you have to but get off the phone before they can trace the number.'

'Don't you worry, I'll hang up before they can even think of it.'

They left Bertholt's after Ashton had paid the bill and walked to the nearest pay phone which happened to be opposite the television centre on the Kaiserdamm, a tidy step from the *Frühstückskneipe*.

It was always going to be a hit or miss affair. If Immelmann was on shift, it didn't automatically follow that he would be manning a phone in the Central Police Station, and if it was his day off, they might never run him to ground. Watching him from outside the kiosk, Ashton could see that Willie was having difficulties. After a brief conversation with someone at the *Polizeipräsidium*, he hung up and consulted the telephone directory. He fed another coin into the box and punched out the number he had taken from the book. There followed another brief conversation with apparently an equally negative result. The same thing happened when he tried a second number and Ashton began to wonder just how many Immelmanns there were in the West Berlin directory with the initial W.

Willie got lucky at the fourth attempt, or so it seemed to Ashton. At least, the exchange lasted a good deal longer than any of the previous calls, but that wasn't saying a lot and it was impossible to tell how it was going from his impassive expression. Finally, Willie replaced the phone and backed out of the kiosk.

'Well?' Ashton demanded.

'You were right,' Willie said and grinned. 'Detective Sergeant Immelmann is the Werner I heard on the tape.'

'Terrific. All I need now are two more copies of the snapshots you gave me the other day.'

'Herr Franklin insisted I gave him the negatives.'

Ashton closed his eyes and reeled off a string of four-letter words under his breath. Whatever else he might be, there were no flies on Head of Station, Berlin.

'You should see yourself,' Willie said, laughing.

'It's not a joke.'

'Yes, it is. I told Herr Franklin there were only twenty-four exposures on the roll of film, whereas there were thirty-six.'

'I always knew you were a crafty old fox, Willie,' Ashton said, patting him on the back.

Before unification, Nicholson had enjoyed a rent-free apartment in Potsdam, courtesy of his joint paymasters in the Stasi and KGB. Following that unthinkable event, he had withdrawn all his savings from the State Bank after the money on deposit had been converted to West German marks, and had become something of a gypsy, drifting from town to town. He had first moved to Dresden, then Karl Marx Stadt that had previously been, and was again once more, known as Chemnitz. Four months ago, he had settled in

Leipzig where as a means of protection in an increasingly hazardous environment, he had two accommodation addresses, one in Gross-Zschocher on the south-western outskirts of the city and the other in Schönefeld to the north-east. While not establishing a recognisable pattern, he generally used these safe houses turn and turn about. However, he had spent last night with a hooker at a flat in the Stadtmitte.

The whore had been walking her beat in a side street near the Hauptbahnhof when Nicholson had picked her up. Her name was Marta and she was a Polish girl from Cracow who had come west eighteen months ago looking for a better life and had discovered the age-old way of making money. In pursuit of the D-mark nothing was taboo – straight, oral, Greek-style, he'd left his calling card in every orifice. The only time she had demurred was when he'd gagged and chained her to the bed before going to sleep. While he rode the S-Bahn home, she was still lying there flat on her back waiting to be released when the cleaning lady showed up, arms raised above her head, both wrists manacled by the pair of handcuffs which had been looped around the metal struts of the bedframe.

Nicholson alighted from the six-car suburban train at Schwartzstrasse, turned right outside the station and walked on past the cemetery to his lodgings in Kulkwitzstrasse. Although unshaven, he looked reasonably smart in a pair of slacks and a jacket that was only slightly creased. But it was the briefcase he was carrying which gave him an air of respectability. In East Germany a briefcase was a badge of office and no one he met on the street gave him a second glance.

Leipzig had had its share of air raids during the war and there were still empty spaces in the town centre, but only a few bombs had fallen on the Gross-Zschocher District and his landlady's house had survived the conflict unscathed, though no one would know it now. Years of neglect had left their mark, a large section of the guttering was missing, the windowframes were rotting and deep cracks had appeared in the concrete façade. Digging out his key, Nicholson let himself into the house. As he stepped inside the gloomy hall, his landlady, Frau Meissener, appeared from the kitchen to ask if he had met up with his friends.

'Friends?' he said blankly.

'Yes, two young men, Herr Neurath. They arrived early yesterday evening. I told them you hadn't returned from work and they left saying they would try your office in Lobauerstrasse.'

Nicholson caught his breath. There was no office but he did have rooms on Lobauerstrasse in the Schönefeld District which meant his visitors knew the location of his second bolthole.

'I obviously missed them again,' he said calmly. 'Did they say who they were?'

'I didn't think to ask for their names. One was about your height, the other was much taller, and thinner too. He had a strawberry birthmark on the right cheek.'

Ilya. It could only be Ilya, the Russian who had supplied him with the sniper's rifle. Nicholson thanked her for letting him know about his friends, then climbed the stairs to his room. Moscow had sold him out; there could be no other explanation for what had happened because only his case officer had known where he was living. Ilya and his unknown partner had been told where to find him and they hadn't dropped by for a quiet chat.

Nicholson raised the linoleum in the left-hand corner of the room, then took out his penknife and unscrewed one of the floorboards. Lifting it clear, he reached inside the cavity for the oilskin packet which contained fifteen thousand Deutschmarks, a 5.45 PSM automatic and an out-of-date British passport. It was, Nicholson decided, time to go home.

Hazelwood entered Montrose Place for the second time just as one of the residents of the square pulled out from the kerb. Tripping the indicator as if to turn right, he shot across the road and squeezed the Rover 800 into the now vacant space between a Bentley and the more modestly priced Jaguar XJ6. He had been about to leave the house with Alice when Stuart Dunglass had telephoned full of apologies for asking him to drop everything, but a problem had arisen which couldn't wait until Monday.

Although he had vehemently denied it when taxed by Alice, the fact was the DG's phone call could not have come at a more opportune moment. If there was one thing Hazelwood loathed, it was the once-a-week shopping expedition to the local supermarket, and the summons from Dunglass had therefore come as a merciful reprieve.

This part of Belgravia was regularly patrolled by traffic wardens and he was more likely to get a parking ticket than have the Rover stolen by some mindless joyrider, but Hazelwood didn't believe in taking unnecessary risks. He set the alarm which automatically locked all four doors, the boot and the petrol tank, then crossed the road and walked up the front steps of the large Edwardian town house. The butler-cum-chauffeur-cum-general handyman met him at the door as he reached for the bell-pull. Rowan Garfield was already present when the former Royal Marine corporal showed him into the study. Dunglass poured him a cup of coffee from an elegant piece of Queen Anne silver, then invited Garfield to give a resumé of what had happened during the night.

'The duty officer received a signal from our friends in Virginia,' Garfield told him with all the spontaneity of a man reading a prepared statement displayed on an Autocue. 'To put it in a nutshell, the CIA wants us to share Zelenov with them. This morning, I had an interesting conversation with their man in Grosvenor Square who virtually told me they wouldn't hesitate to filch him if we turned them down.'

'They can forget about whisking him across the pond,' Hazelwood growled. 'According to Ashton, the old man has set his heart on going home to Moscow.'

Garfield smiled wryly. 'When push comes to shove, they have a lot more money to wave under his nose than we do. And as my American friend pointed out to me, Zelenov has already seen the colour of theirs.'

'They've approached him?'

'Yes, Reindekker has been in touch.'

'I wonder how much good that has done them,' Hazelwood mused. 'Somehow I don't imagine Leonid Nikolaevich is too impressed with Messrs Reindekker and Agostini. One is injudicious enough to start a fire fight, the other finishes it and leaves Ashton to clear up the mess. He might think he would be safer dealing with us.'

'Provided Zelenov knows what it's all about.'

'Of course he does,' Hazelwood said testily. 'Leonid Nikolaevich isn't naïve; he knows it isn't his business expertise we're after. Ashton fed him that line as a salve to his conscience.'

'Aren't we straying from the point?' Dunglass looked at each man in turn. 'What we have to decide is whether to call their bluff or go into partnership. What's your opinion, Victor?'

Hazelwood supposed that if they refused to co-operate with the CIA there was always a chance that Zelenov would eventually succumb to their blandishments. However, if they did take him to America, his value would be degraded to the point where it was practically worthless. The old man had never met Valentin and had no idea who he was.

'I don't think Zelenov will be of use to anyone unless he's in Moscow,' Hazelwood said. 'He's the only bait we have which might draw Valentin out into the open and that isn't going to work if he's on the far side of the Atlantic.'

'After what happened in Tallinn, it wouldn't surprise me if we never heard from the "Insider" again.'

Dunglass had cast himself in the role of the sceptic who wanted to be convinced but had yet to hear a persuasive argument. It was a tactic Hazelwood had seen the DG use on a number of occasions when questioning a Head of Department, only this time he was expected to respond and not Garfield.

'I disagree. I believe Valentin will be anxious to discover why Zelenov returned to Moscow and where he got the money to do so. He won't go himself but he will send one of his minions.'

'You seem very confident, Victor.'

'You're surprised? You shouldn't be, we've got two very important factors going for us – greed and fear. Greed because the hundred thousand dollars he got from Ashton won't go very far in view of the number of helpers who will expect their cut. Fear because if Valentin is the ringleader of some kind of conspiracy, he'll want to satisfy himself that Zelenov is not being used as a weapon to bring him down.'

'So what do you advise?'

'I recommend we allow the Yanks to participate on the clear understanding that Zelenov goes to Moscow and nowhere else.'

'I agree with Victor,' Garfield said, venturing a long overdue opinion.

'Thank you for your support,' Hazelwood told him drily. 'There is however one other proviso I should mention. No matter how many dollars the Yanks may contribute, we must run this operation. If we let the CIA take control, they will want to see an early return on their investment and Leonid Nikolaevich Zelenov will not die peacefully in his bed.'

Ashton worked on the letter to Voigt in the privacy of his hotel bedroom. The envelopes and writing pad were the cheapest money could buy and looked it. He had bought the pastepot, scissors and the packet of Letraset, the last in stock, from a general store in the Prenzlauer Berg District of East Berlin. The large pair of rubber gloves had been purchased in a mini market in the same area and he had obtained the *Berliner Morgenpost, Tagesspiegel* and *Telegraf* at a news kiosk on the Ku'damm. The expensive silk scarf and Chanel No. 5 were get well presents for Harriet, the carrier bag which had also come from the KaDeWe department store had served to hide his other purchases when he'd returned to the Excelsior.

Before doing anything else, Ashton locked the door and slipped the security chain into the slot, then donned the pair of rubber gloves. This was a precautionary measure intended to protect Neil Franklin and Helga von Schinkel in case Voigt became nasty and turned his forensic people loose on the English Bookshop. The Kripo specialists might lift his fingerprints from some object on the premises but they weren't going to find a match on the envelope or the anonymous letter inside.

He ripped the Cellophane wrapping from the packet of envelopes and opening the packet of Letraset, selected the letters he needed. With painstaking care he then rubbed them on the envelope, addressing it to Herr Heinrich Voigt at Pommersche Strasse 136, Wilmersdorf, Berlin 31. Sending the letter to his private residence was a lot safer than mailing it to him at the *Polizeipräsidium* where it could be intercepted by Werner Immelmann, the crime index officer for the Wolff investigation.

The letter itself was far more time-consuming and involved a scissors and pastepot job. By the time he had finished composing it, all three newspapers were in shreds. With capital letters unavoidably appearing in the middle of some words, the note looked a mess but at least it was concise and unambiguous. It read: *Birgit Simon lives on Schiller Strasse. Her phone number is 803–9124. She is a Nazi, so is her boyfriend Detective Immelmann.*

He had put the phone number in hoping the uniformed branch still had the sergeant's private directory where it was listed under Simon's first name. The snapshots of Immelmann taken outside her apartment house was the other vital link but they had to be sanitised first. Using the rubber glove like an eraser, he wiped the photos back and front to smear any latent fingerprints he might have left on both surfaces. He enclosed the snapshots with the anonymous letter and then dug out a fifty-pfennig stamp which he thought would cover the postage.

Before peeling off the rubber gloves, he gathered the remnants of the newspapers together and stuffed them into the carrier bag with the pastepot which he planned to drop in a litterbin on his way to the hospital. He used a handkerchief to tuck the envelope into his jacket pocket and would do the same when he popped it into a postbox.

The task had taken him all afternoon. He just hoped Voigt wouldn't consign the letter to the wastebin when he received it on Monday morning.

Chapter 23

Nicholson surrendered to the British Military authorities at four thirty-five on the Sunday afternoon. At least, that had been the time when he'd walked into Oxford Barracks in Münster and informed the guard commander of the 1st Queens Regiment that he was a long-term deserter. It was the only story he could think of which was likely to make the junior NCO take him seriously and although the army was no longer looking for him, no one in the regiment would know that. In all probability the commanding officer himself had only been about four years old when Nicholson had surrendered to the military authorities in 1958. Furthermore, it was the only story which might persuade Headquarters Rhine Army to check the facts with London since his personal file would have been sent to the MoD long ago.

Plausible though his explanation was, it had almost backfired. The corporal, a twenty-four-year-old irrepressible cockney from Bow, had taken one look at his grey hair and called him 'grandad'. The junior NCO had also told him it was a good joke but would he now kindly run along and try it out on someone else, preferably 1st Coldstream Guards on the other side of town.

Two things had persuaded the corporal to take him seriously; the fifteen thousand Deutschmarks he'd emptied out onto the guard-room table and the sight of the 5.45 PSM tucked into the waistband at the back of his trousers. The Makarov automatic had almost got Nicholson killed, thanks indirectly to the Provisional IRA. Unaware that an active service unit of the Provos was operating in West Germany, he had been totally unprepared for the NCO's reaction.

Before he knew what was happening, every off-duty soldier in the guardroom had grabbed his SA80 automatic rifle and he'd ended up facing enough firepower to blow him away in a million pieces. The corporal had kicked his legs from under him and he had landed flat on his face on the concrete floor, loosening a tooth and collecting a bloody nose as a result. After handcuffing his wrists behind him, the soldiers had bundled him into a cell.

The battalion orderly sergeant had arrived a few minutes later and had subsequently been joined by the orderly officer. A major who had identified himself as the field officer of the week had been his next visitor followed by a medical orderly who had cleaned up his battered face.

Still handcuffed, Nicholson had then been handed over to the Military Police and conveyed to Brigade Headquarters where he had been questioned by the Chief of Staff and the Intelligence officer. Although he had given them his old army number and they had examined his out-of-date passport, which the guard commander at Oxford Barracks had found when he'd searched him, both officers had remained unfriendly. The money and the Makarov pistol had coloured their thinking and there had been some talk of handing him over to the German authorities. He had almost pissed in his pants at that, but somehow he had managed to keep his head and had convinced the two officers that they had no authority to hand over a British citizen to a foreign power without due cause.

After consulting Commander 4 Guards Brigade, the Chief of Staff had informed him that he would be held in the unit guardroom under close arrest pending further enquiries. Sunday supper had consisted of eggs, chips and bacon from the NAAFI. Breakfast that morning had been provided by the unit cookhouse and had included cornflakes, egg, sausages, baked beans and fried bread. At 8.30, he was escorted to the headquarters block and on up to the court martial centre where he was shown into the waiting room for prosecution witnesses. The man seated at the table would never see fifty again and was wearing a dark grey two-piece suit which matched the colour of his hair. Not army, Nicholson thought, eyeing his nondescript tie, nor was he a retread holding down a minor staff job.

'Mr Martin Nicholson,' he said without looking up from the

papers on the table. 'Army number 14484443, National Service release group 51.01, deserted 49 Field Regiment the fourteenth of February 1952, surrendered Royal Military Police Helmstedt checkpoint on the eleventh of October 1958.'

'That's me, squire,' Nicholson said.

'And a right bastard you are too.'

The interrogator leaned against the chair back, arms folded across his chest, eyes glittering. A hard nut of an ex-policeman, Nicholson decided, time-filling towards a second pension with the British Services Security Organisation, the away team of MI5. And the dickhead was pulling the oldest stroke in the book, deliberately needling him in the hope he would lose his temper and let something slip.

'If you say so,' Nicholson said and smiled to show he was unruffled.

'Let's talk about this statement you gave the field officer at 1 Queens.'

'Is there something you don't understand?'

'Yes. Why Münster? If you were living in Leipzig, the quickest route to the West is straight down the road to Weimar and on through Erfurt to the old border crossing point at Eisenach.'

'I know, that's the way I came. I then went on to Frankfurt by bus and train.'

'You haven't answered my question.'

'I wanted to surrender to the British Military authorities. So, at Frankfurt I caught the intercity to Hamburg departing at 7.49 yesterday morning. It got me into Münster just over four hours later. Check it out if you don't believe me – the 639 Germania stopping at Wiesbaden, Bonn, Köln, Düsseldorf-Essen, Dortmund, Münster.'

'You should have got off the train at Bonn and saved us all a lot of trouble.'

'And have the British Embassy hand me over to the German authorities?' Nicholson snorted with derision. 'No thank you.'

'So what held you up after you arrived in Münster? It should not have taken you another four hours to get from the station to Oxford Barracks.'

'I rang the Ministry of Defence in London. I wanted to let

someone with a bit of clout know that I was on the way back in case the army tried to give me the brush-off. Took me a hell of a time to get hold of a duty officer in the Adjutant General's Branch.'

'I bet he was pleased to hear from you, yesterday's no account deserter. Couldn't hack it in 49 Field Regiment, couldn't hack it behind the Iron Curtain, couldn't hack it when you came crawling back, and couldn't hack it the second time around in East Germany.'

'The Russians were after me,' Nicholson told him.

'The Russians? Jesus, that's rich.'

'I worked for the Stasi.'

'Yeah? Doing what?' The interrogator leaned across the table until their faces were only an inch apart and Nicholson could smell the peppermint on his breath. A drinker, he thought, the evidence was there in his florid complexion. 'Cleaning the Stasi's toilets at 22 Normannenstrasse? That would be about your number – shithouse Martin Nicholson, king of the bogs.'

Nicholson clenched both hands, digging his fingernails into the palms. The dickhead on the other side of the table was beginning to get under his skin, which was the whole idea. Injured pride would make him boastful, that was the theory he was working on.

'Where did you get the fifteen thousand marks?'

'From my bank account. I was well paid by the KGB as well as the Stasi.'

'No, you're a car thief, Martin, that's your special racket. You've been nicking Mercs and BMWs off the street, then running them into Poland where it's cash on delivery and no questions asked. Some of the dealers from Moscow are even willing to put money up front for a particular model. You made a contract with one of the dealers and cheated on him. That's how you got the money, that's why the Russians are after you, that's why you did a runner.'

'You can provoke me all you like,' Nicholson told him, 'but you'll get nothing from me. You don't have the clout to grant me immunity and I'm not naming any KGB case officers until I get it.'

The interrogator smiled wryly. 'I'll say this for you, Martin,' he intoned, 'you've certainly got style. But you're still a con man.'

'No, I'm the genuine article, and we both know it.'

'I do?'

'I didn't tell anybody in 1 Queens that I had deserted from 49 Field Regiment which means you'd already checked me out with the Ministry of Defence before starting this interview.'

The nameless security officer left the table to summon two military policemen who were waiting in the corridor. His deadpan expression gave nothing away but Nicholson took comfort from the fact that in place of the two young lance corporals who had collected him from Oxford Barracks, his escort now comprised a sergeant and an equally hard-bitten full corporal. It showed the appropriate authorities were taking him very seriously.

The Joint Intelligence Committee met every Tuesday at ten o'clock. The meeting was chaired by the Secretary of the Cabinet Office and was attended by the Directors General of the SIS, MI5, GCHQ Cheltenham and the Chief of the Defence Intelligence Staff. As had been the practice of his predecessor, Dunglass liked department heads to bring him up to date the day before the weekly gathering. The briefing conference usually started at 10.30 and lasted all morning. However, on this particular Monday, Hazelwood found himself attending a preliminary session with Garfield and the DG minutes after walking into the office.

Garfield had had a busy weekend. After leaving the DG's house in Montrose Place, he had spent the rest of Saturday brokering a deal with the friends in Grosvenor Square. Once that had been secured with no strings attached, he had produced a draft instruction for Head of Station, Moscow, which Dunglass had finally approved late yesterday morning. The fair copy had then been delivered to the Foreign and Commonwealth Office for onward dispatch.

'Fortunately, it arrived in time to be included in the diplomatic bag,' Garfield told him.

'Who's the courier?' Hazelwood asked.

'The retired naval commander – Osbourne. Of course, he hasn't seen the instruction and hasn't been told what it's about.'

'Pity. It would have been helpful to know how it was received in Moscow.'

'You're not expecting Head of Station to make difficulties, are you, Victor?' Dunglass said quietly.

'Depends what restraints we have put upon him.'

'Well, money certainly isn't one of them,' Garfield said, intervening quickly. 'We've practically got a blank cheque from the CIA, and we all know that if you've got the dosh, there's nothing you can't buy in Russia.'

'Dosh?'

'Street talk for money, Director,' Hazelwood growled.

'It's actually found its way into the Concise Oxford Dictionary, Victor.'

'Is that germane to our discussion?'

'Not really,' Garfield said with a nervous smile.

'So what is?'

'Well, I've suggested that one of the commercial attachés should acquire the flat we need for the Zelenovs.'

Hazelwood had no quarrel with that. The embassy's commercial attachés were responsible for promoting trade between the UK and Russia, a duty which included advice to British businessmen on local customs and furnishing such practical assistance as was required. And what could be more practical than finding suitable accommodation in the Moscow area for the Russian-born representative of Stilson Manufacturing? There was another consideration. Head of Station had been in post for nearly four years and had probably been identified as the SIS resident. His involvement with the local housing market might well draw attention to the Zelenovs and place them in danger. In any event, Head of Station would have his work cut out distancing himself from the business of recruiting a surveillance team to keep a protective eye on Leonid Nikolaevich and Vera Vorontsova.

'Has the Ambassador been told we mean to use one of his commercial attachés?'

'He's about to be,' Dunglass said. 'The Permanent Undersecretary wasn't very enthusiastic but in the end he agreed it was the only practical solution.'

There were times when Hazelwood wondered if their appointments had somehow been reversed and he was the DG. Dunglass had cut his teeth in a series of minor engagements during the confrontation with Indonesia when Sukarno had tried to take over the whole of Borneo by force. He had then gone on to spend the greater part of his career in the Far East and had become Deputy Director after a spell as department head of the Pacific Basin. None of his peer group had thought he was being groomed for stardom and his appointment to Director General had come as a complete surprise to many people. Dunglass had a good brain and was nobody's fool, but even after a year in the chair, he was still inclined to seek Hazelwood's approval for decisions he had already taken.

'It may be a little premature,' Dunglass continued, 'but perhaps we should give some thought to Zelenov's reception when he arrives in Moscow.'

'He will be looking for a familiar face, Director.'

'Quite so. How do you feel about sending Ashton to meet him at the airport?'

'I wouldn't be too happy about it, his face is too well known in Moscow.'

'When was he last there?'

'March-April last year.'

'Fifteen months ago,' Dunglass said meaningfully.

'Even so, I don't think we should risk it.'

'Crawford then, the SAS warrant officer?'

'He doesn't speak a word of Russian and Zelenov has no English.'

'In that case, it will have to be Ashton or a complete stranger.'

The phone rang just as Dunglass started to explain why there wouldn't be time to send one of Garfield's desk officers to Tallinn in order to get acquainted with the Russian. Answering it with a terse 'Yes?' he then calmed down and told his personal assistant he would take the call. The ensuing conversation was brief and entirely one-sided.

'That was really for you,' he informed Garfield afterwards. 'The Armed Forces Desk rang your department to say they had just had a call from the Adjutant General's Branch. Martin Nicholson has surrendered himself to 4 Guards Brigade in Münster.'

At first, Hazelwood couldn't take it in, then a dozen questions sprang to mind, but there wasn't anything else Dunglass could tell them apart from the fact that he'd walked into Oxford Barracks on Sunday afternoon.

'4 Guards Brigade will have informed Rhine Army.' Dunglass pursed his lips. 'I imagine someone from the British Services

Security Organisation is questioning him right now.'

'Perhaps we ought to let the firm in Gower Street know we have an interest?' Garfield suggested diffidently.

'We have to do better than that.' Dunglass left his desk to go walkabout, part of the process of thinking on his feet. As was usually the case, he ended up gazing out at the Thames. 'I want Nicholson brought to England so that we can interrogate him in depth over several weeks. We'll have to move fast, but don't involve our people in Bonn. The German Intelligence Service is aware that Nicholson is the assassin the Stasi referred to as "The Englishman". If the BND learns he is in custody, we'll lose him to them. Get on to the training school and tell the Commandant that Crawford is to report here for briefing soonest. He can bring Nicholson home.' He paused, then said, 'I suppose we had better inform the army, Victor?'

Hazelwood told him he would attend to it and returned to his office. He rang the Special Projects branch of Military Operations, briefed Lieutenant Colonel Yeomans and asked him to take whatever steps were necessary to ensure there wasn't a last-minute hitch with 4 Guards Brigade when Crawford arrived to collect their prisoner. That one telephone call should have been enough, but nothing in life was ever simple. Special arrangements had to be made if Nicholson was to be spirited out of West Germany in secrecy, a problem only the RAF could solve. Finally, Dunglass came to the conclusion that two escorts were better than one, a decision which involved Hazelwood making a difficult phone call to Head of Station, Berlin.

The anonymous letter had arrived only a few minutes before Voigt normally left his apartment in Wilmersdorf for the *Polizeiprä-sidium*. The allegations in the almost illiterate note had both angered and sickened him and he had been sorely tempted to destroy it. Then he had read the text a second time and had reluctantly accepted that it was not a poison pen letter.

He had always regarded Sergeant Immelmann as one of the best and brightest officers in the Kripo and had predicted a brilliant future for him. Only the other day he had commended him for the cool way he had handled a dangerous situation when a crowd of

Turkish youths had rioted on Katzbach Strasse. If he hadn't been there, the British Consul in Berlin would have been sending Fräulein Egan back to her native land in a coffin. Unfortunately, it was now evident that Werner Immelmann was not whiter than white.

The snapshots enclosed by the anonymous author had removed any lingering doubt because there was no mistaking the blond man in the foreground. Whether or not Immelmann had been photographed on Schiller Strasse was immaterial; the phone number had been the really damning piece of evidence. The internal investigation of the Kripo Division which the Police President had initiated at his request was still in continuance and he had gone straight to the property room and checked Immelmann's private telephone directory. Birgit – 803–9124; the name and number had leaped at him off the page and he had felt sick and winded as though he had been punched in the stomach.

In a perverse way, he wished Immelmann had destroyed his personal directory. Nobody liked having their worst fears confirmed and he had hoped nothing would come of the inquiry. Every other officer was under the impression that they were being investigated because some smart aleck lawyer had alleged that certain members of the Kripo were on the take, but the detective sergeant should have guessed what lay behind it. As the crime index officer for the Wolff investigation, Immelmann was aware he suspected the assassin had received an update on the security measures in force from someone in the *Polizeipräsidium*. What in God's name had made him hang on to the bloody directory? Arrogance? Stupidity? Or a psychological desire for martyrdom?

Voigt looked at the snapshots again. They had been taken in the course of an unauthorised surveillance operation that smacked of an SIS involvement. The anonymous letter had been sent to his home address which, although known to his own officers, was not accessible to members of the public. Neil Franklin was in fact one of the few outsiders who knew where he lived. And if he was right in thinking the SIS were up to their old tricks, he could guess who had been the real driving force behind the operation. Fräulein Helga von Schinkel had always had a bee in her bonnet about neo-Nazis and he'd heard all about her little black book. With or without

Franklin's knowledge, she had targeted Birgit Simon and had ensnared his detective sergeant as a result. It might be irrational but he hated her for doing that to him. She had made him look at his officers with a jaundiced eye and left him wondering who among them he could now trust.

Voigt crossed the room and fed the snapshots and the anonymous letter into the waste destructor, but it solved nothing. He could not put the allegations out of his mind and carry on as if nothing had happened. Returning to his desk, Voigt picked up the phone, rang enquiries and asked the chief supervisor to identify the subscriber on 803–9124. It took the supervisor less than a minute to access the information on the computer and inform him the subscriber in question was a Fräulein Birgit Simon. He made one further telephone call, this time to the local branch of the Office for the Protection of the Constitution to see what, if anything, they had on her. Although it didn't amount to much, the fact that she was listed as a possible National Socialist was sufficient to leave him with no choice but to send for Immelmann.

'Fräulein Birgit Simon,' Voigt said without any preamble. 'I understand you are acquainted with the lady?'

'Yes, Herr Kommissar. She literally bumped into me one evening about three months ago in a *Gasthof* off the Tiergarten. I think it was the Gasthof Leica in Lenne Strasse. Anyway, we . . . er . . .' Immelmann bowed his head and stared at the floor as if too embarrassed to look him in the eye. 'Became good friends,' he finished.

'Good friends?'

'Lovers,' Immelmann murmured and shifted uncomfortably. 'To be honest, Kommissar, she is a bit of a dog.'

It was, Voigt thought, a class act, an Oscar-worthy performance. There had, however, been one minor imperfection in what otherwise would have been a flawless piece of acting. An innocent man would have looked surprised when asked about his relationship with Birgit Simon, but Immelmann had been ready with an explanation as if the questions had long been anticipated. In a voice that was coldly dispassionate, Voigt informed him that he was suspended from duty until further notice.

'But I don't understand—' Immelmann began.

'Yes, you do; you're the informer and you also did your best to conceal the identity of the assassin.' Voigt raised his voice. 'Now leave your warrant card on the desk and get your miserable body out of my sight.'

Ashton had been about to leave for the hospital when Helga had phoned to say that Herr Franklin wished to see him urgently. He had tried to explain that Harriet was expecting him but she had refused to listen. She had sounded agitated and he had assumed Voigt suspected the SIS had been the author of the anonymous letter he'd received and there had been an almighty bust-up. To be told that Nicholson was in custody was the last thing he'd expected when he'd walked into Franklin's office.

'4 Guards Brigade down in Münster are holding him.'

'Well, bully for them,' Ashton said.

'You're wrong there, he's all yours – and Crawford's, I hasten to add.'

'I must be dense.'

'You and the SAS warrant officer are taking Nicholson back to England. You are to meet Crawford at Köln airport, pick up Nicholson from the guardroom in York Barracks and convey him to Gütersloh where the RAF will have a BAe 146 waiting to fly you out. Your Lufthansa flight leaves Berlin-Tegel at 15.25, one hour and eighteen minutes from now. Collect your plane tickets from Helga on the way out.'

'Harriet—'

'For God's sake,' Franklin said, cutting him short, 'this comes first.'

'You think I don't know that?' Ashton said in a cold fury. 'I was about to ask you to let her know what's happened.'

'That's already been taken care of. I telephoned her parents at the Schweizerhof and explained matters. Do you have any other questions?'

'Only one. Have we cleared this with the German authorities?'

'That's not your problem.'

'In other words, they don't know.'

'The BND have been informed, told Nicholson is the assassin the Stasi referred to as "The Englishman". If there is a warrant out for

Nicholson's arrest, I'm not aware of it.'

'I thought the government wanted us to be good Europeans. I mean, even supposing he didn't kill Wolff, he murdered at least half a dozen people in West Germany, all of them good men. We should hand the bastard over.'

'And we will, just as soon as we've learned the names of his masters in the KGB.'

'I'd like to believe that,' Ashton said quietly.

'Well, you can, you have my word on it.' Franklin paused, then delivered the clincher. 'It's common knowledge that I want to spend the rest of my service in this city. You don't think I would risk being declared *persona non grata* by the Foreign Ministry in Bonn, do you?'

Chapter 24

Heinrich Voigt could not recall a week which had begun so disastrously. He was a man who liked everything to be in order and the collapse of his neat, self-contained little world had been triggered by the anonymous letter. *Birgit Simon lives on Schiller Strasse. Her phone number is 803–9124. She is a Nazi, so is her boyfriend Detective Immelmann.* Those three short sentences had virtually destroyed the Kripo Division and had made him indecisive. He should have raided the apartment house on Schiller Strasse before he had suspended Immelmann from duty, not two hours afterwards. But he hadn't known whom he could trust among his subordinates and had anguished over the composition of the search party.

In the end, he had gone to the Office for the Protection of the Constitution and asked for their assistance which inevitably had held things up. The delay had been fatal because it had given Birgit Simon time to remove any evidence linking her to the New National Socialist Party before he had arrived with a search warrant. She was waiting for him now in one of the interview rooms down the corridor from his office, utterly confident that he would have to let her go. The only reason she had a lawyer sitting in with her was because he had insisted she was legally represented.

Voigt opened the folder containing the artist's impression of Martin Nicholson and a list of names with brief notes. He wished he hadn't fed the snapshots into the shredder because he had precious little in the way of hard evidence to play with and would have to rely on bluff. He had been introduced to the game of poker when on an exchange visit with the NYPD many years ago and had proved to be a surprisingly adept pupil. None of his American friends had ever been able to read what he was holding in his hand and he just hoped the highly intelligent Fräulein Simon wasn't too familiar with the game. Leaving his office, he walked on down to the interview room where she was waiting to be interrogated.

The attorney she had chosen was thought to be politically untainted. He was a large, jovial man in his early fifties who looked as though he would feel more at home running a bistro rather than practising law. On the other hand, his chubby fingers, plump stomach and double chin suggested he would probably eat most of the profit. In Voigt's experience, thin, hungry-looking lawyers were usually anxious to make a name for themselves and were inclined to be difficult, unlike the well-fed and obviously contented variety who didn't have anything to prove and were therefore generally amenable. There was however always an exception to every rule and Fräulein Simon's legal adviser happened to be one.

'I wish to lodge a strong protest, Herr Kommissar,' he said before Voigt could pull out a chair and sit down facing lawyer and client. 'This is a free country and the police have no right to question Fräulein Simon about her political beliefs.'

'This is a murder inquiry,' Voigt said, effectively cramping his style.

'Murder?' the lawyer repeated and gaped at him, fish eyes popping behind his spectacles.

'Joachim Wolff. I presume the case is familiar? It was extensively reported on TV and in the newspapers.' Voigt turned to Birgit Simon. 'I had a long talk with Detective Sergeant Immelmann this morning,' he said. 'I understand he is a very good friend?'

'That's correct.'

'In fact, would it not be correct to say that you are lovers?'

'Is that a crime now, Herr Kommissar?'

'The sergeant has been suspended from duty pending further enquiries. When these have been completed, I expect to charge him with being an accessory to murder. As you might guess, we've had him under surveillance for some time.'

'I don't understand what all this has to do with me.'

'He provided this man with vital information.' Voigt produced the artist's impression and placed it in front of her. 'His name is Martin Nicholson, he is the man who shot Joachim Wolff, he is the hired killer the Stasi referred to as "The Englishman".'

'This is all very interesting but I still don't see—'

'Are you sure Sergeant Immelmann never mentioned his name in your presence? You know – pillow talk?'

'You don't have to answer that question, Fräulein Simon,' the lawyer told her.

'It's all right, Gunther, I've nothing to hide.' She turned to Voigt with a brilliant smile. 'We have this understanding, Herr Kommissar. Neither of us talks shop when we are together. In any case, we are much too busy making love.'

She was very sure of herself and patronising with it. Voigt hoped this overweening conceit might yet prove her undoing because he had precious few surprises up his sleeve. 'How long have you known Sergeant Immelmann?'

'Three months.'

'You are an oddly matched couple if I may say so. A university lecturer and a policeman – how did you come to meet one another?'

Birgit Simon opened her handbag, took out a packet of Turkish cigarettes and lit one from a book of matches. 'I literally bumped into him. I was with a group of my students in this *Gasthof* near the Tiergarten and I was waving my arms about to emphasise a point . . .'

Voigt knew how the story was going to end and didn't bother to listen. Her account of their meeting was a repeat of the one Immelmann had given him almost word for word. She had been well rehearsed and there was no way he was going to catch her out.

'Can you remember the name of this *Gasthof*?' he asked when she had finished.

'I think it was the Leica . . . in Lenne Strasse.'

The momentary hesitation and the puzzled frown were very convincing and Voigt knew his chances of nailing her were dwindling. He opened the folder and looked at the list of neo-Nazis stapled to the cover which the Berlin Office for the Protection of the Constitution had given him. Immelmann had told Birgit Simon what security measures would be in force for the neo-Nazi rally at the *Bierkeller* on Katzbach Strasse and she had passed the information on to a third party. But who? Someone in the movement who had a low profile, someone she could approach without arousing suspicion? He ran his eye down the list again and took a chance on the psychiatrist.

'Let's talk about Leopold Ultich. When was the last time you made an appointment to see him?'

'I don't know anyone called Leopold Ultich,' she told him quickly, but her voice was proof that she was shaken, and Voigt knew he had her by the throat.

'Now you are being very foolish. You will have spoken to his secretary when you made an appointment to see him and your name will be on record.' He pointed to the artist's impression of Martin Nicholson. 'This man has been identified by the Jurgens, there is a warrant out for his arrest and Interpol has been informed. Make no mistake, we shall catch him and when we do, he will talk his head off – names, telephone numbers, everything – no one will be safe. I recommend you give some very serious thought to your own position, Fräulein.'

There was a long pause, then Gunther asked if he might have a word in private with his client.

Although Köln is also the airport for Bonn, it was scarcely in the international league and was no busier than Luton. Consequently, Ashton had no difficulty in spotting Crawford amongst the sparse crowd waiting in the concourse. The SAS warrant officer had flown into Düsseldorf, rented an Audi from the car hire desk and thundered on down the autobahn to arrive roughly twenty minutes before the Lufthansa flight from Berlin touched down.

'How's Miss Egan?' he asked as they left the terminal building and walked towards the short-stay car park.

'Harriet's flying home tomorrow,' Ashton told him.

'That's good news.'

'Yes, it is. She will be convalescing at her parents' home in Lincoln for the next three weeks or so.' Or even longer, he thought. Perhaps she might never return to London? From little things she had said to him, the prospect of going back to work seemed to worry Harriet. Significantly, all the get well cards she had received from colleagues at Gower Street and Benbow House had gone straight into the drawer of the bedside locker with scarcely a second glance. 'I should be with her,' Ashton said aloud.

'Yeah, I know. Somebody gave you the short end of the stick.' Crawford unlocked the Audi and waited until Ashton had got in beside him before continuing. 'But look at it this way, you'll be there to meet her off the plane, once we've delivered this piece of crap who calls himself an Englishman.'

Ashton supposed it was a small consolation. He just hoped Franklin had made it clear to Harriet's parents that he hadn't volunteered for the job.

'Any idea where we are taking Nicholson?' he asked.

'No. All I know is our responsibility ends when we arrive at RAF Lyneham where a reception committee will be waiting for us.'

Crawford drove out of the car park and followed the signs for the autobahn to Leverkusen, Remscheid and Wuppertal. The evening rush hour was at its height and it was stop-go all the way from the moment they left the airport. Road repairs added to the chaos.

'Do you think we'll have any trouble with the German authorities?' Crawford asked.

'Not unless they know Nicholson is in custody.'

'That's what bothers me.'

'Do you know something I don't?'

'Somebody from the British Services Security Organisation was questioning Nicholson this morning. I just wonder who else 4 Guards Brigade have told. If they've informed the Joint Services liaison officer we could be in deep shit.'

Crawford didn't have to spell it out for him. The JSLO was the link man between the local garrison commander and the Burgomeister. He was responsible for ironing out any little difficulties which arose between the army and the local population. And the best way of doing that was to make sure they never surfaced in the first place. Even if the JSLO wasn't aware of Nicholson's history, he might well consider it was his duty to inform the police chief of Münster about the sixty-one-year-old deserter who had surrendered to the military authorities.

'What time are 4 Guards Brigade expecting us?'

'Eighteen forty-five,' Crawford told him.

'Better put your foot down then.'

The SAS warrant officer had every intention of doing just that. Tripping the indicator, he went on down the slip road to the autobahn and moved into the slow lane. Crawford watched the traffic coming up behind him in the wing mirror, saw a gap and pulled out, flooring the accelerator as he did so. Ashton watched the speedo needle climb above a hundred and sixty and mentally converted it to miles per hour.

'They ever tell you what was in that second lot of microfilm that cost the poor old taxpayer a cool hundred thousand dollars?'

'It was a contingency plan in case Boris Yeltsin decided force was the only way he could bring the Ukrainians to heel.' Ashton shook his head. 'And I got that from Valentin.'

'The high-priced help were sheltering behind the need-to-know principle, were they?'

'Damn right,' Ashton said tersely.

It made sense to withhold classified information from people who could function perfectly well without it, but all the same, there had been times when Hazelwood could have been a little more forthcoming and taken him into his confidence. What was so secret about Denista for God's sake? Had she been booted out of the embassy in Sofia or was HMG still thinking about granting her asylum? It would be nice if just once in a while you were allowed a glimpse of the whole picture so that you could see what difference, if any, your contribution had made.

'Has Nicholson got anything to do with our mysterious Russian?'

'Well, I'm told Valentin tipped us off about the Stasi file on him.' Ashton rubbed his chin. 'And I suppose Nicholson might have met Valentin sometime in the distant past.'

'Yeah?'

'Except I doubt if he was aware of it.'

'Terrific,' Crawford grunted. 'I might have guessed there would be a fly in the ointment.'

They drove on, Crawford holding the outside lane until a BMW flashed him to move over. Ashton calculated they were still doing over a hundred miles an hour when the overtaking vehicle shot past them as if they were dawdling along at a sedate thirty.

'There goes somebody in a hurry to meet his maker,' Crawford observed laconically.

Somebody had been. Approximately ten kilometres west of Kamen Kreuz, the interchange for the E3 autobahn to Münster, traffic on all three lanes slowly ground to a halt. Some distance up ahead, a pall of black smoke rose lazily into the evening sky.

Hugo Calthorpe was in his last eight months as Head of Station, Moscow. He had been in post longer than anyone else in the embassy and was fond of telling newcomers he'd had a full head of light brown hair when he'd arrived in the former Soviet Union. He was not, however, the worrying kind and the cares of office were not the cause of his receding hairline. Both his father and grandfather had been completely bald by the time they were fifty and he expected to be similarly afflicted in another four years. Richard Quennell, the current Head of Chancery, was another cross he bore with cheerful fortitude.

Quennell was forty-one, five years his junior. He had left Cambridge with a double first and his star had been in the ascendancy ever since. He had married into an affluent, well-connected family and was widely seen as a future Permanent Undersecretary. In part, this was due to his happy knack of being in the right place at the right time. The previous Head of Chancery had not enjoyed the best of health and as the senior First Secretary, Quennell had frequently deputised for him. His repatriation on medical grounds at the beginning of the year had meant that Quennell had been promoted to Counsellor six months earlier than he might otherwise have anticipated.

The staff list showed that under His Excellency the Ambassador Extraordinary and Plenipotentiary, there was in descending order of importance, one minister and three counsellors. On Orwell's principle that like the pigs in *Animal Farm*, some men are more equal than others, Quennell was apt to treat both Head of Commerce and Calthorpe as if they were his subordinates. Calthorpe remembered a time not so very long ago when Quennell would have trotted along to his office having asked if he could spare him a few minutes, but nowadays it was the other way round.

'Good of you to drop in, Hugo,' he said, welcoming him with a brilliant smile.

Calthorpe was inclined to agree with him. The lights were on in the Kremlin Palace across the Moscow River from the embassy and the golden onion domes of the Cathedral of the Annunciation were floodlit; if he had left just two minutes earlier after working well beyond normal office hours, Quennell would never have caught him.

'I know it's not my province,' Quennell continued, 'but this business with Major General Zelenov is a bit of a shaker. His Excellency and the Minister are not at all keen on the idea. As for Commerce, he's bloody unhappy about it, and who can blame him?'

Calthorpe could sympathise with him. Only a year ago, Head of Commerce had seen his Third Secretary become a cat's paw in the hands of the SIS through a chain of adverse circumstances beginning with a minor breach of security which had not been wholly the junior attaché's fault. Now the same thing was about to happen again, this time on instructions from London.

'The thing is, Hugo, the tradesmen are worried their involvement with the Zelenovs might not end with the acquisition of a suitable apartment for them.'

Tradesmen was the collective noun Quennell applied to the commercial attachés. Depending on his audience, his manner was either jocular, bordering on the affectionate, or else snide and disparaging. Like the SIS, he did not regard them as fully paid-up members of the Diplomatic Corps. With one or two exceptions, the vast majority had been recruited from industry and the business world for a specific purpose and were therefore not as well rounded as the entrant from Oxbridge. The present Commercial Counsellor had graduated in business studies at Manchester University and had then worked for Courtaulds and BP before he was recruited by the Foreign and Commonwealth Office.

'Your master didn't make himself very clear on this point,' Quennell continued, flashing another brilliant smile. 'And of course it was no use asking Reggie Osbourne to enlighten us because he hadn't been briefed. So I wondered if you could set our minds at rest, Hugo? Presumably you've received certain instructions from your people in London?'

'You're right, I have,' Calthorpe told him. 'And it's not the Director's intention to involve the Commercials in the actual operation.'

'It's not his intention,' Quennell repeated thoughtfully. 'Why do I get the impression he's hedging his bets?'

'Perhaps because you've got that sort of mind, Richard.'

'Now I am worried.'

'You've no reason to be. I'm going to be running things this end.'

Calthorpe did not add that his hand would not be directly on the tiller. London had told him to go out and recruit a surveillance team from the indigenous population and he therefore planned to exercise control through Katya Malinovskaya, a former member of the KGB's Criminal Investigation Division. An attractive twenty-nine-year-old brunette, she had been singled out for accelerated promotion in order to give the old Second Chief Directorate a new and acceptable image. But as Calthorpe knew from personal experience, Katya Malinovskaya had been more than just a pretty face and there was no telling how far she might have gone in the service had not a hired killer plunged a knife into her back. Discharged on medical grounds four months later, she had formed her own security firm and was much in demand by local entrepreneurs in need of protection from the *Mafiozniki*.

'Your Director seems to set great store by this old Red Army man, Hugo.'

'Well, he expects Zelenov to lead us to the mysterious Valentin.'

'I wouldn't hold my breath if I were him,' Quennell said. 'He could be in for a long wait. After all, we have been trying to identify this "Insider" ever since he first made contact with us.'

Calthorpe noted the 'we'. Quennell's sole contribution had been to hand over the microfilm which had come into his possession via the wife of the Second Secretary, Information and Cultural Affairs. She had been ice skating in Gorky Park and had been sent flying by some clumsy Russian who had bumped into her. Full of apologies, he had picked her up and in the process had slipped the microfilm into her coat pocket. That first delivery had been in the way of an introductory offer and, in addition to some hogwash about an unnamed British deserter, had included an extract of the evaluation report on the germ warfare trials conducted by the Soviet Maritime Air Force against the UK in 1967. There had been one further contact when Valentin had indicated how future lines of communication were to be established. Thereafter, Valentin had dealt direct with London.

'You have to give our friend this much,' Quennell said. 'He knew what he was doing when he decided to approach us through Laura; the woman's not in this world half the time.'

Calthorpe had never met anyone quite so fey as Laura. She had no memory for names or faces, and stories about her social gaffes were legion. Small wonder then that she had been unable to describe the man who had skated into her other than in the most general terms. Laura hadn't even been able to do that on the second and last occasion Valentin had contacted her. It had happened sometime during a guided tour of the Kremlin which had included the State Armoury, the Cathedral of the Annunciation and the Palace of Facets. She had found the microfilm in her coat pocket later that evening but only after an anonymous caller had phoned the apartment to suggest she might have picked up the wrong tickets at the Bolshoi.

'This UK firm Zelenov is supposed to be representing,' Quennell said, going down another track, 'does it actually exist, Hugo?'

'Yes, it's in Acton. As a matter of fact, we have used Stilson Manufacturing before; they did some good work for us in Czechoslovakia back in the seventies. Their reps used to furnish reports on the war potential of the factories they visited – that sort of thing. It was all low-level stuff but very useful. Moreover, none of their reps ever came to the notice of the Czech Security Service, the *Statna Tauna Bezpecnost*. This means the firm is unlikely to have been carded by the KGB before the organisation became defunct.' Calthorpe smiled. 'I imagine that should reassure our fellow Counsellor.'

'He'll be even happier if his attachés are not required to meet the Zelenovs.'

'They aren't. London will make sure they have somebody on the spot to do that, probably the man who recruited Leonid Nikolaevich.'

'And who was that?'

'Ashton.'

Quennell closed his eyes. 'Dear God, not him,' he intoned. 'Last time Ashton was in Moscow there was bloodshed all over the city.'

★ ★ ★

They left the E3 autobahn at Münster South and headed into town on Route 51a, then made a right turn on to Albersloher Weg for Loddenheide. It had taken the emergency services almost four hours to clear the obstruction and even then, only one lane was open. Ashton assumed the police, fire service and paramedics had had to approach the scene of the accident from the north because the traffic had been triple-banked for miles behind them. A twenty-vehicle pile up, Crawford had observed as they crawled past the tangled wreckage which had been strewn over a distance of something like two hundred yards. One car had somersaulted over the central barrier and collided with the oncoming traffic, which explained why nothing had passed them going in the opposite direction while they had been stuck in the log jam.

'Not much farther now,' Crawford said.

'You know this part of the world?'

'There was a time when I did, but it's changed out of all recognition since my day. York Barracks belonged to the *Luftwaffe* prewar and the other three camps are built on what was the airfield.'

In rapid succession they passed the entrances to Buller, Minden and Waterloo; shifting into third, Crawford tripped the indicator to show they were turning right up ahead. The two signboards fronting the gateposts informed visitors that York Barracks was occupied by Headquarters 4 Guards Brigade and the 1st Battalion The Coldstream Guards.

Although both wrought-iron gates were open, the barrier was down across the road and an armed sentry confronted them from the sangar directly to their front. A second Coldstream appeared from the dark shadows in the lee of the guardroom and moved purposefully towards the Audi, his SA80 automatic rifle at the ready.

Lowering the window on his side, Ashton produced his passport for inspection and vouched for Crawford. 'I believe you've been warned to expect us,' he said.

The army had a way of doing things. The sentry called for the guard commander, and the guard commander in turn sent for the picquet officer. There was a further delay while he phoned the Chief of Staff at Brigade Headquarters. Long before the latter arrived from his quarter in nearby Angelsachsenweg, Ashton sensed there had been some kind of last minute cock-up. When the Chief of Staff swept in through the barrack gates in a Peugeot and told them to follow him round to Brigade Headquarters, Ashton knew he wasn't guilty of being unduly pessimistic.

Chapter 25

Hidden from view behind a dense row of plane trees, Brigade Headquarters was located in a barrack block diagonally opposite and approximately one hundred yards beyond the guardroom. The reserved parking slots in front of the building were marked with neat signs planted in the grass verge bordering the kerb. There were seven in all; Brigade Commander, Chief of Staff, Deputy Chief and one each for the four grade three staff officers responsible for Operations, Intelligence, Logistics and Personnel. Crawford parked their car in the next slot beyond the Peugeot which happened to be the space allocated to the Brigadier commanding 4 Guards Brigade.

'Moving up in the world, are we?' Ashton said.

'Nothing like being ambitious. Should I stay in the car, or what?'

'I think you'd better tag along.'

Ashton got out of the Audi and crossed the narrow internal road to join the Chief of Staff who was waiting for him on the opposite pavement. The offices of the Brigade staff were on the ground floor to the right of the entrance in what was known as the secure area. It was only after they had been admitted to this inner sanctum that Ashton learned officially that there had been a change of plan.

'RAF Gütersloh has been stood down,' the Chief of Staff informed him.

'Do you know why, Major?'

'We've been bombarded with signals from every direction, but it's best if you hear the whole story from Mr Hazelwood. He said you could reach him at the office.'

'When was this?'

'The last time he telephoned was roughly an hour ago.'

Ashton glanced at his wristwatch. Even allowing for the hour difference between the two zones, it was something of a record for Victor to still be in his office at 9.30 p.m. 'Can I use your phone?' he asked.

'Certainly. It's crypto protected and linked to sky net. Just depress the button on the cradle when you want to switch to secure speech.' The Chief of Staff edged towards the door. 'I'll be in the corridor should you need me.'

Signalling Crawford to stay, Ashton lifted the receiver and punched out the international direct dial code for London followed by Hazelwood's number at Vauxhall Cross. The phone rang just twice before Victor picked it up.

'About time,' he growled after Ashton had identified himself. 'What kept you?'

'A traffic accident on the autobahn. Shall we switch to secure?'

'Let's do that.'

As always, there was a noticeable loss of power. Before the scrambler was activated, Hazelwood could have been in the same room, now his voice sounded faint as if there was a fault on the line.

'I expect you already know we've had to cancel the flight to Lyneham?'

'I was told the RAF had been stood down but that's not quite the same thing.' Ashton opened the centre drawer in the desk and found some scrap paper in case he needed to make notes. 'Do I gather Nicholson has become something of a political embarrassment and you want us to back off?'

'That's the last thing I want,' Hazelwood told him, 'but unfortunately we haven't any choice.'

The German authorities were aware that Nicholson was in military custody and they wanted his body. Hazelwood wasn't entirely clear how Bonn had learned that he had surrendered himself to 1 Queens in Münster but word could have reached them from several different sources. Once 4 Guards Brigade had reported the incident to superior headquarters, the number of interested parties had multiplied until every Tom, Dick and Harry had been informed.

'Anyway, there's now a warrant out for his arrest and the Foreign

Office doesn't want us fouling up Anglo-German relations. It's my understanding that Nicholson will be taken to Berlin and put on an identification parade. If the *Polizei* haven't already collected him, they very soon will.'

'I think he's still in the guardroom, Victor.'

'Well, there's German efficiency for you. They make a song and dance about jurisdiction and then, having got their way, it appears they are happy to leave him where he is for the time being.'

'That could be to our advantage,' Ashton said.

'What do you mean?'

'It gives me a chance to see what I can get out of him. I mean, once Kommissar Voigt gets his hands on Nicholson, there's no telling when we shall be able to interrogate him.'

'You'd better get on with it then.'

'You'll need to clear it with 4 Guards Brigade first, otherwise I'll never get near him.'

'Who do I talk to?'

Ashton told him to hang on, then stuck his head out into the corridor and informed the Chief of Staff that Mr Hazelwood wanted to have a word with him. From listening to one side of the ensuing conversation it was evident the Deputy DG had the Guards major eating out of his hand.

'Did you get the gist of that?' Hazelwood asked after the Chief of Staff had handed the phone over to Ashton.

'Nicholson is all mine until the Germans claim him?'

'Right. Phone tomorrow and let me know how you got on.'

'What about inducements, Victor? Can I offer him anything?'

'He wants immunity and we can't give it.'

'So how do I play Nicholson?'

'Tell him he has to persuade us it's in our interest to intercede on his behalf.'

'I'll do what I can,' Ashton said and hung up, then briefly told Crawford what had passed between them.

'A man like Nicholson isn't going to do us any favours out of the kindness of his heart, Peter. We'll have to frighten him.'

'He may not scare easily.'

'We won't know that until we've put him to the test.'

'Let's just play it by ear.'

Ashton motioned the warrant officer to lead on, then switched out the lights and closed the door behind him as he left the office. Before making his way to the guardroom on foot, he sought out the Chief of Staff, thanked him for the use of his telephone, and gratefully accepted his offer of a couple of beds for the night in the mess annexe.

The picquet officer and guard commander had evidently been warned to expect them. At any rate, there were no objections when Ashton asked if he and Crawford could be left to interview Nicholson in his cell.

Until he met him in the flesh, Ashton had thought he already knew everything there was to know about Martin Nicholson. He had, after all, translated the Stasi file, had studied the personal documents Harriet had obtained from the Records Office at Hayes, and had read the proceedings of the Court of Inquiry held by 49 Field Regiment Royal Artillery and the SIB report. He had also listened to what ex-Gunner George Bennett had had to say about him and had seen both his passport photo and the artist's impression of his appearance thirty years on. But the pathetic figure in vest and underpants who crawled out from under the army issue blanket when the guard commander finally succeeded in rousing him was far removed from the mental picture Ashton had formed.

Based entirely on his record as a hired killer, Ashton had seen him as a big man despite the evidence in the medical documents provided by the army. He had also mentally dismissed the fact that, while doing his National Service, Nicholson had been a contender for the bantamweight championship of BAOR, which meant he would have tipped the scales at a hundred and twelve to a hundred and eighteen pounds.

'Come to take me home, have you?' Nicholson sat up on the edge of the bunk yawning. 'About bloody time too. What kept you?'

'You're not going to England,' Ashton told him coldly.

'You're joking.' He turned to Crawford. 'He is joking, isn't he?'

'Can you see a smile on his face?'

'Shit, shit, shit.' Nicholson punched his thigh with a clenched fist.

'You're right about the shit,' Ashton said. 'You're in it up to your neck. The Germans have claimed jurisdiction; they've got you bang to rights for killing Joachim Wolff. Then there's also the little matter of what you did to thirteen-year-old Renate Jurgen. That should be good for a minimum of another five years on top of a life sentence. Yes sir, make no mistake, you are going to die in jail.'

'So how are you going to spring me?' Nicholson asked, looking from one man to the other.

'We aren't,' Crawford said amiably. 'The Foreign Office and our nice Prime Minister are not about to go to town on behalf of a piece of dog shit like you, not when they are having a love affair with Chancellor Kohl.'

'Fuck you, arsehole.'

Nicholson launched himself from the bunk with the intention of throwing a punch at the SAS warrant officer. Forty years ago he might have rocked him with a right hook but time had caught up with him and he was no longer the fast, hard-hitting bantamweight. Knowing that Crawford was likely to break him into little pieces, Ashton moved between them, blocked the hook with his left forearm and moving inside, brought a knee up into Nicholson's groin, then stamped on his stockinged feet.

The long drawn-out cry of pain started low and rose a full octave; with almost contemptuous ease, Ashton picked up yesteryear's championship contender and dumped him on the bunk, then told Crawford to get out and leave them alone. Before the SAS warrant officer could knock on the door to attract the attention of the guard commander, the Lance Sergeant unlocked the cell and demanded to know what all the noise was about.

'It's all right,' Ashton told him. 'The prisoner's having a spot of hernia trouble. Nothing to get excited about, he'll be as right as rain in no time.'

The Lance Sergeant looked dubious. 'I hope you're right, sir,' he said, 'because I'm responsible for his well-being and I don't want anybody to get the wrong idea.'

Ashton assured the guard commander there was no danger of that and waited until the NCO had left the cell and locked the door before turning the screw on Nicholson again.

'My colleague may have overstepped the mark but he is absolutely right – the British Government isn't going to lift a finger to help you. Of course, their attitude might change if they were convinced you had something they wanted.

'Like what?'

'Like the name of your case officer when you were employed by the KGB.'

Nicholson thought about it for all of ten seconds. 'Okay,' he said, 'you've got yourself a deal. I'll give you his name, contact procedure and the rest of it just as soon as I set foot in England. Until I do, you can go and play with your dick.'

'They are not going to take my word for it. You have to give them a free sample, something which isn't already on the Stasi file.'

'We're back on names again, are we?'

'I'll settle for just one, provided it's the Russian.'

'And that will get me on a plane to London, will it?' Nicholson shook his head. 'Like hell it will,' he snarled. 'You'll conveniently forget all about me once you have his name. I'll be better off making a deal with the German prosecutor.'

Ashton thought he probably would be. Voigt would give an arm and a leg to know exactly who had hired Nicholson and how they had contacted him. If the price of that information was a nominal sentence, that would see him out on the street again within three years but the prosecutor's office might well go along with such a deal. Joachim Wolff was no great loss to society and not too many Germans would demand justice on his behalf. There had of course been seventeen other victims, but the Stasi file was the only evidence against him and that was unlikely to stand up in court unless one of his former case officers was mad enough to testify on oath.

'You seem to have things worked out pretty well,' Ashton told him, 'but I'm not sure I would want to put all my eggs in one basket.'

'Well, you would say that, wouldn't you?'

'You won't hear me denying it but you shouldn't disregard everything I've said on that account. I mean, it wasn't some radical anti-Nazi group who wanted to see Joachim Wolff dead on a slab. You were hired by members of his own party – right?'

'You're telling the story, not me.'

'And they had to find an Englishman to do the job because they didn't want the rank and file pointing an accusing finger in their direction.'

'Keep it up, squire,' Nicholson said with a mocking smile. 'I'm all ears.'

'So they went to the Russians and asked for you.' Ashton saw the obvious question coming and pre-empted it. 'How did they know of your reputation? Well, my guess is they heard about it from a former officer in the Stasi who'd had access to your file and had become a paid-up member of the New National Socialist Party after Germany was reunited.'

'You're off your trolley,' Nicholson said, but his voice lacked bite and Ashton knew the old renegade was just going through the motions.

'Anyway, this Stasi agent knew who to contact in Moscow and your paymaster in Russia agreed to hire you out for a substantial consideration.'

'You're making it up as you go along.'

Ashton saw no point in contradicting him; he was improvising but that didn't alter the fact that he was plumb right.

'I hope the law enforcement officers and the public prosecutor in Berlin take good care of you. I mean, let's face it, even if they charge you tomorrow, it will be months before a trial date is set and you've got a lot of enemies.'

'What enemies?'

'The people who hired you. They're frightened you will blow the whistle on them.' Ashton snapped his fingers. 'My God, why didn't I think of it before? They've already taken steps to protect themselves, haven't they? They sent somebody after you – that's why you surfaced in Münster and surrendered to 1 Queens.'

Nicholson rested both arms on his thighs, bowed his head and stared at the cracked linoleum on the floor. 'I don't scare that easy,' he muttered.

'I never thought you did.'

'So why try to put the fear of Christ up me when you know it's a waste of time?'

'I was trying to bring home to you what a jam you're in.'

'Bollocks. You're after something for nothing.'

'And you've got nothing that's worth having. That's what I am going to tell them at home, that's why you will die in a German prison,' Ashton said brusquely and walked towards the cell door.

'Where are you going?' Nicholson asked, looking up from the floor.

'I'm leaving. We're not getting anywhere so there's no point in continuing this conversation.'

'Wait.'

'What for?'

'You want a name, I'll give you one. Pavel.'

'Pavel who?'

'I don't know his family name but he was the case officer I was assigned to when the KGB took me over.'

'So describe him.'

'I never met the bastard, he was just a voice on the phone.'

'I don't believe you.'

'I don't give a shit what you believe, it was the way he operated. Pavel was the only case officer I ever had who never showed his face.'

'If that's your idea of a free sample, forget it.' Ashton looked over his shoulder and raised a clenched fist as if to hammer on the door. 'I can tell you now, London won't be interested.'

'Pavel got in touch with me again a few weeks ago, only this time he called himself Valentin. First thing he asked me was did I recognise his voice.' Nicholson paused, then said, 'Think your lah-di-dah friends in London will be interested now?'

'It may not be enough.'

'It's all you're getting.'

'Well, if you should change your mind between here and Berlin, you can always ask to see the British Consul.'

'Like hell I will. I'm not saying another word until I get off the plane at Heathrow.'

'You may want to.' Ashton rapped on the door to summon the guard commander. 'Valentin is the man who put us on to you,' he added.

There was a rattle of bolts, then the door opened and Ashton walked through into the guardroom. As the Lance Sergeant started to close it again, he looked back in time to catch one final glimpse of Nicholson. Although prepared to concede it could be wishful thinking on his part, he thought the bastard gave every impression of being deeply worried.

'So how did you get on?' Crawford asked him as they walked towards the officers' mess. 'Was he more forthcoming after you threw me out of the cell?'

'No. All I got from him was the fact that Valentin used to call himself Pavel back in the old days.'

'And we already know there is more than one Valentin.'

'Yes. Do we know what time the *Polizei* are collecting Nicholson tomorrow?'

'According to the picquet officer, 08.00 hours. What have you got in mind?'

'Nothing,' said Ashton, 'apart from something to eat and a place to lay my head.'

The officers' mess was deserted, dinner had finished several hours ago and the cook had gone off duty. The steward had already closed the bar and had only remained behind in order to show them to their rooms. These, it turned out, were part of the overspill accommodation and were located in the headquarter block directly above the court martial centre.

The two police officers from Berlin arrived in an unmarked BMW promptly at 08.00 hours having spent the previous night in the Martinhof on Münster's Hörster Strasse. Ashton had planned to have a quiet word with them before they carted Nicholson off, but somebody with an eye to a public relations photo opportunity had arranged for the local press and TV to be present. In addition to reporters from the *Münstersche Zeitung*, *Kölner Stadt-Anzeiger*, *Rheinische Post* and a camera team representing all three major networks, there was also a host of civil dignatories shepherded by the Joint Services liaison officer. Knowing how the DG would react if his face appeared on TV or in the newspapers, Ashton had taken one look at the three-ring circus and backed off. So had Crawford who, like everyone else in the SAS, was noticeably camera shy. Commander 4 Guards Brigade and his principal staff officer were also conspicuous by their absence.

When the police officers finally departed with their prisoner, it was still only 7.30 in London. Returning to the mess, Ashton settled their bill with the secretary, then spent the next hour in the ante room reading *Country Life*, *Field* and yesterday's newspapers.

The Chief of Staff hadn't expected to see him again but the only other sky net crypto-protected radio telephone was in the Brigade Commander's office. If their positions had been reversed, Ashton doubted if he would have been quite so accommodating had he been required to vacate his office so that a complete stranger could talk to his superior in London in complete privacy. Getting past Hazelwood's personal assistant who considered it was her duty to act as a filter, was never easy. Once through, however, Ashton quickly told him what had happened.

'Nicholson departed from here in a blaze of publicity.'

'How did that happen, Peter?'

'I don't know, the army's pretty mystified too. Anyway, what does it matter how the German media were alerted? The thing is, it's going to make a deal with Bonn virtually impossible. Nicholson is going down for life and it will be light years before they can think of allowing him to serve the rest of his sentence in England.'

'What do you recommend then?' Hazelwood demanded.

'I think Neil Franklin should be told to keep badgering Kommissar Voigt until he agrees to let him see Nicholson.'

There would be no better time to interrogate Nicholson than immediately after the Jurgens had identified him. He had not expected to be handed over to the German authorities and would be feeling especially vulnerable after being picked out on a line-up.

'I think Neil will have something to say about that.'

Ashton was sure he would. Head of Station, Berlin, had always been on his guard where Voigt was concerned and liked to keep his distance from the Kommissar. But there was no reason for him to be coy on this occasion.

'The Kripo owe us one, Victor.'

Hazelwood said he intended to make that very point to Neil Franklin, confirmed that he had nothing else for Crawford and himself and agreed they should return by the first available flight. Because of heavy booking, that turned out to be BA 8092 departing Düsseldorf at 14.30, which put him into Gatwick a good ninety minutes after Harriet had arrived at Heathrow.

Blackboards and easels were not usually in demand and the housekeepers at Vauxhall Cross had had to go cap in hand to the administrative wing at Benbow House in order to produce one for the Deputy DG. Why Victor Hazelwood should want such an old-fashioned training aid was beyond Garfield. The chalk was inclined to skid over a large grease spot making his scrawl even more unintelligible; furthermore, it made a grating squeak that set his teeth on edge. As far as he could see, the one saving grace of the blackboard was that it might conceivably save a lot of scrap paper.

However, thus far all the so-called brains trust had produced after discussing the information Ashton had phoned in was the original heading which read: *Pavel equals Valentin equals who?* At the risk of seeming crass in front of the other two members of the panel who happened to be in charge of the German and Russian Desks in his department, Garfield finally plucked up courage to ask Victor what was the object of the exercise.

'I want to sketch in the blank spaces,' Hazelwood told him enigmatically.

'What blank spaces?'

Hazelwood pointed to the heading on the blackboard. 'In Pavel's career.'

'Ashton believes there is more than one Valentin. I thought we agreed with him, Victor?'

'We do. But Nicholson is telling us that one of them is Pavel, the case officer who ran him when he was working for the KGB.'

'After he had served his appenticeship with the Stasi.'

'Take it a step farther,' Hazelwood said as if encouraging a none-too-bright student.

'Which means Pavel must have entered the picture in the mid to late sixties.' Garfield shrugged. 'Of course, I'm just guessing but it must have been sometime after Nicholson returned from England with his newly acquired British passport.'

'I think we can do better than that. When was the first time Nicholson operated outside the borders of the GDR and Federal Republics?'

Garfield sifted through his photocopy of the Stasi file. 'In 1971, Milan, Italy, Tuesday, July the sixth.'

'Good. Let's say that was his first job for the KGB. What rank would Pavel have held in those days? Lieutenant, senior lieutenant, captain?'

'Go one up,' Garfield said. 'His case officer in the Stasi was a major.'

'A major then.' Hazelwood wrote the rank and date on the

blackboard. 'Assume Pavel is a high-flier – when might he have expected to be promoted to half colonel?'

Suddenly it was a quiz game, the questions coming fast and generating an air of excitement amongst the participants. Would Pavel have been posted outside the borders of the Soviet Union a second time? If so, in what capacity? As an illegal with a false identity like Konon Trofimovich Molody alias Gordon Lonsdale who'd run the Portland spy ring? Or had he served in an embassy in a disguised capacity? Had anyone called Pavel been a member of a delegation visiting one of the former Warsaw Pact countries? Ranks, dates and possible appointments appeared on the blackboard in different coloured chalks as Garfield and the two grade one officers in charge of the Russian and German Desks responded to the questions.

Finally, Hazelwood wrote 1993 in yellow at the foot of the blackboard, then said, 'What rank is Valentin likely to be holding today and how old do we think he is?'

'Lieutenant general, mid to late sixties.' Garfield smiled. 'I've got it,' he said.

'Well, don't hug it to yourself, Rowan.'

'You want us to make a note of everything on the blackboard, then crosscheck the data against the list of KGB personnel we've identified since 1971 to 1993. We're looking for anyone called Pavel, whether this is his first name or patronymic, who more or less fits the career pattern we've mapped out.'

'So what are you all waiting for?' Hazelwood said. 'Let's get to work.'

'You don't believe Valentin will take the bait when Zelenov arrives in Moscow?'

Hazelwood said he had never been one to put his shirt on just one horse in the race and liked to spread the odds. Furthermore, he very much doubted if they would hear from the Russian again after what had happened in Tallinn.

He could not have been more wrong. At 19.30 hours British Summer Time, GCHQ Cheltenham picked up a signal from Valentin transmitted from somewhere near Riga. The message indicated the possibility of another meeting with 'Mercury' in ten days' time. It also warned that Ashton was to come alone this time.

298

Chapter 26

It was the rain driven against the window by the wind which roused Ashton rather than the grey light of dawn that filtered into the room through a gap in the drawn curtains. He turned his head to peer at the luminous face of the alarm clock on the bedside table; ten minutes to five on a dull, wet morning in July, too early to get up, too late to go back to sleep.

Harriet was stretched out on her left side facing the bathroom, her back towards him. Her breathing was shallow and she was utterly still. She was usually a restless sleeper, lying first on one side, then the other, sometimes rolling over on to her back, occasionally ending up in a prone position flat on her stomach. Although certain Harriet was awake, she did not respond when he whispered her name. Tentatively, he reached out for her, gently raising the duvet with one hand while he slid the other over her hip. If she hadn't been wide awake before, the way she flinched at his touch and wriggled irritably confirmed that she definitely was now.

Ashton removed the offending hand. It was not the first time Harriet had rejected him nor was it likely to be the last. Since returning to London, he had lived a bachelor's life from Sunday night to the Friday evening when he would motor up to Lincoln to spend the weekend with Harriet at her parents' house. Strangers observing them together on those occasions would never have guessed that a date had been set for their wedding. Although the neurosurgeon at St Thomas's had warned him what to expect, he had never really believed that Harriet's whole personality would change quite so much.

It had always been a convention that they didn't share the same bed while they were staying with her parents. In the past, this somewhat false modesty had irked Harriet more than it had him but nowadays she seemed to regard the practice as a heaven-sent opportunity to keep him at a distance. He even got the impression that Harriet was relieved when Sunday night came and it was time for him to drive back to London.

But sex was only a minor part of it. Her apparent lack of confidence had been infinitely more worrying. She was reluctant to go out, especially at night when in her imagination every reveller was intent on attacking her. She burst into tears easily and didn't know why, which distressed her even more. Harriet was also irrational where Detective Sergeant Immelmann was concerned; he was the man who had saved her life and she wouldn't hear a word said against him. As for her career, Harriet was coming round to the view that she was in the wrong occupation. Furthermore, she dreaded the thought of going back to work. The fact that she had returned to London with him yesterday afternoon while still on sick leave for a further week was, he had believed, an encouraging sign. Now, in the cold light of day on this Monday morning he wasn't so sure.

The alarm suddenly erupted in a loud discordant jangle that had Ashton wondering where he was. He could not recall nodding off and was so disorientated that he couldn't make out where the noise was coming from. Still half-asleep, he started to crawl all over Harriet to get at it and was sharply asked what he thought he was doing. He turned the other way, threw the duvet aside and sitting up on the edge of the bed, reached out and shut off the alarm.

'Sorry about that,' he said. 'I was dead to the world.'

'You certainly were. Flat on your back and snoring like a grampus.'

'You should have given me a thump.'

'I tried that once,' Harriet told him, 'and you thumped me back.'

'Really? I hadn't realised I was that brave.'

'I'm not surprised, you were asleep at the time.'

She sounded more like her old self, teasing him the way she used to; then her mood changed abruptly and she told him to get shaved and dressed while she prepared breakfast. Tense, mercurial, distant; that was the new Harriet Egan and there were times when he didn't know how to reach her. The only advice he had ever received from her family doctor was not to try. 'Don't let Harriet see that you are worried, it will only make her far worse. Give her room to breathe, she will come out of it eventually.' He had little faith in the remedy which struck him as thoroughly complacent, but the family had complete confidence in the good doctor and he went along with it to please them.

And sometimes it worked, the depression would lift and she would come alive again. When he walked into the kitchen, Harriet was smiling as if she didn't have a care in the world. She bubbled like champagne all through breakfast, full of ideas and plans for the future. Obviously they couldn't go on holiday just yet when she had had so much sick leave but how about another long weekend break in Paris?

'Remember the Commodore on the Boulevard Haussmann?' she asked with a mischievous smile.

Remember? How could he forget? Maybe November wasn't the best time of the year to see Paris but they had been celebrating their engagement and everything had been magic. 'I'll look for some brochures during the lunch hour,' he said.

'No need. I'll pop into the travel agent, it'll give me something to do.'

'Well, okay . . .' He glanced at his wristwatch and hurriedly swallowed the remains of his coffee. 'Time I was going,' he said and stood up.

'Yes, it wouldn't do to be late into the office, would it?' Harriet said teasingly and came towards him.

She was wearing a towelling bathrobe loosely belted at the waist over a white satin nightshirt. No great dexterity was needed to untie the knot and slip his hands under the robe as she embraced him, her mouth open, her tongue actively seeking his. She drew Ashton on, stepping backwards towards the bedroom, her hips thrusting forward as she rubbed her body against his. He stroked Harriet's thighs, then clasped her buttocks and lifted her off both feet as she reached behind her and opened the door. Unable to see where he was going, Ashton cannoned into the bed and fell on top of her.

'You're going to muss your suit,' Harriet said and laughed softly.

'To hell with the suit,' he told her.

'Shall I put my wig on?'

He knew instinctively that Harriet was testing him and it was vital he chose his words with care. Her hair was growing back but it was still very short and close to her skull. Outside the house, Harriet either wore a headscarf or the wig she had purchased in Lincoln.

'What for?' he said lightly. 'You look dead sexy.'

'That's because I am dead sexy.' She reached down, unzipped his fly and stroked his erection, then scissored her legs behind his back, locking them at the ankles as he entered her. 'Do it to me,' she urged through clenched teeth, 'do it, do it, do it.'

There was a savage intensity about their love-making which he had never experienced before. It was almost as if Harriet wanted to devour him in the shortest possible time. There was no doubting who was in control and there was no way he could hold himself back so that it was over sooner than he would have wished.

'You're a lovely man,' Harriet told him when he finally left for the MoD.

'Are you going to be okay on your own?' he asked.

'Of course I will.'

'I'll phone you later on this morning.'

'There's no need,' she said and kissed him gently on the lips.

It did not occur to Ashton that from the moment he had walked into the kitchen, Harriet had been putting on an act entirely for his benefit.

Ashton never did get around to making the phone call before lunch. His first hour in the office was devoted to bringing Yeomans up to date on his return from leave. The few days' sailing had at last come off, but not in the Solent. Instead, Yeomans had enjoyed almost two weeks off the Côte d'Azur crewing a yacht belonging to some Greek tycoon who was a friend of a friend of his wife's and had come back looking as brown as a berry. Then Hazelwood rang and asked him to come over just as he was about to tackle the files the chief clerk had deposited in his in-tray.

The whole of Vauxhall Cross was a smoke-free zone with the exception of Hazelwood's office. Although some zealous member of the Civil Service Union had put two non-smoking stickers on the wall either side of the entrance, they hadn't made a blind bit of difference. However, as a concession to his more health-conscious colleagues, Victor occasionally remembered to keep the door closed which meant he then had to rely on an extractor fan to clear the atmosphere. As a cost-cutting exercise, the Property Services Agency had bought the smallest appliance on the market and installed it as close to the ceiling as possible with a view to preserving the aesthetic appearance of the room. Consequently, the extractor was not particularly efficient. When Ashton arrived, Hazelwood was on his third Burma cheroot of the morning and Garfield was already beginning to look a bit green about the gills.

'Make yourself comfortable, Peter,' Hazelwood said and waved a hand towards the only vacant chair in the office. 'Thought you'd like to hear what Rowan and his minions have come up with, based on what you learned from Nicholson.'

'That makes a change,' Ashton said quietly.

'What does?'

'Well, it's not often someone like me gets to know what it's all about.'

'Would you care to enlarge on that rather cryptic observation?'

'I never thought you'd ask, Victor, but since you have, what is the Foreign Office going to do about Denista? Are the Bulgarians any closer to discovering who might have murdered de Vries? Has anyone assessed how much bum information de Vries fed us during the forty-something years he was working for the Soviets? And how about all those British prisoners of war who are known to have fallen into Russian hands in late '44 and early '45 who are still unaccounted for? Has anyone thought to ask Mr Yeltsin to look into it like he's doing for the Americans?'

'Four questions,' Hazelwood said ponderously.

'I hadn't realised I was going to be rationed, Victor.'

'Denista left the embassy at her own request and is now living at home with her parents. Mike Pearman is satisfied that she is not in any kind of danger.'

Captain Ivan Khristov was still in charge of the investigation but the number of officers assigned to the de Vries case had been reduced; the Captain was however currently following a new line of enquiry which looked quite promising. As for de Vries himself, he had really only been active during the Greek Civil War; after the United States had taken over responsibility for that commitment in 1947, thereafter his importance to the SIS had steadily diminished.

'The world's a different place these days,' Hazelwood continued. 'Anyway, the Director decided it would be a waste of time, effort and resources if we appointed a committee to assess how much damage de Vries might have done to us so long ago.'

'And our missing POWs?' Ashton persisted.

'That matter is being pursued by the Foreign Office. Now can we hear what Rowan has to tell us?'

'By all means.'

Garfield glanced at the notes he'd made on his millboard as if to refresh his memory, then cleared his throat. 'I expect you remember our rogues gallery from the days when you were on the Russian Desk?'

'It's only two years ago,' Ashton reminded him.

'Quite so.' Garfield cleared his throat a second time, then said, 'We went through the list of KGB officers we've managed to identify over the years looking for a man called Pavel. We found two – Sergei Semyonovich Pavel and Pavel Trilisser. Sergei Semyonovich was a major in the NKVD who first came to our notice at the time of the Nuremberg trials in 1946 when he was keeping an eye on the Soviet Prosecutor. He then resurfaced in North Korea in 1951 where he supervised the brainwashing of Allied prisoners of war.'

'Christ, he must be in his eighties, if he's still alive.'

'Yes, that's why we eliminated him, which brings us to Pavel Trilisser. He was an official at the Moscow Olympics in 1980 and was employed as a sports liaison officer. He looked after the British Archery Team; it was his job to ensure the competitors got to the right venue on time. He was very shy, didn't like having his photograph taken but one of our lot managed to get a snapshot of him with the team.'

'One of our lot?'

'A national coach who does us the odd favour. The next time we see Pavel Trilisser it's eleven months later and he's the Second Secretary, Cultural Affairs at the Soviet Embassy in Damascus.'

Long before Ashton had even joined the SIS, it was policy to get a photographic record of as many Soviet officials as possible, then wait for their faces to show up again some place else. Trilisser would have been spotted by the Mid East Department which would explain why he hadn't come across the name when he had been on the Russian Desk.

'The dates fit,' Garfield continued. 'Nicholson did his last job for Valentin in 1978.'

'According to the Stasi file,' Ashton said.

'I thought you and Harriet Egan had decided that the KGB worked through the East German Ministry of State Security when they took Nicholson over?'

'It was the only logical explanation we could think of which wasn't at odds with the facts. But you have to remember it was Valentin who put us on to "The Englishman".'

'I hadn't forgotten, and I don't know why he did it. However, we came to the conclusion that our mysterious Russian was probably a major when he was running Nicholson. Taking that as a starting point, we plotted a theoretical career graph for Valentin and reckoned he would almost certainly have moved up at least one rank after they parted company. Second Secretary, Cultural Affairs equates to a lieutenant colonel. You follow me?'

Ashton nodded. He could see what the Head of the European Department was getting at but he didn't personally agree with his reasoning. You couldn't ascertain the rank of a KGB officer simply by his diplomatic appointment. He knew of a case where one of the embassy chauffeurs had outranked the Ambassador. If Pavel Trilisser was being groomed for stardom back in the early eighties, his then superior officers were going about it in a very public manner. On the other hand, the higher up the ladder you went, the more of an administrator you became and they might have been giving Trilisser a practical insight into how a diplomatic mission actually functioned.

'How long was he in Damascus?'

'Thirteen months.' Garfield smiled. 'We were meant to believe that the Ambassador had asked for him to be relieved because he was rogering the wife of the Deputy Trade Representative.'

Thirteen months as a pseudo diplomat was probably about right for what Trilisser would need to know in the future. And the reason given for his premature recall had that ring of authenticity typical of a KGB cover story.

'And after Damascus?'

'Well, that's what clinched it for me,' Garfield told him enthusiastically. 'He dropped completely out of sight.'

'But he stayed in touch with Nicholson one way or the other.' Ashton rubbed his jaw. 'Has Franklin managed to have a word with him yet?' he asked.

Hazelwood crushed what was left of his cheroot in the ashtray. 'He's working on it, Peter. As it happens, we have another iron in the fire.'

The other iron in the fire was Leonid Nikolaevich Zelenov, and Garfield was only too eager to let him know that the embassy had managed to obtain a flat for the old man in the Kuncevo District of Moscow. Meanwhile, the consular affairs officer in Tallinn was keeping him sweet with regular payments in US dollars.

'And Stilson Manufacturing couldn't have been more helpful; they have established Leonid Nikolaevich's credibility with Katya Malinovskaya's security agency after Head of Commerce at the embassy put them in touch with her organisation . . .'

'Just hold it a moment.' Ashton turned to Hazelwood. 'Why is Rowan telling me all this?' he asked.

'Zelenov keeps asking after you.'

'Oh, I get it. He wants to see my face at Sheremetyevo Airport when he arrives in Moscow and you're keen to oblige him.' Ashton shook his head. 'I can't have been your first choice, Victor. I mean, I'm too well known over there.'

'That could be part of the attraction now.'

It wasn't simply another way of saying that he had changed his mind. Hazelwood enjoyed the reputation of being the sort of Intelligence officer who made things happen and it could be he saw Ashton as the vital bit of fissionable material which would produce a chain reaction. He also recalled what Harriet had said of the Deputy DG, that Victor was only too aware of his sense of personal loyalty and exploited it shamelessly when it suited him.

'Am I a conscript or do I have a choice, Victor?'

'I would never order you to go to Moscow.'

Out of the corner of his eye, Ashton could see Garfield opening and closing his mouth like a fish gasping for oxygen. 'I'm glad to hear it,' he said. 'Now find someone else to do it.'

'If we can ensnare Valentin we will know which way the wind is blowing in Russia and how strongly before it even registers on the Beaufort Scale.'

'So what?'

'I want you to think about it before you come to a decision.'

'I've already made it,' Ashton told him. 'So start looking for another foot soldier.'

'Well, if that's your last word on the subject, we won't keep you.' Hazelwood waited until he had reached the door, then said, 'Call me if you should change your mind, Peter. We've got a couple of days in hand.'

From the bewildered expression on his face, Ashton thought it was the first Rowan Garfield had heard about it.

Nicholson stripped off the coveralls he had been issued with as a maximum security prisoner and changed into the civilian clothes he'd been wearing when he had walked into the guardroom at Oxford Barracks over a fortnight ago. He dressed slowly under the watchful eyes of the two escorts Kommissar Voigt had sent to collect him, postponing for as long as possible the moment when they would leave for the Central Police Station on the Tempelhofer Damm. He had tried to discover what sort of unpleasant surprise the Kripo had in store for him ever since he'd learned from the prison governor that he would be attending a further identification parade at 16.00 hours. But all anyone would tell him was that his lawyer would be present.

'Any idea what all this is about?' he asked in German.

'Get a move on,' the older of the two plainclothesmen told him.

'I am, I am.'

'We don't want to be late, arsehole.'

'No, it wouldn't do to keep the Jurgens waiting.'

'You've got the wrong lot, these witnesses have come all the way from Munich.'

Munich? When the hell was that? 1970? No, it was 1971 and the beginning of January when he had electrocuted that Ukrainian bitch who used to broadcast anti-Soviet propaganda over Radio Free

Europe. He had fixed the light switch in the hall so that it was live and had dampened the floor for good measure. But no one had seen him break into her apartment, or had they? Maybe it was time he asked to see the British Consul instead of waiting for the right moment to make a deal with Voigt?

'Hands behind your back,' the senior officer barked at him.

They manacled his wrists, then, grabbing an arm apiece, they hustled him out of the holding cell and on down the gallery to the check gate at the end of the landing. Beyond it, two flights of metal stairs led to the rotunda. The unmarked BMW was parked directly outside the Judas gate which opened into the exercise yard.

As they approached the BMW, the driver got out, walked round the vehicle and opened the rear, nearside door. Ducking his head below the sill, Nicholson climbed into the back and sat down. The senior plainclothesman rode up front with the driver, the younger officer joined him in the back. Exiting from the prison, they headed east on Moabit, then branched off into Invalidenstrasse and drove past the Lehrter Bahnhof.

'This isn't the quickest way to the *Polizeipräsidium*,' Nicholson observed.

'Maybe not, but it's the quietest,' the senior officer told him.

The ambush occurred shortly after they had turned right at the intersection of Invaliden with Müllerstrasse and were heading south towards the Unter den Linden. An Opel truck parked by the kerbside suddenly pulled out in front of their BMW, forcing the driver to stamp on the brakes. As they skidded to a halt, the truck reversed into them, smashing the main beams, radiator grill and both wings. Almost in the same instant, they were rammed from behind. The windscreen shattered under a hail of automatic fire and the two men up front rocked in their seats as they were repeatedly hit in the chest and head. The younger officer sitting in the back screamed and threw up his hands to surrender but as Nicholson was to discover a split second later, the gunmen weren't interested in taking any prisoners that day.

Ashton alighted from the Victoria Line train at Pimlico and made his way to their flat in Churchill Gardens by way of Bessborough,

Lupus and Claverton Streets. As always, he walked round the Vauxhall Cavalier to satisfy himself that the car had not been vandalised while he had been at work. Then he looked up and down the road to make sure no one was watching him when he unlocked the boot and took out the 'peeper'.

The peeper was a stave some four feet long with a mirror slotted into the tip at an angle of five degrees. He pushed the mirror under the car and went round the vehicle again, checking the underside this time in case anyone had attached an unpleasant surprise to the chassis. Such a routine precaution was necessary when there were several IRA Active Service Units operating in the London area. Although he rarely used the Vauxhall on official business these days and it was therefore unlikely that he had been targeted, he continued to act as if he were one of the unfortunates in the high-risk category. It was however necessary to be discreet when inspecting the car, otherwise he would only draw attention to himself with all that implied.

This morning he had neglected to check the vehicle, which was inexcusable because Harriet had a spare set of keys to the Vauxhall and could have driven off thinking he had already looked the car over. He was lucky on two counts; the car hadn't been moved and there was no suspicious object anchored to the underside. Locking the peeper away in the boot, he let himself into the flat and called out to Harriet.

There was no answer. He had walked into an empty flat before when he'd returned from Tallinn but somehow this time the silence was infinitely more foreboding. There was one other difference. This time, the note Harriet had left for him was on the kitchen table and not in the sitting room. It was also longer, full of crossings out and not always coherent.

My dear Peter, she had begun, as if they were just good friends instead of lovers. She feared what she had to say would come as a terrible shock to him but she couldn't remain in the flat. She thought she had tried to do too much too soon, but everybody seemed to expect so much from her that she had felt compelled to return to London and she hadn't been ready for it. Everything was getting on top of her and she needed some time to herself because there were things she had to think about.

I have to decide what I am going to do about us and how I want to spend the rest of my life, she had continued. *I do know I am not going back to Benbow House or Gower Street. That may sound cowardly to you but it's the way I feel. I'm going home. Please, Please, Please don't phone or try to see me. I don't want to be harassed. I'll get in touch once I've sorted myself out.*

She ended with *Love, Harriet* and there was a postscript which Ashton could hardly read that had something to do with borrowing a suitcase from him. He went into their bedroom, opened the fitted wardrobe and found that all her clothes had gone. It was only then that he realised the full significance of the PS.

Ashton blamed himself for what had happened. He should have seen through her air of false confidence. What exactly was it the neurologist had said to him? 'Fräulein Egan will recover but we cannot guarantee she will be as good as new. She may not be as confident of herself as she was before. Also, both her character and personality may change.' Well, he'd certainly been spot on there. Ashton clenched his right fist and smashed it against the wall, hard enough to break the skin on every knuckle. But the pain solved nothing. And it didn't alter the fact that having rung Harriet twice after he had returned to the MoD, it hadn't occurred to him that anything was amiss when she didn't answer. He told himself he shouldn't have left it at that, then suddenly recalled he had tried once more towards late afternoon. And she had been at home that time because he'd got an engaged tone.

Or was there a more devious explanation? Ashton went into the living room and discovered that the phone was off the hook. Pure absent-mindedness? He didn't think so. The glass on the low table hadn't been there last night. Harriet had fixed herself a strong whisky and had sat there staring at the phone while she decided whether to stay with him or leave, and once she had made up her mind, she had made sure he couldn't get through to her. Ashton picked up the phone and slammed it down on the cradle. What had she been afraid of? That he might sense something was wrong and come running to her? Well, nothing really mattered now.

He lifted the receiver and punched out Hazelwood's number in

Willow Walk. 'Hi,' he said, 'it's me – Peter. I've thought it over, you've got yourself a volunteer.'

'Good.'

'So when would you like to lay it all out for me?'

'Tomorrow morning, nine o'clock,' Hazelwood said and hung up.

Chapter 27

Ashton was getting used to seeing Sheremetyevo 2 from the air. This would be the fourth time he had been to Moscow. He had first visited the city in 1991, officially as a tourist but with Hazelwood's knowledge and tacit approval. Twelve months later, when Head of the Security Vetting and Technical Services Division he had returned in the guise of a Queen's Messenger to carry out the annual security check of the embassy. With one notable exception, no one had known about the third and wholly illegal trip he'd made with a false passport and forged visa. Roy Kelso had had his suspicions and had tried to nail him; Victor had been damned certain but had turned a blind eye. The notable exception had been Harriet and only she could have proved it.

He wasn't sure how to describe this fourth excursion. It was totally above board as far as the SIS was concerned; he was going with their express agreement and they had set it up with Stilson Manufacturing. If there was a close working relationship between the Russian Intelligence Service and the Ministry of the Interior, which had taken over the former Second Chief Directorate of the KGB, then quite a number of people were going to be decidedly unhappy when they learned that Mr Peter Ashton was back in town. And he would come to their notice because he was travelling under his real name with his much-used passport and a visa that had been issued by the Russian Consular Section at 5 Kensington Palace Gardens. Usually, it took between a fortnight and three weeks to obtain the requisite visa, but if you were a businessman with hard currency to spend, you could get one on the spot. Furthermore, you didn't have any problem obtaining hotel accommodation in Moscow.

He hoped the SIS had done right by Stilson Manufacturing because it was extremely unlikely that they would be able to sell so much as a grub screw to the Russians when the authorities in Moscow rumbled this little caper. The company had even written to Leonid Nikolaevich Zelenov with a translation attached to express their pleasure that he had agreed to represent them in Moscow. Moreover, they had gone so far as to give him a contract to make everything look authentic. A second letter enclosing the plane tickets and the address of the flat in Moscow would have been delivered to him yesterday morning.

For sheer professionalism, the European Department was hard to beat. Rowan Garfield might give the impression of a man who didn't have much to say for himself but anyone he sent into the field was well equipped, well organised and well briefed. He had, in fact, spent two whole days taking Ashton through his song-and-dance routine.

The Boeing 767 of British Airways touched down ten minutes ahead of schedule. By the time his suitcase appeared on the baggage carousel, those few minutes in hand had been more than wiped out. There were, of course, no carts readily available in the immediate area. Passport, visa and briefcase in one hand, luggage in the other, Ashton fought his way through Passport Control and Customs and then the milling throng in the concourse.

If the officials inside the terminal hadn't made him feel particularly welcome, it was a very different story when he emerged from the building. The clothes he was wearing identified him as a man with hard currency in his wallet and he was almost trampled underfoot by an army of taxi drivers anxious to get their hands on some of his money. Freedom of choice was an unheard of expression. Before he knew what was happening, a middle-aged man in a check shirt and a pair of old trousers that had gone shiny with age, grabbed his suitcase and bear-led him to his Mercedes.

'You like?' he asked.

No doubt the Mercedes 190 had been the original owner's pride and joy but it had clocked up a lot of miles and had changed hands several times since leaving a showroom in 1985. The car was beginning to show its age, the paintwork had lost its gloss, the chrome was pitted with rust and some backstreet mechanic had knocked out a dent in the wing with a hammer, rounding off what had been a botched job with Polyfilla.

'Will it get me to the Pekin Hotel on Sadovaya?' Ashton asked in Russian.

'Like a rocket,' the cab driver told him.

'I'd rather we didn't go into orbit.'

'That's good, very good.' The Russian grinned, unveiling two rows of bad teeth, then opened the boot. 'We go – yes?' he asked and heaved Ashton's suitcase into the trunk and closed the lid before he could say no.

'How much to the Pekin?' he asked.

'Twenty dollar.'

'Make it ten.'

'Fifteen.'

'Done,' Ashton said and climbed into the back.

The driver paid the official dispatcher the usual fee and the militiamen controlling the traffic on the sliproad stuck him for a thousand roubles which was about the equivalent of twenty pence. Once on the motorway, the Russian put his foot down and held it there, hellbent on overtaking everything on the road. The Pekin was a shade over fifteen miles from the airport; the cab driver tried to make it in the same number of minutes which meant that Ashton had his heart in his mouth for most of the journey.

There was a time not so very long ago when tourists and businessmen alike didn't know which hotel they would be staying in until they arrived in Moscow. There had been a big turn around since Yeltsin had come to power and Stilson Manufacturing had been able to telex the Pekin direct, make a reservation and receive confirmation all within the space of twenty-four hours. But some things hadn't changed; checking into a hotel was still a time-consuming process and was further complicated by the fact that the receptionist dealing with his reservation wasn't familiar with the computer program in use and had to call for assistance before she could retrieve his particulars from the data base.

Once in the privacy of his room, Ashton picked up the phone and rang Katya Malinovskaya's security agency on Gorky Street, completely forgetting Moscow was three hours ahead of London. The chances of finding anyone in the office at 18.40 hours were less than remote, but he was lucky enough to catch the lady herself just as she was about to leave. After referring to the letter Katya Malinovskaya had received from Stilson Manufacturing, he was able to persuade her to stay on.

It was the first time Neil Franklin had been in London since he had been appointed Head of Station, Berlin; it was also the first time he'd set foot in Vauxhall Cross. Given any choice, he would sooner have stayed in Berlin. Unfortunately, the Director had suggested it might be a good idea if he submitted the results of his inquiry into the ambush on Müllerstrasse in person and a suggestion from the DG was as good as an order. This morning he had caught the British Airways flight departing at 08.00 hours for a meeting scheduled to start three hours later. Although he had packed an overnight bag, he hoped to catch a plane which would get him into Berlin in the early evening. However, much depended on the number of questions he would have to field and with Hazelwood in the audience, there was no telling when he would get away.

Hazelwood was the one person Franklin hadn't bargained for. Apart from Dunglass, he had assumed Garfield as Head of the European Department would have an interest, as would the officer in charge of the German Desk. Perhaps it had been wishful thinking on his part, or his ingrained antipathy towards the man, that had made him overlook the Deputy DG. Whatever the reason, he was careful not to let his animosity show when he shook hands with Hazelwood.

Twenty people could sit round the table in the conference room. Dunglass suggested that to make it a little more informal, he and Hazelwood should sit together at one end and facing Garfield and Franklin. Once they had taken their seats, the DG invited him to carry on.

Franklin opened his briefcase, took out a batch of photographs he'd received from the Kripo and passed them round the table. Taken at the scene of the ambush, they showed the driver of the unmarked police car slumped over the wheel, his head on one side as if looking inwards at his companion who was still held more or less upright by the seat belt. The officer in the back had evidently tried to get out of the BMW after being wounded and had died half in half out of the car, his forehead resting on the road, his knees in the well between the transmission tunnel and the door sill. Nicholson had fallen sideways across the seat and was staring up at the roof. A large part of somebody's brains was in his lap.

'The ambush was well planned and well executed,' Franklin told them. 'Seven men are known to have been involved, three in the Opel truck, two in the transit van which rammed the BMW from behind and the drivers of the two getaway cars parked in Clara-Zelkin Strasse, a side street fifty metres beyond the scene of the ambush. It is likely there was an eighth man who acted as a lookout and gave the order to spring the ambush.'

On the basis of statements obtained from eye witnesses, the police had calculated that the attack had started at 15.39 hours and had ended approximately ninety seconds later. A total of one hundred and three empty cases of 9mm had been recovered from the scene of the ambush of which over two-thirds had been found in the back of the Opel truck.

'According to Ballistics, the terrorists were armed with the micro version of the 9mm Uzi sub-machine-gun. This weapon has a twenty-round box magazine and a cyclic rate of one thousand two fifty rounds a minute. The two getaway cars were abandoned in the Marzahn District of East Berlin and set on fire. Both vehicles had been reported stolen a week before the ambush. The Opel truck and the transit van were taken earlier that day.'

Hazelwood looked at the photographs again. 'When was Nicholson told that he would be attending this latest identification parade?'

'Shortly after 08.00 that morning. The prison governor was informed the previous afternoon.'

'Who by?'

'The Public Prosecutor's Office of the First Judicial District. They told Kommissar Voigt at the same time.'

'It was the Public Prosecutor's Office and not the police who organised the parade then?'

Hazelwood again, tenacious as a bulldog. Franklin gave him a tight smile and agreed that indeed that had been the case. Anticipating what he thought would be the next question, he did his best to pre-empt it.

'The Central Police Station was judged to be the most secure as well as the most convenient place to hold the parade.'

'Nicholson was lodged in Moabit Prison after he had been identified by the Jurgens. Right?'

'Yes.'

'So how many times prior to the fatal ambush was he taken to the Central Police Station from the jail?'

'He was interviewed at length on three separate occasions.'

'Did the police always take the same route there and back?'

'Put it this way, they had never gone via Invaliden and Müllerstrasse before.'

'Were they instructed to use that route?' Dunglass asked, suddenly coming to life.

'No one will admit to it but obviously the terrorists knew the police would be coming that way, otherwise they wouldn't have laid the ambush where they did.'

'Why do you keep referring to them as terrorists, Neil?' Garfield asked diffidently.

'Because that's what they are in Voigt's opinion. The motive for killing Nicholson is certainly political.'

'We're talking neo-Nazis?' Hazelwood growled.

Franklin nodded. 'They're the favourites.'

'And they got their information from whom? A sympathiser in the Kripo or the Public Prosecutor's Office?'

'I believe it was the latter organisation. The Chief Public Prosecutor knew a week in advance when the witnesses from Munich would arrive in Berlin. I think one of the lawyers or legal secretaries in his office must have leaked the details.'

'Would the police escort have taken their instructions from the Public Prosecutor?'

'No, someone on the staff of the Police President's Office would have done that,' Franklin said and hastened to explain why this should be so before Hazelwood could begin to grill him about it.

Until that last fatal afternoon, Voigt, as head of the Berlin Kripo, had been responsible for safeguarding Nicholson while he was in transit between the jail and the Central Police Station. He had been relieved of the commitment because the Berlin Kripo were not involved in the Munich case. After arriving at this decision, the Police President had assigned the task to the Moabit Precinct.

'And Voigt comes out of the whole messy business smelling like a rose,' Hazelwood observed bluntly.

'He can hardly be held to blame, Victor.'

'He made sure you didn't get to see Nicholson while he was still responsible for him.'

'It wasn't like that at all,' Franklin said angrily. 'Your protégé, Ashton, might have urged Nicholson to get in touch with the British Consul but he never acted on his advice. But we didn't lose out; Kommissar Voigt made a point of briefing me after each interrogation. Anyway, what did it matter who saw Nicholson when we and Voigt had an identical list of questions to put to him?'

The SIS had wanted to know how the people who had hired Nicholson had learned of his reputation and secondly, who had told this rag-bag collection of neo-Nazis where they might find him.

'But he never confided in Voigt, did he?' Hazelwood said abrasively.

'Not entirely.'

'What does that mean? A little bit? Or what?'

'He expressed a willingness to talk but only if he was given immunity or just a nominal sentence. Voigt told him he had no authority to give such an undertaking but said he would put it to the Public Prosecutor.'

'When did this conversation take place?' Dunglass asked quietly.

'Ten days ago, Director, towards the end of the third and final interrogation. He had dropped several hints during the other two sessions.'

'Did Voigt mention this to the Public Prosecutor at the time?'

'I don't know.'

'Well, when did he first tell you about it?' Hazelwood asked, chipping in again.

'After the last session.'

'And this is the man who made a point of briefing you each time he interrogated Nicholson, is it?'

'I don't know what point it is that you are trying to make, Victor,'

Dunglass said in a mildly reproving tone. 'But the fact is, Kommissar Voigt needn't have mentioned it at all and we would have been none the wiser.'

Franklin was grateful for the Director's intervention. It wasn't often that Hazelwood was put in his place. Certainly the previous DG had never sat on him, not even back in the old days when Victor had been a middle-ranking officer in charge of the Russian Desk.

'Am I right in thinking Voigt is heading the investigation into the ambush?'

Franklin nodded. 'That's correct, Director. Of course he is answering to both the Police President and the Public Prosecutor.'

'Could they point him in a certain direction or turn him away?' Dunglass smiled briefly. 'In other words, could they control the investigation?'

'In theory, but anyone who tried to control Heinrich Voigt would be given short shrift. He's very much his own man.'

'Incorruptible?'

'Absolutely.'

'Good.' Dunglass leaned back in his chair. 'Are there any other questions we should ask Neil while we have him to ourselves?' He looked first to Hazelwood, then Garfield. 'No? Well, that would seem to be it, Neil. All that remains is for me to thank you for giving us such a lucid briefing.'

Franklin could hardly believe his luck. He was after all going to make the British Airways flight departing at 15.35 hours and would be home by 7 p.m. at the latest. Assuring the DG that he would be in daily contact with Voigt and would keep everybody informed, he started towards the door.

'There is just one thing more, Neil,' Dunglass said, halting him in his tracks. 'I'm sure your faith in the Kommissar is entirely justified but I hope we aren't going to sit back and leave it all to him.'

'I'm sorry?' Franklin said, genuinely puzzled.

'I'd like you to make use of your own resources.'

'Resources?' Franklin hoped he didn't sound too obtuse but he still didn't really understand what the DG expected him to do, at least he hoped he didn't.

'I'm referring to Helga von Schinkel, Willie Baumgart and all your other helpers. Surely you don't want me to spell it out for you in words of one syllable?'

Franklin would have liked him to put it in writing, but that was too much to hope for.

Number 124 Gorky Street was a grey anonymous building near the top of the incline some four hundred yards from what used to be Marx Prospekt. Either side of the entrance, there were two large square-shaped windows at hip height above the sidewalk which looked as if they hadn't been cleaned since the beginning of spring. The wide swing door weighed a ton and appeared to be designed for the express purpose of discouraging people from entering the building. A cracked and uneven tiled passageway fronted the half-dozen shops and offices on the ground floor. From the central hall, a staircase led to the minuscule two- and three-room apartments on the upper storeys. Katya Malinovskaya's security agency was situated to the right of the entrance between a bookshop and an arts and crafts emporium.

Katya Malinovskaya was an attractive brown-haired woman who would not have looked out of place on the front cover of any of Moscow's newly emergent fashion magazines. Although they had never met before, Ashton knew a good deal about her. She was twenty-nine years old and had been chosen to represent the more acceptable face of the KGB's Second Chief Directorate with the coming of Perestroika. But Katya had always been more than just a pretty face. Until a near-fatal knife wound in the back had put paid to her career, she had been one of the coming stars in the Criminal Investigation Division which had grown out of the former Twelfth Department.

'I'm Peter Ashton from Stilson Manufacturing,' he said, introducing himself. 'It's very good of you to stay on.'

'Not at all, business is business,' Katya said and invited him to sit down. 'I looked up the letter we received from your company before you arrived.'

'Well then, you know my employers are a little worried about the safety of our local rep in Moscow.' Ashton frowned. 'One hears so many stories about the *Mafiozniki* and the crime rate in this city.'

'What precisely does your company manufacture, Mr Ashton?'

'Industrial tools, dies, all kinds of precision instruments.'

'I would not have thought the *Mafiozniki* would be interested in such merchandise. You are not making anything they could sell to the ordinary consumer.'

'Really? Well, we know of other companies who have been forced to do most of their business through the *Mafiozniki* and it has cost them a small fortune. That's why we are recruiting our own indigenous sales force, starting with Mr Zelenov.'

'And you don't want him to come to any harm?'

'We'd never get anyone else to work for us if he did.'

'So what exactly do you want us to do?'

'We want Mr Zelenov protected round the clock, alarm systems, physical and electronic surveillance – the lot.'

'It will be expensive,' she warned.

'It will be even more expensive if we have to pay a levy to some crime syndicate,' Ashton told her.

Whether or not Katya Malinovskaya had believed a word of his story was immaterial. According to Head of Station, Moscow, she had acquired expensive tastes since going into business on her own account and had just bought herself a brand new top-of-the-range Porsche 911 Coupé which would have cost her more than eighty thousand pounds in England. To finance her new life-style no job was outside the bounds of acceptable behaviour. In Hugo Calthorpe's opinion, the only thing which interested Katya Malinovskaya these days was the colour of a client's money. As proof of this contention, he had cited the fact that at least two members of the Commodities Exchange who had used the services of her agency were about to appear before a tribunal charged with bribery and corruption.

'I need some more information before I can give you an accurate quote, Mr Ashton.'

'Of course, that's understood. What would you like to know?'

'The address of your company's office in Moscow.'

'Mr Zelenov will be working from his home in the Kuncevo District. We've obtained a flat for him in the apartment house at 636 Jel' Ninokaja.' Ashton watched her make a note of the address on a scratchpad, then said, 'I thought we might take a run out there tomorrow morning so that you can assess the task at first-hand.'

'Sounds a good idea.'

'Of course, I will have to pick up the keys to the flat from the District Housing Authority first, but that will only take a few minutes.'

'More like a few hours, Mr Ashton.'

'I don't think so. My company has greased the right palms and they know I'll be giving them a bonus.'

'I see.' She gazed at him steadily. 'Where are you staying in Moscow?'

'The Pekin Hotel.'

'Good. I'll collect you from there. Is 8.30 too early for you?'

'That's fine,' Ashton assured her.

'How did you get here?'

'By taxi.'

'I'll run you back to the hotel,' Katya told him and wouldn't hear of it when he said there was no need. Opening the top drawer of her desk, she took out a Makarov 5.45 PSM automatic pistol and tucked it into her Gucci handbag. 'One never knows who might walk into the office,' she said enigmatically.

Ashton picked up his briefcase, moved ahead of Katya and waited outside in the passageway while she locked the office. In high-heeled shoes made of fine leather, sheer nylons and a blue and white polka-dot silk dress that was obviously very expensive, she was easily the best dressed woman on Gorky Street that evening.

'Your Russian is very good,' Katya said as they walked towards her Porsche.

'Thank you.'

'Have we met before?'

'Regrettably not.'

'Funny,' she said, 'I could have sworn your voice was familiar.'

Ashton steeled himself not to look at her. Either Katya Malinovskaya had a phenomenal ear or else she had somehow discovered that a year ago he had spoken to her on the telephone while on the illegal trip to Moscow.

'I don't know what to say,' he told her in all honesty.

The complex housing the Russian Intelligence Service at Yasenevo on the outer Moscow ring road had formerly belonged to the First

323

Chief Directorate of the KGB. However, apart from operating under a different name, the basic structure of the organisation was unchanged. Computer Services, Signal Intercept and Crypto Analysis were still located in the Technical Services building north-east of the twin car parks fronting the headquarters block.

The tape of the intercept picked up by a mobile monitoring station near Riga the previous evening was delivered to the officer in charge of the Crypto Analysis Department at 16.00. When decoded, it read: *For attention Valentin. With reference to your request transmitted 02 July 19.34 Zulu hours. MERCURY restored to health and currently staying Pekin Hotel Moscow. ENDS.*

In keeping with established practice, the tape and clear text were subsequently handed over to the Deputy Chief of the RIS by the OIC Crypto Analysis Department.

Chapter 28

In the age-old battle of the sexes, punctuality was not something most men associated with the female of the species. There were, of course, exceptions to any generalisation and Katya Malinovskaya was a prime example. Ashton could have set his watch by her; at exactly 8.30 she walked into the lobby of the Pekin Hotel.

'If you're ready, Mr Ashton,' she said and turned on her heel.

Yesterday's blue silk dress with the motif of white polka dots had been replaced by a loose-fitting cotton garment that resembled a toga. The same high-heeled shoes were still in favour as was the Gucci shoulder bag containing the essential piece of hardware that a surprising number of citizens were carrying in Moscow these days. There were other pointers to show that Katya Malinovskaya was not inclined to leave things to chance. Although the Porsche couldn't have been left unattended for more than a couple of minutes, she hadn't been content just to lock the car and set the alarm, she had also clamped the steering wheel.

'This is a very expensive coupé,' she told him. 'I do not want to lose it.'

'I can see that,' Ashton said.

She barely gave him time to clip the seat belt home. Firing the engine into life, Katya engaged first gear, let the clutch out and put her foot down. Eighty thousand pounds worth of machinery responded with a deep-throated snarl. The hotel sat back from the Garden Ring Road. Without any loss of momentum, she glanced right and left, then made a right turn onto the fourteen-lane highway that had the tyres screaming in protest and left particles of burning rubber on the asphalt in their wake. Lane-hopping, she went on down the boulevard past the planetarium and made another right turn to cross the Moscow River by the Kalinin Bridge. Some landmarks such as the vast wedding-cake structure of the Ukrainia Hotel were familiar sights, others like the Borodino Panorama Museum on Kutusov Avenue were not. Up ahead, a signboard informed them they were on the right road for Minsk, Brest Litovsk, Warsaw and Berlin.

'Do you know how to find the Municipal Housing Authority in Kuncevo?' he asked.

'But of course.' Katya looked surprised that he should ask, as if the housing authority in Kuncevo District was a must for every tourist.

'Whereabouts do you live in Moscow?'

'Chinki-Chovrino,' she told him and kept her eyes on the road ahead. Presently she made yet another right turn, this time into Republic Boulevard.

The Municipal Housing Authority for Kuncevo was located in an undistinguished building in an equally once seen quickly forgotten street. Finding her way there wasn't a problem for Katya. The difficulties arose when Ashton walked into the building to collect the key to the flat at 636 Jel' Ninokaja. The commercial attachés had done everything that had been asked of them and the necessary documents couldn't be faulted, but that didn't stop a myopic official examining the papers line by line. Ten minutes into this bravura performance Ashton took out his wallet, extracted ten dollars and was rewarded with an understanding smile and the keys to Zelenov's flat.

The apartment house on Jel' Ninokaja was not one of the drab multi-storey barrack blocks that disfigured the northern suburbs. Although the architect would have won few laurels at an Ideal Homes exhibition, the five-storey apartment house was not totally displeasing to the eye. Zelenov's flat on the second floor consisted of a medium-size bedroom, a kitchen-diner, a sitting room and a bathroom/lavatory, which was an almost unheard-of luxury. The previous occupants had left the place in a good state of repair but the decoration left something to be desired.

'What do you think of it?' he asked.

'It looks very bare,' Katya said.

'Well, it would, the furniture hasn't arrived yet. What I want you to do is make the flat secure – spyhole in the door, security chain, locks on all the windows, intruder alarm system with panic button—'

'Do you do this for all your local representatives?' Katya asked, interrupting him.

'You have some objection?'

'No, I'm just naturally curious.'

'I also want all three main rooms bugged. I guess that makes you even more curious?'

'No, it doesn't. I imagine you would want to eavesdrop on Mr Zelenov in case he went into business on his own account.'

'So have you seen enough or do you want another guided tour?'

'That won't be necessary.' Katya took a pocket calculator out of her shoulder bag. 'How would you like to pay?' she asked. 'Dollars or pounds?'

'Dollars.' The CIA was funding half the cost of the operation and he had departed from London with a hefty down payment, courtesy of Garfield's friend in Grosvenor Square. 'And I want the job done in a hurry,' he added.

Her fingers stopped flying over the buttons. 'What do you call a hurry?'

'It has to be finished by tomorrow evening.'

Her fingers flew over the buttons again, inflating whatever figure she had dreamed up in the first place. 'Two thousand seven hundred and fifty.' She pulled a face. 'I warned you last night it would be expensive.'

'You certainly did.'

'And that doesn't include the bodyguards. A team of three will cost you seventy-five dollars a day.'

'We'll run them for a week, starting at twelve noon the day after tomorrow. Ashton took out his wallet and gave Katya ten one-hundred-dollar bills. 'Consider this a down payment.'

He waited while she held each note up to the light. Evidently, in her book, the fact that they were all well used and had random serial numbers didn't mean they weren't counterfeit. The inspection over, he gave her the spare key to the flat.

'I'll have it back off you when you pick me up from the hotel tomorrow evening at five o'clock. Okay?'

'No problem.'

'Good. Now you can drop me off at Ehrensvard on Kalinin Prospekt.'

'Ehrensvard?' she repeated, frowning.

'It's a new furniture store – a joint venture with the Finns.'

'How I envy Mr Zelenov,' Katya said drily. 'He's a very lucky man to be working for a company like Stilson Manufacturing.'

The weathermen had called it a summer storm in their forecast which was a bit of a misnomer because summer hadn't been much in evidence so far. The black thunder clouds were however an appropriate reflection of Hazelwood's anger and the explosive energy he was about to release. None of his colleagues had ever seen him in a really foul mood; consequently, Garfield had no idea what he was walking into when he received a brief note from the Deputy DG inviting him to step along to his office.

'You wanted to see me, Victor,' he said brightly and closed the door behind him.

'*For attention Valentin*,' Hazelwood grated, reading the file copy from the Signals Centre. '*With reference to your request transmitted 02 July 19.34 Zulu hours. MERCURY restored to health and currently staying Pekin Hotel Moscow. ENDS.*' He threw the signal at the younger man. 'You want to tell me what that's all about?'

Garfield turned a delicate shade of pink. 'We're telling Valentin where he can find Ashton.'

'Jesus Christ.' Forked lightning cleaved the black sky; an instant later there was a rolling clap of thunder as if God had been angered by the blasphemy. Although the violent din made Garfield flinch, it had no effect on Hazelwood. 'Amazing as it may seem to you,' he continued, 'the true meaning of that coded message had dawned on me. What I want to know is why it was sent and on whose authority?'

Garfield bent down and picked up the file copy of the signal which had fallen at his feet and placed it on the desk. 'We thought it would give the operation a kick start,' he said carefully, then pulled up a chair and sat down without waiting to be asked. 'As things stood, too much was being left to chance. Let's face it, Victor, if Zelenov is to be the honey pot, the bees have to know he's in town.'

'So the idea is to put Valentin on to Ashton who will lead him to the old war horse?'

'Well, he is going to meet Zelenov at the airport.'

'I don't believe I'm hearing this,' Hazelwood told him with barely suppressed fury.

'I don't understand why you are so angry, we haven't put Ashton in jeopardy. On the second of July, Valentin indicated that he wanted to meet him in ten days' time and we put him off and kept on doing so. All we've done is explain why Ashton hasn't been available until now.'

'Stick to the original excuse about kick-starting the operation, it has more validity.' Hazelwood picked up the signal on his desk. 'This was dispatched the day before Ashton left for Moscow. Did anyone tell him he had been sick?'

Garfield didn't answer, there wasn't anything he could say. What angered Hazelwood was the fact that he had only discovered the signal by chance. If he hadn't sent for the Valentin file to bring himself up to date, he wouldn't have known of its existence.

'You should have consulted me before you drafted that signal, Rowan.'

'The DG knew about it,' Garfield said sullenly.

'Are you saying he okayed the text?'

'Not exactly, but he appreciated that we had to give Valentin a gentle prod.'

'You keep saying "we". Who's the other genius?'

'Hal Reindekker.'

'Dear God.' Hazelwood closed his eyes. 'Reindekker.'

'The operation is being financed largely by the CIA; Hal Reindekker is their case officer.'

And it seemed he could do no wrong in Garfield's eyes. He had been introduced to the American by the friend in Grosvenor Square when he had been brokering a deal with the CIA's man in London and had been suitably impressed. Reindekker had travelled from Tallinn to London by way of Helsinki to attend that first meeting and had become something of a commuter since then. And with each visit he had grown in stature. Listening to Garfield's eulogy about how the American had won his spurs in Vietnam and the terrific work he had done in the Baltic States, especially in Lithuania when the Russians had tried to bring the country to heel, Hazelwood could see that his words of advice had fallen on deaf ears.

'Remember that small proviso I made?' Hazelwood said, interrupting him in full flow. 'I told you that no matter how many dollars the Yanks might contribute, we had to run the operation.'

'Yes, I know. If we let the CIA take control they will want to see an early return on their investment, et cetera, et cetera. But I happen to agree with their point of view, and so does our Director. We just can't sit back and hope Valentin will somehow discover that ex-Major General L. N. Zelenov is now residing in Moscow. We're playing a big enough longshot as it is. Our old Red Army man may have commanded an élite airborne division with distinction in Afghanistan but it doesn't follow that he had any dealings with the KGB's hierachy. That's why we have to put the players into juxtaposition and then wait to see what happens.'

'I don't like it.'

'With respect, Victor, you can't keep changing your mind.'

'What exactly do you mean by that?' Hazelwood asked sharply.

'First you tell the Director that Ashton can't go to Moscow because his face is too well known over there, then suddenly he volunteers and it's okay. Valentin sends word he wants to meet Ashton and we prevaricate because we want to make him realise that we are not going to jump through the hoop every time he snaps his fingers. You tell me it's all part of the softening up process before we throw Zelenov at him. Only now it seems you don't want to engineer a confrontation.'

There was, he recognised, some truth in Garfield's allegation. He had changed his mind several times, but not because he was indecisive. He had kept Valentin dangling in the hope that Nicholson would eventually crack and provide them with the information they needed to identify the 'Insider'. And by playing for time, there was a chance that instead of sending Ashton into the lion's den, he could find a new friend for Zelenov.

'I think you are worrying yourself unnecessarily, Victor.'

'Oh, do you!' Hazelwood pointed a finger at him as if it were a pistol. 'Well, you'd just better pray that nothing happens to Ashton.'

'You won't find me running for cover, if that's what's bothering you.'

'It isn't, and you wouldn't get a chance to duck below the parapet.'

'Is there anything else you want to say to me?' Garfield asked stiffly.

'Yes. Next time you have an urge to signal Valentin, make sure you consult me first.'

'Right.' Garfield stood up, put the chair back where he had found it and started towards the door, then turned about to deliver a parting shot. 'I know you think we've virtually put a pistol to Ashton's head, but this won't be the first time you've been wrong, Victor. I remember you telling us that we would never hear from Valentin again after what had happened in Tallinn and that same night he signalled us from Riga.'

Taken aback, Hazelwood could only watch the door close behind Garfield as he left the office. He was getting old, losing his grip. Opening the carved box, he took out a cheroot and lit it, savouring the aroma as he blew a smoke ring towards the ceiling. It was raining heavily now but the thunder had moved away. He hoped it was a good omen.

Appearances were often misleading and this was particularly true of Pavel Trilisser. A lean, aesthetic-looking man, he was often taken for a member of the Academy of Sciences, an academic, a high-ranking judge or a distinguished physicist by strangers encountering him at a social function. Now aged fifty-four, he was in fact the deputy head of the Russian Intelligence Service which was the same post he'd held when the RIS was known as the First Chief Directorate of the KGB.

Trilisser was rightly regarded as a brilliant officer. He had received accelerated promotion to Lieutenant General and had been the youngest deputy head of the Foreign Intelligence Service when he was appointed to the post in 1987. From such a platform he'd had every expectation that one day he would become Chairman of the KGB. However, six years later, he was still two rungs from the top of the ladder. His career had suffered a set-back when the hardliners had turned against Gorbachev in August 1991.

Although internal security was the responsibility of the Second Chief Directorate in what used to be Dzerzhinsky Square, a number of Yeltsin's supporters felt that he should have intervened much earlier than he had. His detractors had been convinced that Pavel Trilisser had waited until it was evident that the coup was going to fail before he arrested his own chief and sent word to the Minister of the Interior, Boris Pugo, that he should surrender himself to the paratroops of the Ryazan Division who were about to surround his apartment. Victor Ivanenko, whom Yeltsin had installed as his Chairman of the KGB, had invited a select audience to witness the arrest of the Minister of the Interior. The spectacle had backfired; when a neighbour had let them into his apartment with a spare key, they had found Pugo lying on the bed dying from a self-inflicted gunshot wound in the mouth. From his seriously injured wife, they had learned of Trilisser's phone call.

Neither black, nor white, Trilisser had been classified as grey in the aftermath of Yeltsin's victory. In keeping with this assessment, he had been left in post and a younger, less competent but more politically reliable officer had been promoted over his head to command the RIS.

He had shown no resentment towards his new chief and had uncomplainingly carried through a number of far-reaching reforms which had made the Service more accountable but less effective. Of the various RIS departments, he was responsible for overseeing Operational Planning, Technical Support, Counter Intelligence and Computer Services, previously known as Directorates E, OT, K and I respectively.

Counter Intelligence was headed by Vasili Petrovich Urzhumov, one of Trilisser's hand-picked subordinates. In common with the other department heads, Urzhumov was required to give a verbal situation report covering the previous twenty-four hours at the daily morning conference at 07.30 hours. However, in the last eight months, the workload of Counter Intelligence had become the heaviest of any department and it was not unusual for him to meet the deputy head of the RIS on a one-to-one basis later in the day. This usually involved a short walk from his own office to the main building. But on that particular afternoon, he had to drive out to Novo-Yasenevo, a training camp a hundred and forty kilometres north-west of Moscow in order to meet Trilisser. He found him in a clearing of the birch forest, watching a group of men and women stripping and re-assembling a variety of semi-automatic weapons while blindfolded.

'You have news for me, Vasili Petrovich?' he asked quietly.

'About Mercury – yes.' Urzhumov backed away, drawing Trilisser on until they were out of earshot of the others, then told him that Ashton had checked into the Pekin Hotel yesterday evening under his own name. 'This morning he was collected from the hotel by Katya Malinovskaya and taken to the Municipal Housing Office for the Kuncevo District. They then drove on to an apartment house at 636 Jel' Ninokaja . . .'

'Katya Malinovskaya?'

'She used to be a sergeant in the Criminal Investigation Division; now she runs her own security agency. *Pravda* did a piece on her in their Moscow business page a few months ago.'

'I wonder why Ashton should need her services? He's not planning to move into this flat on Jel' Ninokaja, is he?'

'I don't know. Could be he's obtained it for somebody else? I suppose we could ask the officials at the Municipal Housing Office?'

'I don't think so, we don't want to draw attention to ourselves. Our best course is to keep the apartment house under observation and await developments.'

'They're already in motion. When they left the flat an hour later, Katya Malinovskaya dropped Ashton off at Ehrensvard furniture store in Kalinin Prospekt. Ehrensvard is a joint venture with a Finnish company in Helsinki; they import Scandinavian furniture.'

'I wish I knew what London is up to.' Trilisser aimed a kick at a tuft of couch grass. 'Hitherto, they've always responded to Valentin's instructions, now it looks as if they are trying to control events.'

'Will Valentin do business with them again?'

'Look around you, tell me what you see.'

Five dachas dotted haphazardly about in a forest clearing, a path meandering through the birch trees towards a lake hidden from view. An under-strength platoon being exercised in basic weapon-handling skills.

'How many foot soldiers do we have, Vasili Petrovich?'

'Three hundred and twenty-five,' Urzhumov told him promptly, 'organised in teams of five led by a senior lieutenant with a sergeant as second in command.'

'And what are their rates of pay?' Trilisser asked quietly.

'Officers get forty US dollars a week, sergeants thirty, enlisted men twenty.'

It didn't sound a lot but converted to roubles, twenty dollars represented a small fortune and was more than enough to keep a family of four in comfort.

'And that doesn't include the specialists in the upper echelons, Vasili Petrovich.'

Urzhumov knew what was coming even before he was asked how long they could keep going on a hundred thousand dollars. 'Not quite ten weeks,' he murmured.

'Well, there you are,' Trilisser said irritably. 'Valentin has to do business with London. But in the meantime, we watch Ashton and walk in his shadow until we know what is happening, and then we make our move.'

The entrance to Deep Shelter Four was located in the grounds of what had been the Moscow residence of the Stroganov family before the October Revolution of 1917. To the casual observer, it appeared to be a stable block that had been allowed to fall into disrepair by the clerical staff of Tusino District Council who now occupied the house. No stranger to the site, Urzhumov drove straight there after leaving the training camp, showed his building clearance pass to the duty gateman, and parked his modest Lada saloon behind the stables where it was out of sight from both the house and the approach road, then went into the building.

All twelve stalls appeared to be in a dilapidated condition. Opening the one facing the entrance to the stable block, he stepped inside and went on down two narrow flights of steps which ended at a steel door. Urzhumov took out a key and unlocking the door rolled it back on its bearings. He switched on the lights, entered the open lift facing him and closed the gate, then pressed the button for Level Two.

Deep Shelter Four was one of six nuclear bunkers sited around the periphery of Moscow. Work on these had started when Stalin was alive and had been completed under Brezhnev. Each bunker provided shelter for one thousand VIPs, had its own emergency generator, air recycling plant, heating, ablution and sewage systems. The bunkers were also stocked with six months' supply of fuel and provisions. Thanks to a remarkable feat of engineering, each shelter was connected by underground Metro to the major government buildings in the city centre utilising existing track where possible. Deep Shelter Four was on a direct line to the Russian Parliament and Ministry of Defence some fifteen miles away.

Alighting from the lift at Level Two, Urzhumov followed the directional signs for the emergency hospital. It was his job to check that the latest batch of medical supplies had not been tampered with. The chests were arranged in stacks of fifty but instead of surgical instruments, field dressings, splints and drugs, they contained AK47 Kalashnikov assault rifles, 7.62mm RPK light machine-guns, RGD-5 hand grenades and AT-3 Manual Command to Line of Sight wire-guided anti-tank missiles.

Chapter 29

Attractive as the view was from the British Embassy on the Maurice Thores Embankment south of the Moscow River, Hugo Calthorpe did not usually make a habit of coming into the office on a Sunday morning. He did so today in order to check that everything was up and running. He went to his combination safe and rotated the dial in clockwise and counterclockwise directions until he had worked through the sequence of numbers which made up the setting. He lined up zero with the benchmark on the rim, moved the dial forward one more time, then yanked the handle down when he heard the tumblers click. Reaching inside the safe, he took out a small short-wave transmitter identical in appearance to a Cellnet phone and pulled out the extending aerial.

The transmitter had been provided by the US Army's Signal Corps. It had been passed to him at an official reception to mark the Fourth of July by one of the CIA operatives on the staff of the American Embassy, a good fortnight before the operation had been finalised. Fitted with a built-in scrambler and with a range in excess of ten miles, the transmitter would enable him to function as a case officer without ever coming into physical contact with the agent in place.

At exactly 10.45 the transmitter started bleeping like a Cellnet phone. Calthorpe picked up the transmitter and, holding the mike close to his mouth, gave his fictitious extension number.

'How do you hear me?' Ashton asked.

'Loud and clear.'

'You too. You'll be pleased to hear that the decorators have done a first-rate job, so have the removal men.'

In veiled speech, Ashton was telling him two things about the flat in Kuncevo. It was now protected by a highly sophisticated intruder alarm system and had been fully furnished. 'No problems then?' Calthorpe said.

'Not so far. I'll be leaving shortly to meet our friends.'

'Good. Please give them my regards.'

'I'll be sure to do that,' Ashton said.

A faint click told Calthorpe that he had signed off. Before leaving for the airport, Ashton would establish contact with the American Embassy and the lines of communication would then be firmly established. Whether they would remain open after Zelenov had been familiarised with the system was another matter. But if there was a foul-up and the operation became public, at least there would be nothing to implicate the embassy. The commercial attachés might have started the ball rolling with the housing authority but Stilson Manufacturing had done all the spadework thereafter. The same applied to Katya Malinovskaya's security agency to an even greater extent. Calthorpe had simply given Stilson her business address together with a list of satisfied clients. Their personnel manager had then written direct to the agency giving Katya Malinovskaya the impression that her firm had been recommended to him.

As Head of Chancery, Richard Quennell had taken it upon himself to express his satisfaction that Calthorpe had managed to put the two interested parties in touch without drawing attention to himself. London too was pretty satisfied with the way he'd handled matters. If he said so himself, Calthorpe reckoned he'd brought off a minor miracle.

Domodedovo, one of two airports south of the city used purely for domestic services, was much quieter than its international neighbour, Sheremetyevo 2. It hadn't always been that way. Before Aeroflot had been split up among the newly emergent independent states, before a cash crisis had forced national carriers to cancel many of their scheduled flights, the airport had been really jumping. Ashton had thought he would be meeting Leonid Nikolaevich Zelenov and Vera Vorontsova at the international airport until he'd checked with the enquiries desk at the hotel and learned that the flight from Tallinn would be landing at Domodedovo. 'Estonian Airlines,' the girl had added, leaving him to draw the conclusion that this was the way the Russians were getting even with the Balts.

The elderly Tupolev Tu154 from Tallinn had arrived half empty which meant that Ashton was spared a long wait. Barely twenty minutes after the plane had touched down, the Zelenovs appeared in the Arrivals Hall carrying all their worldly goods in two battered-looking suitcases.

'I hope this flat of yours is well equipped,' Zelenov said as they shook hands.

'I think you'll find we have thought of most things,' Ashton told him.

'I hope so, because Vera Vorontsova sold all our household utensils before we left. I told her we wouldn't need them in Moscow.'

'And you were right.' Ashton relieved Vera Vorontsova of her suitcase and then found himself carrying the General's as well.

'Yours?' Zelenov enquired when he led them towards the BMW.

'Rented.'

'Thought so.'

'How was your flight?'

'Not bad. Saw your American friend at the airport. I thought he had come to see us off but it seems he was waiting for the Finnair flight to Helsinki.'

Zelenov's tone of voice made it clear that he hadn't believed a word Reindekker had told him. Without comment, Ashton unlocked the car, put the suitcases in the trunk, then opened the door for Vera Vorontsova.

'I'm riding up front with you,' Zelenov announced and promptly got into the car. Apart from observing that it was good to be back, he didn't say another word until they reached the apartment house on Jel' Ninokaja. 'Looks a nice neighbourhood, Mr Aak . . . sh . . . ton.'

'I'm glad it meets with your approval, Leonid Nikolaevich.'

Ashton lifted the suitcases out of the boot and carried them up to the flat on the second floor, then let the Zelenovs into their new home. 'These are yours now,' he said and gave Vera Vorontsova the keys.

Compared with what they had been used to at 21 Vanu Viru, the flat was a veritable palace. Everything about it thrilled Vera Vorontsova, the bathroom, large bedroom, kitchen-diner, living room, the Scandanavian furniture, the well-stocked refrigerator and larder. It didn't take Zelenov long to find the bottle of vodka in the sideboard.

'Stolichnaya. Now that's what I call the real thing,' he said appreciatively. 'Where did you get it? At one of the Beriozka shops?'

'Yes.'

'Thought so. That bloody Siberian arsehole believes in looking after the tourists before his own people.' Zelenov found a couple of glasses, broke the seal on the bottle and poured two very large measures. 'I'll give you a toast,' he said and passed a tumbler to Ashton. 'Fire in your belly.'

'And yours.'

'Good. Now that we've sealed our friendship, perhaps you will tell me what all that shit is doing in the corner of the room up near the ceiling?'

'It's part of the security system. With the exception of the bathroom, there's a magic eye in every room.' Ashton opened the centre drawer in the sideboard and took out one of the control units which was about the size of a matchbox. 'Press the white button once as you leave the flat and the alarm is set. To switch it off, you do the same thing the moment you open the front door. The red button is the panic alarm. Someone breaks into the flat while you're at home, you press that and the warbler starts shrieking loud enough to split your eardrums and make the intruder piss in his pants.'

'Tell me something, Mr Englishman. Why do I need it?'

'Moscow's a dangerous place these days; makes Washington, Miami and New York seem almost tranquil. That's why I've had locks put on all the windows, and there's a spy hole in the door.'

'I've got nothing worth stealing, Mr Englishman.'

'Maybe not, but some people are going to think you are a very wealthy man.'

He wasn't fooling Zelenov; it showed in his eyes and the way he now addressed him as Mr Englishman. Putting a brave face on it, Ashton showed him the transmitter.

'It's a battery-powered radio telephone,' he explained. 'It's tuned to a single fixed channel. You switch it on, punch out double two, double four and you're through to the Moscow office. Any time of the day or night someone will be there. Watch me.' Ashton tapped out the four figure number, spoke to Calthorpe in English to let him know their guests had arrived safely, then handed the phone to Zelenov. 'Say hello to the man, he can speak your language.'

The Russian looked at him with deep suspicion, then cleared his throat and growled a hello into the microphone. 'You are a friend of Mr Aak . . . sh . . . ton?' he asked.

'We work for the same company,' Calthorpe told him.

'So who are you?' Zelenov demanded rudely.

'I'm the marketing director for Stilson Manufacturing with responsibility for Eastern Europe.'

'You have a name?'

'I'm Henry Stilson,' Calthorpe said, lying effortlessly. 'My cousin owns the firm and we're delighted that you're joining us.'

'Thank you,' Zelenov said and returned the phone to Ashton, leaving him to sign off.

'Easy, wasn't it?' Ashton said, collapsing the aerial and moving the switch to the 'off' position.

'Will this Mr Henry Stilson always be there when I phone?'

'No. He's the marketing director and you wouldn't expect him to be chained to a desk all the time. But one of his assistants will certainly answer the phone in his absence.'

It wasn't only the British Embassy who responded to 2244; the same number also activated a listening post in the US Embassy. If Hugo Calthorpe or one of his minions failed to react within fifteen seconds, someone on the CIA team would.

'I'm impressed.' Zelenov stepped into the kitchen, told Vera Vorontsova in a loud voice that they would like some coffee later but in the meantime she was not to disturb them. Having issued his orders, he returned to the living room and took Ashton aside. 'Now, suppose you tell me what I am being paid to do?'

'Interest potential clients in our machine tools and dies. I've left some sales literature for you to study—'

'Cut the shit, Mr Englishman, you must think I'm still suckling at my mother's breast. I know fuck all about your products and all my friends are in the army.'

'That's why we need you,' Ashton said quickly. 'We want to tap into the old military industrial network. We'd like you to visit your old haunts, renew acquaintances . . .'

'You want me as a spy.'

'No.'

'I won't betray my country.'

'No one's asking you to.'

'You are not a businessman.' Zelenov wagged a finger under his nose, almost sprayed him with spittle in his anger. 'You're not *Mafiozniki* either.'

'You knew that in Tallinn,' Ashton said coldly, 'so don't get on your high horse with me, old man.' He adopted a more conciliatory approach and softened his tone a little. 'Now, you settle in, read those brochures, and we'll talk about this again tomorrow morning. Okay?'

Zelenov took his time before answering and sounded less than enthusiastic when he did, but he was not about to go a hundred per cent patriotic on him and that was what mattered to Ashton.

'That's the spirit, Leonid Nikolaevich,' he said and patted the old warhorse on the shoulder, then asked him to give his apologies to Vera Vorontsova for not staying for coffee.

Ashton left the flat, went downstairs and got into the BMW. It was almost one o'clock. The bodyguards Katya Malinovskaya had contracted to provide at twenty-five dollars a day were supposed to come on duty at noon, but as of that moment there was no sign of them anywhere on Jel' Ninokaja.

Sunday evening in Moscow was like Sunday evening anywhere else – dull, flat, depressing. Ashton dined early, then went up to his hotel room and played around with the TV, switching from channel to channel in the hope of finding some programme that was mildly entertaining. His personal transmitter started bleeping in the middle of a panel game that had been derived from *What's My Line?* back in the fifties.

Answering the signal, he heard a familiar voice say, 'Hi there, how are you doing?'

Reindekker was in town; he had seen the Zelenovs off in Tallinn and had then come on by road.

'I'm okay,' Ashton told him.

'How about our friends?'

'Settling in. Leonid is having a bit of trouble with his conscience.'

'He can't afford to have one,' Reindekker said and laughed.

'I may have to point that out to Leonid when I see him tomorrow morning.'

'Do whatever you have to, Peter, just so long as we get a result.' Reindekker paused, then said, 'Does anyone know he's back in Moscow yet?'

'It's possible.'

'Let's hope you're right. Talk to you tomorrow.'

Ashton heard a click and switched off his transmitter. At his request, Katya Malinovskaya had bugged the flat in Jel' Ninokaja. Although she had turned the receiver over to him, it didn't mean she was unable to eavesdrop on the Zelenovs and he knew there were some people in London who were counting on her to do just that.

Of the department chiefs who answered directly to him, the Head of Computer Services was the one man Pavel Trilisser didn't trust. He had been brought in from the Ministry of Science and Technology when Yeltsin had purged the RIS, and that made him suspect. It was for this reason, rather than the strict observance of the need-to-know principle, that he had forbidden Vasili Petrovich Urzhumov to raise anything relating to the Mercury file at the daily conference. He was therefore not surprised to receive a phone call from the Head of Counter Intelligence half an hour after the meeting had dispersed asking if he could spare him a few minutes.

Ashton, he learned, had been particularly busy during the past seventy-two hours, starting on Friday afternoon when he had returned to the apartment house at 636 Jel' Ninokaja to accept delivery of a van load of furniture from Ehrensvard. He had arrived without Katya Malinovskaya in a BMW which he'd hired through the car rental desk at the Pekin.

'That evening he visited the Beriozka shop at the Minsk Hotel in Gorky Street,' Urzhumov continued. 'He purchased two cartons of Marlboro cigarettes, then proceeded on foot to the nearby Kino Rossija. After the performance, he left the movie theatre carrying the same plastic bag.'

'Did he meet anyone in the auditorium?' Trilisser asked.

'If he did, it went unobserved.'

'I wonder why he went to the Kino?'

'Perhaps he was bored and had nothing better to do?' Urzhumov suggested.

'There is a Beriozka shop in every hotel, there was no need for him to patronise the one at the Minsk. He chose to do so for a reason.' Trilisser suddenly looked up from his desk and gazed at Urzhumov. 'Did any of the tourists who were shopping in the Beriozka when Ashton was there also go on to the Kino?' he asked.

'It's possible. I do know a woman was observed leaving the Kino carrying one of their distinctive bags.'

Counter Intelligence had slipped up. She had probably been there when Ashton had bought the damned cigarettes and they had worked a switch, the oldest trick in the book. And what annoyed Trilisser even more was the fact that they had pulled it off under the noses of the surveillance team.

'I'd give a lot to know what was in that bag,' he said.

'Could it have been a transmitter?'

'What prompted that thought, Vasili Petrovich?'

'Nothing, it was just a shot in the dark,' Urzhumov said, then hastily corrected himself. 'Well, perhaps an informed guess.'

'So share it with me.'

'Ashton returned to the flat on Saturday evening and was joined by Katya Malinovskaya. There is reason to believe that the purpose of his visit this time was to inspect the work that had been carried out by some of her operatives.'

'What sort of work?'

'I would guess they had installed some kind of electronic protective system. Naturally we haven't been inside the flat because that would have been too risky, but if the length of time they spent in there is anything to go by, it has to be more than just the peephole which has appeared in the door.'

'When did they start?'

'Friday afternoon about 13.00 hours.'

Urzhumov was right; they had had plenty of time in which to install some pretty complicated gadgetry. He wondered why Ashton should have wanted to turn the place into a fortress and for whom? If the *Mafiozniki* had been involved he could have understood it, but Ashton was SIS.

'Interesting,' he said in a non-committal tone of voice.

'There's more. After Katya Malinovskaya had departed, Ashton unloaded a large box of groceries from the car and carried it into the flat.'

'And what happened yesterday, Vasili Petrovich?' Urzhumov's reluctance to look him in the eye was an ominous sign; it almost certainly meant that the fuck-up factor had been at work. 'Tell me the worst.'

'Ashton left the hotel shortly after ten in the morning and drove straight to the flat. He only stayed a few minutes before going on to the airport.'

'To meet someone,' Trilisser said, drawing the only possible conclusion, then found himself listening to a lengthy explanation from Urzhumov about how his men had neglected to inform him of Ashton's movements until a good quarter of an hour after the Englishman had arrived at the Domodedovo terminal.

'By the time I got there, he had already departed.'

'I don't want to hear your excuses,' Trilisser said icily. 'Just tell me who he met.'

'There were two of them, an old man and his wife. They arrived on the plane from Tallinn.'

Tallinn: merely to hear the name was enough to make his stomach churn.

'Describe them,' he snapped.

Urzhumov reared back as if he'd been struck. 'They were both old. The man was thickset, had short legs, broad shoulders, and walks with a slight stoop.'

'And the woman?' Trilisser continued remorselessly.

'I was told she had a round, doughy face and small eyes. Her nose looks disjointed as if it had been broken sometime in the past, and she's rather on the large side.'

'Leonid Nikolaevich Zelenov and Vera Vorontsova.'

'That's what I thought,' Urzhumov said eagerly, 'soon as I learned they had arrived on an internal flight by Estonian Airlines.'

'I think we had better check to make sure. Forget what I said on Friday and ring the Municipal Housing Authority in Kuncevo.'

'I already have. I phoned them this morning after the daily conference.'

Urzhumov had spun the officials a tale about trying to find accommodation for an old hero of the Great Patriotic War of the Fatherland.

'Soon as I gave them his name, they told me a Mr L. N. Zelenov had already been allocated a flat at 636 Jel' Ninokaja.'

Trilisser wasn't listening. Ashton had turned the old Red Army man around because British Intelligence believed Zelenov could lead him to Valentin. But that didn't make a lot of sense; Ashton had met two men on successive nights in Tallinn, both of whom had claimed to be Valentin. Ashton wasn't stupid; the high-grade intelligence he had received from those two would have led him to conclude that Valentin was simply a collective name.

So what was the SIS hoping he could do for them? Zelenov had commanded an élite airborne division in Afghanistan and before that when the formation had been stationed in Moscow Military District where he had met a number of the Politburo and their acolytes. Perhaps the British were using the old General as bait, tethering him like a sacrificial goat to draw the first tiger which picked up the scent into the killing ground? They might bag something but not the particular tiger they were after. Or had they made the connection? Were they aware that he and Zelenov had met briefly when the airborne had been stood down for two weeks and a large part of the division had been on R and R in Kabul? Trilisser dismissed the possibility out of hand because he was convinced there was no way British Intelligence could have got on to that.

'Has Ashton contacted the British Embassy since he arrived in Moscow?' he asked.

'He hasn't been near Maurice Thores Embankment.'

'That isn't what I asked you. Has he phoned the embassy, written a letter, sent a message through a third party?'

Urzhumov gave the question a great deal of thought this time before he attempted to answer it.

'In his place, I wouldn't make a phone call from the hotel. I'd find a pay phone, and he hasn't done so. He hasn't been near a mailbox and I would know if he had tried to post a letter in the hotel. Apart from the Zelenovs and Katya Malinovskaya, Ashton hasn't met anyone else.'

Except for the unknown person who had switched shopping bags with him in the Kino Rossija. Trilisser scowled. And if he had been supplied with a short-wave transmitter, contacting the British Embassy would be child's play. However, as yet, Ashton had very little hard evidence to give them and if ever there was a time to deal with him, it was now.

'Is Ashton aware of being under surveillance?' Trilisser asked.

'He's given no sign of it and I would be very surprised if he was. There's a small army shadowing him and I've been ringing the changes to make sure he never sees the same face twice.'

'I think he should meet Valentin again.'

Urzhumov blinked. 'When?' he asked in a low voice.

'This evening,' Trilisser said, then told him what had to be done and how it was to be accomplished. 'Nothing must go wrong.'

'Don't worry,' Urzhumov assured him. 'Nothing will.'

'I'm glad to hear it,' Trilisser said, dismissing him.

There had been too many mistakes already, starting with de Vries and culminating with the near-disaster of Nicholson. The offer of five hundred thousand Deutschmarks for his services from a former Stasi officer had been impossible to refuse. The approach had been made through one of the 'Illegals' the RIS had left in place in the old East Zone as the Russian Armed Forces were withdrawn. Satisfied that his own security had not been compromised, he had agreed to reactivate "The Englishman", seeing in his decision a brilliant way of killing two birds with one stone. He could sell Nicholson to British Intelligence as well as the neo-Nazis while at the same time silencing the one man who had it in his power to expose Valentin. If things had gone according to plan, Nicholson should have been gunned down minutes after he had assassinated Joachim Wolff, but the Germans had fucked it up and he had been living on a knife edge ever since.

Maybe with hindsight he should have thought longer and harder about the offer, but would he have come to any other decision? Obtaining surplus weapons to arm the Secret Special Action Force he had established within the RIS had never been a problem. Finding the money to keep the unit in being until Parliament decided to topple Yeltsin was however an altogether different matter.

Trilisser left his desk and went over to the window in time to catch a final glimpse of Vasili Petrovich Urzhumov before he entered the Technical Services building. A good man, he thought, loyal, patriotic, but as in any game of chess it was sometimes necessary to sacrifice a major piece for the greater good.

Chapter 30

Ashton left the Pekin for the second time that day and walked to Mayakovskaya Metro station. He had spent a couple of hours with Zelenov getting nowhere and had then had a less than satisfactory meeting with Katya Malinovskaya when he'd dropped by her office in Gorky Street. Things hadn't improved thereafter. Lunch in the main dining room had finished by the time he had returned, and he had been having a quick wash and brush up in his room prior to trying the snack bar when Reindekker had paged him on the short-wave transmitter. Entering the station, he fed the turnstile with twenty kopeks and rode the escalator down to the platform below ground.

He took the train for Dinamo and got off at Belorusskaya, the next stop and interchange for the Circle Line. Following the signs for Park Kultury, he boarded a southbound train and started ringing the changes, alighting at Kievskaya to catch a train out to Kutuzovskaya before doubling back to pick up the Circle Line again for Oktyabrskaya where the American was waiting for him on the platform.

'You got anyone on your tail?' Reindekker asked him.

'I don't think so.'

'You mean you don't know?'

'Precisely,' Ashton said irritably.

'What the hell, I thought you were a pro.'

'Listen, it may only be three o'clock in the afternoon and the rush hour doesn't start until five, but in case you haven't noticed, the Metro isn't exactly deserted. It's difficult to tell whether anyone's

349

following you when there are a fair number of people about, and the bigger the surveillance team, the harder it gets. Now, what do you want to do?'

'There's a train coming,' Reindekker said, 'and we're going to get on it and ride the Circle Line. Okay?'

Ashton looked up and down the platform and saw no one he remembered alighting from the train he'd been on. Cool air brushed against his legs, and two pinpoints of light in the tunnel grew larger and brighter, then an eight-car unit pulled into the station. Half a dozen people left the car facing them; boarding it, Reindekker and Ashton turned left inside the doors and moved down the coach until they found a couple of seats away from the other passengers. Even then, the American waited until the train was on the move before he mentioned Zelenov.

'So how is the old s.o.b.?' he asked in English.

'He's not very happy.'

'I thought you were going to put him straight?'

'You don't hold a pistol to the head of a man like the Major General,' Ashton said quietly.

'No? What's he going to do if we lean on him? He can't shoot his mouth off to State Security without incriminating himself. He can't return to Tallinn because the Estonians won't have him back and he sold everything he owned before coming to Moscow. Leonid Nikolaevich is dependent on us for the roof over his head, the bed he sleeps in, the money in his pocket and the food in his belly.'

'I'm sure he already knows that, he's just finding it hard to accept his situation. Give him time and he'll gradually come to terms with it.'

'Time is a luxury we can ill afford. We've got Mr Yeltsin running around with a begging bowl and twisting our arm to put something in it otherwise democracy in Russia will go down the pan. Well, I'm telling you that before we start shelling out, we want to be damn sure the Siberian messiah is here to stay.'

The train rolled into Oktyabrskaya and came to a halt. As the doors opened, Reindekker made inconsequential small talk, his eyes on those entering and leaving the car. Ashton wondered what he would do if some Russian decided to sit next to him, but the situation didn't arise. Once they were on the move again,

Reindekker back-tracked and went on from where he had left off.

'We figure Valentin is the leader of a group of diehards who are determined to bring Yeltsin down. Now the sooner we discover what sort of asset we've got in this old soldier, the better it will be for all of us. If he can't point us at Valentin, we should dump him.'

'I bounced a name at him,' Ashton said.

'Yeah? Whose?'

'Pavel Trilisser. You heard of him?'

'Sure, your Rowan Garfield believes he is Valentin. The question is, how did Leonid Nikolaevich react?'

'He claimed he'd never heard of the man but his eyes didn't back him up. He has met Pavel Trilisser somewhere. I'm sure if you work on Zelenov after I've gone, he will eventually tell you where and when their paths crossed.'

'Fill me in,' Reindekker said. 'When are you returning to London?'

It was inconceivable that he hadn't been told. Garfield's friend from Grosvenor Square had been present at the final briefing and would have informed him that Ashton would spend exactly one week in Moscow easing Zelenov into place. After he had departed, the American would take over. Reindekker was just anxious to make sure the ground rules hadn't been rewritten.

'It's okay, Hal,' Ashton said, 'nothing's changed. I'm still leaving on Thursday.'

Reindekker started to say that he hoped Ashton didn't think he was anxious to see the back of him and was just getting into his stride when the train pulled into Dobryninskaya. This time, a burly middle-aged Russian plumped himself down in the adjoining seat and made it impossible for him to continue. For some reason the car became even more crowded at the next stop. At Taganskaya they got out, walked through the connecting subway and caught the first train heading in the opposite direction.

'There's something else you should know,' Ashton said when he judged it safe to resume their conversation. 'I had a difference of opinion with Katya Malinovskaya. She was contracted to provide a team of bodyguards to watch over Zelenov. I couldn't spot them yesterday and there was no sign of them this morning. All right, they're professionals and the ordinary Joe wouldn't know what to look for, but I do, and I'm telling you they weren't around. Naturally she said they were and claimed her people had rented a room in one of the flats across the road from 636 Jel' Ninokaja. Hard currency will buy you anything in Moscow, that was her line.' Ashton smiled. 'Sound familiar to you?'

'Are you saying she's lying?'

'Put it this way, if there are no bodyguards, Katya is either conning us or her people have been warned off.'

Reindekker said he would bear that in mind, made a few appreciative noises, then parted company with him at the next stop. Ashton went on to Belorusskaya and took a cab back to the Pekin. When he collected his room key, the girl on reception said there was a message for him and produced an envelope from one of the pigeonholes behind the counter.

Although the envelope burned a hole in his pocket, Ashton didn't open it until after he'd let himself into his hotel room and put the security chain on the door. The envelope contained a photocopy of a signal that had been received from London. The date/time group showed that it had been transmitted the night before he had left for Moscow, the message itself was prefixed with a caveat which read *For attention Valentin*. Ashton would have said it was a fake but for the sentence informing Valentin that Mercury had recovered and was now staying at the Pekin Hotel.

It angered him that Garfield had been less than frank at the briefing. Although he had told him just how the Russian Desk had been stalling Valentin, not one word had been said about this particular signal. There was, he thought, nothing like taking a calculated risk when you were over three thousand miles from the firing line.

Ashton went into the bathroom, took out a small penknife and crouching by the bath, used a blade to unscrew the side panel, then reached between the supporting cradles for the transmitter. He switched it on, extended the aerial, tapped out 2244 and got a bleep. He didn't know which embassy had acknowledged the call, but that wasn't important. Someone out there was on listening watch.

He returned to the bedroom, sat down in the easy chair and waited for the telephone to ring. There was every prospect that it would be a long vigil.

★ ★ ★

The sudden burr-burr of the telephone made Ashton jump. He had no recollection of falling asleep. When last awake, the evening shadows had been stealing across the room, now it was pitch-dark and he couldn't locate the phone. He got up, blundered into the bed, turned half right, groped for the table lamp. His hand encountered the light and almost swept it on to the floor, then he found the press button and the sixty-watt bulb seemed as bright as the noonday sun. He lifted the receiver and sat down on the edge of the bed. The combined clock and wake-up alarm showed that it was 21.14 hours.

A voice with a mid-Atlantic accent said, 'Good evening, Mr Ashton, I hope I haven't disturbed you.'

'Do I know you?'

'We haven't met yet but we soon will. Valentin wants to see you.'

Ashton tranferred the receiver to his left hand and bending forward, grabbed the transmitter which was lying on the floor by the easy chair. Bringing the radio close to the telephone, he held the transmit button down. 'What makes you think I want to see him?' he asked.

'Why else are you in Moscow?'

'To drum up some business for Stilson Manufacturing.'

'Take another look at that signal and save yourself a lot of time and effort. Your head office wants you to do business with us.'

'I don't always listen to London.'

'You'd better do so this time otherwise you'll be on the next flight to Heathrow. Also your friend Leonid Nikolaevich will find himself under house arrest pending further enquiries.'

'You're very persuasive,' Ashton said acidly.

'The hard currency bar in three minutes,' the caller told him and hung up.

Ashton replaced the phone and then spoke into the transmitter. 'Is anyone out there?' he asked.

'I am,' Reindekker answered.

'Okay. I don't know how much you heard but Valentin wants to see me and I'm on the move.'

Ashton switched off the set and collapsed the aerial. Conscious of how little leeway the messenger had given him, he shoved the radio under the bath, put the side panel back in place and forced the screws home. By the time he made it down to the hard currency bar on the mezzanine floor, he was still a good five minutes late.

Ashton stood in the entrance and looked slowly round the bar. As he did so, a man at the back of the room waved a hand, beckoning him to come on over to his table. The stranger was wearing a double-breasted brown pinstripe that was only a shade lighter than the colour of his hair. He had a pleasant, homely looking face and a friendly smile to complement it. When he stood up to greet him, Ashton saw that he was roughly an inch shorter than himself.

'I am Vasili Petrovich,' he announced. 'We haven't met before but I have studied your photograph many times.'

'I imagine you have.'

'I've ordered you a Scotch,' the Russian said and pointed to the spare glass. 'All the English like whisky – yes?'

'A lot of us do.' Ashton sat down at the table and leaned forward. 'Now suppose you forget the social niceties and tell me what is going on?'

'We are going to meet Valentin.'

'I don't have the kind of money he wants with me.'

'Oh come now, Mr Ashton, that isn't the way we do business. He merely wants to tell you what is available and how much you will have to pay for it. This is what we did in Tallinn, remember?'

'Yes, but I'm not going on a blind date with you,' Ashton told him, 'not unless I know what's in it for me.'

'I have no money to give you.'

'But you have some idea of what Valentin has for sale?'

The Russian hesitated and went through a whole series of facial contortions that were intended to convince Ashton that he would find himself in hot water if he said too much. 'He will tell you why Lieutenant Colonel Alexei Leven was executed,' Vasili Petrovich said at last.

'Leven was GRU – Military Intelligence.'

'No, he was always KGB. We put him in the GRU to look out for dissidents in the armed forces. Now we go, yes?'

Ashton reached for the glass of whisky and knocked it back in one. He hoped Reindekker wasn't too far away and had his wits about him because he couldn't stall Vasili Petrovich any longer.

'Why not?' he said.

They went down to the lobby and out on to the forecourt where the Russian had parked his car, an eight-year-old Lada. Despite its age and run-down appearance, he listed its plus points with all the fervour of a born-again salesman as he headed towards the intersection of Gorky Street with the Garden Ring Road. From time to time, Ashton glanced at the rear-view mirror but all he got was an oblique view of a stream of headlights as vehicle after vehicle overtook them on the outside lane. At the Gorky Street intersection the Russian turned right at the traffic lights.

'Did you know they had filmed Leven's execution?' Vasili Petrovich asked, abruptly changing the subject.

'Yes, I saw the movie.'

'You shouldn't believe everything you see on the screen, the camera can lie.'

Ashton stared at the road ahead. Hazelwood had suggested the execution might have been a fake and now it seemed he had been right. 'Are you saying Alexei Leven is still alive?' he asked.

'No, he went before the firing squad after the film had been made. The men who are hunting Valentin are brutal, ruthless and efficient. What you saw was a mock execution designed to break his resistance to interrogation.'

'What had Leven done?'

'He worked for Valentin.' Vasili Petrovich took one hand off the wheel and pointed to the glove compartment. 'You'll find a blindfold in there,' he said.

'What do I want with that?'

'You object? I can't see why, we're only observing the same procedures we used in Tallinn. Of course, if you refuse to accommodate us, my instructions are to turn back and drop you off at the Pekin Hotel.'

Ashton opened the glove compartment and took out the blindfold. He slipped the elastic band over his head and then fiddled around with the two large circular pads until they fitted snugly over his eyes.

'Now you are being sensible,' Vasili Petrovich told him.

'And Lieutenant Colonel Alexei Leven wasn't?'

'He was careless and also very unlucky. There were a number of officers in State Security who were convinced that you had turned him around, Mr Ashton. They became even more convinced of this when de Vries signalled Moscow querying the instructions he'd received and Leven tried to suppress the message. He was virtually a dead man when they searched his quarters and found he had microfilmed a large number of Top Secret documents.'

Nothing more was said. The last time Ashton had glanced at the speedometer, they had been doing the equivalent of forty miles an hour and he estimated some five minutes had elapsed since he had been required to blindfold himself. Based on those two factors, he reckoned they had covered a further three miles when the Russian eventually slowed down and made a left turn across the oncoming traffic.

The uneven surface told Ashton they were now on a minor road. They crossed several bridges and at one stage he heard a train in the distance. Occasionally, another vehicle passed them going in the opposite direction. Some twenty minutes after leaving the highway, Vasili Petrovich stopped the car and lowered the window on his side. Then someone opened a large iron gate and he drove on for a short distance before leaving the road to head cross country. After roughly fifty yards in first gear, he stopped again and this time switched off the engine.

'Please remain seated, Mr Ashton,' he said and got out.

Ashton heard Vasili Petrovich walk round the car, then the Russian opened the door and helped him out of the Lada. They walked ten paces, wheeled left and wheeled left again fifteen paces farther on, then stopped briefly while Vasili Petrovich unlocked a wooden door and pushed it back. Once inside the building, the Russian took his arm again and led him forward.

'There are some steps in front of us, Mr Ashton,' he said, 'but don't worry, I'll walk in front and guide you down.'

The staircase was narrow and consisted of two flights of concrete steps. At the bottom, Vasili Petrovich stopped to open some kind of lattice gate. It was only after the Russian had closed the gate behind them and Ashton heard the distant hum of an electric motor that he realised they were standing in a lift. The floor shuddered under his feet, then the lift began to descend.

Fear kept him rooted to the spot and paralysed his natural instinct for survival. Then Harriet entered his thoughts and he told himself that if he wanted to see her again, he had better do something and fast. As the lift bumped to a stop and the Russian released him while he opened the gate, Ashton surreptitiously pushed the blindfold up on to his forehead and saw they were in what appeared to be a large fall-out shelter. Three men were waiting for them and although no weapons were in evidence, he knew they were armed. He also knew that if he threw Vasili Petrovich out and closed the gate, he would be dead before he could set the lift in motion.

Ashton chose to do the unexpected. Keeping his head down, he stepped out of the lift and allowed Vasili Petrovich to close the gate behind them before he grabbed one of his arms and swung him into the other three Russians. He broke to the left because everywhere else was bathed in light. Head up, arms pumping across his chest, he ran for his life. Ten, fifteen, twenty, twenty-five, thirty yards; nothing but confused shouting to his rear. Fifty yards and the darkness closing in around him, then the first round came down the tunnel and he threw himself flat.

Someone opened up with an automatic and ripped off a long burst. Ricochets from the strike of shot whined above his head and he rolled over and over to get out of the beaten zone. The ground suddenly fell away beneath him and he landed heavily on his back between two steel bars. Then it rapidly dawned on him that he was lying on the Metro track and he couldn't tell which was the live rail.

The firing gradually died away and finally ceased altogether. In the ensuing silence, Ashton thought he could hear the lift moving either up or down the shaft. Presently the sound of voices reached him and moments later there was a crash of gunfire punctuated with shrill, agonised screams. Although the fire fight was over in a matter of seconds, it seemed the newcomers were not satisfied that everybody had been accounted for. Glancing back over his shoulder, Ashton saw two flashlights bobbing towards him. There was, he decided, only one thing he could do. Surrendering was always a dangerous business and he took care to do it before the flashlights illuminated him.

'Don't shoot,' he shouted in Russian, then repeated it in English before he stood up and raised his hands.

The militiamen were not exactly gentle with him after he had climbed back onto the platform. Once they had manacled his wrists behind his back, they urged him towards the lift, using their Kalashnikovs to butt-strike him about the head and ribs. But at least he was alive, which was more than could be said for Vasili Petrovich and the other three Russians. When they halted, Ashton found himself standing in front of a lean, aesthetic-looking man who had once appeared in a photograph of the British Archery Team at the Moscow Olympics.

'You must be Mercury,' Pavel Trilisser said. Without waiting for an answer, he added, 'That corpse behind you was Valentin, otherwise known as Vasili Petrovich Urzhumov.'

'Thanks for telling me,' Ashton said drily.

The militiamen shoved him into the lift and had a lot of fun slapping his face, bloodying his nose and splitting his bottom lip on the way up. By the time they bundled him into the waiting prison van, Ashton had also collected two black eyes. With his impaired vision, it was some moments before he realised he was not alone.

'Well, hi there,' Reindekker said. 'How're you doing?'

Ashton peered at him through narrow slits. The American had a nasty-looking gash high up on the left side of the skull and his hair was matted with blood. 'About as well as you,' he told Reindekker.

'Yeah, I guess it hasn't been our night.'

'So how did you get swept into the bag?'

'I followed you out here,' Reindekker said, 'and I was having this slight altercation with the gate guard when the 7th Cavalry arrived. Unfortunately, they weren't on our side.'

Chapter 31

Ashton and Reindekker were taken to Moscow's Lefortovo Prison where they were put in solitary confinement and questioned repeatedly over the next seventy-eight days. Unlike the arresting officers, the interrogators who grilled Ashton never resorted to violence. They were however very good at applying psychological pressure and he wasn't allowed much sleep.

They appeared to want confirmation that V. P. Urzhumov was the Valentin who had been passing information to the SIS and he was happy to go along with that. Six weeks into the interrogation, his inquisitors suddenly changed tack and talked about the arms cache they had found in Deep Shelter Four. Time and again Ashton was told that the British, with the backing of the CIA, were planning to overthrow Yeltsin. When he denied it, he was informed that Reindekker had already confessed and had been shown a signed statement which implicated him. But they made sure he never saw the American, which was enough to convince him that both the signature and the document were forgeries.

August came and went, so did September. No one from the embassy visited him which his interrogators said only went to prove that he had been abandoned. Although he never saw a newspaper and had no idea what was going on in the world outside, he sensed a change of mood in his interrogators and knew something must have happened to make them feel uneasy. One day in early October, Ashton thought he could hear cannon fire in the distance, but his guards insisted it was only thunder.

On Monday, October the eleventh, he was released from the

Lefortovo and handed over to the consular affairs officer at the British Embassy. That same evening, he was put on the BA flight to Heathrow where he was met at the airport by one of Garfield's people and taken to the safe house in Chiswick.

In the boom years, the eighty-year-old semi-detached at 84 Rylett Close in Chiswick had changed hands for two hundred thousand. The property had been repossessed by the building society in 1991 when the young couple who had purchased it on a hundred per cent mortgage had fallen seriously in arrears with their payments. Kelso had bought it on behalf of the SIS twelve months later at a knockdown price. The Technical Services Division had then turned the place into a veritable fortress.

To Ashton it was another prison. It was of course much more comfortable than the Lefortovo and the régime was definitely benevolent, but he resented the fact that he couldn't take a walk in Ravenscourt Park unless he was accompanied by a Special Branch officer. He was also denied access to a telephone. However, apart from these minor irritations, he had no complaints about his treatment.

There was nothing to touch the SIS when you went missing. Twenty-four hours after the embassy had lost track of him, Kelso's men had cleared out the flat in Churchill Gardens and removed the Vauxhall Cavalier. Kelso had also arranged to have all his mail redirected to the Post Office Box Number for Benbow House and had subsequently settled his gas, electricity and telephone bills. An itemised account of these expenses had been presented to Ashton on his arrival at Rylett Close together with a detailed questionnaire from the European Department which he had duly completed.

Supplementary questions had arrived by hand of special messenger. In between answering these, Ashton had watched TV and caught up on all the news from Yeltsin's dissolution of parliament to the storming of the White House and the capture of Aleksander Rutskoi.

Ashton was relaxing over a coffee in the front parlour when a dark blue Rover 800 and a Vauxhall Cavalier pulled up outside the house. Although he did not recognise the man who was driving his car, there was no mistaking the rumpled figure of the Deputy DG.

'Surprised to see me?' Hazelwood asked when Ashton let him into the house.

'A little. I thought Rowan Garfield might want to see me.'

'He's not anxious to collect a bloody nose.' Hazelwood went into the parlour and plumped himself down in an easy chair. 'Mind if I smoke?' he asked and produced a Burma cheroot from the top pocket of his jacket.

'Be my guest,' Ashton told him, but he had already struck a match and was puffing away contentedly.

'Pity we lost Valentin,' he said reflectively.

'You don't believe that crap about Urzhumov, do you? Pavel Trilisser is our man; he framed Alexei Leven and had Urzhumov killed to protect himself.'

'He also finked on Rutskoi and is now the hero of the hour, sitting at the right hand of Yeltsin as his special adviser on external affairs. He's in the Kremlin, that's why we can't get to him.'

'I bet the CIA isn't happy about that; they put up most of the cash to run the operation. By the way, how is Reindekker?'

'Surviving, he's been promoted and is running the South American Department at Langley.' Hazelwood tapped his cigar over the fireplace and managed to spill ash on the carpet. 'Still, the Director thinks you did a good job and should take a break. How does ten days grab you?'

'When can I leave?'

'Soon as you're ready.' Hazelwood reached into his pocket, took out a bunch of car keys and threw them to Ashton. 'I've had the Vauxhall filled up.'

'Thanks, Victor.'

'Where are you going?'

'Lincoln,' Ashton told him and went upstairs to pack.

Amongst the mail that had been waiting for him, there had been a brief letter from Harriet. She had resigned from the Security Service and had taken a job with one of the local estate agents but would have to leave in March because she was pregnant. It was, she wrote, the best thing that had ever happened to her.

Ashton threw a few clothes into a holdall and walked out of the house into a bright sunny morning. He hoped it was a good omen.